She sure didn't need his crazy accusations...

JC bit her tongue before she told him everything. How she was unprepared to become a mother. And worse, how unhappy she was about this pregnancy...and how guilty *that* made her feel.

"Why on earth would you think I did this on purpose?" she finally spat out.

Brady looked at the glass in his hands and, as if only just realizing he was still holding it, set it on the counter. "When you were a kid you seemed to have a...a crush on me."

"You knew?" she asked weakly. "Did my sister know?"

He gave one quick nod.

Buzzing filled her ears. "I can imagine how much fun you two had laughing about it, about me. Poor chubby, silly Jane."

"Neither one of us laughed at you," he said. "I was flattered."

"Flattered?" she repeated tonelessly. Groaning, she covered her face with her hands, her curls falling forward to hide her face. "Oh, my God. Just kill me now. You're a marine—you must know a hundred different ways to do it quickly and painlessly."

Dear Reader,

"Life is what happens to you while you're busy making other plans." —John Lennon

As we're all well aware, life does not follow a set road map—no matter how much we'd like it to. There are bumps that leave you flat and broken down. Turns that lead to wonderful new destinations. You may find yourself at the top of a high hill, joyous and certain that if you reach up, you'll touch the stars. Or in a valley so low you wonder how you'll ever climb out.

Ex-marine Brady Sheppard is in one of those valleys. The woman he loves has married another man. He's drinking too much and is also suffering post-traumatic stress disorder from his time served in Afghanistan. Too full of pride and anger to ask for help, he spends his days bitter and alone. Until he finds out he's going to be a father. Too bad the mother of his child, Jane Cleo (JC) Montgomery, is his ex's kid sister.

Let me just confess right here and now that Brady was no walk in the park to write. He was harsh and angry and dealing with some very big, very real issues. But as I wrote him, I fell for him in a huge way, because somehow he finds a way to deal with those issues. To overcome his anger and ease his bitterness. He learns that life goes on.

I love to hear from readers. Please visit my website, www.bethandrews.net, or write to me at P.O. Box 714, Bradford, PA 16701.

Beth Andrews

A Marine for Christmas
Beth Andrews

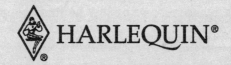

HARLEQUIN®

TORONTO • NEW YORK • LONDON
AMSTERDAM • PARIS • SYDNEY • HAMBURG
STOCKHOLM • ATHENS • TOKYO • MILAN • MADRID
PRAGUE • WARSAW • BUDAPEST • AUCKLAND

Recycling programs
for this product may
not exist in your area.

ISBN-13: 978-0-373-71670-8

A MARINE FOR CHRISTMAS

Copyright © 2010 by Beth Burgoon

ABOUT THE AUTHOR

Beth Andrews loves Christmas, wine and chocolate—though not necessarily in that order. During the writing of this book she listened to hours of Christmas carols, visited a local winery (several times) and made many, *many* homemade chocolate truffles. All for research purposes, of course.

Beth is a Romance Writers of America RITA® Award finalist and Golden Heart winner. She lives in northwestern Pennsylvania with her husband and three teenagers, who claim they are her children but are a far cry from the sweet, quiet babies she gave birth to. Learn more about Beth and her books by visiting her website, www.BethAndrews.net.

Books by Beth Andrews

HARLEQUIN SUPERROMANCE
1496—NOT WITHOUT HER FAMILY
1556—A NOT-SO-PERFECT PAST
1591—HIS SECRET AGENDA
1634—DO YOU TAKE THIS COP?

Don't miss any of our special offers. Write to us at the following address for information on our newest releases.

Harlequin Reader Service
U.S.: 3010 Walden Ave., P.O. Box 1325, Buffalo, NY 14269
Canadian: P.O. Box 609, Fort Erie, Ont. L2A 5X3

For my fabulous critique partner Tawny Weber.

Thanks for always finding something to love in my stories and for being such a wonderful friend.

Acknowledgments

My sincere gratitude to Mitzi Batterson of James River Cellars Winery in Glen Allen, Virginia, for taking the time to answer my questions about running a family-owned winery in Virginia.

CHAPTER ONE

IT MIGHT HAVE BEEN the numerous shots of whiskey and the goading of his fellow drinkers down at The Empire Bar, but Brady Sheppard thought crashing his ex-fiancée's wedding was the best idea he'd had in years.

Too bad he wasn't drunk enough to believe he'd gone through the side entrance of the First Presbyterian Church undetected because of his stealth and military training. He'd caught a break, that was all. It'd been bound to happen eventually.

The sounds of a string quartet masked the soft click of him pulling the door shut. Bracing his weight on his crutches, he slanted forward. To his left, waning sunlight filtered through two stained-glass windows, breaking up the shadows of a long hallway. Glancing around the corner, he spied five women in identical dark purple gowns lined up in a haphazard row, flowers clasped loosely in their hands as they chatted in hushed whispers while waiting for their cue to walk down the aisle.

The door at the end of the hall opened and Brady's heart rate picked up. Backing against the wall, he stayed hidden in the shadows as Jane Cleo Montgomery stepped into the hall. She, too, had on a purple dress and held flowers, her brown, corkscrew curls piled on top of her head. As she passed him unaware, she said something over her shoulder and laughed.

And that was when he saw her. Liz. *His* Liz.

He didn't move, barely breathed as the woman he was supposed to marry glided toward him, a serene smile on her beautiful face. His hands tightened on the crutches. Of course she was happy. She was getting what she'd always wanted. A fancy, summer wedding in her hometown, surrounded by family and friends. Except he wasn't the groom.

Ignoring the throbbing pain in his knee, he hobbled out into her path. "Hello, Lizzie."

The color drained from her face as she pulled up short, stumbling over her long train. "Brady."

That was it. After everything they'd meant to each other, the years they'd been together, all she could give him was his name. He wanted to shake her. Demand that she take back everything in that goddamn letter she'd sent him over a year ago when she'd blown his life apart. Wanted to see more in her eyes than nerves. Something that told him she regretted what she'd lost. That she was hurting, even just a little.

And how pathetic was he that he'd take whatever scraps she tossed his way?

"I'll get Dad," J.C. said from behind him.

Swinging his crutches forward, he backed Liz down the hallway. Her familiar floral scent confused his already muddled brain. Her gown had a fitted, beaded bodice and puffy skirt that accentuated her hourglass figure. She'd swept her glossy, dark hair up and wore one of those tiara things attached to a veil that ended below her small waist.

She was the most beautiful thing he'd ever seen.

"Glad I'm not too late," he murmured.

She swallowed, her hazel eyes wide. "Too...too late?"

"For the ceremony."

"Brady, please..." She held out her hand only to curl her fingers into her palm and lower it back to her side. "Please don't do this."

He went hot, then cold, trembling with the effort to contain his anger. Those were the exact same words he'd said to her after he'd read that damn letter. He'd called her from his base in Afghanistan, begged her to give him another chance.

He moved even closer, crowding her. She gasped, her warm breath washing over his face. "What do you think I'm going to do, Lizzie?" he asked quietly.

"I...I'm not sure." Her voice was as quiet as his. And when she met his eyes, the strange intimacy of their conversation reminded him of how he used to hold her after they'd made love. How it seemed as if they were the only two people in the world. "Make a scene or... or interrupt the ceremony..."

He shook his head to clear it. The ceremony. Right. He stepped back, grimacing with the pressure on his left leg.

"Are you all right?" she asked. As if she cared about him. Dr. Elizabeth Montgomery, trying to heal the poor Jarhead's injuries.

He glared at her. "Afraid I'm going to stand up when the minister asks if anyone objects?"

Someone laid a heavy hand on Brady's shoulder. "Son, you need to leave."

Brady glanced at Liz's father. Don Montgomery, tall and pudgy with intelligent brown eyes and thinning dark hair threaded heavily with gray. The physician's round face was red above his starched collar.

"I'm not your son," was all Brady said. Though, until recently, he'd considered Don to be like a second father.

Jane Cleo brushed past them to stand next to her sister, looking from him to Liz and back again.

"Go home," Don said, not unkindly. "Don't make this harder than it has to be." When Brady didn't so much as blink, the older man sighed and reached into the inside pocket of his dark suit jacket. "I'm afraid if you won't leave on your own, I'll have to call the police."

"No," J.C. and Liz said at the same time.

Liz pushed between them, facing her father. "Brady would never do anything to hurt me." Then she turned to him, pleading with her eyes. It just about cut him off at the knees. "Would you?"

Damn it. *Damn it!* She was right. No matter how much he'd had to drink, no matter how pissed he was, he'd rather die than hurt her.

He was as big of a fool for her as he'd always been.

"Goodbye, Brady," she said softly before linking her arm through her father's and tugging him down the hall, J.C. following.

He stood in that dark hallway while the music changed to a classical song he'd heard before but never in a million years would be able to name. All he knew was that as that song played, Liz was walking down the aisle toward the man she was going to marry.

He wiped a hand over his mouth. He wanted a drink. Needed it to dull his mind.

Instead, he found an empty spot in the back where he could stand unnoticed. And torture himself by watching the woman he'd loved for half of his life become someone else's wife.

"I NEED A FAVOR."

J.C. licked sweet buttercream icing off her fork. "I'm not holding your dress while you pee again," she told Liz quietly, hoping the other members of the bridal party seated next to her at the head table couldn't hear. "Once in a lifetime is one time too many."

An elderly couple walked past, congratulating Liz. She thanked them before turning back to J.C. "This is serious," she said in a harsh whisper.

"More serious than wedding cake?"

Liz had detached her veil but kept the tiara firmly in place. She always had liked to pretend she was a princess. Which left J.C. to play the role of lady-in-waiting.

Liz picked up J.C.'s plate and carried it with her as she pulled her sister to her feet. "Come on."

They made their way across the large room, weaving around the tables and chairs tied with wide, purple taffeta. The tables were topped with narrow glass jars of varying heights filled with water, lavender rose petals and lit, floating white candles.

Liz stepped behind a large column. "Get him to leave."

J.C. didn't need to be told who *him* was. Brady Sheppard. She peeked around the column. Yep. There he sat at the end of the bar, all scruffy and brooding in his rumpled T-shirt and faded jeans, his dark blond hair still military-short. He stared at the spot where she and Liz stood. No surprise, given he hadn't taken his eyes off the bride ever since he'd hobbled into Pine Hills Country Club a few hours ago.

Poor Brady. She should be ticked at him for crashing her sister's wedding—and she was. A little. But after everything he'd gone through, everything Liz had put him through, it was tough to work up a good mad. Especially when he seemed so...lost. So alone.

Taking her plate back from Liz, J.C. scooped up a small bite though she could no longer taste the delicious vanilla cake and milk chocolate ganache filling. "Ignore him. Don't let him ruin your special day."

It was a refrain she, the other bridesmaids and the mothers of both bride and groom had repeated numerous times already.

"I have ignored him and he's already ruined my day. And now it's time for him to leave." She nodded toward the other side of the room. "Before Carter's frat brothers talk him into doing something stupid."

J.C. looked over to where her new brother-in-law stood by the presents table. Pale blond hair, green eyes, chiseled features...Carter Messler—make that *Dr.* Carter Messler—was not only handsome, funny and smart, he was also the most easygoing guy J.C. had ever met. Usually. Surrounded by his groomsmen, though, they had one thing in common: they were all scowling at Brady. Carter's scowl was the darkest.

"But...Carter's a pediatrician," J.C. said. "Pediatricians don't go around getting into fistfights."

"I've never seen him so angry." Glancing nervously at her new husband, she lowered her voice. "Brady could get hurt."

J.C. smashed the remaining cake crumbs under her fork. Brady had never backed down from a fight. Which was probably what had made him such a good Marine. And she doubted he'd let a bum knee and crutches stop him from taking a swing or two.

Liz was right. He had to go. And not just because J.C. didn't want to see him get his stubborn head bashed in. The disheveled, ex-Marine partaking in the open bar was preventing Liz and Carter from enjoying their day.

"What do you want me to do?"

Liz squeezed J.C.'s hand. "Whatever you have to. He'll listen to you," she said desperately, as if willing it to be true. "He's always liked you. He used to tell me you were like the little sister he never had."

And wasn't that enough to make her ego take a serious nosedive.

"I'm not making any promises" she said, handing her plate to Liz. "But I'll do my best."

J.C. resolutely kept her gaze forward instead of glancing at her reflection as she passed the mirror behind the polished bar. She didn't need visual confirmation that her hair was rebelling against the dozens of bobby pins the stylist had used. Unlike Liz, ignoring problems usually worked pretty well for J.C.

She stopped in front of him. "Hello, Brady."

"Janie." He sipped from a squat glass of amber liquid. "You look different."

She'd heard a variation of that statement all day from numerous friends and relatives who hadn't seen her in the past two years. And while it usually pleased her to have people notice the sixty-five pounds she'd dropped, she could've sworn she'd run into Brady since then. "I lost some weight."

His narrowed eyes roamed from her head to her feet

and back up again. "I was talking about the dress." Her skin prickled.

"Oh," she said breathlessly as she wiped a damp palm down the front of the simple, halter-style gown. "Is there someone I can call to come get you?"

Resting one arm against the bar, he leaned back. "Am I going somewhere?"

"I think it's for the best if you did."

His light blue eyes sharpened. "You do? Or Lizzie does?"

"Me. Liz. Carter. My parents. The other bridesmaids... I'd say it's unanimous."

"What if I'm not ready to leave?"

She fisted her hands around the material of her skirt. She felt for him. Honest, she did. But just because Liz had moved on with her life didn't give Brady the right to act like an ass. It wasn't as if he was the only person in the world to be in love with someone who didn't love him back.

Moving to his side, she was careful not to touch him. "I get it. You're upset and you want to hurt her back. Well, congratulations, you succeeded. But enough's enough."

Other than a momentary twitch of his left eye, he remained expressionless.

After a moment, he raised his glass to her, downed the remaining drink, then set the glass on the bar. "Don't bother calling anyone on my account. I'll see myself home."

Positioning the crutches under his arms, he stood, gazing somewhere over her left shoulder. She glanced back to see Liz and Carter, arms around each other as they swayed to the band's version of "Unchained

Melody." When she turned back, Brady was already halfway to the door.

What she wouldn't give to have Brady look at her with even a fraction of the longing she'd seen in his eyes when he stared at Liz. To have him see her as Jane Cleo instead of just Liz's little sister.

Lips pressed together, she watched him until he went out the side door of the clubhouse. Could he drive with his injured knee? Would he? No. The Brady she'd known most of her life would never drink and then get behind the wheel. She pushed a loose bobby pin into her hair, jabbing her scalp in the process. Of course, the old Brady didn't have a permanent glower, would never crash a wedding or suck back whiskey as if it were the only thing getting him from one minute to the next.

She headed to the rear of the bar where the bridal party had stashed their personal items. No one would miss her if she slipped away for a little bit. Long enough to make sure Brady got home safely.

Twenty minutes later, J.C. wondered which of them of them was the bigger idiot. Him for thinking he could walk the ten miles home on crutches. Or her for leaving her sister's wedding to give him a ride, all because she still hadn't gotten over her stupid, childhood crush.

Her. Definitely her. She'd not only driven him, but helped him inside and onto the couch and even made coffee.

She frowned as it dripped into the pot. Well, wasn't that what people did when they cared about someone?

Carrying a cup of coffee, she made her way to the living room where Brady was slumped on the couch, his head resting against the back of it, his left leg out straight.

"I thought you could use this," she said, holding the mug out as she sat next to him. When he made no move to take it, she put it on the coffee table and then clasped her hands together in her lap.

Other than to tell her he was staying at the cottage on The Diamond Dust, the historic plantation the Sheppards called home, he'd remained silent on the drive over. So there she was, in the middle of the woods in a sparsely furnished living room with her sister's stoic, drunk ex.

Finally she cleared her throat and made a move to leave. "I'd better get going."

Nothing. No "Thanks for getting me home." The man didn't even blink. She'd taken one step toward the front door when his gravelly voice stopped her.

"I didn't want to hurt her."

"Excuse me?"

He finally sat up and took a long gulp of coffee. Stared down at the mug. "I didn't go there to hurt her."

Her heart racing, she retook her seat. "Why did you do it then?"

"I had to see."

"Had to see what?"

He set his coffee down then rolled his head from side to side. "I had to see it happen. Had to watch her marry someone else. So I'd know it was real. And that it really is over between us."

She laid her hand on his forearm. "Brady, I...I'm so sorry."

He looked down at her hand then up at her face, his gaze hooded. "You're still as sweet as you always were, aren't you, Jane?" he murmured.

His tone was low and dark. Dangerous. Gooseflesh rose on her bare arms. "I…I hate that you're…" In pain. Broken. Unable to see beyond Liz. "That you have to go through this."

He shifted, his knee bumping hers. She slid over several inches. But…was it her imagination, or did he keep getting closer?

"Like I said, sweet." He skimmed the tip of his forefinger down her cheek.

She sat motionless, her mouth dry as he cupped the back of her head. Then he tugged her head down and kissed her, his lips brushing hers once. Then again. The third time, he slowly deepened the kiss, his lips warm and firm, the rough pad of his thumb caressing her jaw. His tongue slipped between her lips, coaxing a response.

He eased back, his eyes searching hers. "Okay?" he asked softly.

She exhaled shakily. Was it okay? She'd dreamt of this, of him touching her, kissing her…wanting her… her entire life. Almost as long as she'd loved him.

Ignoring all the reasons why they couldn't do this, she pressed her mouth to his.

Brady groaned and speared his fingers into her hair, scattering bobby pins across the couch. When his other hand cupped her breast through the silk of her gown, she almost jumped out of her skin. But then he lightly pinched her nipple and she arched her back, fitting herself more fully into his palm.

Willing herself to relax, she tentatively smoothed her palms over the hard contours of his chest up to his shoulders. He lifted his head long enough to strip his shirt off, tossing it behind him before kissing her again.

She couldn't stop touching him. Couldn't believe she really was touching him. He was so beautiful, his body lean but muscular. His skin soft. And hot.

Still kissing her, he grabbed hold of her underneath her thighs, tugging her down until she lay flat on her back. Lifting her dress, he swept his hand up to her hipbone, leaving trails of warmth in his wake. He parted her legs and lightly stroked her through her panties. She squirmed. Her thigh muscles clenched.

Before she could raise her hips in a silent demand for him to touch her harder, he pulled her panties down, leaving them around her ankles. Then he lifted his mouth from hers so he could unfasten and shove down his jeans. Her head was still spinning as Brady thrust her dress up around her waist. Cool air washed over her.

Slow down. She brought her legs together. And for the first time, she noticed Brady's features etched in pain.

"Your knee," she said. "Are you—"

He kissed her again. Settled on top of her, spreading her legs insistently, keeping most of his weight on his right side. And then he was at her entrance. Hot. Hard.

He didn't return her feelings. But she couldn't refuse him.

He pushed into her, his thickness stretching her. He gave her a moment to adjust to his size. His hardness. Then he took her hips in a viselike grip and began to move.

Unlike her fantasies, there were no tender words. No lingering looks. None of the fireworks she'd imagined. There was no connection between them other than the joining of their bodies.

Oh, God. She'd made a huge mistake.

Her throat burning, she stared up into his handsome face, her hands clutching the cushion beneath her. His mouth was a thin line, the hair at his temples damp with sweat. And no matter how hard she silently willed him to, he never once opened his eyes.

Finally, after what seemed like an eternity, his pace quickened and his body grew taut. Emptying himself inside her, he gave a guttural growl.

And called out her sister's name.

CHAPTER TWO

Three months later

SEVEN O'CLOCK in the morning—on Thanksgiving, no less—was way too early to start throwing up.

Bent over the porch rail, J.C. wiped a shaky, gloved hand over her mouth. Wrinkling her nose at the bushes below her, she straightened. At least she hadn't thrown up in her car. Again.

Her stomach still churning, she crossed Brady's porch and pounded on the door before digging into the pocket of her bulky coat for a mint. She would not freak out. She could handle this. And once Brady knew, he'd help her. He'd figure out what to do.

But first he had to answer the damn door.

Wrapping her arms around herself, she scanned the surrounding woods. A blanket of damp leaves covered the forest floor and not even the sun shining in a gorgeous blue sky could pierce the darkness of the trees. She'd parked behind Brady's silver pickup, so it stood to reason that if his truck was here, he was here.

She rattled the doorknob—only to have it turn easily in her hand. She blinked, then slipped inside and shut the door. "Hello? Brady? It's me. J.C."

The living-room blinds were drawn, but she had no trouble making out the shape of the cream sofa. The sofa where what should've been her dream come true had turned into her greatest nightmare.

The blinds to her right were drawn, but sunlight shone through the tiny window above the kitchen sink. She crept through the small foyer toward it but stopped at the doorway.

The cottage had seemed sterile, just-moved-into, when she'd last been there three months ago. But now the kitchen was a mess. And not your ordinary, didn't-do-the-dishes-last-night-and-left-the-empty-milk-carton-on-the-counter mess she often made in her own apartment. Dirty dishes were piled high in both sides of the sink and took up half the counter space. Garbage overflowed from the bin in the corner and crumbs littered the hardwood floor. Cupboard doors hung open as if someone had ransacked the place. And it would take a jackhammer to chisel through the food on the stovetop.

And she didn't even want to know what that awful smell was. Covering her nose and mouth with her arm, she ducked her head and rushed down the hallway, careful not to brush up against anything lest she risk some sort of infectious disease.

"Brady," she called again as she passed the small bathroom, her eyes straight ahead. After the horror of that kitchen, you couldn't pay her to look in the man's bathroom. At least, not without some sort of Hazmat suit on. She stopped at the closed door to his bedroom and knocked. "Brady, are you up?"

No answer. She twisted the silver stud in her left earlobe. She'd already let herself into the house, no sense stopping now. She opened the door but couldn't see a thing. Did he have something against mornings?

Or just sunlight in general? She found the light switch and flipped it on.

The bedroom was as messy as the kitchen, minus any decaying food or garbage. Clothes were tossed on top of and all around the three-drawer dresser. A sock hung from a hardback chair in the corner and a lamp lay on its side on the carpet next to the bed, where a large lump snuffled softly and then began to snore.

She stepped hesitantly into the room. "Brady," she whispered. He continued snoring. With the toe of her sneaker, she nudged a white T-shirt out of her way, then stepped over a pair of dark boxer briefs to the head of the bed.

She picked up an open bottle of whiskey from the nightstand and wasn't sure if she should be relieved it was still half-full. Finding the cap behind a digital clock that blinked twelve, she screwed it on.

Brady slept on his stomach, his long body stretched diagonally across the bed. A sheet covered him from the waist down, leaving his naked back and one bent leg exposed. His shoulders were broad, the lean muscles clearly defined. He had a black vine tattoo that started at his right hip, wound its way over his back and up to his shoulder before curling out of sight. His right arm hung limply off the side of the bed, his left held a pillow over his head.

Too bad or she might have poured the rest of the whiskey over his face.

"Brady." Nothing. If not for his soft snores, she'd think he was comatose. "Wake up."

Other than a twitch of his toes, he didn't move. Holding the whiskey bottle by the neck, she nudged his shoulder with the bottom of it. "Wake—"

Brady's hand shot out and grabbed the bottle, tossing it onto the bed at the same time he wrenched her forward. Before she could so much as open her mouth to scream, he flipped her onto her back and pinned her to the mattress, his muscular thighs straddling her hips.

His large, strong hand was around her throat.

Panic shot through her as his fingers tightened, cutting off her airway. She bucked wildly underneath him, clawing at his wrists, but she may as well have been fighting a statue. The wild tangle of his shaggy, wheat-colored hair and the darker stubble on his cheeks and chin sharpened the already sharp lines of his handsome face. His blue eyes were like ice chips, cold and empty.

"Brady...stop...it's me," she managed to spit out, though it hurt to talk. To breathe. "Jane Cleo. Please..."

He blinked, and his hold on her loosened. Realization flashed across his face and he leapt off her to the other side of the room. She rolled onto her side as she gasped for breath.

"Damn it, J.C.! What the hell are you doing?" Brady demanded, the hint of Southern accent doing nothing to soften his harsh, sleep-roughened voice. "I could've killed you."

"I...I was trying to wake you," she rasped.

He pressed the heels of his hands against his eyes. "How did you even get in here?"

Her arms shaking, she pushed herself up into a sitting position, keeping her gaze off his naked body. "The door was unlocked."

"That didn't give you the right to come in."

"No. Of course not. But I wanted..."

"What? A repeat of the last time you were here?"

he asked, then gave one quick shake of his head. "Not interested."

Tears stung her eyes, made her already sore throat burn. "I didn't come here for a repeat of anything, you bastard," she said fiercely, her hands gripping the crumpled sheet. "I came to tell you I'm pregnant."

BRADY REARED BACK, hitting his already spinning head against the wall behind him with a dull thud and jolt of pain. "What?"

"I'm pregnant."

Oh, shit. He swallowed, but his tongue felt as if it were wearing a fur coat. "How?"

"The usual way."

"Who?"

She struggled to her feet, her arms crossed against a coat bright enough to burn his retinas. "A traveling salesman," she snapped. "Who do you think?"

That was the problem. He couldn't think. Not with his head pounding. And a panic unlike he'd ever felt crawling up his spine.

He stared at her stomach, but her coat was too bulky to discern any changes in her body. "Are you sure?"

She threw a sandwich bag at him, hitting him in the chest. "See for yourself."

Shoving his hand through his hair, he frowned down at the bag where it'd landed by his feet. "What are those?"

"The pregnancy test I took last night, along with the two I took this morning. You'll notice every last one of them has a stupid plus sign."

He dropped his hand, hitting his bare thigh. And realized she'd literally caught him with his pants down.

Searching for and finding a pair of gym shorts, he jerked them on, ignoring the throbbing in his bad knee. He took a deep breath and held it for the count of five.

"No," he growled. "Are you sure it's mine?"

She bristled, reminding him of some mortally offended, overgrown Shirley Temple impersonator with her round face and her frizzy curls smooshed down by an ugly, piss-colored hat. "Of course I am."

And with those words, any hope he might've had that he hadn't royally screwed up yet again flew out the window. Just proved how useless and cruel hope could be.

Instead of kicking a hole in the wall like he wanted to, he shrugged. With his bad leg, he probably couldn't do much damage anyway. "Can't blame me for asking."

But the look she gave him said she not only could blame him, but likely would for a hellishly long time.

He worked to not limp as he crossed to the bed. Told himself it didn't bother him when she darted away like a rabbit. His stomach roiled from not having anything in it other than the Jim Beam he'd downed last night.

The idea of having a kid should make him feel something besides disappointment. Even the angry red marks on J.C.'s slender throat, the marks he'd put there, should make him feel something. Guilt, at least. But to feel guilty about any of it would mean he'd have to have some semblance of conscience, of humanity, left.

Sitting on the bed, he reached back for the Jim Beam before picking up a spotted water glass with smudged lipstick on the rim from the floor.

"Do you think that's going to help?" J.C. asked, disgusted.

He flicked her a glance, then poured two healthy shots into the glass. "Can't hurt."

She made a sound, sort of like his mother's teakettle right before it starting whistling. But thankfully, she kept her mouth shut. He gulped his drink, savoring the burn as it hit the back of his tongue.

He carefully stretched his left leg out in front of him. And noticed J.C.'s eyes lock on the webbing of scars. The raised, white welts were from the shrapnel when the roadside bomb had gone off. The thinner lines were from the two surgeries he'd endured only to be told his leg would never be one hundred percent.

His fingers tensed on his glass and he debated risking another death glare from J.C. to get a second shot. As if the pain and stiffness could let him forget he wasn't whole anymore, the scars reminded him.

As did the pity in people's eyes.

Wiping the back of his hand over his mouth, he worked to keep his expression bland.

She blew out an exasperated breath. "Well?"

"Well what?"

"Don't you have anything to say?"

He scratched the side of his head. Realized he never did make it to that barber appointment his mother had set up for him last week. Or had it been two weeks ago? "Can't think of anything."

Her mouth popped open. "You can't think of anything?" she repeated, her voice rising. "Don't you think we should discuss this?"

"Seems a little late for that."

"But what are we going to do?"

"That's up to you."

She stepped back, her hand to her heart. "Me? Don't you have an opinion?"

He turned his attention to pouring more whiskey into his glass. "Your body. Your decision."

"I am not having an abortion, if that's what you're getting at." Underneath the slight tremble in her voice was a determination that he'd never before heard from Jane Cleo.

"Like I said, your decision."

Whipping her hat off, she crushed it in her hand, her hair poofing out around her head as if it had a life of its own. "But what are we going to do now?"

He drained his glass as he stood. "I'm not sure about you, but I'm going to hit the head and then go back to sleep."

She blocked his exit. "That's it? You don't have any reaction to the fact that you're going to be a father?"

His skin grew clammy. "I'm not going to be a father."

"I told you," she said, speaking through her teeth, "I'm sure it's yours."

"I don't doubt that." His memory of what had happened between them was blurry at best, but he knew she was telling the truth. Even if he'd spent the past few months pretending that night had never happened. That he hadn't taken advantage of J.C. That he hadn't slept with Liz's sister.

That Liz hadn't married someone else.

But that didn't mean he was going to saddle some poor kid with him as a father. And he sure as hell didn't need the added responsibility of a child. Especially when Liz wasn't the mother.

"What I mean is," he continued, "I don't plan on being a father. Not to your baby or any other kid."

"You want me to handle this alone?"

He slammed the bottle down on the nightstand. She flinched. "What do you want from me?" he growled. "You can't show up here, wake me up and throw something this huge in my face and expect me to take care of it. To take care of you. Because if that's what you expected, you're talking to the wrong man."

She shut her eyes. "This isn't happening. This isn't happening."

What was she doing? J.C. had always been a bit... eccentric. Which was fine when she'd been a teenager and had staged a one-person sit-in at the high-school cafeteria to protest the school's refusal to offer meat-free lunches once a week. But this was just plain weird.

And if that one word didn't sum up Jane Cleo Montgomery, nothing did.

She opened her eyes and walked away. Finally, his torment was ending. Except, she whirled back around and threw her hat. It sailed over his head and hit the wall behind him.

"Do you have any idea what I've been going through?" she asked quietly, but his headache spiked just the same. "How scared I've been? For over a month I told myself that I couldn't really be pregnant. But now, well—" she gestured to the bag of pregnancy tests "—there's no more denying it. My worst fears are confirmed and now I get to deal with the joys of an unexpected pregnancy, which includes puking every morning, no matter what I eat or even if I eat."

Brady rubbed the back of his neck. "What do you

want me to say, Jane? That I'm sorry? Okay, I'm sorry."

"I don't want an apology. I want you to get your head out of that bottle and help me. How am I going to tell my parents?" she asked, her voice breaking. "How am I supposed to face Liz?"

Grinding his back teeth together, he reached over for the whiskey bottle and added more to his glass. Ignored the unsteadiness of his hand as liquid splattered over his fingers. Damn it, did she think this was easy for him? Any of it? He wiped his hand on the sheet. He'd regretted what had happened between them the moment he'd come to. The last thing he wanted was for Liz—the woman he'd sworn to love for the rest of his life—to find out he'd slept with her kid sister.

"Your family's close," he said. And they'd coddled J.C. her entire life. They wouldn't let her go through this alone. "I'm sure once they get used to the idea, they'll help you out."

"Thank you for sharing that brilliant piece of logic," she said so coldly, so sarcastically, he raised his eyebrows. "Tell you what, when you figure out what, if any, part you want to play in this baby's life, let me know. In the meantime, you can go to hell."

He saluted her with his glass. "Already there."

With a low growl, sweet Jane Cleo Montgomery, the girl who was so bubbly and happy it was as if she'd swallowed a goddamn beam of sunshine, stormed out. A moment later, the front door slammed shut, followed by a dull thud. Which was probably one of the framed family photos his mother had hung in the living room falling.

Brady finished his drink and hung his head, his hands

between his knees. Once she thought things through, she'd agree he shouldn't have any part of this kid's life. And he sure didn't want any part of it. Yeah, he used to think about having kids, of becoming the type of father his own dad had been, but that was before. Before his knee, and his life, had gone to hell. Before Liz decided he wasn't enough.

WHO SAID SHE DIDN'T have a backbone?

So what if Brady was no help to her at all? Or that he didn't want anything to do with the baby she was carrying? Or with her, J.C. thought late that afternoon as she ignored the heated debate her mother and grandmother were having next to her over whether to thicken the turkey gravy using cornstarch or flour. J.C. shut off the flame under the huge pot of boiling potatoes. She'd handled Brady's rejection. Not only handled it, but told him where to get off.

Too bad her backbone turned to Jell-O whenever she thought about telling her family she was pregnant. She sipped from her glass of ginger ale, but it did little to soothe her suddenly dry throat. Picking up two pot holders, she hauled the heavy pan of potatoes to the sink and dumped them into the waiting colander, leaning back from the steam in an effort to keep her hair frizz-free, if even for just an hour.

Well, she just had to suck it up and tell them. It wasn't as if she could hide it much longer anyway. When she'd put on her long suede skirt earlier, she hadn't been able to button it around her rapidly expanding middle. Which had resulted in a fifteen-minute crying jag and her re-thinking her stance against elastic waistbands. A stance she'd taken up after she'd lost weight and had worn her first pair of size-six jeans.

Now she had a large safety pin holding the two edges of her skirt's waistband together and it still dug into her with every inhalation.

Would the indignities of this day ever end?

She poured the potatoes back into the pot and carried it over to the counter. Giving up this round of culinary battle, Grandma Rose carried a tray of her homemade angel biscuits to the living room, a pinched expression on her wrinkled face, her heavily shellacked blue-tinged hair bouncing with each step. J.C.'s mother, Nancy, stayed at the stove stirring the gravy. And humming.

"What did you do to Grandma?" Liz asked as she came into the room. "She's in there mumbling about the sad state of the world today and how the youth of America have no respect for the traditional way of doing things."

"Mom schooled Grandma in the art of gravy making," J.C. said.

"I didn't school anyone." Nancy adjusted the heat beneath the pan with one hand while stirring with the other. "I just pointed out that I've thickened my gravy with cornstarch for the past thirty-four years and that her son has never had any complaints about it."

"Ooh…burn," J.C. mouthed to Liz.

Liz's sleek chestnut hair swung as she nodded. "Second degree," she mouthed back. They shared an easy smile.

Until J.C. remembered what she'd done. How she'd broken the number one rule of sisterhood: no going out with your sister's ex.

J.C. wiped the back of her hand across her damp

forehead. It had to be one hundred degrees in her sister's cramped kitchen. It didn't help that she'd had to wear her heaviest turtleneck sweater today, an oversize, soft cable-knit that covered her stomach. And hid the slight bruising from her encounter with Brady. And while she sweated in clothes that added at least ten pounds to her curvy frame, her mother and sister were both cool and stylish. Nancy in trim dark pants and a V-neck top, her short, layered hair was a shade darker than Liz's with only a few strands of gray. Liz had on skinny jeans and a gorgeous billowy mauve top with a wide band at the bottom that accentuated her tiny waist.

Not that J.C. was bitter or anything.

They usually had Thanksgiving dinner at their parents' spacious house, but Liz had wanted to host her first official holiday dinner in the house she and Carter were renting while their dream home was being built. And since Carter's family was in Ohio, it was going to be him, Liz and J.C., their parents and Grandma Rose.

J.C. poured cream over the potatoes, then shook in salt and pepper. All the people she loved the most in this world, everyone she needed to tell about the baby, would soon be gathered around the table. She'd get to face them over plates filled with green bean casserole, sweet potatoes, turkey and stuffing, and then see their shock turn to disappointment when they heard about her latest screwup.

What better way to spend the holiday?

She threw a stick of butter into the pan. Then, seeing the amount of potatoes, added half of another stick before shoving her sleeves up to her elbows, picking up the masher and mixing it all together.

Her mother, obviously satisfied no lumps would dare

appear in her gravy, poured it into a gravy boat and peered over at J.C. "Honey, are you feeling all right? You look a bit flushed."

"I'm fine," J.C. said. "Just…it's hot in here." Okay, so there was a definite edge of whining in her voice. Her life was falling apart and so far she'd had a really crappy day. She deserved a pout.

Nancy laid the back of her hand against J.C.'s forehead, the gesture bringing tears to J.C.'s eyes. "I don't think you have a fever," Nancy decided. "Are you sure you're over that stomach bug?"

She averted her gaze. "Definitely. It was probably something I ate," she said, referring to the lie she'd told her mother last Sunday when she'd gotten sick after they'd had brunch.

Nancy smiled and rubbed J.C.'s arm. "Good." She glanced at the potatoes. "You need to scrape the sides down or you'll miss lumps. Here, I can finish—"

"I've got it." J.C.'s grip tightened when her mother tried to take the masher from her. "Why don't you go on out and save Dad and Carter from Grandma's lecture about the merits of thickening with flour?"

"Be careful you don't overmash them or they'll get gluey," her mother warned. "And remember, you can always add a little milk if they're too thick."

"I've got it, Mom. Really."

Though she seemed conflicted about leaving the fate of the potatoes in J.C.'s hands, Nancy nodded and then walked away.

Her mother's back disappeared around the corner and J.C. let go of the masher as if it had caught fire. God. As if she needed an advanced degree to mash potatoes. And considering it was the one task her family entrusted her to handle for family dinners, you'd think they could give her more credit. Picking up a large spoon, she scraped down the sides and then began pounding away in earnest.

By the time Liz came back into the kitchen, J.C.'s arms were aching from the effort and sweat was trickling between her shoulder blades.

"You can stop now," Liz said as she attempted to work a few potato pieces out of J.C.'s curls. "Those vicious potatoes are dead."

"Just making sure I got them all."

"I think that's a safe bet. Here," she added, handing J.C. a large blue serving bowl. "Put them in this."

"Did you have to cook the entire ten-pound bag?"

"I didn't want to run out."

"Who did you think was coming? The Jewell High School marching band?"

"If they do," Liz said, shutting off the oven, "we'll be covered."

J.C. scraped the last of the potatoes from the pan and added them to the mountain already in the bowl. "We could cover ourselves with mashed potatoes and still have enough to eat."

"Now I know what Carter and I can do with all the leftovers."

"Eww… Please. That's one visual I really don't need."

"Wait," Liz said, when J.C. picked up the heavy bowl. "I made something special for you."

J.C. set it back on the counter. "What?"

"Close your eyes."

J.C. squeezed her eyes shut. She heard the oven door being opened and then shut.

"Ta-da!" Liz said.

"Uh…" J.C. studied the brown, football-shaped loaf in the baking pan. "I repeat, what is it?"

"Tofurkey."

"Is that like a contagious disease? Because that thing looks like a breeding ground for bacteria."

"It's not a science project, it's a tofu turkey." Setting the pan down, she used a large metal spatula to transfer the loaf onto a small serving platter. "Mom and I didn't think it was fair that you got left out of the biggest tradition of Thanksgiving, so we decided to make you a vegetarian turkey. I found the recipe online. It's basically tofu wrapped around stuffing—Mom made a special version of her bread stuffing using vegetable broth instead of chicken broth."

J.C. blinked and for some reason, the blob of browned tofu didn't look half as bad as she'd first thought. At that moment, it looked downright delicious. "You made that for me?"

"Well, I'm sure not going to eat it and I doubt anyone else here is, either."

"I think it's beautiful," J.C. managed, unshed tears thickening her voice.

There were times, more than a few, when they were growing up when J.C. thought she hated her sister. Times when she'd wanted to hate her, if only to try to ease the jealousy that came with having an older sister who was smarter, prettier and more popular than J.C. could ever hope to be.

But the truth was, J.C. loved Liz. There was no way she could harbor any animosity toward the person who was not only her sister but also her best friend.

She threw herself at Liz, knocking her sister back a full step as she clung to her.

"Hey," Liz said, returning the hug, "what's this?"

And Liz's concern made J.C. feel even worse. "You made me a tofu turkey."

Liz smoothed J.C.'s curls away from her face. "It's tofu and stuffing, not a cure for cancer. Now come on, what's wrong? It's not like you to get emotional over a meat substitute."

God, how she wanted to tell Liz everything. And maybe if she told Liz about the baby, then Liz could break the news to their parents.

But while that had worked when J.C. had been fifteen and had gotten her belly button pierced, she doubted she could get Liz to bail her out of this situation.

J.C. stepped back. "I always get emotional at the holidays."

"Yes, but usually you reserve it for sappy commercials."

"That one where the college kid comes home to surprise his family and makes coffee to wake them gets me every time," she said lightly, picking up the potatoes again. "Now come on. Let's get these real potatoes and that fake turkey on the table."

And the sooner they all sat down, the sooner she could admit she'd had a one-night stand with her sister's ex-fiancé and was now pregnant. Pregnant and scared out of her mind.

CHAPTER THREE

J.C. PUT THE POTATOES on the table and sat next to her mother. Even though they were eating at the picnic table Carter had brought inside, it somehow still looked like one of those fancy layouts in a home and garden magazine. Liz had covered it with a red tablecloth and then added a white runner down the middle. On the runner, gourds and a few pinecones were scattered around glass bowls filled with bright red and green apples, cranberries and minipumpkins.

J.C. unfolded her red-and-white cloth napkin onto her lap and tried not to think about how the last time she'd hosted a family dinner, they ate off paper plates. And her mother had provided most of the food.

Ten minutes later, grace had been said, dishes had been passed and her plate was piled high with food. J.C. nibbled at a flaky, buttery biscuit but couldn't seem to swallow properly. If she didn't come clean to her family right now, she'd never be able to eat her meal. And she was starving.

Setting her biscuit down, she brushed the crumbs off her fingers. "I have an announcement," she said but her voice was so reedy, no one heard her over their laughter and conversation. "I have some news," she yelled, blushing when everyone quieted and stared at her.

To her left, Grandma Rose peered at J.C. over her glasses. "Did you get fired again?"

Jeez. You get fired a few times—okay, five times, but that third time was *not* her fault—and suddenly it's, what, a habit?

"No. I'm still employed." J.C. drank some water. "I..."

"Come on, sweetie," her dad said, giving her a wink as he scooped sweet potatoes onto his fork. "Whatever it is, it can't be as bad as when you stopped going to college but didn't officially drop out, leaving me to foot the bill for a year's worth of classes you didn't take."

"Daddy," Liz admonished while Carter ducked his head and coughed—the sound suspiciously close to a laugh. "We all promised not to talk about that again, remember?"

J.C. twisted the napkin around her fingers. "I told you I'd pay you back."

"We've been through this," Nancy said, shooting her husband a loaded look. "You can worry about paying us back once you're on your feet." She sipped her wine. "Now, what is it you want to tell us?"

"You...you and Daddy..." Her voice shook so she took another drink, and then, staring at the table, said, "You're going to be grandparents."

When no one spoke, J.C. raised her head.

A huge, proud smile broke out across her dad's face. He pumped Carter's hand, not noticing his son-in-law was too flabbergasted to return his handshake. "Congratulations. When are you due?" Don asked Liz.

"Due?" Carter repeated, his gorgeous face devoid of color, his green eyes panicked as he gaped at his wife. "What's due? Who's due?"

"I thought you wanted to wait a few years before having children," Nancy said to Liz.

"Yeah," Carter choked out, his hand still being pumped by his father-in-law, "me, too. Why didn't you tell me?"

"I didn't tell you," Liz said slowly, "because I'm not pregnant."

Frowning, Don let go of Carter's hand and sat back. "What? But Janie said…"

Staring at her plate again, J.C. felt five expectant gazes turn on her.

"Jane," her mother said sharply, "are you pregnant?"

Biting down on her lower lip, she nodded.

"Oh, dear Lord," Grandma Rose murmured.

"But…but I didn't realize you were seeing someone," Don said, sounding lost and hurt. J.C. winced.

"I'm not." Raising her head, she sent Liz a beseeching look. "It was a…a mistake."

"Oh, Lord Almighty," her grandma cried, throwing her hands up as if she were at a tent revival meeting.

Her mom shook her head, her disappointment palpable. "Didn't we teach you to have more self-respect than that?"

J.C.'s throat constricted. "It wasn't like that," she whispered.

No, it was worse. Because even though she'd known Brady was using her as a substitute for Liz, J.C. had gone along with it.

Liz rushed around the table and, crouching next to J.C., put her arm around her sister and squeezed. "Now, let's all calm down. This can't be easy for J.C."

Don stood. "What's his name?" he asked in a low,

deadly tone J.C. had never heard before. Not even when she'd sold the car they'd bought her as a high-school graduation present to pay for a trip to Europe.

"It doesn't matter. He doesn't want anything to do with me or the baby."

He slammed his palm down on the table, and they all jumped.

"Don!" Nancy admonished, catching her wineglass before it fell. "Calm down."

"I want his name, Jane Cleo, and I want it now," her father said.

J.C. wound the napkin around her finger so tightly, her fingertip went numb. "I… It…" Her stomach burning, she forced herself to meet Liz's eyes. "It was Brady."

Liz jerked as if she'd been slapped. "Brady? You… you and…" She shook her head slowly. "You slept with Brady? With *my* Brady?"

"Your Brady?" Carter asked, his eyebrows shooting up.

And with that, all hell officially broke loose. Don wanted to force Brady to "do the right thing" while Nancy tried to calm him down. Grandma Rose was worried what her Bunco group was going to say when this got back to them, and Liz and Carter were having a heated argument off to the side over Liz's lingering feelings for her ex-fiancé.

J.C. slouched down in her chair so far, her chin was level with the tabletop. For half her life all she'd wanted was Brady Sheppard to notice her. To want her. And now that he'd slept with her—albeit he hadn't exactly wanted *her*—this was what she got.

Her mother had always warned her to be careful what she wished for. As usual, she'd been right.

TWO HOURS LATER, Liz was elbow-deep in a sink of soapy water and seriously regretting not taking her mother up on her offer to stay to help her clean. But after the dinner disaster, she'd needed some peace and quiet.

Though peace seemed to be out of the question, she had more than her share of quiet.

"I've already apologized," she said, proud of how composed she sounded when all she wanted to do was hit something. Or someone. Or burst into tears. "Several times. How long are you going to continue with the silent treatment?"

Setting leftovers in the refrigerator, Carter glanced coolly at her over his shoulder. "You're the one who said you didn't want to discuss it."

Since when did he use that biting, condescending tone? She couldn't say she cared for it much. She threw the tofurkey into the sink. Shoved it down the disposal with a wooden spoon. As the whirring sound filled the air, she tapped the spoon repeatedly against the sink. And to think, she'd been so excited about hosting her first holiday as a married woman. Thrilled to be able to spend one of her precious few days off from the E.R. with her family.

Now she didn't think she'd ever be able to look at J.C. the same way again.

Liz turned off the disposal. "There's nothing to discuss. I made a mistake. A slip of the tongue." She tossed silverware into the water. "I don't see where you have any right to hold it against me."

Shutting the fridge door, he faced her, his shoulders rigid, his pale hair sticking up from where he'd run his fingers through it. "Some would say that slip of the tongue indicates your true feelings. Such as you still considering your ex as belonging to you."

"You're a pediatrician, not a psychiatrist. Don't try to analyze me. And I didn't appreciate you humiliating me in front of my parents by accusing me of still having feelings for Brady."

His expression darkened. "You were humiliated? How did you think I felt when your ex-lover crashed our wedding?"

She blew the hair off her forehead. "What did you want me to do, Carter? Let your idiot friends throw him out?"

"No, but you could've trusted me to handle it."

"I didn't want a scene."

"Right," he said, his sarcasm setting her teeth on edge. "But it didn't bother you that I was embarrassed in front of three hundred people."

Of course it'd bothered her, but how could she worry about something that happened three months ago when all she could think about was what had happened at dinner? She scrubbed the bottom of the roasting pan. No, she shouldn't have reacted that way but she'd been… shocked…hearing that J.C. and Brady had…been together…she hadn't been able to censor herself.

Still, it wasn't like Carter to get so angry. To treat her so coldly.

When they'd first met while doing their residency training at George Washington University Hospital, she'd immediately been attracted to him. And guilt-stricken over that attraction since, at the time, she'd been wearing Brady's ring. For months she'd deluded herself into believing the pull between her and Carter was just physical, a result of only seeing Brady a few times a year. She'd tried to ignore the attraction, tried to think of Carter as only a friend, but after working with him day in and day out, her feelings for him became too big. Too real. She found his intelligence, sense of humor and easygoing attitude impossible to resist.

Especially after years of Brady's quiet intensity.

She wished Carter would display some of that laid-back attitude now.

"I'd think you'd be happy Brady has moved on," Carter said as he began drying dishes. "Weren't you the one who was worried he wouldn't be able to let you go?"

"I want him to move on. Just not with J.C."

"Why not?"

She gaped at him. How could he be so intelligent and still be so clueless? "Because it's not right. She's my sister."

Drying a handful of spoons, he glanced at her. "Because it would be uncomfortable—for all involved."

"Exactly," she said with a sigh. Now this was more like it, and more like the man she'd fallen for so hard for. The man she'd chosen.

Carter nodded. "I get that. But from what J.C. said, he's not going to be involved with her or the baby."

The baby. Brady's baby. With her sister.

God, why did it hurt so much?

She swallowed past the lump lodged in her throat. "Brady would never abandon his own child."

"You sound pretty convinced of that."

"I am. I know him."

Carter tossed the towel over his shoulder and stood eyes downcast, feet apart, hands braced against the edge of the sink. "Do you still love him?"

She blinked. He'd never asked her that before. Not on their wedding night when they'd argued over her not wanting him to confront Brady. Not almost two years ago when she'd gone to him in tears because she'd ended her relationship with Brady. Ended it so she could be with Carter.

"Wha-what?"

He faced her. "Do you still love him?"

"I love *you*," she said, taking his hand in her wet one.

He shook his head and stepped away from her. "That's not what I asked."

Suddenly chilled, she crossed her arms. "I…I don't understand."

"I need to know if you still have feelings for Brady."

"Of course I do," she said carefully. "I'll always… care…about him. I was with him half my life."

"But you're not with him now," Carter said quietly. "You're with me. And I can't help but wonder if with me is where you really want to be."

HEADLIGHTS CUT THROUGH the darkness as the car pulled into the short driveway. A motion-detection light above the garage came on, illuminating the bottom half of the stairway on the side of the building. Where Brady sat at the bottom of those steps. He didn't move. Wasn't sure he could so much as stand since his leg had stiffened up during the two hours he'd been waiting in the cold for J.C. to come home.

She opened her car door, grabbed something from the seat next to her and then got out of the car. She took two steps before she noticed him and stopped, a huge purse clutched to her chest. Her gaze flicked from him to her apartment above the garage, then behind her to her car.

"If you take off," he said, figuring she was thinking of doing just that, "I'll still be here waiting when you get back."

She turned back to her car anyway but didn't get in. After a moment, she mumbled to herself and started walking toward him again. "What do you want?"

Gripping the wooden railing, he put all of his weight on his right leg and stood. "Things got out of hand this morning and I wanted to make sure we're on the same page."

"As much as it may shock you, I'm not a complete idiot. You don't want anything to do with me or with this baby. See? Same page. Now, I've had a really craptastic day and all I want is for it to be over. Goodbye."

Then she brushed past him and climbed the stairs, another motion-detecting light coming on when she reached the top. As he watched, she went inside and shut the door. No slamming this time, but somehow the quiet click was just as final.

That hadn't gone quite as planned. He shoved his frozen fingers into the pockets of his jacket. After J.C. left his house earlier, he'd tried to forget she'd been there in the first place. Forget what she'd told him…and how shitty he'd treated her.

While he'd sat in his living room staring into a glass of whiskey, she'd more than likely been telling her family—telling Liz—he'd gotten her pregnant. And that he didn't want anything to do with his own child.

Oh, yeah, he'd wanted to forget all of it.

Unfortunately, his usual method of temporary amnesia hadn't worked.

He scanned the long, steep staircase. At least thirty steps.

Shit.

The railing was on the wrong side to be of any help to him but he'd have to make the best of it. Have to take it one step at a time. Literally. He debated getting his cane from his truck, but when he faced J.C. he wanted to do it on his own two feet.

Clutching the rail, he leaned on his arm to take some of the weight off his left leg while he lifted his right onto the first step. He gritted his teeth against the pain and stepped up with his left leg.

He repeated the process. Then again. And again. Halfway up, he stopped to catch his breath. To think, less than a year ago he was running top speed up mountainsides in full combat gear. With that cheery thought still in his head, he glanced toward the dark house to find J.C.'s grandmother glaring at him from a bedroom window. From what he could remember, J.C. had moved into the apartment above her grandma's garage a few years ago after her latest attempt at college had failed.

He was just thankful Mrs. Montgomery hadn't come home with J.C. It was going to be hard enough to fix things with J.C., he didn't think he could handle facing anyone else in the Montgomery family.

By the time he reached the top, his shirt clung to his sweat-soaked skin and he had an inch-long sliver imbedded in his palm from his death grip on the wooden railing. But hey, at least he'd made it. Bracing his shoulder against the door, he wiped the sweat from his face with the bottom of his T-shirt before knocking. After a minute, he knocked again. Another minute, another knock.

He'd forgotten how, underneath that sunny personality, J.C. was as stubborn as they came.

"Last winter I waited in a cave in southern Afghanistan for over fourteen hours," he said, pitching his voice so she'd be sure to hear him through the door. "Sitting out here until you go to work tomorrow won't be a problem."

A moment later, the door opened to reveal a pinched-face J.C. holding the fattest white cat he'd ever seen. She stepped aside to let him in. "Like I said, I'm tired so wh—"

"I thought you were allergic to cats."

"What?"

"I remember you wanting a cat when—" When he and Liz were together. Seemed as if his life could be defined in two ways: when he and Liz were a couple, and now. "In high school. But you couldn't get one because you were allergic."

"I couldn't get one," she said with enough frost to cause the temperature in the apartment to drop at least ten degrees, "because Liz is allergic to them." The cat gave Brady a sneering, you-are-a-dumb-ass look, then leaped to the ground and waddled off. "I didn't get a chance to finish my dinner, so I'm going to make a sandwich. Do you want one?" she asked so grudgingly that even if all he'd had to eat for the past week were MREs—meals ready to eat, the packaged, precooked meals given to military personnel out in the field—he would've said no.

"I'm good."

"I guess you might as well sit down, then. I'll be back out in a minute."

But when she would've walked away, he grabbed her by the wrist. Ignoring how she went as stiff as a new recruit at attention, he lightly tugged her forward, hooked his finger under the edge of the neck of her sweater and pulled it down. She swallowed and tried to step back but he didn't loosen his hold. All day long he'd tried to convince himself that he hadn't hurt her, that his hangover had dulled his recollection of what had happened. Of how bad it'd been.

The cat was right. He was a dumb-ass.

He brushed his thumb over the light bruises on her pale, delicate skin, his stomach turning. "I didn't mean to hurt you."

Apprehension flashed in her eyes. "I'm fine."

This time when she pulled away, he let her go. She disappeared through a doorway, and he crossed over to the white couch. He sat on the edge—the only spot available among six pillows of varying shapes, sizes and colors. Stretching his left leg out, he rubbed his knee and glanced around.

Her apartment was a good deal smaller than his house, so how did she get so much stuff in it? He remembered the squat, light blue chair he used to sit in in her parents' living room next to her sofa. But not the two red velvet ottomans on the other side of a chipped, painted coffee table. Or the two hardback chairs on either side of a round table underneath the window. A large, glass-fronted case took up an entire corner, its shelves filled with everything from ceramic animal figures and music boxes to tea cups, crystal bowls and books, both paperbacks and hardcover. As if a rummage sale had blown up.

The cat padded in and jumped onto a low stool and then up onto the blue chair. J.C. followed a minute later, one hand curled into a loose fist. In the other she carried a glass of water with a sandwich balanced on top. She set the water on the coffee table in front of him and picked up the sandwich.

"Here," she said, holding out her hand to show him the two small, white pills in her palm.

"What are those?"

"Acetaminophen. It's all I have." When he didn't move, she shrugged irritably and set them next to the water. "From the look on your face when I opened the door, I thought you could use them."

Tossing the yellow pillow from the chair to the floor, she nudged the cat onto the arm rest and then sat, curling her bare feet under her. She took a bite of her sandwich and stared straight ahead.

Brady scratched his cheek. Realized he forgot to shave again today. He supposed he appreciated her bringing him the pills—though he knew from experience a few over-the-counter pain relievers would barely take the edge off. But she was too generous. Too sweet. After everything he'd done, she shouldn't give a crap if he was in pain or not. Not to mention how humiliating it was that he'd been so easy to read.

"Thanks." He took the pills and washed them down with the water. "Did you... Have you told your parents?" She gave a terse nod. Leaning forward, he picked up an ugly ceramic duck, turned it in his hands. Cleared his throat. "And Liz?"

J.C.'s mouth flattened. "Is that why you're here?

To see how Liz reacted to finding out that we slept together?"

"No." Maybe. He rubbed his thumbnail over a chip on the duck's beak. "How did…your family…take the news?"

"About as well as you'd expect." She bit into her sandwich again. "And so you won't be wondering…Liz didn't take *the news* well."

Okay. And what the hell was that supposed to mean? Not that he dared ask. "I didn't handle things as well as I could have this morning."

"You don't say," she said dryly.

"I've done some thinking and…I'm not going to shirk my responsibility."

She set the remainder of her sandwich on her lap. "What do you mean?"

Talking about this made it hard for him to breathe. Hell, it was as if his lungs were being squeezed by a vise. "That I'm willing to support you and the baby."

Her eyebrows drew together. "Support?"

"I'll call my lawyer tomorrow. We'll figure out some sort of financial agreement." He rubbed his damp palms up and down the front of his jeans. This was for the best. For J.C. and the baby. And for him. "I'll make sure you and the child are provided for, but…I won't be in Jewell much longer."

"Where are you going?"

He had no idea. "I'd only planned on staying until I was back on my feet." Which would probably happen faster if he showed up at his physical therapy sessions. "I'll probably be doing some traveling, so it'd be best if we don't set up any type of…shared custody or visitation rights."

"This is perfect," J.C. muttered as she got to her feet, her sandwich falling to the floor. The cat pounced on it and began eating while J.C. paced on the other side of the coffee table, swerving to avoid the ottomans. "So what am I supposed to say in a few years if your child asks about its father?"

The idea of J.C. having to tell her kid—their kid—he'd essentially abandoned them... He set the duck down with a sharp crack. "You can tell it whatever you want."

She shook her head, her dark curls bouncing on her shoulders. "What happened to you?"

What happened to him? He went to hell and he didn't think he'd ever get out. His hands fisted, so he forced himself to relax. To stand with no sign of weakness—when all he felt was weak. And out of control.

She wanted him to be the man he used to be. Someone honorable. The type of guy who did the right thing no matter what the cost.

"People change," he said flatly. "Look, I'm willing to take responsibility—"

"But not too much responsibility, right?" She rubbed her temple and exhaled heavily. "You know what?" she said, dropping her hand. "Forget it. Let's just pretend I never came to you this morning."

"What the hell are you talking about?"

"Don't bother meeting with that lawyer tomorrow. I don't want your money."

He pinched the bridge of his nose as he focused on keeping his voice even. "Then why did you come to me this morning?"

"Because I…God…I'm such an idiot." Then she met his eyes and shocked him for the second time that day. "I wanted you to ask me to marry you."

CHAPTER FOUR

BRADY GRIMACED. The man actually grimaced, his face going so white, J.C. thought for sure he was about to pass out. At the thought of marrying her.

Jerk.

"I don't think marriage is the best thing," Brady said in a low rumble. "For either of us."

Yeah, no kidding. But he didn't have to act as if it were the worst thing, either.

"I wouldn't marry you even if you tied me up and threatened to force-feed me a hamburger," J.C. said. "I wouldn't marry you if we were the last two humans left and the only way to save mankind was—"

"I get it. Then why did you say you did?"

"I said I wanted you to ask me." Noticing Daisy devouring the remainder of her peanut butter and jelly sandwich, J.C. bent and picked it up, much to her cat's annoyance. She met Brady's eyes. "You should've at least asked."

She went into the kitchen, tossing the sandwich into the garbage before getting herself a glass of water from the sink. Staring at her reflection in the small window, she held her glass with two hands to steady it as she drank when what she really wanted was to put her head on the counter and weep.

God, could this day get any worse? Her grandmother

was ashamed of her, her parents disappointed. And while she'd certainly disappointed them in the past, her failings—while numerous—had never been anything of this magnitude. But the worst part had been Liz's reaction. Her sister was hurt. So hurt J.C. wondered if she'd ever forgive her.

Which was a crazy thought. No matter how badly J.C. screwed up, Liz was always there for her.

And Liz always forgave her.

Brady's reflection joined hers as he stepped into the doorway.

"Why did you sleep with me, J.C.?"

She choked and bent over the sink to spit out the water in her mouth. Coughed to clear her airway. "What?"

"Did you..." Walking into the room, he shoved a hand through his hair, causing it to stand on end. "Did you do this...on purpose?"

Her eyes widened. The glass slipped out of her fingers, but Brady caught it. Not that it mattered. What was a broken glass when her life was falling apart?

"You think I wanted to get pregnant? I'm only twenty-six. That's way too young to become a mother. I hadn't planned on kids until I was older." Her voice rose and she waved her hand in the air. "Mid-thirties, maybe. *Married*. I have plans. Dreams I need to fulfill before I get tied down with motherhood."

She bit her tongue before she told him everything. How she was unprepared to become a mother. And worse, how unhappy she was about this pregnancy. How guilty she felt over feeling the way she did.

She sure didn't need his crazy accusations adding to her stress. "Why on earth would you think I did this on purpose?"

He looked at the glass in his hands and, as if realizing he still held it, set it on the counter. "When you were a kid you seemed to have a...a crush on me—"

"You knew?" she asked weakly. "Did Liz know?"

He nodded.

Buzzing filled her ears. "I can imagine how much fun you two had laughing about it, about me. Poor chubby, silly Jane and her unrequited love for one of the beautiful people. Doesn't she have delusions of grandeur?"

"Neither one of us laughed at you," Brady said. "I was flattered."

"Flattered?" she repeated tonelessly. Groaning, she bent at the waist and covered her face with her hands, her curls falling forward to hide her face. "Oh, my God. Just kill me now. You're a Marine, you must know a hundred different ways to do it quickly and painlessly."

She heard him step forward but before she could move, he wrapped his fingers around her wrists and gently pried her hands from her face. "Did you sleep with me so we could...because you hoped we'd get together?"

Straightening quickly, the blood rushed to her head and she swayed. "You got me," she said, tugging free of his hold. "What started out as a childhood crush developed into a mad infatuation that's lasted all these years. So when you showed up at my sister's wedding, uninvited, unwanted and drunk, how could I resist? And the rumors about you drinking every night, getting into fights and sleeping your way through the females of Jewell make you all the more enticing. Now I not only get an unwanted pregnancy, but I'm also a notch on Brady Sheppard's bedpost. It's like a dream come true."

"I'm trying to understand how this happened. Didn't we use a condom?"

"What do you remember of that night?" she asked, her stomach sinking.

"You came up to me at the bar at the country club and asked me to leave, so I did." He frowned and stared off in the distance. "Then, when you found out I planned on walking home, you offered to drive me..."

She waited. And waited. "You don't even remember."

"Bits and pieces," he admitted, having the decency to look abashed.

"Let me give you the CliffsNotes version. I took you home and made you some coffee. We started talking and then you kissed me. You. Kissed. Me." She pointed her finger at him with each word. "Not the other way around."

"Janie, I—"

"It was sort of...intense. One minute we were kissing, and the next..." She shrugged. "The next we were having sex."

And she'd been so wrapped up in the fact that Brady wanted to be with her—and then so devastated by how it'd ended—she didn't even realize they hadn't used protection until she got home.

"Did I hurt you?" he asked quietly, his expression giving none of his thoughts away. "I didn't...I didn't force you, did I?"

"No. Of course not."

He shut his eyes briefly. Had he seriously thought he'd forced her?

"I knew what I was doing," she continued. And now she had to take responsibility for that decision. "But I didn't get pregnant on purpose and I have no desire to trap you into marriage. Right now I'm not even sure I want to see you again." She pushed herself upright, locked her knees so they wouldn't tremble but couldn't stop her voice from shaking. "So now would probably be a good time for you to leave." When he didn't so much as blink, she pointed to the door. "Get out."

"Not until we come up with the terms for a financial agreement."

"The terms are I'll take care of this baby and you can pretend we don't exist." Because the reality was, she didn't know if she wanted to keep this baby. The poor thing hadn't been born yet, and so far neither its mother nor father wanted anything to do with it. How messed up was that?

There was so much involved in having a baby. Diapers. Doctors' visits. Day care. And she'd never once considered being a single parent, of being solely responsible for another life. She had enough trouble taking care of herself.

"Having a child is expensive," he said as if she hadn't spoken. "How are you going to manage?"

She swallowed. Worked to keep her expression disdainful so he couldn't see the terror she was trying to hide. "Unlike you, I have a job."

Nothing. No reaction to her dig. The man really was made of stone. "I'm guessing tellers aren't the highest paid employees at the bank."

True. Another point to consider if she decided to keep the baby. She had a hard enough time making ends meet now. The only reason she could even afford this apartment was because her grandmother was her landlord. How would she support not only herself but a baby?

She clutched his arm above his elbow and pulled him toward the door. His muscles tensed under her fingers but he didn't resist.

She opened the door, and the cool rush of crisp autumn air helped settle her stomach. And her nerves. "Goodbye, Brady."

"I want to help."

"Why?"

He seemed taken aback. "Because it's my responsibility."

More exhausted than she'd ever been in her life, she shook her head. "I'm officially absolving you of any and all responsibility, then."

Yes, she usually accepted any and all help getting herself out of the many jams she managed to get into, but she didn't want him trying to assuage his guilt by tossing money her way. Bad enough he'd only slept with her because he'd been drunk…and that she'd slept with him when he'd really wanted Liz. She'd be damned if she'd take his pity, too. And that was all this was. But it wasn't enough.

Seemed she had some pride, after all.

"Damn it, Jane, you're—"

"You've done your part. If anyone asks, I'll be sure to tell them how you tried to get me to see reason. Go back to feeling sorry for yourself in your dark, dirty house. Drown yourself in Jim Beam for all I care." She nudged him outside so she could shut the door and put an end to this horrible day. "This baby doesn't need anything from you. And neither do I."

BRADY PULLED UP to the cottage and shut off the ignition. Every light in the place was on, and seeing as how they'd all been off when he'd left, that—plus the black sports car parked out front—meant one thing. He had company.

Damn, he hated company.

As he got out of the truck, his leg buckled. He tried to catch himself on the door but wasn't fast enough. He fell on his bad knee, landing hard on the cold ground. Gulping down air so he wouldn't howl with the pain, he pulled himself back up and reached into the cab for his cane. Slowly he made his way across the gravel to the front door.

He heard them as soon as he stepped inside. Seemed both his brothers had come calling. He stood there for a moment, the front door still open in case he changed his mind and decided to make a run for it anyway.

A nice dream, considering he could barely stand.

One of them—Matt, from the sound of it—laughed, the sound easily carrying throughout the small house. Brady scowled. How many times over the past few years had he wished he could be home for the holidays? Times when he would've given anything to come back to Jewell, if even for a day, to see Liz and his brothers and mother. Now he'd do anything to avoid them.

Too bad a few of them couldn't take a freaking hint.

Leaving the cane by the door, he went into the kitchen. Aidan, his older brother, leaned against the sink, his legs crossed at the ankles, not a wrinkle on his khakis or dark blue dress shirt. He didn't say a word when he noticed Brady, just raised an eyebrow over eyes the same light blue as Brady's.

"Why are the windows open?" Brady asked.

Sitting on the counter, wearing dark jeans and a

lightweight, V-neck sweater, his light brown hair pulled back into a stubby ponytail, the youngest Sheppard grinned. "Because it smells like you're hiding a dead body in here," Matt claimed.

"Not yet," Brady muttered. "But the night's young." He tossed his keys onto the cluttered table. "Why are you here?"

"Happy Thanksgiving to you, too." He slid off the counter, landing with an ease Brady hated him for. "Missed you at dinner."

Brady grabbed a bottle of pain relievers from the table. He couldn't take one of his prescriptions, not with Aidan watching, but maybe adding a few of these to the ones J.C. had given him would do the trick.

Opening an upper cupboard, he frowned. He could've sworn he had a bottle of Jack Daniel's in there. Shoving aside a box of cookies he didn't even remember buying, he shifted his weight onto his right leg. "You two ever hear of a little thing called trespassing?"

"Heard of it," Matt said with his usual freaking good cheer. "But it doesn't count when we're all equal owners in this place."

"Your leg bothering you?" Aidan asked.

"It's good."

"You sure? Because you seem—"

"I said it's good." And since he was being watched, being judged, he carefully shut the cupboard door before opening the next one to find a few mismatched plates and bowls. But no bottle. His hand shook as he moved on to cupboard number three. "I'm not in the mood for company."

"There's a news flash," Aidan murmured.

"Go away."

"Now is that any way to treat the people who brought you Thanksgiving dinner complete with half a pumpkin pie?" Matt asked.

"I don't like pumpkin pie," he said, searching the meager contents of his fridge for the six-pack of beer he'd bought the other day. Damn but he needed a drink.

"I do." Matt reached over Brady's shoulder and took out the pie. "Don't worry, Mom sent over two big slices of pecan pie, too."

"Looking for something?" Aidan asked.

It was his tone that clued Brady in. He leaned his arm against the fridge. Shit. They'd cleaned him out.

"This your idea of an intervention?"

"What do you mean?" Aidan asked, unbuttoning a sleeve and rolling it up.

Brady's eyes narrowed. The smug son of a bitch. "What's the matter?" he goaded. "You're not man enough to admit you snuck in here and hid all of my booze?"

Repeating the process with the other sleeve, Aidan stepped forward, his unhurried strides at odds with the cold, hard expression on his face. "I didn't hide it. I trashed it. Dumped it down the sink. When are you going to be man enough to admit you've got a problem?"

Hands fisted at his sides, Brady limped forward until he and Aidan were nose to nose. "Why don't you go—"

"Back it up," Matt said, stepping between them. A surreal experience considering Brady used to be the one breaking up fights between the other two. "Remember Mom and Dad always said you have to set a good example for me."

The urge to throw a punch still vibrating through him, Brady went back to the fridge. He took out several of the plastic containers his brothers had brought along with a half-empty jar of mayonnaise. "What do you want?"

"Why didn't you show up for dinner?" Aidan asked. He sounded so much like their deceased father.

Sounded like Tom Sheppard, but wasn't. No matter how hard he tried.

"I was busy."

Setting everything on the counter, he swallowed a couple of the pain relievers before shoving aside a dirty frying pan and a stack of plates. He pulled out a few slices of bread from the loaf behind the toaster, checked for mold then searched for a halfway clean knife.

"You're lucky Mom didn't come here instead of us," Matt said. "She'd kick your ass if she saw this kitchen."

Sweat broke out above his lip at the thought of his mother seeing firsthand how messed up he was. "I'm all sorts of lucky," he agreed, slathering mayo on the bread.

"Mom cried."

Brady froze, his grip tightening on the knife. "I told her I couldn't come."

"It's Thanksgiving," Aidan continued. "The first one in years where you've been on the same continent and you didn't show up."

Brady slowly, deliberately, set the knife down. Opening all the containers, he found turkey, stuffing and sweet potatoes. He piled turkey onto a slice of bread. "Don't push it," he said, his voice quiet. "I've had a really shitty day."

And he didn't need his sanctimonious brother heaping the guilt on, he thought as he topped the turkey with stuffing and another slice of bread. Hell, he felt so much guilt right now, any more and he'd explode.

"Worse than watching your mother leave Thanksgiving dinner in tears because your selfish, idiot brother didn't bother to show?" Aidan asked.

Brady sat at the table, took a bite and pretended to think that question over as he chewed. "Yeah. Worse than that. Besides, something came up that I had to take care of."

"What could be so important that you skipped out on a holiday family dinner?"

Taking his time, Brady had another bite of sandwich before he answered. "I'd say the woman who's going to have my baby was more important."

Blessed silence.

"You're kidding," Matt finally said.

"Serious as Aidan gets about…well…everything."

"Who?" Aidan asked.

A piece of turkey seemed to be stuck in his throat. He cleared it. "Jane Montgomery."

Another beat of silence. Then Aidan shook his head. "You slept with J.C.? Are you insane?"

"I'd sleep with her," Matt interjected.

Both Brady and Aidan stared at him. "What?" he asked, offended. "I would. She's got a body like one of those old-time movie stars. And that mouth of hers? The combination of that sexy mouth with those big brown eyes?" He nodded, a half smile on his face. "Oh, yeah, I'd—"

Aidan gave him a hard smack upside the back of the head. "Shut up."

Matt rubbed the spot. "I'm just saying…"

Sexy mouth? Brady frowned, picturing the way J.C. had looked when she'd shoved him out of her apartment. There hadn't been anything sexy about her then. He could see where some guys might find her attractive and she did have a certain…warm appeal. But compared to Liz, she was ordinary.

Aidan crossed his arms and glared at Brady. "What are you going to do?"

"Nothing."

"What do you mean, nothing?"

"J.C. said she and the baby didn't need me."

Which should be a relief, right? And what he wanted. No obligations. No ties to either J.C. or the baby.

"Doesn't matter," Aidan insisted. "You have a legal right to your child. And now is the perfect time to re-think that job offer we discussed."

Right. The job offer.

A few weeks ago, Aidan had driven Brady to the V.A. hospital for a checkup. On the way home, he'd offered Brady a position at the Diamond Dust Vineyard, the winery their father had started more than thirty years ago. Aidan had pointed out that Brady had been away from the wine business a long time. And while he'd worked at the winery as a teenager—all three broth-ers had—a lot had changed in the past twelve years. Change that would take Brady time to catch up on. So he'd suggested Brady ease back into the swing of things by taking over the bookkeeping of the Diamond Dust.

His brother wanted him stuck in some office behind a desk taking care of invoices and orders and adding figures. Trying to keep him away from alcohol, most likely. Sounded like hell.

"I don't need to think about it," he said. "I'm still not interested."

"You have other prospects?"

Brady snorted. He used to have prospects. He'd always planned on joining the Virginia State Police after he got out of the service. But like all his goals and dreams, that idea went up in smoke, starting when Liz decided he wasn't enough and ending with his knee getting shot up.

"I think I'll take some time to work on finishing my great American novel."

"How are you going to support a kid—"

"I'm not." He shrugged as if it didn't matter, but deep down, he knew it did. "J.C. doesn't want anything from me. Including child support payments."

Aidan's lips thinned. "So that's it? You're just going to abandon your own kid?"

"I'm thinking about leaving—"

"To go where?" Aidan asked.

Brady stretched out his leg. "North. New Hampshire, maybe. Or Maine."

Somewhere far from Jewell. Where there wouldn't be a chance of him running into Liz and her new husband. Or J.C. and the baby. So his kid wouldn't have to grow up in the same town as him, knowing his father didn't want anything to do with him. Or her.

Even he wasn't that big a prick.

He wasn't trying to hurt J.C. or the kid or make their lives more difficult. He just…couldn't be what they wanted. What they needed.

"You are some piece of work," Aidan said, staring at him as if he were a lowlife. "Why did you even come back?"

"Now that's an easy one," Brady said, working to keep his voice even. "I had nowhere else to go."

Instead of laying into him like Brady expected him to, Aidan snatched his jacket from the back of the chair so quickly, the chair toppled over.

"You need to get your head out of your ass," Matt said before following Aidan to the door.

Brady slouched in his chair. What he needed was for his family to leave him alone instead of trying to bring him back into the fold like a goddamn sheep. He had no interest in joining the winery. Having all three sons run it had been his father's dream.

But his father wasn't here anymore.

And just because Aidan had quit law school after their dad died to run the Diamond Dust Vineyard didn't mean Brady had to follow his footsteps. Matt hadn't. He'd lit out of Jewell right after graduating high school and hadn't looked back. He now made bucketfuls of money advising top wineries around the world. Brady wasn't about to cave, either.

Even if he didn't have any other options.

And he didn't. Not in Jewell, anyway.

Standing, he picked up a dirty coffee mug, rinsed it out and hobbled to his room. He grimaced as he stepped inside. His brothers hadn't bothered opening the windows in here...but he wished they had. The room smelled like his high-school gym locker. Maybe he'd do a load of laundry, he thought as he sat on the bed and picked up the almost full bottle of whiskey on the floor between the nightstand and bed.

He filled the mug halfway and drank deeply, ignoring the tremor in his hand. He concentrated on how the alcohol seemed to wash away his anxiety. Leaning back against the headboard, he took another, slower sip.

Tomorrow he'd worry about dirty laundry. About what he was going to do with his life now that his knee was useless and the woman he loved had exchanged him for some overeducated brainiac doctor. Tomorrow he'd think about what to do about J.C., with her warm brown eyes and huge expectations of him.

He finished the drink. Debated all of two seconds before pouring more into the mug. Yeah, he'd figure it all out.

Just not tonight.

CHAPTER FIVE

SHE DIDN'T USUALLY MAKE mistakes. More like...missteps. Paired the wrong shoes with an outfit. Picked up a real soda instead of sugar-free after a bad day. And when she was fourteen, there had been an unfortunate decision to perm her hair. But overall, Dr. Elizabeth Montgomery-Messler made the right choices.

Screwing up was J.C.'s department.

But as soon as the door opened, Liz knew she'd made a mistake, a huge one, in coming here.

"Good morning," she croaked, her face heating.

Linking her hands together in front of her, she tried to give Brady her professional smile—cool, calm and detached—but couldn't manage it. Not when he glowered at her, his hair tousled, his eyes red-rimmed.

Not when he stood in the doorway wearing a pair of low-slung, faded jeans. And nothing else.

"Liz," he said in his low voice.

"How...how are you?"

Widening his stance, he crossed his arms, the muscles in his arms bulging, the eagle tattoo on his left bicep shifting. "Cold."

If the goosebumps covering his arms were anything to go by, he was freezing. But he didn't shiver. Didn't give any indication he was uncomfortable at all. At least not enough to invite her inside.

"Yes...it's quite...chilly this morning," she said lamely. Though it was almost 9:00 a.m., frost still covered the ground, the sun unable to penetrate the cloudy, gray sky. "We're due for some rain..."

He raked his gaze over her. "Why are you here, Liz?"

"I...I'm running errands... I don't have to work until this afternoon and I...I came here to..."

He raised one eyebrow. She'd forgotten how much that annoyed her. "To...? To discuss the weather?"

She stuck her hand into the pocket of her brown leather jacket, her fingers closing around the velvet jeweler's box. "I wanted to see you. To see how you're doing," she amended quickly.

"Never better."

"Good. That's...good." The breeze picked up, blowing her hair into her face. She tucked the errant strands behind her ear.

"How's your knee?" she asked.

He seemed upset by the question. "It's fine."

"Are you taking physical therapy here in town or at the V.A. hosp—"

"Don't," he warned quietly.

"Don't what?"

"Don't pretend you give a damn."

Her throat constricted. "I...I wanted to visit you," she confessed, "when you were in the hospital."

"But you didn't." He leaned against the doorjamb, studying her in that way that used to make her feel like he could read her thoughts—when all she'd wanted was to keep a few of her thoughts to herself. "I guess your husband wouldn't have been too happy with you sitting by your ex's bedside."

No, Carter probably wouldn't have been happy, but he wouldn't have stopped her, either. When she'd discovered Brady had been injured, that he'd almost died, Carter had told her he understood if she needed to go to him. But she'd been too afraid to face him again.

Afraid he'd ask her to take him back. Terrified she'd say yes.

"After the way things...ended...between us," she said, staring at a point over his shoulder, "I thought a clean break would be best."

"And yet here you are."

She squeezed the box. Then pulled it out. "I wanted to give you this."

He went very still. "You've got to be kidding."

"I can't keep this, Brady. I...I want you to have it back."

"And you always get what you want, don't you? Sorry to disappoint you, but not this time." He pushed himself upright. "Toss it in the garbage. Hell, flush it down the toilet for all I care. But I'm not taking it back."

Her hand trembled. She should've returned his ring long ago but she hadn't wanted to send it overseas and risk it being lost or stolen. And she hadn't been brave enough to drop it off at his mother's house, knowing how angry his family must be with her.

But now she needed him to take it back. Things were still...tense...between her and Carter and if he discovered she still had it, he'd see it as a sign she hadn't let go of Brady. Not completely. She had to show her husband she'd moved on. That she didn't regret the choice she'd made.

"I'm not taking it back," Brady repeated. "So, if that's all..." He started to close the door.

"Did you sleep with my sister to hurt me?" she blurted, then bit the inside of her lower lip. Hard. "Never mind. Let's forget I was even here."

Shoving the ring back into her pocket, she hurried down the steps, the high heels of her suede boots sliding on the wet wood. And wouldn't landing on her rear be the perfect ending to this misadventure?

She wrenched open her car door.

"No."

Her heart pounded against her ribs. "What?"

He looked down at the porch, his hands on his hips. "No," he repeated, lifting his head. "I didn't sleep with Jane to hurt you."

She nodded, got into her car, started it and drove down the gravel road. Well, that was a relief. Brady hadn't become the kind of man who'd deliberately set out to cause pain. Who'd use J.C. as a tool to get back at Liz. He hadn't slept with her sister out of revenge.

He'd slept with her because he'd wanted to. Because he'd wanted J.C.

Her vision blurring, she wrung the steering wheel. Yes. That certainly was a relief.

BRADY'S TOES WERE NUMB. The tip of his nose tingling with cold. But he didn't move, couldn't force himself to turn from the sight of Liz driving away.

He did a few slow neck rolls. She thought he'd take it. Well, why wouldn't she want to get rid of it? She couldn't still wear it, not when she had another man's ring on her finger. Yeah, he'd noticed. Hard not to notice a rock that size. One that made the diamond he'd spent three months' salary on look like a freaking speck.

Guess better jewelry was just one of the perks of trading up from a grunt Marine to a doctor.

A car came barreling toward the house and his heart beat faster but it wasn't Liz coming back. No, it was worse than seeing the woman who was everything he'd always wanted and couldn't have.

It was his mother.

Diane pulled to a stop and got out of her big boat of a luxury car. "You're up," she said, striding toward him. "Good."

"Mom."

By choice, he'd hardly seen her since he'd moved back to Jewell. Her mouth was set in a disapproving line, and her frame was a few pounds heavier than he remembered. But with her graying blond hair cut in a new style and the remnants of the tan she'd acquired on her trip to Florida a few weeks ago, she looked good.

Ready to tear him apart limb from limb, but good.

"Shall we stand out here staring at each other all day," she asked, "or are you going to invite me in?"

He shifted his weight. Let her inside? Now? Before he'd had a chance to rent a backhoe to clean the place out? "Do I really have a choice or is that one of those trick questions?"

She went in ahead of him—straight to the kitchen.

"Oh, Brady," she called in disgust. "Look at this mess."

"I've seen it," he said as he entered the room.

Her eyes narrowed behind her glasses. "Are you sassing me?"

"No, ma'am," he responded automatically.

"Go put a shirt on while I make some coffee…you do have coffee, don't you?" He pointed toward the container next to the coffeepot on the counter. "You and I," she continued, "are going to have a little chat."

Aw, hell. This couldn't end well for him.

By the time he came back, wearing a Carolina Panthers T-shirt, Diane had the coffeepot scrubbed, a fresh pot brewing and was at the sink tackling his mountain of dirty dishes.

"I was going to get to those," he said, brushing crumbs off a chair before sitting.

She didn't even glance at him. "I could see it was high on your to-do list."

He slouched down and stretched his leg out. "I've been busy."

"You obviously have some free time this morning," she said, not mentioning that without a job, he had free time every morning. "And I could use some help."

He wasn't stupid—or brave—enough to point out that they could air dry. He got up again and found a towel at the bottom of a drawer. They worked in silence while the coffee finished brewing.

"You haven't returned any of my phone calls," Diane said, rinsing a heavy white mug.

And here they went. "I meant to—"

"No. You didn't. You're avoiding me." She scrubbed at a spot of dried ketchup on a plate. "When you first came back to Jewell and insisted on living here instead of at the house with me, I thought you just needed time and space to accept all the changes you've gone through."

"I appreciate it," he said, guessing that her giving him space was about to come to an abrupt end.

"But," she continued, stressing the word, "when you didn't show up at Thanksgiving, I realized I was wrong."

Noticing he'd twisted the towel in his hands, he smoothed it out before drying a glass. "I didn't want to do the whole celebratory dinner, that's all. Don't make more of it."

"The problem is, I haven't made enough of it. That needs to change." Her voice softened. "Let me help you."

"I'm fine."

"If you're so *fine,* then tell me why you've been avoiding your family." She tossed the dishcloth into the sink with enough force that water splashed them both. "And while you're at it, you can also explain why I had to hear from someone else that you're going to be a father."

Wincing, Brady scratched the back of his neck. This had to be some sort of gossip speed record.

"I was going to tell you…" In a few weeks. As soon as he'd figured out a few things. Like how to get J.C. to accept child support without wanting more from him. And what he was going to do with the rest of his life.

"Now you don't have to. Shirley Hanold down at the coffee shop told me, in front of my entire walking group, no less."

And so his day continued to get worse. He poured himself a cup of coffee so he wouldn't have to look at her. "Things are…complicated right now."

"Getting the sister of the woman you'd once planned to marry pregnant certainly is complicated. What are you going to do now?"

"About?"

"Don't play dense with me, Brady," she snapped. "Are you, or are you not, going to take responsibility for this baby?"

"I've offered J.C. child support."

His mother waved that away with one hard stroke

of her hand through the air. "Raising a child is about more than money. It's about being there, day in and day out. Nurturing your son or daughter. Loving them…no matter what mistakes they may make."

"Subtle," he muttered.

"You're too stubborn for subtlety." She poured herself a cup of coffee. "Your father and I raised you to be the type of man who steps up and takes responsibility for his actions."

He was willing to support the child for the next eighteen years. To make sure he…or she…was provided for. Wasn't that enough? He chugged a quick gulp of coffee and succeeded in burning his tongue.

"Does this have anything to do with Liz?" Diane asked.

And that was the last place he was going. Bad enough he still loved the woman. He wasn't about to admit it to his mother.

Besides, Liz was married now.

"Liz and I are over."

"Then why did I pass her car on my way here?"

His answer was a hard stare.

"That's it. I've had enough." Setting her cup down, Diane braced her arms against the table, getting right in her son's face. "You live like an animal. You refuse to go to physical therapy. When you're not ignoring your family, you're arguing with us. And your drinking is out of control."

He kept his expression blank. As if it didn't bother him that his mother knew how low he'd sunk. At least she didn't know about his nightmares. That he woke up in a cold sweat. He sipped his coffee.

"I'd think a winery owner would be all for drinking," he said.

"I'm disappointed in you, Brady." She cleared her throat and when she spoke again, her words were louder. Stronger. "I've never said that to any of my sons, never thought I would have reason to, but it's the truth."

What she'd said ripped him through him like a razor. He stood. "If that's all, I think I'm going to go back to bed."

"I'm not finished. You've done nothing to help yourself heal."

"The doctors at the V.A. hospital said my knee will never be a hundred percent."

"I'm not talking about your physical wounds." Hands trembling, she took her coat from the back of the chair and put it on, her movements jerky. "Every day I thank God your life was spared. That I'm not one of those mothers who's had to bury a child. You were given a gift, but instead of embracing your second chance, you'd rather dwell on the past. On what you lost. As much as I love you—and I do love you—I can no longer sit back and watch you self-destruct."

Damn it, that was not what he was doing. He may not be dealing with things how his family thought he should, but he was doing the best he could.

"Get yourself the help you need," his mother continued. "If you don't…" She swallowed.

"Don't stop there," he said softly.

The woman who raised three boys with equal doses of love and discipline stared him down. The woman who was as formidable and implacable as a drill sergeant. Who didn't make idle threats.

"If you don't, you'll have to find somewhere else to waste your life. Because you'll no longer be welcome here."

THE THIRD STREET DINER was packed with a boisterous lunch crowd, but J.C. spotted Liz seated in a small, two-person booth in the back. Hard to miss her, what with that halo highlighting her perfectly straight hair.

Okay, the halo was just the sun shining through a skylight. Still.

J.C. patted her hair. Yes, it was as big and frizzy as she feared. She made her way through the restaurant. She smiled and said hello to a few people but she didn't stop. She had to get her sister back.

"Hi," J.C. said when she got to the booth.

Even though she was sitting—and J.C. was a good three inches taller than her—Liz managed look down her nose at J.C. "You're late."

She checked her watch, then shrugged out of her coat. Bit her tongue instead of pointing out that anything under five minutes shouldn't be considered late. "Sorry. My last customer had a couple savings bonds and…"

And her sister didn't give a rat's behind about her job.

J.C. hung her coat on the metal pole next to the bench seat before sitting down. "I'm glad you came."

Liz folded her hands on the table. "I'm only here because Mom asked me to hear you out."

"Oh. Right. Well…" So she'd had to get her mother to talk to Liz for her. She didn't have a choice. Liz had ignored all of her attempts to explain. J.C. couldn't remember a time when they'd gone five days without speaking.

Couldn't remember there ever being a time when Liz was so angry with her that she didn't want to talk to her.

Their waiter, a short, stocky college kid, took their

orders. Once they were alone again, J.C. cracked her thumb knuckle. "So...how are you?" she asked awkwardly.

"Fine."

J.C. drummed her fingers on the table. This was going to be harder than she'd thought. While she had plenty of experience apologizing for her blunders, she didn't know how to be the one who smoothed things over. She'd always relied on Liz for that.

The waiter delivered their drinks and J.C. unwrapped a straw and stuck it in her ginger ale. Took a sip to calm her churning stomach. She'd had her first prenatal visit yesterday and Dr. Owens had assured her the morning sickness would end soon, it being the second trimester.

And then, after receiving that hopeful news, J.C. had been informed by the doctor's office manager that her medical insurance would barely cover sixty percent of the expenses she'd incur during this pregnancy. No wonder she still felt sick.

"How's Carter?" J.C. asked. She'd been worried about the two of them ever since that awful Thanksgiving scene. When she'd left their house, she'd overheard them arguing in the hallway about Liz's reaction to the news of J.C.'s pregnancy. And who the father was. "Is...are you two okay?"

Liz, her mouth set in a thin line, squeezed a lemon slice into her water. "Of course," she said, but wouldn't meet J.C.'s eyes.

J.C. leaned across the table and covered Liz's hand with her own. "Lizzie, I...God...I'm so sorry."

Liz eased her hand away. "I knew you had a crush on him when you were a kid." She shook her head. "What did you do? Wait all these years for your opportunity? For us to break up?"

"It wasn't like that. And it's not as if he ever would've looked at me twice—at any other woman—if you two were still together." She lined the salt and pepper shakers up with the front corners of the napkin dispenser. "It just sort of…happened."

Liz pursed her mouth. "How exactly does that work? You and my ex-fiancé were both naked and one of you tripped and fell on the other?"

"It was a mistake." She took another drink but it did little to ease the dryness of her throat. "One I'd give anything to go back and undo. It was wrong. *I* was wrong. I…I convinced myself it wouldn't matter to you because you'd broken up with him. That you didn't want him anymore."

"I don't." Her cheeks colored. "That's not what this is about."

"No. Of course not." Liz couldn't still want Brady. Not when she had Carter. Could she? "I didn't mean to hurt you."

"You never mean to do the things you do. You don't think about the consequences of your actions. You just charge forward, not caring about anything except what you want. Then, when it blows up in your face, you expect someone else to pick up the pieces."

Stunned, J.C. sat back. That wasn't fair. She could fix her own messes. She just never had to before.

That part about her only thinking about what she wanted? Total crap. Of course she'd thought of Liz, of her reaction, that night she'd slept with Brady. Had thought of her sister but hadn't let anything stop her, she realized, her queasiness now having nothing to do with being pregnant. She'd betrayed Liz because Brady had wanted her.

Because she'd wanted him.

"I thought I could do this, but I can't," Liz said, sliding out of the booth as she dug into her purse. She tossed some cash onto the table but J.C. got out and stopped her.

"What about lunch?" she asked. What about their relationship?

"I'm not hungry."

"I'm sorry," J.C. rushed to say, her throat so tight it came out as a croak. "Please…can you forgive me?"

Liz slowly looked at her. "Not today," she whispered.

Their waiter passed Liz as she walked out. "Everything all right here?" he asked, setting their food on the table.

Sitting back down, J.C. gave him a pathetic excuse for a smile. "Fine. Thanks."

He took the hint and didn't press. "Let me know if you need anything else."

This was bad. Real bad. Liz hadn't forgiven her. What if she never did? J.C. studied her cheese and mushroom quesadilla and then shoved it aside. Liz just needed more time. To…work through her hurt and anger. She'd forgive J.C.

Because J.C. couldn't get through this without her.

CHAPTER SIX

J.C. LEANED AGAINST the steering wheel and stared up at the white Colonial house that had been in the Sheppard family for five generations. It was lovely with tall, narrow windows, black shutters and wide porches on both the ground and second floors. The front door was a deep, inky shade of blue and had leaded glass windows on both sides, another one shaped like a fan on top. Listed on the Historical Register as one of the oldest structures in the county, there was nothing even remotely intimidating about it.

Right. That was why she'd been sitting there for twenty minutes.

She unbuckled her seat belt. After the week she'd had, failure was not an option.

Too bad. Failure was the one thing she excelled at.

Taking a deep, fortifying breath, she stepped out into the bright midday sun before she could change her mind. She tucked a small, white bakery box under her arm and crossed the cement drive. Once on the porch, she lifted her hand to knock only to lower it again.

Why did last-ditch efforts have to be so difficult?

Shutting her eyes, she rapped on the door. Maybe no one was home. Maybe they were all out in the vineyards doing…whatever people who had vineyards did. Pruning. Or…or fertiliz—

Someone tapped her on the shoulder.

"God!" J.C. whirled around, her heart racing.

A sleek, long-legged brunette in tight jeans and T-shirt proclaiming Conserve Water, Drink Wine smiled. "Not even close. But it's better than a lot of other things I've been called. I'm Connie."

Still trying to catch her breath, J.C. shook the woman's hand. "J.C. Montgomery."

Connie tipped her head to the side, the sunlight picking up reddish highlights in her short, choppy dark hair. "Montgomery, huh? Liz's sister?"

If she had a dollar for every time someone asked her that, she wouldn't have to look for ways to supplement her income. "Yes."

"I was a few years ahead of Liz in school. Plus, she used to come out here before…"

Before she broke Brady's heart.

Connie tucked her fingers into her jeans pockets. "So, is it J-A-Y-C-E-E or just the letters?"

"Uh…the letters."

"Well, J.C. just the letters, is there something I can do for you?"

She glanced at the door. "I'm looking for Aidan Sheppard."

"I need to see him, too. So what do you say we go in and track him down?"

Connie let herself in and J.C. followed her into a two-story foyer with elegant wainscoting, rose-colored walls and a wooden staircase leading to the second floor.

"Shouldn't we wait for someone to let us in?" she whispered.

Humor lit Connie's blue eyes. "I run the vineyards

for the Sheppards. They're used to me coming and going."

Oh. Well. That made sense, then. At least J.C. wasn't letting herself into another house belonging to the Sheppards. The one time she'd done that, things hadn't worked out so well for her.

Connie pulled out a cell phone and pressed a number. "Aidan's office is upstairs. I'll call him." She lowered her voice conspiratorially. "He gets grumpy when people barge in on him."

J.C. smiled weakly. Of course he did. "Yes. That's so rude."

Maybe she shouldn't have come without an appointment.

"He's not answering, which means he's probably on the office line. Let me text him that we're here—" she flipped her phone the other way, her fingers flying over the keys almost as quickly as the words coming out of her mouth "—and he can come down when he's finished."

Then, sticking the phone back into her pocket, she walked around a corner. J.C. switched the box to her other hand. Should she follow? Sit on the cute wooden bench against the wall and wait for Aidan to come downstairs? Take her impetuous self and this whole crazy idea and get out there?

Connie poked her head back around the corner. "You coming?"

She sighed. "Right behind you."

They went into a family room so big, J.C. could've fit her apartment in it. And still have space left over. A stone fireplace took up most of the wall to the left while sliding glass doors led to a bricked veranda at the back of the house. The room opened up into a large kitchen with ceramic tiles on the floor, oak cabinets and stainless-steel appliances—including a double wall oven and a six-burner range top like the ones J.C.'s mother had been bugging her father to get for their own kitchen. Passing a small breakfast nook with three sides of floor-to-ceiling windows, J.C. crossed to the granite-topped island in the middle of the room. After setting the box down, she lovingly ran her hands over the cool surface.

"You want me to give you two a few minutes alone?"

J.C. returned Connie's grin. And how sad was it that she couldn't remember the last time she'd smiled? "Do you have any idea how many truffles I could shape on this much counter space?"

Connie tapped a forefinger to her lips. "Quite a few?"

"Eight...maybe even ten dozen. And I wouldn't even have to set cookie sheets of them on the coffee table or washer and dryer. I can't even reach the edge," she said, stretching her arms across the width of the counter.

"It truly is an amazing structure." Connie carried a large, frosted glass jar with a silver lid over to the island. "Which is why Diane likes it so much. She doesn't make truffles, but she's big on baking."

J.C. blanched. She'd been so worried about meeting with Aidan she hadn't even considered running into Brady's mom. "She's not...she's not here, is she?"

Connie shook her head. "She and Al are spending the weekend up in D.C."

Al being Al Wallace, Mrs. Sheppard's boyfriend—if you could call a sixty-something retired senator some-one's boyfriend—and God bless him for taking Mrs.

Sheppard away for the weekend. J.C. would gladly avoid Brady's mom for...oh...forever would work.

Not that she was afraid of her or anything. Ha.

Diane Sheppard had a reputation for getting what she wanted and had no qualms about stomping on anyone who got in her way.

What if she wanted to be a part of the baby's life? What if...what if she wanted to have a say in any decision she made regarding the baby?

J.C. rubbed her temples. Mrs. Sheppard might not even know about the baby. And if she did, well, this was J.C.'s body. Her baby. And ultimately her decision whether she kept the baby or not.

"Here," Connie said, holding out a thick, pumpkin-shaped sugar cookie with orange frosting. "You look like you could use a sugar rush."

J.C. reached for the cookie only to remember how, when she'd stood on the stupid scale at Dr. Owens's Monday, the nurse had moved the little metal slide up. Then she'd moved it some more. And yet some more.

"I'm good, thanks," she managed to say, lowering her hand. She may be eating for two, but that didn't mean she had to eat everything. Besides, being this virtuous was almost as good as a giant sugar cookie.

And the day she believed that was the day she hoped she stopped breathing.

Connie shrugged, then polished off the cookie before reaching for another one.

J.C. hiked herself up onto one of the two high-backed, black stools. "Even though we just met, I already hate you. But it's nothing personal."

Connie's laugh was deep and husky—and the perfect fit for someone so sexy.

"I'm guessing you're one of those women who can eat anything she wants without gaining weight," J.C. continued. Connie grinned and went for a third cookie. "See? I have to hate you. It's the principle of the thing."

"A girl's gotta have her principles." Connie put the lid back on the cookie jar when the sliding glass door opened.

Brady stepped inside and stopped abruptly when he saw J.C. "Everything okay?"

She twisted her fingers together in her lap. Crap. She'd gone seven days without any more fun-filled run-ins with him. And she'd like to keep that streak alive for the next eighteen years or so.

"Everything's fine," she said.

His hair was mussed, the black T-shirt he wore underneath an open gray and black checked flannel shirt was wrinkled and the stubble from the last time she'd seen him had grown into a full-fledged, if scruffy, beard.

Not even glancing at Connie—who watched them intently—he crossed to the end of the island. Close enough that J.C. could smell the fresh air on his skin.

He studied her as if he were a scientist and she were some perplexing, never-before-discovered insect. "Why is your hair like that?"

"You are such a moron," Connie murmured.

J.C. couldn't agree more. She lifted a hand to her hair. "I straightened it."

"I called you a few times," he said, obviously not having anything else to say about her hair. Like how nice it looked.

Not that she cared. She certainly hadn't spent a solid hour and a half ironing her hair into submission for him. "I got the messages."

All seven of them. He'd called once a day since leaving her apartment Thanksgiving and each time he said the same thing. "It's Brady. Call me."

"You two together?" Connie asked.

J.C. snorted. "No."

"Beat it, Connie," Brady said.

"But I don't want to leave. Not when this is so fascinating."

Brady glared at her. "Goodbye."

She held her hands up in surrender. "I can take a hint." She gave J.C.'s arm a quick, reassuring squeeze as she walked past. "I'll go up and see what's taking Aidan so long."

He frowned. "Aidan? So you're not here because you've changed your mind?"

Please. Even if she wanted his money, she couldn't accept it now.

"I'm not here to see you," she said, glad to hear a touch of ice in her voice. "I'm here on business."

He raised his eyebrows. "Business?" She nodded. "With the Diamond Dust?" Another nod, this one jerky. "Is that why you're dressed like that?"

"What's wrong with how I'm dressed?"

She forced herself to remain still and not fidget or tug at her clothes while he slowly inspected her from the tips of her pointy-toed shoes, up the black, wide-legged pants and over her small baby bump currently covered by a loose white button-down shirt. When she thought he was done and she could breathe again, his gaze lingered at the black lace peeking out of the top of her shirt.

Her breasts had already gone up a cup size and since she liked being able to breathe, she'd left the top three buttons undone and worn a silk camisole underneath. Now, as her skin warmed under his scrutiny, she wished she had on a sweater. Preferably with a high neckline.

He jerked his eyes up, his jaw tight. "You don't look like yourself."

That'd been the point. The hair, the clothes, they were supposed to show Aidan she was a businesswoman. Professional. Capable. Confident.

Someone he would want to do business with.

"YOU'RE NOT HERE to see me?" Brady asked, trying to wrap his head around what she was saying. Why was she dressed like some sort of naughty librarian? With her hair straightened, there was a noticeable resemblance between her and Liz. A resemblance that was eclipsed by the way J.C. filled out that damn shirt.

"I'm really not here to see you. I was hoping to talk to Aidan."

"About doing business with the Diamond Dust?"

"Yes," she muttered.

What sort of business could J.C. have with his family's winery?

"Why don't I wait in the foyer for Aidan?" she asked. "I'm sure you have…things…to do."

He shrugged and went to the refrigerator. Out of the corner of his eye, he noticed J.C. pick up the white box from the island.

"Do you have an appointment?" he asked.

"An appointment?"

Brady took a container of some sort of leftover pasta out before closing the fridge door. "An appointment with Aidan."

She didn't. For one thing, if she had an appointment,

Aidan wouldn't have told her to come to the main house. His brother used their father's home office upstairs, but he held all meetings down the road at the converted farmhouse where the Diamond Dust's main offices were located.

And he never would've let her wait this long. Aidan was nothing if not organized. He'd be willing to bet Aidan scheduled every minute of his day, including his trips to the bathroom.

J.C. fumbled the box in her hands before setting it back on the island. "No. Do I…do you think that'll be a problem?"

"Only if you're serious about doing business with him."

She blanched. No, Aidan wasn't that big prick, to hold something like an impromptu visit against her. But the truth was, Brady didn't want her to go to his brother.

Not when she wouldn't even take his phone calls.

"Maybe I should leave," she said, biting her lower lip, her brow furrowed.

"You're already here," he pointed out. His knee began to ache so he lifted himself up to sit on the counter. "You might as well do what you came here to do."

"But if it's going to make Aidan angry—"

"You don't need Aidan." Brady took the lid off the container. Lasagna. Great. Even better. He opened the drawer between his legs and grabbed a fork. "You've got me."

She wrinkled her nose. "I've got you for what?"

He waved the fork. "To discuss your business idea."

"Have you been drinking?"

She didn't add *again*, but sure as hell implied it. "Not yet."

He would've started already but he'd been starving and all he had at the cottage was cereal...but no milk. Guess he needed to make a trip to the grocery store. The grocery store where he could limp behind a cart while everyone stared. Or asked him how he was doing, what his plans were next.

Better yet, he could have a flashback, proving to everyone how little control he had over himself.

Was it any wonder he needed the oblivion alcohol provided?

The only reason he'd come to his mom's house was because he knew she wouldn't be there. Despite her being pissed at him, she still kept him informed of her comings and goings and two days ago, she'd left him a message saying she was spending a long weekend in D.C. with Al.

"Are you working for Aidan?" J.C. asked.

He could be. If he gave in to his mother's threats and Aidan's pressure.

Brady scooped up more cold lasagna. "Tell me."

She tucked her hair behind her ear—just like Liz always did. "I've had some unexpected expenses. And I need to supplement my income."

He narrowed his eyes at her hesitant tone. "What kind of unexpected expenses?"

"It doesn't matter. But I—"

"Jane. What expenses?"

She shrugged, the movement causing her full breasts to rise and lower. He averted his gaze. "Some...doctor bills."

For the baby. *His* baby. "I'll pay them."

"No. You won't."

"I want to," he said, realizing it was true. He wanted to help her, even if all he had to offer was a few bucks.

"I told you, I don't want your money." Her hands were clenched at her sides, her shoulders rigid. "I have to do this on my own."

And that was when he saw the real reason she wouldn't accept his help.

Pride.

Hell. He knew a thing or two about that. And he wasn't about to try to injure hers.

"Go on," he said quietly.

She looked at him with such gratitude, he felt like a complete ass. Damn it, she shouldn't be willing to accept so little from him.

"When I saw that first bill," she said, "I was a bit stressed so I did what most women do when they're stressed."

"Found some poor bastard to castrate?"

"Ha-ha. No, but only because I didn't think you'd let me within ten feet of you if I happened to be carrying a machete."

He grimaced. "Ouch."

"I searched for some chocolate. But I didn't have any so I decided to make some." She took the lid off the box and carried it over to him.

He set the lasagna aside. "I didn't know you made chocolates." He inspected the candies set on waxed paper.

Then again, there was plenty he didn't know about her. Like why she'd slept with him. Or what her plans for the future were. How she would raise their baby on her own.

But being this close to her he did find out a couple of things about her. She smelled sweet, like vanilla. Her eyes weren't plain brown as he'd always thought, but a deep, rich caramel.

"I usually make them as gifts," she said, "for holidays and birthdays or if a friend needs a pick-me-up. And I made them for—" she dropped her eyes "—for Liz's wedding and they went over pretty well and I…I started to think maybe I could sell them. So, I took some down to Horizons—"

"Is that the gift shop Sandy O'Donnell owns?" he asked, remembering the one time he'd gone into the small store on Main Street. He'd been on leave from basic training and had stopped in to buy a Mother's Day gift. But being surrounded by all those chick gifts—crystal glasses, tableware, picture frames and ceramic figurines—had given him the hives.

"Yes. She carries chocolates from a candy maker in Danville during the holidays and Easter, so I thought she might be interested in selling mine, as well. But she has an exclusive contract with the other guy." J.C. rolled her eyes as if her encounter with Sandy hadn't been all that pleasant. "I tried Kent Goodwin at the Main Street Mercantile and he said he would've been interested…if I'd contacted him back in August when he was accepting inventory for the holiday season. Then he gave me the old 'if I make an exception for you, I have to make an exception for everyone' speech and—"

"The point of all this?" he asked, pinching the bridge of his nose.

"I'm getting there. Rhonda, the manager at Country Crafts, declined because she'd tried gourmet food at her store before and it hadn't sold well. Of course, she didn't tell me that until *after* she ate half a pound worth of samples. I went to Delgato's but he wouldn't even hear me out. You'd think, seeing as how I was the one he fired, *I'd* be holding the grudge and not the other way around."

Couldn't she have just said all three gift shops in town and the only gourmet grocery store within an eighty-mile radius had turned her down? "And now you're here…?"

"I'm here because when I left Delgato's, I saw the flyer for the holiday open houses the Diamond Dust is hosting and I had an epiphany."

"An epiphany on Mechanic Street. That's not something you hear every day."

"That's what makes it special," she assured him solemnly, but her eyes were lit with humor. "I think my chocolates and the Diamond Dust would be a perfect match. Sell the chocolates in the gift shop."

He carefully slid off the counter landing with his weight on his right leg, the box still in his hands. "You want to start making chocolates—"

"Gourmet chocolates." She closed the distance between them and picked out a candy. "Here. Try one." She popped it into his mouth.

The outer shell was dark chocolate, the inside a creamy milk chocolate that melted on his tongue. Damn, that was good. He looked into her eyes and found it difficult to take a full breath.

He pushed away from the counter, set the box down and took a glass from an upper cabinet. "Let me see if I've got this straight," he said as he filled it with water from the sink and took a long drink. "You couldn't find anyone in town willing to sell your chocolates so you decided the best place for them would be at the Diamond Dust?"

She crossed her arms, which drew his attention again to that damn lace covering her breasts. "You make it sound like this is my last resort."

"Is it?"

"So what if it is?" she asked irritably. "It's not like it's the end of my world if this doesn't pan out. I'm sure I can get a part-time job somewhere."

"You don't sound very convincing."

"It's just...I've had some trouble finding a job that suits me. And when some employers see my employment history they're not real anxious to give me a chance."

"How many jobs have you had?"

"Total?"

Sleeping with her was the biggest mistake of his life and she was a pain in the ass for wanting more from him than financial support with this pregnancy. For expecting more from him than he could give. So why did he find her amusing as hell? "How about you give me a rough estimate?"

She pursed her lips. "Around a dozen. Give or take one or two."

Twelve jobs in less than what...ten years? There was no way Aidan would go for any sort of deal with her no matter how good her candy tasted.

Luckily, Aidan wasn't here.

"You've got a deal," he said. "You can sell your candy at the Diamond Dust gift shop."

For a moment, she seemed confused, but then she broke into a grin. "Really?" she asked breathlessly.

"The details will still have to be ironed out." Which would be the perfect job for Aidan. His older brother loved nothing more than ironing out details. "But, yeah, really."

Her cheeks flushed with pleasure. "This is so great. You won't regret it, I promise." He ground his back teeth together when she did a little hip-shaking, shoulder-wiggling dance that brought her closer to him. "Thank you, thank you, thank you!"

Then she grabbed his face with both hands, pulled his head down and kissed him.

CHAPTER SEVEN

J.C. STOPPED DOING her victory dance when Brady's hands tightened on her hips as she pressed her mouth against his. There she went again, throwing caution aside and letting her spontaneity get the better of her. She'd meant for it to be nothing more than a celebratory kiss. Light and fun. To express her gratitude—and relief.

But as soon as her mouth touched Brady's, she knew it could never be any of those things. Not when her heart stuttered at the feel of his lips against hers. Not when warning bells were clanging in her head.

Not when fixing things with Liz meant she had to stay away from him.

She fell back on her heels.

You just charge forward, not caring about anything except what you want.

No. Not anymore.

"Don't take that the wrong way," she warned him in a raspy whisper.

His eyes hooded, he studied her. "How should I take it?"

She shivered. And realized she was touching him, still cupping his face.

She dropped her hands and stepped back. But she could still feel the scratchiness of his beard on her palms. "It's been a tough week and I'm...grateful...

and…" And she was babbling like an idiot. She held her breath for the count of five. "I'm happy. That's all."

"Do you kiss a man every time you're happy?"

"Every chance I get," she assured him soberly. "You should've seen the lip-lock I laid on Marty Boyd last month when he told me my car passed its inspection."

"That impressive, huh?"

"Well, I hate to brag, but it was enough of a kiss that I'm pretty sure he thinks we're engaged now."

And then, to her amazement, Brady smiled. Disheveled, miserable and, if she wasn't mistaken, broken Brady Sheppard smiled. At her. It didn't last long and for a moment, it seemed as if even that small bit of happiness pained him, but what else could she do but smile back?

Someone behind her cleared their throat. "I hope I'm not interrupting anything."

J.C. whirled around. Aidan stood at the other end of the kitchen, gazing shrewdly from her to Brady and back again. Her face flamed.

"Nothing that meant anything," Brady said. "Isn't that what you said, J.C.?"

"Uh…right."

"Connie said you wanted to speak with me?" Aidan asked J.C.

Like Brady, Aidan was tall with broad shoulders and blond hair, but that was where the differences ended. His eyebrows were heavier, his lips fuller, his eyes more green than blue. And though it was the end of the day, his button-down shirt and khakis were still neatly pressed, as if wrinkles dared not mess with this cool-eyed man.

Thank God she and Brady had made the deal and she

didn't have to try to convince Aidan to do with business with her. Though Aidan was polite, the way he scowled at his brother made him seem about as approachable as a wolverine. And not the Hugh Jackman kind.

"No." She cleared her throat. "I mean, yes, I did want to speak with you but now I guess I don't have to…" The tension between the brothers was palpable. And nothing she wanted to get in the middle of. "I'd better get going." She smiled at Aidan as she sidestepped him toward the family room. "I have…things. To do."

"I'll walk you out," Brady said.

"Oh. That's not necessary."

But the expressions on the brothers' faces told her it was. And far be it for her to argue.

"Bye, Aidan," she said.

He nodded. "Nice to see you, Jane."

As they walked back toward the foyer, she snuck a glance at Brady. He reached past her and opened the front door. "I'll have Aidan call you with the details."

"Thank you," she said, careful not to touch him as she passed. She stepped off the porch and into the sunshine.

"I opened a savings account. For the baby."

Shading her eyes with her hand, she looked up at him. He didn't know how important it was for her to prove she could take care of herself. And the first step was to be able to pay her own way. When the office manager at Dr. Owens's office had told her that her insurance wouldn't cover all her expenses, she hadn't been too worried. No, she'd done what Liz accused her of doing. She'd gone to her parents to take care of her.

While her parents were far from thrilled with the situation, they'd told her they'd support whatever decision she made regarding the baby. And that they'd be more than willing to cover her medical expenses.

But she wasn't going to be that person anymore, the one who let everyone else take care of her. "We've been through—"

"My attorney will send you the account information. I'll deposit money into it each month." He stood gripping the porch rail, the muscles of his arms knotted. "You can do what you want with it. Use it or not. Either way, it'll be there. And whatever's left when the kid is eighteen will be turned over to him."

"I don't want to go over—"

"Do you really hate me so much that you'd deny your baby financial security?"

She made a soft sound of surprise. Was that what he thought? That she was doing this as some way to get back at him? That couldn't be further from the truth. But really, what was it hurting if he put money into a bank? She was still trying to figure out how she was going to pay her doctor bills. Knowing she had a cushion for the future would be a huge relief. And as he pointed out, she didn't have to use it.

She could still keep her pride.

She nodded. "Okay."

"Thank you," he said, as if she were the one doing something for him.

"Listen, you said you weren't staying in Jewell and, well, in case I don't...see you again...I want to wish you good luck. With whatever you do. And I...I want you to know...I don't hate you," she blurted. "I could never hate you."

He regarded her intently, his eyes a brilliant blue. Her

cheeks warmed. Her breath clogged in her lungs as the silence stretched on.

"Not that it matters," she added feebly.

Okay, then. She gave him a half-hearted wave and walked away, hoping he couldn't tell how unsteady her legs were.

As she opened her car door, his voice carried to her, soft as the cool breeze.

"It matters."

"YOU MUST BE MAKING PROGRESS," Aidan said when Brady came back into the kitchen. Aidan popped the top of a can of cola and took a drink. "I'm glad you're stepping up and doing the right thing."

Brady grunted and rolled his head side to side so that his neck cracked. Progress? He'd agreed to a business deal he wasn't entitled to make and had told J.C. about the account he'd set up for the baby.

But he was ditching her, leaving her to raise their kid on her own. He wouldn't blame her if she did come after him with that machete.

And what had been up with that kiss? It'd taken every ounce of control he still had left not to pull her closer.

"When's everything going to happen?" Aidan asked.

Brady picked out a dark chocolate from the box next to him and tossed it in his mouth, hoping to replace the lingering taste of J.C.'s kiss. "Everything?"

"You need to tell Mom." Aidan waved his can. "It shouldn't take too long to plan the wedding—"

"Wedding?" Brady choked out.

"Stop repeating everything I say. It's pissing me off."

Aidan's lips thinned and he straightened. "Aren't you and Jane getting married?"

"No."

"No? That's it?"

Brady pretended to consider that. "How about, hell no."

Aidan tapped his fist against his thigh. "Then why did she seem so happy? Did you finalize a financial agreement about the baby?"

"We did." Brady put the lid back on the half-eaten lasagna. Since there was no food at the cottage, he might as well take it back with him. If he took enough of his mom's leftovers home, he could put off the inevitable trip to the store for another day or two. "I'm going to pay child support." Whether she ever used his money, he had no way of saying.

"We'll name you Father of the Year," Aidan said.

And Brady wasn't about to get into it again with his sanctimonious brother.

"As to the reason she seemed happy, that's probably because I told her the Diamond Dust would purchase some of her homemade candy to sell."

The silence was broken only by the soft ticking of the antique wall clock that'd belonged to their mother's great-grandmother.

"You did what?" Aidan finally asked softly, a muscle jumping in his jaw.

"I told her we'd buy her chocolates. We can sell them in the gift store, offer them at the open houses."

"We? I hadn't realized you were on the payroll."

Brady went back to the fridge to see what else he could take home to stock his own fridge. "I'm going to need you to draw up a contract—"

"No way."

"What's the problem? You wanted me to step up and do the right thing with J.C. and I am. Besides, you've been bugging me to get more involved in the Diamond Dust for months. So, I got involved."

"I wanted you to work for the company. Maybe pitch in with some paperwork. Handle some shipping issues we've been having. Not offer someone a deal behind my back."

"It wasn't behind your back," Brady muttered, irritated. "I just told you, didn't I?"

"You made a deal on behalf of the Diamond Dust without discussing it with me or Mom."

Brady grabbed a container of cheese spread, some lunch meat and a half-empty carton of eggs, shutting the door with enough force to shake the condiments. "Isn't that what you've been doing all these years? You've never once asked for my opinion on anything you wanted to do with the Diamond Dust."

"I'm the president. Mom's the owner. You don't even work for the winery. The way I remember it, both you and Matt couldn't wait to get away from Jewell and the Diamond Dust fast enough."

"Dad didn't have a problem with my decision to join the Corps," Brady said, carefully setting the egg carton on the counter instead of hurling it at his brother's head like he wanted. "Just buy the candy from J.C. It's good. Which means we're sure to make a profit. It's a win-win situation."

"Doesn't matter how good it is. Our budget for holiday spending is already set. Tell her you can't keep your end of the bargain."

"No."

Aidan shifted into what Brady recognized as his fighting stance—legs wide, hands loose at his sides, weight on the balls of his feet. "That wasn't a request. That was me not giving you a choice."

Aidan picked up his soda dismissively. As if whatever he said was the last word on the subject. Brady wanted to go after his brother and knock his fat head in. Too bad that, with his bum knee, he didn't have a chance of beating up his brother.

Aidan did whatever it took to win. Even if it meant fighting dirty.

Maybe Brady should consider going to his physical therapy sessions once in a while. The pain would be worth it if he could kick Aidan's ass.

"Just try one." He shoved the box at Aidan.

Even as Aidan chewed, his expression remained sour. Which was nuts considering how good those chocolates were. Then again, ever since their dad died and Aidan's wife left him a month later, he always looked as if someone had switched his favorite Petit Verdot with grape-flavored children's cough medicine.

"Well?" Brady asked when he couldn't stand it any longer.

"You're right. It's good. But that doesn't change anything."

"I already told J.C. we'd do this."

"And your word is your bond?" Aidan asked dryly.

"When I say I'll do something, I do it," Brady managed through gritted teeth. He may not be living up to his family's high ideals but he kept his word.

He just didn't give it very often.

"Sorry," Aidan said, not sounding sorry at all, damn

him. "But it's not going to happen. You'll have to assuage your guilt some other way."

"DO YOU HAVE any chocolates?"

J.C. blinked at Brady. Why was he at her apartment... carrying a large pizza box, no less? When she'd left his mother's house earlier today, she'd figured, other than occasionally running into him while he was still in town, she'd never see him again.

She nudged Daisy back into the apartment with her foot before the cat could slip out into the dark. "Halloween was last month. And you're about twenty years past the normal trick-or-treating age."

"I'm not out begging for treats," he said in his rough voice. "Aidan didn't go for it."

So much for being able to pay her doctor bills with the money she'd get selling her chocolates. So much for trusting Brady Sheppard. "But you said..."

Wait a minute. What exactly had he said? She'd asked if he worked for Aidan and he'd said... She searched her memory. Nothing. He'd said nothing.

"You have no authority to decide anything about the winery, do you?" she asked.

"No."

Guess she should've asked him that question earlier. "Then why did you act as if you did? Why did you say it was a deal?"

He glared, as if he had a right to stand on her doorstep all big and imposing and fierce. "Do you have any chocolates made or not?"

The strap of her tank top slid down her arm and she pulled it back up. "A few, but—"

"If you still want to sell your chocolates at the Diamond Dust, we need to do a pairing."

"I thought Aidan wasn't—"

"We're going to change his mind."

She crossed her arms. As if she'd accept his help after he lied to her about the deal in the first place. "How?"

"I thought we could discuss the particulars over dinner." He held up the pizza box, his expression unreadable. "What do you say? Can I come in, Jane Cleo?"

She felt warm, tingly. She'd never heard her name sound so...so sexy...before. Was that how Liz felt when he said her name, too?

How would Liz react if she knew Brady had come to J.C.'s apartment on a Friday night, even for reasons that were decidedly nonpersonal? Then again, Liz didn't have to find out. Not if J.C. didn't tell her. She stood on her tiptoes and peered at her grandma's house. Except for the porch light, it was dark. Grandma Rose must still be at dinner. And J.C. really had pinned her hopes on selling her chocolates.

She stepped aside.

"Bring them up," Brady called down the stairs.

Peeking around the corner, she saw a kid taking the steps two at a time, a large wooden crate in his skinny arms, a dark blue ball cap on his head.

"Where do you want it?" he asked Brady when he reached them.

Brady gestured with his chin. "On the table is fine."

The kid glanced up at J.C., then did a double take. "Hey," he squeaked, blushing. He cleared his throat. "How's it going?"

She smiled at him and his eyes seemed to cloud over.

"Uh…I'm fine. Thanks." Had his voice gotten deeper from when he'd spoken to Brady?

"Eyes straight ahead," Brady said, then nudged the kid's shoulder.

As Brady and the boy walked over to the table, J.C. bent and scooped Daisy into her arms. The sound of someone choking made her spin around and she saw the boy staring at her, his mouth hanging open.

She took a hesitant step toward him. "Are you all right?"

"Don't make eye contact. He'll see it as encouragement," Brady said under his breath as he took a hold of the kid's arm and steered him past her. At the door, he shoved some money at the boy and practically pushed him outside. "Thanks. I appreciate it."

Now standing at the top of the stairs, the teen tore his eyes away from J.C. long enough to check out the amount of cash in his hands. "Hey. Thanks a lot. If you need anything else, call me." Then he grinned sweetly at J.C. "Or I could hang around. In case you—"

Brady shut the door in his face.

"Well, that was rude." J.C. stroked Daisy's soft fur. "What was that all about anyway?"

"You really don't know?"

"Know what?"

Brady set his hands on his hips, his jaw tight. "You made his night. And gave him enough material to stoke his sexual fantasies for the next year or so."

She almost dropped her cat. She set Daisy down on all fours but the feline didn't take well to nearly landing on her head. Sticking her chin in the air, she meowed and then took off like a shot.

"First of all," J.C. said, her nose wrinkling, "ewww.

Second of all, I'm at least ten years older than he is. Why on earth would he…" She gestured vaguely with her hands. "About me?"

Brady's mouth quirked. So glad to see her confusion amused him. "Maybe he'd want to…" He repeated her hand gesture. "Because you smiled at him. Or maybe it's because when you bent over in those shorts you're barely wearing, that kid thought he'd just seen heaven."

Her face flamed. "They're pajamas," she said in a strangled voice, tugging on the hem of her purple cotton shorts.

And she had on the loose—albeit tiny—shorts and matching tank top with eyelet trim because it felt as if her internal body temperature had gone up twenty degrees since she got pregnant.

Brady shrugged, his intense gaze never veering from her face. "Doesn't matter what you call them. They don't leave much to the imagination. And believe me, teenage boys have vivid imaginations, especially when it comes to barely dressed women."

Great.

She hoped the kid wasn't scarred for life.

J.C. crossed her arms and frowned at Brady's back as he went into the kitchen. She wasn't going to apologize for putting on her pajamas after she'd taken an early shower. She was in her own apartment, after all. And she'd seen no reason not to answer the door when she was just as covered as she'd be if she had on any other pair of shorts and tank top.

She went in after him. "What are you doing?"

He opened the top cupboard to the right of her stove and took down two of her mismatched plates. Held them up to her. "Plates." Taking the roll of paper towels off the counter, he brushed past her, his movements slow, his limp slight but still noticeable. He set the items on the table, came back into the kitchen and took milk out of the fridge.

"I never said I'd eat with you," J.C. pointed out.

In the act of pouring milk into a tall glass, he glanced at her. "Not hungry?"

Hungry? She shouldn't be. She'd had dinner a few hours ago. But the rich scent of tomato sauce and melted cheese made her mouth water. "I don't want to have dinner with you, that's all."

"You're willing to lose out on a chance to make that deal with the Diamond Dust?"

Possibly. Because at the moment, it felt as if she had to decide between making the deal that would enable her to prove to her family she could take care of herself, and loyalty to her sister.

"Will any of this even make a difference?" she asked. "And can I trust what you say?"

He flinched. Well, well. What a shock. Maybe he wasn't completely dead inside after all.

"I messed up," he said, putting the milk back in the fridge. "I never should've let you believe I had the authority to make a deal on behalf of the winery."

"Why did you?"

He tugged on his ear. "I wanted to help you."

He seemed sincere. As sincere as a hard-eyed, hard-drinking man could get.

"Fine. You can tell me about this idea you have while we eat. But," she stressed, "then you have to go."

Before Grandma Rose came home. If she found out he was here, it was sure to get back to Liz.

He didn't look relieved or particularly happy about

her acquiescence. "I appreciate you hearing me out." Then his hooded gaze raked over her, from the tips of her brightly polished toes to the top of her still-damp hair. "Before we eat," he said gruffly, "could you put something...else...on?"

CHAPTER EIGHT

BRADY WATCHED J.C. walk away, his gaze locked on the sway of her hips, the curve of her ass in those damn shorts.

Pregnant women weren't supposed to be so...sexy... were they? He even found the slight roundness of her belly alluring.

He scrubbed a hand over his face. Alluring. J.C. Montgomery. Sweet God, but he needed a drink.

He set the milk on the table when she came back out. She'd put her damp, curly hair up into a knot on top of her head but a few spirals had already come loose. She wore a boxy sweatshirt and loose black sweatpants.

Too bad he was still imagining her in those pajamas.

He cleared his throat and handed her the glass of milk. "Here."

She looked at it suspiciously. "What's this for?"

"I thought maybe you'd want some." He felt like an idiot. Weren't pregnant women supposed to drink a lot of milk?

"Oh. Sure. Thanks."

His neck warm with embarrassment, he put a slice of cheese pizza onto a plate before handing it to her. "I got half plain cheese in case you were still doing the vegetarian thing."

"I can't believe you remembered that."

He sat and helped himself to two pepperoni slices. "Hard to forget you with that duct tape over your mouth at Easter dinner."

"I'd forgotten about that. As a protest against my mom's baked ham." She tore off a piece of crust. "It took two weeks for the skin around my lips to grow back."

He and Liz had been seniors that year, J.C. a freshman. "Liz did your makeup every morning so no one could tell what happened."

"Right." J.C. tossed the crust back onto her plate then brushed her hands off. "Look, you don't have to worry about getting Aidan to change his mind. It's not like I've always dreamed of being a candy maker. It was a spur-of-the-moment idea. Believe me, another one will come along. They always do."

He scowled at his half-eaten slice of pizza. She'd always been that way. Brimming with plans, abandoning one grandiose scheme for the next.

Perfect. He had an out. She didn't want his help. Now maybe his guilt over making her a promise he couldn't keep would ease. Maybe now he could go back to not giving a damn about anything or anyone. It sure made it easier to get through the day.

"Do you always roll over when you don't automatically get what you want?" he asked more harshly than he'd intended.

Her nostrils flared and two spots of color stained her cheeks. "No. But that doesn't mean I go around knocking my head against walls, either."

"When those other stores turned you down, did you even try to convince them to change their mind?"

J.C. shifted her chair to the side, and the cat leaped

onto her lap. "What's the point? They already said they weren't interested."

"The point is to stop taking the easy way out and fight for what you want."

"Wow," she said through tight lips. "That's great advice coming from the man who either ignores his problems or drowns them."

Other than his fingers flexing on his thigh, he showed no sign she'd just made a direct hit. "When I want something badly enough, nothing stops me from getting it."

He just no longer let himself want.

She licked her lips nervously. "Aidan's already made up his mind—"

"So we get him to change it."

"How?"

"By proving your chocolates will sell."

The cat nosed J.C.'s plate, and J.C. moved her barely touched pizza out of reach. "Except I can't give him a guarantee people will buy them."

He finished off his first slice and dug into his second. "But we can market them so they tie in with the wines. Aidan will see an opportunity to increase sales. And believe me, nothing makes him happier than increased sales."

"But I thought wine went with real food. Not candy."

"It can go with sweet or savory. We figure out which of the Diamond Dust's wines go best with each flavor." He nodded toward the crate. "I brought the wine so we can do pairings."

"We?" she asked as if he'd suggested they take jobs as targets at the rifle range. "As in, you and me, we?"

He scratched his cheek. "I was thinking me and the cat. But you'll do in a pinch."

Her lips twitched. "You might be better off with Daisy, seeing as how I don't know anything about pairing wine with...well...anything. Besides, last I heard, pregnancy and alcohol don't mix."

"You're not going to drink. You tell me about the chocolates, what's in them and we'll go from there."

"But...are you sure you can do this? I mean...you don't work at the winery..."

"I grew up working there. Dad taught us every aspect of running the business."

"Right. Of course, but it's...you've been away from it—"

"It's not brain surgery, Jane," he said, keeping his frustration out of his voice. "What's the problem?"

She methodically stroked the cat's back, one hand over the other. "I don't want to be part of anything that encourages you to drink." She cleared her throat. "No offense."

He leaned back, stretching his leg out. "I won't get drunk."

As if he had such little control he'd get wasted sipping what would probably amount to a couple glasses of wine. When he wanted to get drunk, he went straight for whiskey.

Like the bottle he'd picked up at the liquor store earlier today.

"If it'll make you feel better," he said, "I'll use a spit bucket."

"That's disgusting."

"You don't taste with your stomach," he pointed out. "So there's no reason to swallow."

"I guess not," she said, sounding unconvinced. "But there's no way I'm dumping spit."

He closed the pizza box lid and set his empty plate on top of it. "When Dad held private tastings, that was our job, mine and Matt's."

And as usual, no matter what the job, Matt had complained the entire time.

"I haven't seen Matt in years," J.C. said, her elbow on the table, her chin resting on her hand. "How is he?"

He ducked his head so she wouldn't see his frown. He hadn't realized she had any interest in his long-haired, love-'em-and-leave-'em, too-pretty-for-his-or-anyone-else's-good brother. The brother who thought J.C. had a sexy mouth.

"He's fine," Brady said. "He was home Thanksgiving."

And gone the next day. Matt came back to Jewell for the holidays and their mother's birthday, but he never stayed more than a few days.

"Not long ago, the paper ran an article about him," she said. "About his job and all the awards he's won and how one of his wines made it onto some sort of top one hundred list—"

"*Wine Spectator*'s annual Top 100," Brady said, unable to stop staring at her mouth now. "He's doing well for himself."

Giving him a half smile, as if unsure if he deserved a full one, she used the back of her hand to brush her hair back. "I'll say. Funny that he works for wineries all over the world when his family owns one right here."

No, what was funny was how at ease she was now that they were talking about his brother. How, sitting this close to her, he could smell the soap she'd used in the shower. See the tiny freckles dotting her nose. And that with her eyes bright and those few loose curls framing her face, J.C. looked fresh and soft and…pretty.

"If you want," he said mildly, "I can tell Matt to call you next time he's in town. I'm sure he'd be more than happy to get together with you."

J.C. blanched. "Thanks, but I'll pass. So far my experience with the Sheppard men has sucked." Though her words were cold, he detected a slight tremor in her voice. "I'll get the chocolates. I wouldn't want to keep you any longer than necessary."

This time when she walked away, he studied the wall in front of him. Once she disappeared into the kitchen, he tipped his head back, hitting the chair. Then he did it again.

And because his hands were twitching, because he felt unsettled and edgy, because panic was there, right there at the back of his mind, he pulled a bottle out of the case. Merlot. Not his favorite—and a far cry from the whiskey he preferred—but it would do. He just needed it to get him back on an even keel. With that promise, he took the wine and the corkscrew he'd brought and headed to the bathroom.

Where he could have one drink without worrying about J.C. and her disappointment in him.

LIZ COULD THINK OF NOTHING better than coming home after a grueling twelve-hour night shift to the smell of bacon and Carter's special buttermilk pancakes. Unless it was the sight of him standing at the stove wearing nothing but a pair of red and green checked pajama pants.

"Hi," she said cautiously. He may be making her

breakfast and, she glanced at the set table, bought her a dozen red roses, but that didn't mean either of them had forgotten the tension between them was still as strong as it'd been on Thanksgiving. "What's all this?"

A cup of coffee in one hand, a spatula in the other, he said, "It's breakfast." Liz's heart did one slow roll.

"I can see that," she said, tracing her fingertip over a silky rose petal. "But…why?"

On the Saturday mornings when Carter didn't have to make rounds at the hospital, he was usually still in bed when she got home from work. She'd slide under the covers and, more often than not, they'd make love before she drifted off to sleep.

After shutting off the stove, he transferred the pancakes to a tray and carried them to the table. "Because I wanted to do something for you." He took both of her hands in his, brought them up to his mouth and kissed her knuckles. "And because I hate this distance between us."

She squeezed his fingers. "Me, too."

"I've missed you."

She nodded. Though they'd been together the past week, they'd barely spoken. And when they did, their conversations were stilted. Overly polite. The only time they touched was when they slept. They'd wake up wrapped in each other, but it never went any further.

It'd been torture.

He sat and pulled her onto his lap. "I blew it all out of proportion, what happened on Thanksgiving. I was…" He exhaled and shook his head, his hair tickling her cheek. "I was jealous."

She couldn't catch her breath. That wasn't what she

wanted. She didn't want Carter to be jealous. Didn't want him to doubt her love, not even for a second.

But she couldn't tell him the truth, either. How betrayed she felt. The thought of Brady and J.C. together infuriated her. She couldn't even face her own sister. Couldn't forgive her.

Worse was that she'd dreamt of Brady, of the way they used to be together. The way he'd kissed her. Touched her. Made love to her.

"You have nothing to be jealous of," she promised. "Brady and I are over. We've been over a long time."

He slid one hand up to her rib cage, his thumb brushing the side of her breast through her long-sleeved T-shirt. "I'm afraid I'm going to lose you," Carter said, his eyes searching hers.

"Never." She pressed her lips to the side of his neck, inhaled his familiar scent. Caressed the warm skin of his shoulders.

And thought of how Brady had looked the other day when she'd gone to return his ring. Angry. Lonely.

Tears stung the backs of her eyes. No. She wouldn't think of him. Not when she was in her husband's arms. Not ever again. She needed to get Brady out of her system. Before she lost everything. Her sister. Her husband. Herself.

"You'll never lose me," she repeated firmly.

Shifting so that she straddled him, she trailed biting kisses up his neck. He moaned, his hands going under her shirt to smooth her back, down her stomach. She trembled and pressed against him. Kissed him hungrily, loving how solid he was beneath her. How hard. How he was all hers.

"Liz," he said, cupping her breasts. "I love you, baby."

She arched into his touch, her hands gripping his shoulders. "I want you, Carter," she told him, gasping when he grazed her nipple with his thumbnail. "Only you."

His eyes flashed and then he kissed her again. Grasping her under her rear, he stood and swept one arm over the table. Plates and food crashed to the floor, the vase of roses shattered. And as her husband laid her among the ruins of their breakfast, Liz had one man in her thoughts. In her heart.

Him.

"Has hell frozen over?"

Brady glanced at Aidan sitting behind their dad's large mahogany desk, his cell phone up to his ear, one hand covering the mouthpiece.

"Why?" he asked as he entered his dad's—now his brother's—office. "Did you get laid?"

Aidan grinned as he leaned back in his leather, ergonomic chair. "It's not even eight—"

"Don't remind me." Brady slouched in one of the matching checked armchairs facing the desk.

"It's just…unusual…for you to be lurking outside your hovel before— Zachary," he said, turning back to his phone conversation. "It's Aidan Sheppard. Sorry to call you so early on a Saturday but…"

Zoning his brother out, Brady tipped his head back. Aidan's Irish setter, Lily, padded over and nudged his hand until he scratched behind her ears.

Aidan needed to redecorate. The room was the same as when his father had been alive. Sunlight shone in the large window to his right, splashing light on the cream area rug and the wide board oak floor. The built-in bookcases on either side of the window still held his father's books—everything from his favorite author's political thrillers to biographies to books on horticulture and winemaking techniques. Interspersed among them were framed family photos, a few knickknacks and Tom's prized baseball trophy.

Even the bronze statue of a frog, standing on two legs, dressed in knee-high boots and tunic playing a guitar—the statue their mother had claimed too ugly to be seen in any other room—stood in the spot Tom had proudly picked out for it.

And people accused Brady of not being able to let go of the past.

With Aidan's voice no more than a soft murmur in the background, Brady let his eyes drift shut. When he'd come out of the bathroom last night, he'd been steadier. Ready to deal with J.C. and, more importantly, ready to ignore the feelings she evoked.

He wasn't sure if she realized what he'd been doing in the bathroom, how he'd gulped down one glass worth from the bottle of merlot as some sort of anesthetic. But she didn't kick his ass to the curb.

By the time he got home, he was trembling with the need for a drink. After his first shot, he poured himself another and…hadn't been able to drink it. Because he'd had too much to do to get ready for this impromptu meeting with Aidan, he reminded himself. Not because he kept seeing J.C.'s face. Not because every time he lifted his glass he felt as if he was failing himself.

His body relaxed, the constant tension that tightened his shoulders finally eased. Until the first memory hit him, hard and fast like a bullet. Thad's laughter as they drove down the dirt road. The cloud of dust kicked up from the tires. The old man who'd stood on the side of the road, his face lined and weary.

The images came faster, flashing through his mind. The explosion. The sharp pain in his knee, his head smashing against the pavement. Coming to, his leg mangled. Through the thick echoing in his ears, women and children were screaming and comrades shouting, crying out for help. Smoke. Burning bodies.

His buddy lying in the street, his eyes sightless.

Lily whimpered. Brady was clutching the dog's fur. Breathing hard, he forced his fingers open and the dog slunk over to Aidan. He gulped in air, his shirt clinging to his sweat-soaked skin.

"You okay?" Aidan asked quietly.

Damn. How long had his brother been off the phone? Resting his elbows on his knees, his head lowered, Brady nodded.

"Here."

"Thanks," he said, taking the coffee Aidan offered and downing half of it. Lukewarm.

"Want to talk about it?"

Talk? Hell, all he wanted was to forget it. "I'm good."

Aidan studied him, his hands clasped together on top of his desk. "All right," he said slowly. "But if you ever do—"

"Yeah. Thanks," he forced himself to add before finishing off the coffee. He set the cup down and tossed the folder in front of Aidan.

"What's this?"

"It's all the reasons you should reconsider J.C.'s chocolates."

Aidan took off his reading glasses. "As much as I'd like to help J.C. out, I already told you we don't have the money in this year's budget. Besides, I'm not so sure chocolates would sell well, especially with the economy being the way it is."

"Sales of gourmet chocolates have been rising steadily for the past few years," he said. "Plus, twenty-five percent of annual candy sales are made between Thanksgiving and Christmas."

Aidan raised his eyebrows. "You learn about candy in the Marines?"

"In boot camp, right after I learned how to take apart and reassemble my M16." He shifted. "I did some research."

God bless the internet.

"That what this is?" Aidan gestured to the folder. "Your research on chocolate sales?"

"Among other things," he mumbled. He loosened his neck muscles, moving his head from side to side. "Just read it."

Aidan put his glasses back on, opened the folder and began to read the top sheet. It was a far cry from a real business proposal but it was the best he could do without experience.

Brady stretched his leg out and whistled softly for Lily. She hesitated, but when he held out his hand and snapped his fingers, she walked over, her ears back, her head down.

"Sorry, girl," he murmured, rubbing her head. She wagged her tail and dropped beside him. And as easy as that, she forgave him.

If only humans were that easy to placate.

After what seemed like an eternity, Aidan set the papers down and studied Brady over his glasses. "You did all of this?"

"J.C. came up with her projected costs. My pairings."

Aidan tapped a mechanical pencil against his desk blotter. "Expensive candy. I can go to the convenience store and pick up a candy bar for under a buck."

"She's making a quality product with high-end ingredients." According to J.C., anyway. Brady had been impressed with her refusal to use cheaper ingredients. "Don't you appreciate her high standards?"

"I do. I even agree with them. But that doesn't mean I want to do business with her. What if we agree to a deal and she can't hold up her end of the bargain? Or decides she's bored and would rather move on to something else?"

"She won't." Although for all he knew, those were very real possibilities. And if Aidan didn't stop tapping that damn pencil, Brady was going to shove it up his—

"You haven't been back long," Aidan said, dropping the pencil, "so you may not realize that as sweet as J.C. is, she also has a reputation for being unreliable."

"Is that where you get all your information? Local gossip?"

"Does it matter if it's gossip if it's the truth? I don't want to take a chance on conducting business with a vendor who may or may not provide her product."

"She'll provide it," Brady said, pushing himself to his feet. He'd make sure of it. "Make one of those consignment deals. That way you're not out cash and she still gets to sell her candy in the gift shop."

Aidan closed the folder. "Not interested."

Brady linked his hands together on top of his head. Blew out a breath. "What do I have to do?"

"For what?"

He dropped his arms. "To make this happen."

Aidan smiled—never a good sign. "Work for the Diamond Dust."

"That's it?" He'd figured it'd be something...bigger. Stop drinking. Or go back to physical therapy.

Bare his soul to some shrink.

He almost wished it had been one of those stipulations. Then he could've walked away.

"There are a few provisions—"

"Of course there are."

"—such as you, and you alone, are in charge of getting J.C.'s chocolates in the gift shop. I don't care what type of agreement you make with her as long as we don't lose any money."

Brady pinched the bridge of his nose. "No pressure there."

But Aidan wasn't done. "You have to put in eight solid hours of work a day, five days a week. And the first time you show up for work drunk, the deal is off."

"You realize this is blackmail."

"Funny. In business, we call this negotiating. Take it or leave it."

Brady ground his teeth. He couldn't imagine working for his father's company after all these years. Or worse, having Aidan as a boss. And what if he had another panic attack or whatever that had been? He couldn't control when the flashbacks came. Couldn't control how he'd react.

Besides, J.C. told him she didn't need this. And he'd set up that savings account for the baby. She could dip into that anytime she needed. Except she wouldn't.

He shoved his hands into his pockets.

"When do you want me to start?"

CHAPTER NINE

"JANE MONTGOMERY? Is that you?"

J.C.—along with the rest of the people attending the Diamond Dust's Holiday Open House that Saturday—looked toward the sound of the high-pitched voice. A short, busty brunette in dark skinny jeans and killer red leather boots elbowed her way through the crowd.

"If she's not careful," Brady murmured from behind J.C., causing her to jump, "she's going to jiggle right out of that shirt."

"I can see where that would bother a guy," she said, her heart thumping against her ribs.

What was he doing here? She hadn't spoken to him since a week ago when he'd called and told her she could sell chocolates at the Diamond Dust's open houses on consignment.

"I didn't say it would bother me."

She looked up at him so quickly she almost wrenched her neck. "Holy cow. Did you make a joke?"

"I never joke about women and jiggling."

Before she could decide that yes, Brady Sheppard had indeed shown some humor, the brunette reached them. With a squeal guaranteed to ring every eardrum within a five-mile radius, she threw her arms around J.C.

"I can't believe it's really you," the brunette said,

rocking her side to side. "You look fabulous! I hardly recognized you."

Rounding her shoulders and sticking her hips back in an attempt to keep her baby bump from touching the other woman, J.C. met Brady's eyes over the other woman's head. But he held up his hands. The universal signal for, "You're on your own."

"Uh…thank you," J.C. told her new hug-buddy. "Who are you?"

The woman pulled back, squeezing J.C.'s hands. "It's me! Tina Harris."

J.C. blinked. "Tina?"

Last she'd heard, Tina worked in real estate up in Richmond, having lived there since high school. J.C. scanned the other woman head to toe. No wonder she hadn't recognized her. While she could now see Tina in the pert nose and dimpled smile, her hair was shorter and a far cry from the brassy blond she'd dyed it to in high school.

And those boobs? Totally new.

"Wow. It's nice to see you," J.C. said. "You look terrific."

"Forget about me." Tina held their hands out to the sides as if to better showcase J.C. "You look amazing."

"Thank you. Do you remember Brady Sheppard?" She stepped back to include him.

"Of course. You went out with J.C.'s sister, didn't you? You two were such a dream couple. I imagine you're married with a few kids by now, am I right?"

Though nothing in Brady's expression changed, J.C. could feel his tension.

"Brady and Liz broke up over a year ago," she mumbled.

Tina's dimples disappeared. "That's such a shame. The same thing happened to me and Mike...you remember Mike Nivens, don't you?" she asked J.C. before turning to Brady. "Mike and I were high-school sweethearts like you and Liz except we dated a few months, not years and years like you two. But after graduation, we went our separate ways. Which worked out for the best," she said with a giggle, holding her left hand out.

Good God, how did she even lift her hand with that rock on her finger?

"Congratulations," J.C. said.

"I'm so lucky. Shawn...that's my fiancé...is the best. Guy. Ever. He's an orthodontist in Richmond...there he is now." Tina waved. "Honey? Honey, we're over here!"

J.C. winced and lifted her shoulder to her ear. For such a small person, her voice carried.

"There you are." Tina's great guy came up to J.C.'s chin, had a pot belly and a comb-over that started at his left ear. He smiled and wrapped his arm around Tina's waist. "I thought I'd lost you."

"Honey, I'd like you to meet Brady Sheppard—his family owns this winery. Isn't that cool? Brady," Tina continued, cuddling against comb-over's side, "this is my fiancé, *Doctor* Shawn Connolly. Shawn is the number one orthodontist in Richmond. If you're ever in the market for braces, be sure to look him up."

Brady shook Shawn's hand. "Nothing I'd like better than driving three hours to get metal bands slapped on my teeth."

J.C. reprimanded him with a slight shake of her head.

Shawn shared a look with Tina. "I'm sure you can find quality dental care right here in Jewell. It seems like a beautiful little town."

"It is," Tina said, ignoring Brady's slight. "It was the best place to grow up, so safe...why...everyone was like family. And this is Jane Montgomery, an old friend of mine from high school. But I tell you, I couldn't believe it when I first saw her! She's lost a ton of weight."

J.C. gritted her teeth. "Actually, I didn't lose quite that much."

And she and Tina sure hadn't been more than acquaintances. Cute cheerleaders didn't hang out with chubby girls who'd rather volunteer at the local ASPCA than work on homecoming floats.

Tina hugged Shawn around his middle. "Well, however much you lost doesn't matter. You look so much better."

She didn't need to be reminded that she'd spent most of her life overweight. Especially in front of Brady.

Brady laid his hand on the small of her back and she almost jumped out of her skin. "What brings you to Jewell?" he asked the couple in front of them.

Tears stung her eyes. She blamed it on hormones. She couldn't even listen to love songs on the radio without getting all blubbery. Not because the warmth of Brady's hand seeping through the silky fabric of her dress made it easier to pull her shoulders back and pretend Tina's comments didn't bother her.

"We're going on a cruise for Christmas so we're doing the holiday thing early with my family," Tina said. "But I still need to get my sister-in-law's gift and was hoping to find it here. She's such a snob. She returns everything."

"Chocolates," Brady said.

Tina looked at him as if he'd lost his mind. "Excuse me?"

"We now carry a line of locally produced gourmet chocolates," he clarified, sounding as if he'd memorized a brochure. Reaching behind J.C., he picked up the tray of samples she'd set out and held them out to Shawn and Tina.

"None for me, thanks," Shawn said. "My teeth are like a walking billboard for my business."

"I don't have his willpower," Tina confessed, scanning the tray. "I can't pass up chocolate. Ooh…what's this one?" She pointed to a glossy dark chocolate truffle with a drizzle of white chocolate.

Brady nudged J.C. "That's cappuccino," she said. "The…uh…ganache is milk chocolate, coffee and cinnamon."

"Sounds yummy." Tina picked it up and bit into it, her hand underneath the candy to catch any loose bits. The expression on her face was practically orgasmic.

"The cappuccino flavor is one of the top sellers in J.C.'s line," Brady said.

"You made these?" Tina asked. As if J.C.'s candy-making ability ranked up there with walking on water and being able to yodel.

"It's just a—"

"Yes," Brady said, not even glancing her way. "She makes them all."

Ten minutes later, Dr. Shawn walked over to the gift wrap table with three boxes of mixed truffles. Tina waited in line at the checkout counter with a bottle each of the three wines Brady suggested made the best pairings.

And Brady was still by J.C.'s side, all silent and grim-faced in his worn jeans, faded Marine Corps T-shirt and work boots. His hair was beyond shaggy and getting close to unmanageable. She'd say he hadn't shaved in a week.

"I appreciate the sales job you did with Tina," she said.

He leaned back against the thick, wooden beam next to her table and inclined his head. The Brady Sheppard way of saying *you're welcome.*

Well, if he couldn't take the hint that she wanted him gone, she thought irritably, she'd just ignore him. Humming "It Came Upon A Midnight Clear" with the two violinists playing softly in the corner, J.C. pulled on clean gloves and arranged a trio of her extra dark truffles on the silver tray then checked her watch. With less than thirty minutes left until closing time, she wasn't sure how many more she'd need to set out, but there were still at least twenty customers milling around the gift shop and tasting room in the large farmhouse.

Two walls were all windows, with silver pendant and gooseneck lights hanging from the exposed ceiling beams. Wide, wooden beams showed where original walls stood and ancient-looking narrow boards made up the floor.

Finger foods, catered from The Old Library, the fanciest restaurant in Jewell, were presented on a covered board over three large wooden wine barrels.

"Why'd you let Tanya upset you?"

She dropped a chocolate on the floor. Picking it up,

she tossed it into the garbage can under the table. "Her name's Tina. And I wasn't up—"

"Bullshit."

Sighing, she turned, only to find him standing too close to her. "I… It's hard for me to…to know what to say when someone comments on my weight. It's… awkward," she finished, her gaze on the table.

And she hated that there were days she still felt like that overweight girl. Self-conscious. Second-best to Liz.

"Seems to me," Brady said after what had to be the longest moment of her life, "you've done something to be proud of."

"All I did was lose weight." It wasn't as if she'd graduated from college. Or gone to medical school. She didn't help save people's lives every day she went to work.

"Was it easy?"

"What?"

"Was it easy to deprive yourself?"

"It's not about deprivation. It's about making better choices." She took the gloves off and crumpled them in her hand. "Everything in moderation. Fruit instead of junk food. Exercise more."

"You still needed willpower. Dedication. Determination. And these?" he asked, gesturing at the candy before settling his right hand on the table. "They're good. Tanya—"

"Tina."

He shrugged. "She bought three boxes because they're good. Not because of anything I did."

"Well," she said, warmth spreading throughout her chest, "you sure told me."

"You don't give yourself as much credit as you deserve."

"That has to be one of the nicest things anyone's ever said to me. Except for when I was in third grade and Davey Rodgers told me my hair made me look like a little lion."

"Not a lion," he said, studying her intently. She would've stepped back except he lifted his free hand to her hair and wrapped a curl around his finger. "More like a sunburst around your face."

J.C. JERKED HER HEAD BACK, her hair tightening around Brady's finger before sliding away. She tucked it behind her ear. "So, is this how you usually spend your Saturdays?"

He fisted his hand. "I'm working."

She tipped her head and studied him. "You get paid to stand around and look…"

He raised an eyebrow. "Intimidating?"

She opened a bottle of water and gestured at him with it. "I was going to say grumpy but intimidating works, too."

"I didn't say I was happy about working. And I sold three bottles of wine, didn't I?"

"That you did." She crouched to pull a box out from underneath the green cloth covering her table. "Do you get a commission?"

"Just a regular paycheck," he said absently, his attention caught by the way her bright pink dress swirled around her knees when she straightened.

"You're working here for real? That's great. You must not be—" She blushed and concentrated on setting out more of her candy. "Your knee. It…uh…must not be bothering you as much."

And if that was what she'd meant to say, he'd kiss bin Laden's ass. "I don't drink on the job."

As per his brother's instructions, he'd been sober every day. Hungover, but sober.

"I never realized you were interested in working here," she said, choosing to ignore him.

"I'm not." He helped himself to a white chocolate truffle. "It's temporary."

"Do you still want to go into law enforcement?" At his sharp look, she shrugged. "Liz mentioned you wanted to attend the police academy when you got out of the service."

"I'd never pass the physical."

Not to mention the psych evaluation.

"Maybe if you find a good physical therapist—"

"My knee will never be a hundred percent," he said, tossing a second half-eaten chocolate in the garbage.

"I'm sorry," she said, laying her hand on his forearm. His muscles tensed under her warm fingers. "Now stop wasting my inventory."

He stepped back and her hand fell to her side. He nodded to the middle-aged couple approaching them. "Customers."

As J.C. went into her sales pitch—offering them a sample, explaining the different flavors and wine pairings—Brady edged away.

He didn't need her pity. He'd known the risks going in. Those risks were part of the reason Liz hadn't wanted him to join up. For as long as he could remember, he'd wanted to be a Marine. To be in the middle of the action.

Right. *Action.* He saw a snow-covered road carved from the side of a mountain. Heard the echoing, rat-a-tat of machine gun fire. His commander's shouts. His buddies' curses. Felt the surge of adrenaline as he dove for cover. Returned fire.

His mouth dried and his heart began to race. Taking J.C.'s water, he drained it, his fingers denting the plastic.

"I could've gotten you your own water."

He lowered the bottle. "Sorry."

J.C. regarded him seriously. "Hey, are you—"

"Another sale?" he asked, motioning to the couple walking off.

"No," she said, drawing the word out. "But they seemed to like the Turtles."

He twisted the cap back on the bottle. "Can't win them all."

"That's so inspiring," she said. "I think I'll put it on one of those needlework samplers and hang it in my living room." She moved an oblong red ceramic tray of white chocolate dipped pretzels an eighth of an inch to the left. "Is there a reason you're standing watch back here instead of…whatever else you're supposed to be doing? That can't really be your job."

"As far as Aidan's concerned, anything and everything he doesn't want to handle—and thinks I can—is my job."

Pam, the gift shop's superefficient manager, needed him here as much as Aidan needed help being uptight. Pam had no sooner given Brady his first assignment—making sure all the chardonnay bottles were label side out—than he'd realized that Aidan had asked him to work an extra day to keep Brady busy.

As if he were a kid who needed to be entertained or else he'd get into trouble.

He'd been about to walk out, he should've walked out. But then he'd spotted J.C. at the back of the store setting up her table.

"I like it back here."

She smacked his arm. "Yeah. For the free chocolate."

"Among other things."

She caught her breath.

And someone cleared a throat. "Are we interrupting?"

J.C. GROANED AND QUICKLY stepped away from Brady. What had so far been a pretty decent day was about to go downhill. Fast.

"Liz. Hi," she said, her voice strangled. "Wha-what are you doing here?"

Crossing her arms, Liz glanced at Brady and then back at J.C. "We ran into Lori Crandall at the grocery store and she mentioned you were selling chocolates here. I can't imagine why you didn't tell us yourself."

"Right. I saw Lori in here earlier." J.C. wiped her palms down the side of her dress. "I…I would've told you…" she lied, "but I figured you'd be…too busy…to come."

"Hey," Carter said as he joined them, a grin on his movie-star-handsome face, "we're never too busy for you."

Then he pulled her into a warm hug. Out of the corner of her eye, J.C. saw Brady roll his shoulders back as if preparing to go a few rounds.

Winner got Liz.

Luckily, if Carter had any violent thoughts about Brady, he hid them well. "How are you feeling?" he asked as he released her.

"Fine. Good. It's okay if you have to go," she told Brady in a rush. "I'm sure you have a lot to do."

"Nothing that can't wait. Aren't you going to introduce us?" he asked in a deadly soft tone as he inclined his head toward her brother-in-law.

"Not on your life." Taking him by the arm, she pulled him to the other end of the table. "Stay here. Please," she said, when he looked ready to argue. "Please, Brady."

He looked over her head at Liz and Carter. His mouth flattened. "Where are your boxes?"

"What?"

"The store closes soon. If you get the boxes, I can start packing up your stuff."

"You don't have to."

He sent another fleeting look at Liz. "All part of the job description, Jane."

J.C. felt numb. Still thinking of her sister but willing to settle for her. Well, at least he got her name right this time. "Sure. Whatever. They're under the table."

"I can't...I don't think I can get them," he said tightly, stopping her before she could walk away.

She shut her eyes for a moment. She could do this. She could act as if him sending longing looks her sister's way—after he'd touched her hair so sweetly—didn't bother her. Grabbing the boxes, she set them on the table and then deliberately turned away.

Liz, in her black skinny jeans, white top and red jacket, and Carter, with the barest hint of stubble and his striped scarf tucked under the collar of a caramel-colored suede coat, could've been in the picture accompanying one of those fashion magazine's articles: How The Perfect Couple Dresses, Weekend-Style.

But on closer inspection, J.C. could see perfection was an illusion. There were tension lines around Carter's mouth. Liz held herself stiffly. And while Carter kept his gaze on the candy display, Liz kept looking at Brady only to drop her gaze when she thought someone noticed.

"It was really…great…of you both to take the time to…support me like this," J.C. said when she reached them.

"I have to admit," Carter said, "once I found out what you were doing, I had an ulterior motive for wanting to come out here."

She swallowed and peeked at Liz, but her sister wouldn't look her way.

"I was hoping you'd have some of that chocolate bark with the cashews available," Carter continued. "The last time you gave me some to take to the office, I was a real hero."

She exhaled shakily. "Sure. I think I still have a few boxes left…" Before she could look over her products, Brady slid two, one-pound boxes down the table.

Wonderful. He could not only hear every word they said, but he wanted them to be aware he was listening.

She tried to return Carter's smile but failed miserably. "Here you go. There's one milk chocolate and one white chocolate."

"Perfect," he said, the unusual edge to his voice the only indication Brady's presence still bothered him. "Do I pay here or up front?"

"Oh, no. They're my treat."

"You can't be giving away all of your profits," Carter said.

"We'll pay for them," Liz said firmly, finally meeting J.C.'s eyes. "We insist."

"Okay, then. Thanks." J.C. swallowed but it felt as if she had one of her truffles stuck in her throat. "You can…uh…pay at the cashier."

Carter pulled out his wallet. "Looks like they're getting ready to close." He shot a glance over J.C.'s head— presumably to where Brady still lurked. "Will you be all right here by yourself, J.C.?"

She could've sworn she heard Brady growl.

"Sure. I get to keep most of my stuff here—they're going to set up a small display of the chocolate I have left to sell during the week," she said, purposely misinterpreting his question. Would she be all right alone with Brady Sheppard? "I'll be fine."

Though he didn't seem convinced, he didn't push it. "I'd better get in line, then." He kissed her cheek. "And in case we don't see you before then, good luck Tuesday."

"Thanks."

"You ready, honey?" he asked Liz.

"I'd like to speak with J.C.," she said. "I'll catch up with you in a minute."

"I hate this," J.C. blurted as soon as Carter walked away. She lowered her voice so Brady couldn't hear. "Can't we please discuss this?"

Liz frowned at J.C. "What's Tuesday?"

And that had been the last question she'd expected. "Nothing. Just…I have an appointment with Dr. Owens…"

"And you told *my* husband about it?"

"*Your* husband," J.C. whispered, her movements jerky as she swept pieces of the curly gold ribbon she'd scattered across the table into a pile, "is the only person at your house who'll talk to me when I call."

Liz drummed her fingers on the table, next to the base of a glass pedestal holding the remaining bite-size samples of J.C.'s Turtles. "What's this really about? You selling chocolate here?"

"I need extra cash. For the holidays."

"Do you really think orchestrating it so that you're around him more is going to change anything?"

J.C.'s head snapped back. "I…I didn't orchestrate anything." But…but hadn't she let him talk her out of speaking with Aidan? And then she'd jumped at the chance he'd offered to sell her chocolates at the Diamond Dust. She'd even spent the evening with him pairing the wine and chocolates after he'd been so ugly to her. "He just happened to be working—"

"Isn't that how it always is with you? Things *just happen*."

J.C. winced as she remembered how she'd tried to explain why she and Brady had gotten together.

It just sort of…happened.

"I didn't even know he was going to be here," J.C. insisted.

"You've always wanted whatever I had," Liz said, her hushed voice sounding thick. "And Brady is no different."

J.C.'s scalp tingled and she snuck a look over her shoulder. She edged closer to her sister. "I don't want Brady."

"Even if you did, he's not the right guy for you. You deserve someone who'll put you first."

She knew that. She didn't need Liz and her condescending attitude to remind her.

"Because no way a man could possibly want me after they were with you," she said, her hands fisted. "Mediocrity just doesn't cut it after you've had perfection, right?"

Liz blushed. "I didn't say that."

And then, Brady was there, his hands on her shoulders. "Your husband's waiting for you," he told Liz. "You'd better go."

Liz blinked several times, but J.C. caught the sheen of tears in her eyes before her sister walked off.

For several heartbeats, J.C. didn't move.

Brady squeezed her shoulders. "You okay?" he asked, his mouth close to her ear.

She cringed. As if he gave a damn. As if his whole show of support hadn't been for her sister's benefit. It was as fake as Liz's so-called concern.

Trembling with anger, with humiliation, she jerked away from him. "Do me a favor. The next time you want to try to make my sister jealous, leave me out of it."

CHAPTER TEN

WELL AWARE OF THE INTEREST they were getting from the people left in the store, Brady wrapped an arm around J.C.'s waist. Though she stiffened, she didn't fight him as he led her down a short hallway and into the stockroom. They'd no sooner stepped inside when she twisted away from him.

"Is there a problem?" he asked.

She stared at him incredulously. "You used me as some sort of...of..." She glanced around, as if she'd pick the right word out of the air. "Tool...to get back at Liz. Did you think she'd toss Carter aside and jump into your arms because of me? I hate to break it to you, but I'm the last person Liz would ever be jealous of."

How he'd stepped on this landmine, he had no clue. He hadn't been playing games and he sure as heil hadn't been trying to make Liz jealous.

He scratched the underside of his jaw. Playing hero brought a man nothing but grief.

Sure, he may have felt a slight surge of satisfaction at Liz's reaction to him coming to J.C.'s aid. But that only proved he was human.

And not as dead inside as he'd like.

"I don't want to get back at Liz," he said.

"Then what was with all that touchy-feely stuff? You

deliberately made it seem as if there was something going on between us."

"By telling her she should leave?"

"You touched my shoulders," she said with as much indignation as if he had pinched her butt.

Behind him, someone rapped lightly on the still-open door.

"Sorry to…interrupt," Pam said curiously, glancing between them, "but I need to get—"

"Later," Brady said before shutting the door and leaning against it.

No doubt when Aidan heard about it, he'd rip Brady for being so rude to a valued employee.

"Your fight was starting to draw a lot of attention," he said with what he considered remarkable calm in the face of her irrationality. "I thought it best to intervene before it came to blows."

"We weren't fighting. We were…having a discussion. A private discussion that you were eavesdropping on."

"Seeing how I was the main topic, I'd say I had a right to overhear."

You've always wanted whatever I had.

I don't want Brady.

J.C. rubbed her temples. "She hates me."

Impossible. Liz had always doted on her little sister. She'd been J.C.'s biggest champion.

He shrugged. "She's pissed. She'll get over it."

"That's a big help," J.C. said acidly. "Thanks so much."

"You want a shoulder to cry on," he said before he could stop himself, "try your brother-in-law."

She looked at him as if he was a few rounds short of a full clip. "What?"

"Nothing."

Damn it. Maybe his paranoia was getting worse. How else to explain him taking issue with J.C. cozying up to Liz's husband? Just because she'd been thrilled to see him and had asked Brady to back off when he'd been itching to take the guy down a peg didn't mean anything. It certainly couldn't mean that Liz had been right about J.C. wanting whatever her sister had.

Even if she had told that bastard about her doctor's appointment Tuesday. An appointment Brady had no idea about.

"You're tired…" Didn't pregnant women get tired easily? And cranky? And blow things out of proportion? "Why don't we finish packing up your stuff then I'll drive you home."

"I don't need your help getting my stuff together and I sure don't want you taking me home."

Damn but she was stubborn. And starting to seriously tick him off. "You shouldn't drive when you're so upset."

"I've been upset before," she said as she stalked toward him, "and unfortunately, I'll be upset again. But I'm still capable of taking care of myself."

In other words, he could take his help and shove it.

He opened the door and stepped aside so she could pass. He watched her walk away, her hair bouncing to her long strides, her arms swinging.

I don't want Brady.

Looked like the Montgomery sisters had more in common than anyone realized.

"I WAS THINKING we'd try that new salmon recipe tonight," Liz told Carter as she set the last of the bulging cloth grocery bags on the kitchen table. "Unless you think it's too cold for grilling."

"That's fine," he said, not even pausing as he carried the dry cleaning into the living room.

She squeezed the package of salmon fillets. If he'd at least try to keep up his end of the conversation, maybe she wouldn't have to continue with her inane chatter. The sound of her own voice was grating on her last nerve. But she couldn't shut up, either. Not when the silence was so tense. So…uncomfortable.

Not when she was afraid of what Carter would say if she'd stop talking long enough for him to get a word in edgewise.

Laying a loaf of French bread aside, she unpacked the baked chips and organic eggs. He'd been fine all day. They'd slept in, enjoyed a leisurely brunch at their favorite restaurant and then ran their errands. Up until they'd gone to the Diamond Dust, Carter had been… himself.

Lips pursed, she shook her head as she stacked yogurt containers in the fridge. Naturally he'd been upset about seeing Brady. She never would've guessed he'd be at the gift shop, let alone hovering over J.C. If she had, she would've put up a bigger fight about going there. But Carter had insisted she at least take a hold of the olive branch J.C. had extended with her daily phone calls. Though Liz wasn't ready to make peace yet, she hadn't wanted Carter to think her resistance had anything to do with Brady.

Rinsing the salmon at the sink, she heard Carter's footsteps as he came back into the kitchen.

"I'll make the marinade," she said, laying the fillets

on a clean towel, "and you can put together a salad. And do you want rice or potatoes?"

He came up behind her and shut the water off.

She laughed nervously. "What are you—"

"We need to talk."

Her stomach dropped at his serious tone, his carefully schooled expression. She kept smiling. "If we want to make it to that movie…" But he just continued to watch her. She couldn't escape what was going to happen next. "All right."

Taking her time, she patted the salmon dry and set it in a plate. After washing her hands, she put the fish in the fridge.

Carter sat at the table, his hands in his lap as he stared out the window above the sink. The evening was darkening.

What had she done? She'd been careful, so very careful, not to show any reaction to finding Brady and J.C. together.

She pulled out the chair opposite him.

"Honey, what is it?" she asked, certain she'd be better off not knowing. "What's wrong?"

He dug something out of his pocket then laid it in the center of the table between them.

A small velvet blue box.

Brady's ring.

Her lungs squeezed painfully and she couldn't draw a full breath. "Where… How…"

"Mr. Sandburg found it in your coat," Carter said quietly.

She shut her eyes. While she'd run into the pharmacy for a few items, Carter had gone next door to pick up their dry cleaning. Including her brown leather jacket, the one she'd been wearing when she'd gone to see Brady.

Sitting on the edge of her seat, she leaned forward. "It's not what you think."

"What is it I think?"

"I…I'm not sure. Maybe you see my having that ring as a way of holding on to…to him."

He linked his hands together on top of the table. "Is it?"

"No. No of course not. I…I was giving it back—"

"You were carrying it around with you in case you bumped into him?"

Her vision blurred and she blinked furiously. "I saw him last week," she whispered.

His body twitched. "When?"

"Monday."

"You weren't going to tell me."

"I didn't want to upset you." She reached out but he slid his hands back to his lap. "I tried to give him the ring but he wouldn't take it so I…I stuck it in my pocket. That's all. Look, it's so insignificant, I forgot it was even there."

She held her breath. He remained motionless, his face drawn. Had she thought his anger at Thanksgiving was bad? She'd take it any day over this.

"I saw how you looked at him."

Her blood chilled. "What?"

"Today. You kept watching him."

"I didn't—"

"And at the end, when he came up behind J.C., when he stood so close to her, you were upset."

"I was…I hadn't realized they were there…" And

that shock, along with her hurt and anger, had almost brought her to her knees. "That they were…together."

That it seemed as if they were together. Or could be.

Carter wiped a hand over his mouth. "It might not seem like it, but I'm trying to understand why you can't let this thing between Brady and your sister go. Why it upsets you so much."

Tears ran down her cheeks. She knuckled them away. "I don't know."

"If I thought it was just the fact that she was with your ex, it'd be different but…" He shook his head. "There's more to it than that."

"No. I—"

"You kept his ring. You went to see him without telling me." Carter's voice turned gravelly. "You look at him the same way you look at me. The way you're only supposed to look at me."

Stunned, tears running unheeded down her cheeks, she watched as he walked out the door. She wished she could call him back. Tell him that she needed some more time to adjust to…everything. But she'd be lying. She wasn't sure she'd ever be able to accept J.C. having Brady's baby. Or Brady being a part of her sister's life.

And because of that, she couldn't even tell her husband what he needed to hear most. That he was the only man she loved.

J.C. ARRIVED FIVE MINUTES LATE for her appointment with Dr. Owens on Tuesday to find the waiting room filled with women of all ages. Several were way more pregnant than her, and two had recently given birth—as evidenced by the newborns in their arms and their post-baby bodies. To her left, a middle-aged woman read a pamphlet on improving your sex life after menopause. And all of them were shooting glances at the corner.

She followed their gazes…and tripped over her own feet. Brady Sheppard, his left leg out straight, his hands linked on his flat stomach, watched her steadily.

Unreal.

"What are you doing here?" she asked.

"Waiting for you."

"Why?"

"I didn't want you to have to do this alone."

Her jaw dropped. *This* as in her doctor's appointment? Or could he possibly mean…? No. He'd made his stance about the baby very clear. And seeing as how he hadn't so much as mentioned her pregnancy recently, she doubted he'd changed his mind. That he'd ever change his mind.

"How did you even know I have an appointment today?" she asked.

He tipped his head to the side. "I heard you and your brother-in-law talking about it at the gift shop."

She switched her purse strap to her other shoulder. "It's…nice…of you to…think of me but I won't be alone. My mom is supposed to meet me."

He sat up. "I'll wait until she gets here."

"Oh, but—"

"Jane?" Rhonda Darcy, her round body stuffed into an impossibly cheerful set of Snoopy scrubs, stood in the doorway leading to the examination rooms. "Come on back, hon, and we'll get your vitals."

"You don't have to stay," J.C. told Brady.

She didn't want him to stay, she told herself as she

followed Rhonda down the hallway to a small, window-less room. Not after how he'd acted at the gift shop. Not when he'd heard what Liz had said to her. How her sister had practically accused her of throwing herself at Brady.

As if she'd throw away her relationship with her sister for a man. A man who didn't even want her.

"Weight first," Rhonda said.

J.C. toed off her shoes and stepped onto the scale. Staring straight ahead, she could see Rhonda's hand moving the lever to the right but couldn't make out the numbers.

And if Rhonda so much as breathed what those numbers were, J.C. might resort to violence.

Rhonda noted J.C.'s weight in a small laptop. "Hop on down." She gestured for J.C. to sit in the chair next to a metal table where she sat to put her shoes back on. "I'm sure glad we didn't call the police on your young man out there."

J.C. about fell right off the chair. "Did...did he do something wrong?"

He hadn't seemed drunk but their conversation had been brief. And as she'd learned, he didn't need alcohol to say incredibly stupid things.

"All that boy did was wait." She moved J.C.'s hair aside and checked her temperature with an ear thermom-eter. "Even when Missy told him she couldn't give out your appointment time, he just thanked her and took a seat. Didn't kick up a fuss like some folks would. But after two hours, Dr. Owens started getting nervous about him being here so long."

"Wait," J.C. said, her head coming up in surprise. Two hours? "How long has he been waiting?"

Rhonda wrapped the blood pressure cuff around J.C.'s arm. "He showed up right when we opened at nine."

While Rhonda took her blood pressure, J.C.'s head spun. Nine. It was now after four. Brady Sheppard had spent the entire day sitting in her obstetrician's waiting room.

For her.

"Anyway," Rhonda continued, hooking her stethoscope around her neck, "The doctor pointed out how you might not want him here and maybe we should call the police to escort him home. Which we can certainly do if that's what you'd prefer."

"No." She cleared her throat. "No, he's…fine. He's…"

Rhonda took a hold of J.C.'s wrist. "With both Missy and I knowing him—Missy went to school with one of his brothers, and Diane Sheppard and I go way back—so we convinced Dr. Owens he wasn't hurting anyone."

Hurting anyone, no. Confusing the hell out of her? Definitely.

Rhonda finished checking her pulse and sent her back out to wait for the doctor. J.C. walked down the hall. Just because Brady showed up here didn't mean anything. She wouldn't let herself read more into it than a sign he was curious about the baby. Or that he was crushed over her being upset with him, and he'd wanted to make amends.

She snorted softly. That would be the day.

And since she'd told him to leave, she doubted she'd ever find out.

She opened the door and sure enough, his seat was empty. But, as she stepped out of the exam room, she saw that it was only because Brady was on his feet, his expression pained as he faced her parents.

J.C. hurried over and stepped between them. "Mom. You made it." She winced at her own false cheeriness. "Hi, Dad. I hope Mom didn't drag you away from the office early."

"Your father insisted he wanted to be here," her mom said, equally chipper. Equally false. "Isn't that nice, dear?"

"Great," she croaked.

"It's not every day a man's baby girl gets to see the ultrasound of her own baby," Don said gruffly, glancing at her.

"Daddy…" She stood on tiptoe and kissed his cheek.

But when she fell back to her heels, his expression hardened. "Move aside, Jane. Brady was about to explain what he's doing here."

As much as she'd love to hear that as well, she didn't want to hold this particular discussion in the middle of one of Jewell's busiest doctor's office.

"Now, Don," Nancy said. "I'm sure Jane asked him to be here."

They both looked at her. She felt Brady's gaze, too, burning a hole in the back of her head. All of their expectations weighing down on her.

"Yes," she said. "I did. Ask him, that is." And while that might not be true, her next words were. "I want Brady to go in with me for the ultrasound."

BAM…BAM…BAM…

Twenty-five minutes later, Brady stood next to an examination table in the cold, sterile ultrasound room.

Bam…bam…bam…

If she didn't stop making that racket, he was going to lose his mind.

His head pounded. Memories circled the edge of his mind, waiting to overwhelm him. Because J.C., sitting at the edge of an exam table, kept swinging her feet, her heels hitting the metal with a resounding bam. Like bombs going off.

Brady shot his hand out and grabbed her knee. "Do you mind?"

She stilled. "Sorry."

He released her. Her skin had been warm through the soft fabric of her black pants.

"I'm nervous," she blurted. "About…" She gestured to the ultrasound machine next to the bed. "Seeing the baby."

"You worried something will be wrong?"

"No," she said so quietly, he had to lean forward to catch the rest of what she said. "That it'll make it real." She stared down at her clasped hands. "I…I don't know if I want this."

He straightened. "The ultrasound? If you're not feeling up to it—"

"The baby."

His head snapped back. He stepped around in front of her. She stared at the floor. He gently took a hold of her chin and raised her face. "Talk to me."

She pulled away from his touch. "How can I raise a child? I've never seen anything through in my life." She rubbed her palms up and down her thighs. "God, this is so selfish but…I'm not sure if I'm ready, or even capable, of committing the next eighteen years of my life to someone else."

"What are you thinking? Adoption?"

The thought of it left him cold. Of having a child out there, not knowing where he or she was, if the kid was safe. He shoved a hand through his hair. As if he had a right to be upset. As if he had the right to tell her what she should or shouldn't do with their child.

A child he'd already walked away from.

"No. Maybe. It kills me to think about giving this baby away," she said. "But I have thought about it. I'm afraid if I keep it, I'll mess up both our lives."

Damn. He should've seen this coming. All this time when she spoke about the pregnancy it was *this* baby. Or *the* baby.

Never her baby. Never their baby.

She was being torn up by the distance between her and Liz and her fears of raising a baby alone. And he'd been so focused on himself, on his own problems, he hadn't even noticed.

"Whatever you decide," he said, forcing out the words she needed to hear, "you have my support."

Words that gave her permission to put their child up for adoption. Words that were unbelievably hard to say.

"But…what about our families?" she asked in a rush.

"This isn't about them. It's about what's best for you and the baby."

She brushed her hair back and gave him a shaky smile. "Thanks."

"Could you… When you make the decision, could you let me know?"

She frowned. "If you want me to. But…aren't you leaving town? How will I get a hold of you?"

"I'll be here until after the first of the year." And when he'd made that decision, he had no idea. "But when I do leave, I'll make sure you have a way of reaching me. In case you need anything."

In case she needed him.

Before they could respond to a knock at the door, a short blonde in black heels and a red and black dress covered by a lab coat came in.

"Hello, Jane," she said warmly. "How are you feeling?"

"Fine. You were right, the morning sickness went away."

"Wonderful." She offered her hand to him. "I'm Nanette Owens."

"Brady Sheppard."

Dr. Owens opened a small laptop, scanned the screen and shut it again. "Your blood pressure's normal. Pulse was a bit elevated but that's not unusual." After using some hand sanitizer she clapped her hands. "Now let's check out your baby."

Brady eased back a step as the doctor had J.C. undo the bottom buttons of her white blouse and fold her shirt back.

"Okay," Dr. Owens said, "go ahead and pull your pants down to your hips."

He jerked his eyes up, stared sightlessly at the plain gray wall. But he could hear J.C. rustling around.

Sweat beaded on his forehead.

The doctor tucked a disposable sheet around J.C.'s pants and Brady glanced down. J.C.'s stomach protruded slightly, as if she'd swallowed a water balloon. The doctor squirted gel a few inches below J.C.'s belly button, then flipped a few switches on the ultrasound machine. After typing for a minute, she picked up a wand and placed it over the gel.

"Showtime." Dr. Owens moved the wand. Blurry black and gray images filled the screen and Brady looked away. "And there's baby."

Brady went numb. He couldn't look. He needed to keep some distance. It was his only protection.

"I don't see it," J.C. said.

"Here's the head." The doctor pressed something on the machine that made a clicking sound. "And here are the arms." More clicking. "From what I'm seeing here, I'd say you were right on about the date of conception. Baby's at seventeen weeks."

J.C.'s arms were straight by her sides, her hands clenching the sheet under her. He lightly traced a finger over her knuckle. Bent close to her head. "Breathe," he said into her ear.

She exhaled, her fingers relaxing.

And he couldn't resist any longer. He had to see. It wasn't the clearest image but he could make out a head. Moving arms and legs.

Damn. J.C. had been right. This made it much too real.

Dr. Owens worked the machine for another five minutes. When he looked over at J.C., he could've sworn she wiped the side of her face…as if she was crying. But with her head turned away from him, he couldn't be sure.

"Everything's fine," the doctor said, using paper towels to wipe the gel off J.C.'s stomach. "Heartbeat is strong, growth right on track. Do either of you have any questions?"

"When's it coming out?" Brady heard himself ask.

His neck warmed. "I mean, when's J.C.'s...what do you call it?"

Dr. Owens smiled. If she found it odd he had no clue when the baby was supposed to be born, she didn't show it. "Her due date?"

"May fourth," J.C. said tonelessly as she buttoned her shirt.

May. Where would he be then? What would he be doing? Used to be he knew exactly what his life would be like. Who he'd be with. What kind of man he'd be.

"Would you like to know the sex?" Dr. Owens asked.

J.C. stood and pulled her pants up and though he tried not to look, he caught a glimpse of the curve of her hip. "Isn't it too soon to tell?" she asked.

Brady didn't blame her for sounding incredulous. He could barely make out the baby's head, let alone anything else.

"It's early, but the baby was positioned right for me to tell..."

Brady bit the inside of his cheek to keep from saying anything. Bad enough he'd seen the ultrasound. He didn't want to know any more about their baby. Not if he wanted to walk away.

But he'd lost the right to offer an opinion.

Nibbling her lip, J.C. nodded.

The doctor grinned. "Congratulations. You're having a son."

CHAPTER ELEVEN

FRIDAY EVENING, Brady sat at his kitchen table, a bottle of whiskey at his elbow, a spotty water glass in front of him, his cell phone in his hand. He'd left the window above the sink open, hoping some fresh air would help ease the tightness in his chest. The feeling that he was suffocating.

Pressing Redial on his phone, he held it to his ear, ground his back teeth together as it rang. And rang. When J.C.'s recorded voice came on and told him to leave a message, he hung up. Turned the phone end to end a few times and then tossed it aside.

The wind picked up, blew the take-out menu from his favorite Chinese place onto the floor. The evening air was thick with the threat of rain. A storm was coming. Several, if the local weather forecaster was to be trusted. Southern Virginia was in for a long night of violent weather.

His hand shook as he poured whiskey into the glass. As a kid, he'd loved a raging thunderstorm, especially the raw power of it. If the electricity went off, all the better. He'd stare out his bedroom window, watch the sky light up. Press his cheek against the glass to feel the vibrations shake the house from a strong rumble of thunder.

He heard thunder in the distance.

His breathing felt ripped from his lungs. The nape of his neck tingled. The edge of his vision grew dark. He inhaled for the count of five. Exhaled for the same amount. And told himself that no matter how much it sounded like an IED—improvised explosive device—it wasn't.

Goddamn, he hated storms now.

He lifted the glass to his lips. Set it down again and ran a hand back and forth, back and forth through his hair.

He wanted a drink. Hell, he needed ten of them. The oblivion they promised. The relief. He needed something to get him through the next few hours while the storms raged. More to get him through the night.

Congratulations. You're having a son.

He shoved away from the table and stood. The bottle tipped. Instead of catching it, he watched dispassionately as it fell, whiskey pouring onto the table. At the last second he remembered to grab his phone. Shook off a few drops of alcohol, then tried J.C.'s number again. Still no answer.

He gripped the sink and stared out at the rain. It blew through the screen and he lifted his face, letting it dot his skin. Then another muted boom of thunder. He slammed the window shut and pressed the heels of his hands against his eyes as he bent at the waist, rocking slightly. His head pounded. His stomach roiled. Sweat soaked through his shirt as terror beat down on him.

It was bad. Real bad.

He glanced over at the glass on the table. If he drank it, he'd stop shaking. The gnawing, endless craving would end. And maybe he'd even have a dreamless night. Instead of tossing and turning. Sleeping only in the few reprieves when his brain shut down enough to pause the nightmares. He went back to the table. Sat down. Jumped back up and paced the length of the kitchen.

Last night had been the worst. He'd spent a fitful night, not falling asleep until a few hours before dawn. When he'd finally drifted off, he'd dreamt of Liz. Of the way they used to be. The way he'd always thought they would be forever.

It was their wedding night and Liz had her back to him, her dark hair over her shoulder so he could unfasten the buttons running down her gown. He'd kissed the nape of her neck, flicked his tongue out to taste her and she'd shivered. Taking his time, he'd pushed each tiny button free, trailing his lips over each inch of skin he exposed until finally the gown had slid down her naked body. She stepped free of the silk pooled around her feet and turned to him, but she wasn't Liz anymore.

She was J.C.

J.C. with her wild curls and sensuous curves and warm smile. And when she stepped up to him in his dream and kissed him, he didn't back away. He didn't wake up when, in the dream, his clothes somehow disappeared. No, he remained in that dream as J.C. pushed him back onto a large bed. As she straddled him, her breasts swaying, her eyes closed.

Then he'd woken up, hard and aching for her.

His body stirred at the memory of it.

And he looked at the spilled whiskey and realized exactly what he needed to help him get through the night.

"IN MY DAY," Grandma Rose said, "expectant mothers took care of themselves. They rested. They certainly didn't work all day and then spend all night on their feet."

As the soapy water drained from the sink, J.C. rolled her eyes at the ceramic Victorian Santas lined up on her grandma's windowsill. Funny how Grandma Rose hadn't complained about J.C. staying on her feet when she'd offered to do the dinner dishes.

J.C. dried her hands and then folded the towel. "Didn't everyone smoke and drink while they were pregnant, too?"

Like the drum roll punctuating a joke, thunder rumbled in the distance.

Sitting at her kitchen table as regal as a queen, Grandma Rose sniffed delicately. "I don't understand why you'd choose to spend your Friday night making chocolates."

"I told you, I made a commitment to the Diamond Dust." And while the commitment part usually didn't mean all that much to her, she was determined to see this project through. To just once, complete a task she'd set for herself.

"But you could be out—"

"I thought you wanted me to rest?" she asked with an exasperated laugh.

"If you were out with some nice young man, you could rest. You could have dinner. Or see a movie."

"I just had dinner, I'm too busy for a movie and from my personal experience so far, nice young men don't ask out pregnant women."

"They might if you took some care with your hair," she said, eyeing J.C.'s frizzy ponytail, "and didn't wear such awful clothes. Why, that shirt needs to be thrown out. And it wouldn't hurt you to put on some makeup."

Used to her grandma's nit-picking about her appearance—at least this time she hadn't asked her why she couldn't be more like Liz—J.C. kissed Rose's soft, wrinkled cheek. "I'd better get going. Thanks for dinner."

"Wait." Rose stood and hurried to the refrigerator, where she pulled out a plastic container. "Take some pasta home. You can have it for lunch tomorrow."

"Great." Smiling, she took the leftover fettuccine in alfredo sauce. "Thanks."

They walked past the living room. Her grandma's artificial tree, complete with festively wrapped packages underneath, was done up in blues and silver. Green garlands, white lights and silver and blue candles decorated the mantel over the fireplace.

J.C. tightened her ponytail. She'd been too busy or too plain exhausted to think about putting up her own decorations but seeing as how Christmas would be here in just over two weeks, she should get a tree. And maybe start shopping for a few presents.

In the foyer, she slipped on her pink and white polka-dot flip-flops. "I'll see you Sunday at Mom and Dad's."

Lightning flickered.

"Oh, dear. You'd better take an umbrella," Rose said, hurrying over to the umbrella stand in the corner.

"I don't need one." J.C. raised the hood of her light blue sweatshirt and, looking back at her grandmother, opened the door. "'Night," she called over the heavy rain and wind, then turned.

She squeaked at finding Brady standing on her

grandmother's porch. "Brady. God. Don't scare me like that."

"Brady?" Rose repeated sharply as she peered past J.C. "What's he doing here?"

She shrugged. Rain dripped off his hair. Ran in rivulets down his cheek. The bottoms of his jeans were as soaked as his jacket. And as usual, he was scowling.

"My grandmother would like to know what you're doing here," J.C. said.

"Evening, Mrs. Montgomery."

Grandma Rose pulled her shoulders back. "Don't you 'evening' me, Brady Sheppard. I'm not some impressionable young girl. You can't charm me."

He shifted. "No, ma'am."

"And don't for one second think that I don't know what you're after." Rose shook her finger at him. "Well, you're not going to get it. Not again. You hear me?"

He glanced at J.C. "Yes, ma'am."

"And you," she said to Jane, "need to remember what my own grandmother told me—no man buys the cow when he gets the milk for free."

J.C. considered pointing out that she'd already given him the whole farm. Instead, she nodded somberly. "No free milk. Got it."

And before J.C. could be taken to task for being cheeky, she slipped outside and shut the door. The strands of white Christmas lights decorating the porch swayed in the breeze. Cold, needlelike rain hit J.C.'s face. She turned her head and hunched her shoulders.

"Did you need something, Brady?"

He wiped the rain off his face. Stared at a point above her head. "I wanted to make sure you were all right."

"Why wouldn't I be?"

"You seemed upset. At the doctor's office." He met her eyes. "You're disappointed the baby's a boy."

"Don't be ridiculous," she snapped, then pressed her lips together. Lightning lit the sky. "Look, I appreciate you coming over here to check on me—three days after the fact—but I'm fine. And I really have a lot—"

Thunder cracked sharply. Brady shivered. "Do you think I could come up...? For a towel," he added at her hesitation. "And maybe...a cup of coffee?"

Bad idea. Bad, *bad* idea. She'd bet a week's pay her grandmother was already on the phone with J.C.'s mom. And while she could easily excuse his presence at the doctor's office as her giving him his parental rights, and their pairing wines and being at the gift shop together as purely business, this was different.

She'd have no excuse for being with him tonight.

"It's getting pretty late—"

"Please," he said quietly. Gruffly. "Please invite me up, Jane."

Slowly she nodded. Then she raced down the porch steps and into the pouring rain. Water ran down the sleeve of the hand holding her hood in place. Cutting through the front yard, she rounded the corner to the garage and climbed the stairs as quickly as possible.

At the top, her flip-flop skidded on the wet wood, her foot shooting out from under her. Her arms flailed, and the plastic container flew out of her hand as she pitched backward. Her hand hit solid wood and she latched on to the railing, the sudden change in momentum causing her to lurch forward. Her legs buckled and she twisted so she wouldn't land on her stomach. Instead, her shin hit the sharp edge of the stair. Pain shot through her. Left her gasping.

Getting unsteadily to her feet, she picked up the plastic container and glanced behind her. Brady was halfway up the stairs, his face in shadow. She limped inside and left the door open for him—Daisy wouldn't go outside, not if it meant getting wet. As she went into the kitchen, she unzipped her soaking sweatshirt and peeled it off, letting it drop onto the floor. The T-shirt she wore underneath it was wet, as well, but she wanted to check her leg before she changed into dry clothes.

After wiping her face on a hand towel, she sat at the table. "You okay in there?" she whispered, rubbing her stomach. She didn't feel any different. Other than her leg, she had no pain. No cramping.

She shuddered out a breath. Thank God.

She gingerly pulled her pant leg up to her knee. A fist-size bruise was already forming. But there was no blood. Just some slight scraping of the skin.

"You all right?"

Brady stood in the doorway, his hair matted to his head. Water dripping off him, forming a small puddle at his feet.

"Yeah. It's not so bad," she said, twisting so he could see her shin. "It hurts but I don't think there's any major damage."

"The baby?"

"Fine. I didn't hit my stomach." She stood. "Before I make the coffee, I'll get you a towel and then change."

But when she went to move past him, he didn't budge. Lightning flashed, illuminating his harsh expression. He looked…dangerous. And pissed off.

"Give me your shoes," he ordered.

She glanced down. She hadn't even bothered to kick them off when she got inside. "What?"

Another rumble of thunder. "You almost fell because you're wearing those damn things. You could've broken your neck."

"But I didn't."

He stepped toward her, his movements menacing, his expression hard. "The shoes."

"You... You're nuts," she said, edging away from him until her spine hit the edge of the counter. "Look. I'm cold. I'm wet. And I need to call the doctor to see what, if any, pain relievers I can safely take. So why don't you—"

"Hold on."

Hold on? To what...him? Not likely. Not when she just wanted him out of her way.

Wrapping his fingers around her uninjured leg, below the knee, he lifted her foot off the ground.

"Hey!" She clutched the counter for balance. "Watch it, grabby hands."

He plucked off her flip-flop and tucked it under his arm. He very carefully lifted her other leg and took off that shoe, as well. All she could do was stare as he searched through her kitchen drawers. When he finally found what he was looking for—a paring knife—she drew her shoulders back.

"You wouldn't dare," she breathed.

He raised one eyebrow. Then he held up a flip-flop, tilted his head and...with his eyes locked on hers...sliced through the strap. Tossing the flip-flop over his shoulder, he repeated the process with the second one then laid the knife on the counter and gave her a look that told her he'd not only enjoyed destroying her shoes, but he'd do it again in a heartbeat.

She shook her head. "There is something seriously wrong with you."

He closed the distance between them. Water dripped from his coat onto her bare feet. "You're the one stupid enough to wear those shoes."

She pressed back against the counter again. "At least I don't go around dismembering people's shoes."

"Damn it, you could've been hurt," he snapped, grasping her upper arms and lifting her on tiptoe.

A lump formed in her throat. He'd been scared for her. How awful it must've been for him in that split second when it'd seemed as if she was going to fall backward. How helpless he must've felt. How angry because he couldn't race up the stairs.

Thunder shook the apartment.

Brady shuddered, his fingers tightening on her arms. His breathing grew rapid.

She remembered his violent reaction that morning she'd first told him about the baby. How he'd seemed to space out at the gift shop last week.

All this time she'd thought the changes in him, his drinking, were because of Liz. Because he couldn't let her go. And maybe that was part of it. But it wasn't all of it.

"Hey, it's okay," she soothed him. She laid her hands on his chest. Under the soggy, cold shirt, his muscles tensed. His heart raced. "It's just a storm. Everything's fine."

A muscle jumped in his jaw. He slid his hands up to her shoulders. Brushing his thumbs against the sides of her neck, he tipped her head back and met her eyes. She dug her nails into his skin. His narrowed gaze dropped to her mouth.

And any hope she'd had about truly being over her feelings for this man died when he swore under his breath and then kissed her.

His mouth against hers, Brady swallowed J.C.'s gasp. He kept the kiss gentle. Almost…reverent. He was afraid if he pushed for too much, too fast, she'd pull away. Tell him to go.

He couldn't let that happen. Not when the panic was already receding. He was able to blot everything else out because she was in his arms. Kissing him back.

He had no right to touch her, to discover that she tasted as sweet as he'd imagined. To sink into her kiss and forget how screwed up his life had become. But he couldn't stop. He needed to surround himself with her warmth. It was the only way to get rid of the fear that gripped him every day.

He slid his tongue along the seam of her lips and she pulled back slightly, but not far enough away to break contact. Forcing himself to slow down, he skimmed his lips across her jaw, over her chilled cheeks to her temple and down along her hairline.

Her skin was cold, so he rubbed her arms. Pressed closer to her as his own body heated despite his wet clothes. He wanted to tear her hair band out. Watch her shake her head so the curls framed her face. But he didn't have the patience for it.

He pressed an openmouthed kiss behind her ear. Her head fell back on a soft moan that seemed to wash over his body, caress his skin.

He kissed her mouth again. Her lips parted and the tip of her tongue touched his tentatively and about blew his mind.

He yanked her against him. Speared one hand into the damp hair at the nape of her neck to hold her still for his kiss. His other hand slid under her shirt to her waist, the curve of her belly pressing against his palm.

Deepening the kiss, he shifted his weight off his bad leg by slipping it between her thighs. She wrapped her arms around his neck, her fingers combing through his wet hair. The movement brought their bodies center to center. He hissed out a breath. Her breasts rubbed against his chest, her beaded nipples burning through his shirt.

He shifted to the side and broke the kiss long enough to wrench his coat off. Letting it fall on the floor, he raked his gaze over her and his body tightened. She was...stunning. Her lips were red and swollen, her breasts, the roundness of her belly pressing against her shirt. Her cheeks flushed, her eyes dark with desire.

He took her mouth in another voracious kiss. Grabbing her ass, he pulled her even closer. She was all soft, lush curves. And the mewling sounds she made in the back of her throat were driving him crazy. Unable to resist, he rolled his hips and almost whimpered himself. He needed to be inside her. Right now. Or else he'd lose his mind for good.

He would've dragged her down and made love to her there on her kitchen floor, was in the process of doing just that, when she stopped kissing him.

He lifted his head. "What's wrong?"

"I...I don't want this," she said, holding herself as stiffly as possible in his arms.

"Are you sure?" he murmured, unable to stop himself from trailing a finger down the smoothness of her cheek. "I want you."

She laughed harshly. "You don't want me. You want a warm body." When she pushed him, he dropped his arms and stepped back. "I'm convenient."

"What the hell is that supposed to mean?"

"It means you're looking for someone to help you through the night."

No. Not anyone. Her. But she'd never believe it.

"Is that so wrong?" he asked. "We're both adults. Both unattached."

"It wouldn't be wrong," she said with a sigh, "except you'll never be unattached. You're always going to be in love with Liz."

He wanted to deny it. Wanted his denial to be the truth, but he wasn't sure it would be. "She has nothing to do with this."

"How can she not have everything to do with this?" J.C. crossed her arms. "She's my sister and the woman you've loved half your life. What happens between us affects her, too."

"So I'm supposed to…what? Let Liz vet all the women I might sleep with? Because she sure as hell didn't ask my opinion when she decided to dump me for her husband."

"There's too much between us. Call it history or family ties…or whatever. All I know is I've already let you use me once," she said wearily as she straightened from the counter. "I'm not about to make that mistake again. Especially not for a man who only wants me so he can pretend he's with my sister."

CHAPTER TWELVE

"YOU'RE EITHER the world's most patient man," J.C. said in exasperation, coming back to the kitchen when he'd refused to leave, "or the most stubborn."

"Both," he admitted.

She'd swept out of here twenty minutes ago, no doubt hoping that if she took long enough changing into dry clothes, he'd give up, maybe even get pissed and take off. But he wasn't going anywhere. Not when she had such a messed-up view of what'd happened between them. Of why he'd kissed her.

"Here," she said, tossing him a dark blue towel and a gray sweatshirt.

He caught one in each hand. "Thanks."

She shrugged and brushed past him, close enough he could smell a light vanilla scent as she went to a corner cupboard. She'd changed into a pair of striped pajama pants and an oversize, stained shirt with a scowling Garfield holding a coffee cup above the words *I Don't Do Mornings*. She must've redone her hair because the sides were smoothed back, the ponytail higher on her head. Several curls, having escaped confinement, trailed along the back of her neck.

The skin he now knew was soft and warm and sensitive to his touch.

Squeezing the towel in his hands, he stepped back so he wouldn't pull her against him.

She turned—spray cleaner in one hand, a dry cloth in the other—and, without so much as a glance his way, went back to the table. Rain pelted the roof, its intensity waning as the storm moved past. But another one would follow. And if he was alone, he didn't think he could make it through the night. At least not sober.

By the time he'd peeled off his damp shirt, rubbed the towel over his chilled arms and chest, and dried his hair, she'd wheeled a small, three-tiered cart between the table and wall and taken a round, plastic container from the fridge.

"Thank you," she said, still not looking at him, "for cleaning up the floor."

"No problem." Since she'd left him to stew, he'd had plenty of time.

He tugged on the sweatshirt, shoving up the short sleeves. Sitting to her left, he clasped his hands between his knees. Inhaled deeply. "When I'm with you," he said slowly, his gaze fixed on her profile, "I don't pretend you're Liz. And I sure as hell wasn't thinking of her when I kissed you."

"You sure about that?" she asked, spraying cleaning solution over the table. The harsh, chemical scent stung his nose. "It wouldn't be the first time."

"Whatever I did the night of Liz's wedding, I didn't mean to hurt you."

"It wasn't all your fault." She wiped the table with brisk, rough strokes. "I convinced myself you wanted to be with me. And I kept on believing. Right until the end when…" Her voice broke, and she vigorously scrubbed the same spot. "When you called out Liz's name."

He linked his hands at the back of his neck and leaned back. Blew out a heavy breath. "Shit."

His memories of that night were blurry. Disjointed. He'd known he'd used J.C. to help him through his pain and anger. But he hadn't realized how low he'd sunk. Wincing, he shut his eyes. How low he was still sinking. Not thirty minutes ago he'd had her in his arms wanting only to shove aside his panic, to ignore the memories for a little while.

She unfolded a plastic tablecloth. When she spread the material over the table, he sat up and snagged her hand. She froze, her fingers curling. He traced his fingertip over the delicate skin of her inner wrist. Back and forth. Back and forth. Finally, she raised her head.

He wrapped his fingers around her wrist. Felt her pulse beat. "I'm sorry, Jane."

"Sometimes…" she said softly as she withdrew her hand. "Sometimes being sorry isn't enough."

J.C. DIDN'T SO MUCH as glance Brady's way as she set out what she needed—gloves, wax paper, tape, melon ball scoop, cookie sheets. After taping wax paper to the cookie sheets, she opened the container of ganache she'd made earlier. Wind rattled the windowpane.

"Won't be long before another storm comes," she said casually. As if having him sit there wearing her University of Virginia sweatshirt, all big and male and brooding, didn't bother her in the least. As if it hadn't taken all of her willpower to push him away. "If you don't want to get caught in another downpour, you'd better get going."

"Last time you wanted me out of your apartment, you told me outright."

"Fair enough," she said, pulling on a pair of gloves. "I'd like you to leave."

Scooping up a small amount of the dark ganache, she rolled it lightly between her palms, then set it on the wax paper. Repeated the process.

Brady stretched his leg out. Bent it again. Drummed his fingers on the table.

She sighed. "Brady—"

"I haven't had a drink in four days."

Her fingers tightened on the scoop and she glanced at him. Four days... She caught her breath. Four days ago he'd accompanied her to her doctor's appointment.

"Are you bragging?" she asked, keeping her tone neutral. "Or complaining?"

He slouched. "Just stating a fact."

"Oh. Well, that's—"

"I wanted to," he muttered. "Every damn day I've wanted a drink worse than the day before."

Using the scoop, she scraped a tic-tac-toe pattern into the ganache. "Maybe...maybe you need to decide what you want more. To have a drink. Or to stop drinking."

He stood. Put his hands into his pockets. Took them out again. The next storm rumbled in the distance and he hunched his shoulders.

"Don't like thunder?" she couldn't stop herself from asking.

"I've been jumpy since..." He shook his head.

"You were hurt?"

"Since I've been stateside." His expression was hard. "Sometimes...loud noises cause me to...zone out."

She frowned. "You mean you have flashbacks?"

He glared at her. "Sometimes I think about what happened back there."

There. Afghanistan. Where his friends had been wounded. Killed.

And now a thunderstorm had the power to cause this strong man to tremble. Her heart broke for him.

"Can I stay?" he asked, his tone belligerent. His feet wide, his arms loose at his sides as if ready for a fight.

"What do you mean?" If he said stay as in stay the night in her bed, she'd kick his butt to the curb—she didn't care how emotionally damaged he was.

He kept opening and closing his fist, like a gunfighter getting ready to draw his weapon. "If I go home now," he said, as if he were forcing the words out, "I'll drink. And I don't want to drink. Not tonight."

She squeezed the last of the ganache between her hands. He was using her. Again. She was his safety net. Except she couldn't save him. And even if she could, she wasn't sure she wanted to.

"Should I be your crutch?" she asked, unable to keep the bitterness out of her voice. "How about if I throw myself on any alcoholic beverages that get within a few feet of you?"

"I was thinking more along the lines of you just… talking to me," he said quietly. "Letting me keep you company while you work or do your laundry or…whatever you had planned."

She tore off her chocolate-coated gloves and dropped them into the empty bowl. She wanted to send him away. To protect herself from him. If she let him too close, he'd hurt her again. But then she met his eyes and, for the first time since he'd come home, glimpsed the man he used to be.

She had to let him stay.

"BRADY," DIANE SAID TWO days later as she passed him the serving bowl of green beans, "there's something important Aidan and I would like to discuss with you."

They were seated at the small table in the breakfast nook rather than in the ornate dining room—the spot for Sunday dinners when he'd been a kid. His mother sat with her back to the dark window, Brady to her left. Aidan, as always, was her right-hand man.

Spooning beans onto his already full plate, Brady raised his eyebrows. "Don't keep me in suspense."

Diane smiled at him. "How would you like to take on a bigger role at the winery?"

His fingers tingled and he set the beans down. Every week since he'd been back in Jewell, his mother had invited him to Sunday dinner. And every week he'd declined. Until yesterday, when his mother had casually mentioned she was making all his favorites.

Damn. Lured into a trap by the promise of fried chicken, homemade buttermilk biscuits and her double fudge brownies.

He picked up his drumstick. "I wouldn't."

"Told you," Aidan murmured before sipping his chardonnay.

"But why not?" she asked. "Now that you're...getting better—"

"She means now that you're not stinking drunk or hungover all the time," Aidan offered.

Diane fixed Aidan with a look guaranteed to make most men feel as if they were ten years old again. "When I need you to help explain what I mean," she said, her slight Southern accent thickening, "I'll ask."

Aidan stabbed a bean. "Just trying to help."

Brady bit into his chicken, determined not to let the topic ruin his favorite meal.

"Your father always dreamt of having his sons work at the Diamond Dust with him," Diane said.

And his food now tasted like sawdust.

"Don't waste your time," Aidan told their mother. "The only reason he's working here in the first place is because I forced him into it."

"I never pretended otherwise," Brady said mildly.

"But it doesn't have to be that way," Diane said. "Won't you at least consider it?"

He couldn't. He'd already lost Liz and any chance he'd had of becoming a member of the Virginia State Police. If he stayed in Jewell, if he worked at the Diamond Dust, it'd be like admitting he accepted the way his life had turned out.

He wiped his fingers then his mouth on a cloth napkin. "I never planned on working here. Dad knew that."

"Yes, and we fully supported your decision to join the military, but things are different now. You need to start thinking of your future."

"I am," he said. Or he would. Soon.

"Well, then, how are you going to support yourself? And what about Jane and the baby?"

"What about them?"

She seemed taken aback. "I thought you and she were...on friendlier terms."

The memory of how J.C. had felt in his arms, of how she tasted, hit him with great force. "Nothing's changed."

Except that he continued to dream about her. Had kissed her.

Even after everything he'd done, she still let him sit at her kitchen table the other night while she worked on her chocolates. She'd kept up a steady stream of chatter and hadn't seemed to mind when he'd lapsed into silence.

"Everyone in town's talking about how you spent an entire day at the obstetrician's office so you could see her," Aidan said, laying his fork on his empty plate.

Brady rolled his shoulders. Damn small-town gossip, he thought for the nth time. "It wasn't like that."

His brother smirked. "What was it like, then?"

"I think it's wonderful that you and Jane are working out your differences," Diane said, pausing to eat a bite of mashed potatoes. "Especially as I'd like to have some sort of relationship with my first grandchild. You wouldn't believe the horror stories I've heard about grandparents being refused the right to even visit with their grandchildren after a nasty divorce. In some cases where the parents were never married, the mothers disappear with the child. Can you imagine?"

Imagine? He'd been trying not to think about it ever since J.C.'s admission that she wasn't sure she wanted to keep their son.

And he'd told her she had his full support because she'd been so upset, he'd wanted to let her know he didn't judge her. And because... He swallowed the nausea rising in his throat. Because if she did decide to give the baby up for adoption, it'd let him off the hook.

She'd brought up their families and wondered how her decision would affect them. He hadn't wanted to think about it. Hadn't wanted to care.

"J.C. would never keep the baby away from you," he said.

Diane set her water down. "When relationships go bad, some people change."

"Not her."

"I'm sure you're right." Diane cut her chicken into tiny pieces before setting her knife down. "After all, it was your idea to have her sell those chocolates in the gift store. Pam said J.C.'s sales yesterday were up fifteen percent from last week."

Figuring they both needed some space after Friday night, he'd stayed far away from the gift shop yesterday. "Good." He looked over to find Aidan regarding him steadily. "What?" Brady growled.

"I find it interesting how well you seem to have gotten to know Jane."

"I was with her sister for twelve years," he pointed out. "I've always known J.C."

He tapped his fist against his thigh. Just because he'd dreamt of J.C., kissed her, and wanted to take her to bed, didn't change what'd been in his heart since he was sixteen years old.

He would always love Liz.

J.C. WAS FINISHING UP with one of her favorite customers late Wednesday morning when Liz walked into the lobby of Hampton Bank and Trust Company.

"Going to do some Christmas shopping?" she asked Mr. Carns as Liz waited in line at the end of the roped-off area.

Mr. Carns, an elderly gentleman with thinning silver hair and an easy grin, slid his money into a bank envelope. "My wife handles all the gift buying. She leaves me in charge of making sure her wallet's always full of money." He winked.

J.C. smiled. "She's a lucky woman."

"That's what I keep telling her." Hitting the counter with the flat of his hand, he straightened. "If I don't see you before, you have a merry Christmas."

"You, too, Mr. Carns."

As usual for the middle of the week, business was light. "Silver Bells" played in the background and in between each teller's window hung a swag of evergreen boughs tied with a red velvet ribbon. Behind her, Mary Jo Hanold spoke to a customer using the drive-up window. Two windows down in the lobby, Shirley Dodge counted out a deposit from one of the local grocery stores.

"Hello, J.C.," Liz said, stepping up to the window with obvious reluctance.

"It's so good to see you. I've tried calling but—"

"I'd like to cash this." She set down a personal check while seemingly engrossed in watching the hands of the large clock on the wall above the door turn. "Large bills are fine."

J.C. narrowed her eyes. "Yes, ma'am."

Other than the slight stiffening of her shoulders, Liz gave no indication she even heard J.C.

"What do you want from me?" J.C. asked as she processed the transaction on her computer. "Blood?"

"All I want is to cash a check."

"Fine," J.C. said. She was so very tired of being the only one trying to make things right between them.

She quickly counted out the cash, recounted it out loud for her sister's benefit and then tapped it into a neat pile. "Next time," she said, sliding the money across the counter, "try one of our convenient ATM locations."

Liz put the money into her wallet. "Grandma Rose

mentioned Brady spent quite a bit of time at your apartment Friday night."

"Grandma Rose," J.C. said vehemently, "has a big mouth."

"So it's true?"

J.C. straightened a stack of withdrawal slips. "He stopped by."

"Are you...are you two...together?"

Heat washed over her as she remembered how he'd kissed her, as if he could never get enough of her. Held her breast, his voice scraping along her nerve endings when he'd said he wanted her. How...relieved he'd been when she'd told him he could stay through the worst of the storms.

"No." She picked up the withdrawal slips and fanned herself. "Of course not."

When Liz didn't respond, J.C. glanced up, shocked to see her sister fighting tears. Liz must be close to her breaking point to show that much weakness in the middle of the bank lobby.

J.C. set up her Next Window Please sign.

"Don't move," she ordered and then told Mary Jo she was taking a five-minute break.

By the time J.C. had walked out from behind the teller station, Liz's eyes were dry. But she still let J.C. lead her through the lobby to the corner office they used to open new accounts.

J.C. flipped on the light and shut the door. "What is it?" she asked, taking Liz's hand. "What's wrong?"

Liz linked her fingers with J.C.'s. "Carter and I..." She cleared her throat. "We're having some...problems."

"What do you mean by problems?"

"He thinks I have…feelings…repressed feelings…for Brady."

Her mouth went dry. "Do you?"

"If you mean do I still care about Brady, about what happens to him, then yes." She tugged her hand free and began to pace. "After all our time together, how could I not? But Carter refuses to believe it's not more than that. He wants us to go to marriage counseling," Liz said, as if her husband had suggested they join a wife-swapping club.

The idea of admitting her marriage was in trouble must be devastating.

"Maybe counseling's not such a bad idea," J.C. offered.

"It's a horrible idea. We don't need it. Where would we attend sessions anyway? I could never face our colleagues after discussing our most intimate issues with one of them." Crossing her arms, Liz shook her head. "No. We don't need therapy. We'll get through this on our own. But I need you to do something for me."

The hair at the back of her neck stood on end. "I'll do whatever I can—"

"Stay away from Brady."

She licked her lips. Clasped her hands in front of her. "I told you, we're not together."

"But you've been spending time with him and I…I miss you." Liz's expression softened. "So much. But things can't go back to the way they were between us if…if Brady's in your life. And you said yourself that he didn't want any part of the baby, right?"

She remembered Brady's expression when he'd seen the baby's ultrasound—small part wonder, huge part fear. "Right, but—"

"I'm not just asking this for me. I'm asking for Carter, so he doesn't have to risk coming face-to-face with my ex when we see you. And I'm asking for you, too."

"Me?"

"You may not believe this, but I don't want to see you get hurt."

Brady's not the right guy for you. You deserve someone who'll put you first.

Someone who hadn't loved her sister first.

"Okay," J.C. managed to say through the tightness of her throat. "I won't see him anymore."

Liz shut her eyes briefly. "Thank you."

And as her sister enveloped her in a warm hug, J.C. assured herself she'd made the right decision. She'd give Brady up.

As soon as she figured out how to give up a man who was never really hers in the first place.

CHAPTER THIRTEEN

"BRADY," J.C. SAID, when she opened the door Friday evening. "What do you want?"

He raised his eyebrows and she forced herself not to wince. Well, he couldn't show up at her doorstep out of the blue whenever he liked. It wasn't fair to her. And having him standing on her doorstep, clean shaven with his recently cut hair ruffling in the breeze, didn't make keeping her promise to her sister any easier.

"There's a ten-foot Scotch pine strapped to the roof of your car," he said.

She widened her eyes. "It must've fallen onto my car when I drove home from work. Funny how I never noticed."

His eyes narrowed to slits. "How did you think you were going to get it off the car, let alone up the stairs, by yourself?"

"I didn't plan that far ahead." Stopping by the Christmas tree lot on the way home had been an impulse. It had seemed like such a good idea, spending Friday night decorating her tree. With her luck, it'd still be on her car Monday morning. "Is that why you stopped by? To tell me about my own Christmas tree?"

He studied her in that intense way of his that made her blush. "Did I do something between last week and today to piss you off?"

"You haven't even spoken to me since then. What could you have done?"

That sounded as if she'd expected him to call. She grimaced.

"So there's no reason for you to not invite me in," he said.

She lightly hit the dangling silver earring in her left ear with her fingertip, set it swinging. "Actually, there is. A reason."

"Should I guess?" he asked when she remained silent.

"I…" She swallowed. "I just got home," she said on a rush. "I haven't even changed yet."

His gaze skimmed over her black pants. Lingered on her shiny burgundy top before meeting her eyes. "I don't mind."

Her mouth dried and she stepped behind the door, closing it slightly, showing only her face through the small opening.

"Since I'm not going to see the other side of your door any time soon, you might as well take this now," he said, holding out a plastic shopping bag.

She eyed it suspiciously. "What is it?"

He pulled a large, plain cardboard box out of the bag. "Do you want it or not?"

She took it, flipped it over then back again. Letting go of the door, she lifted the lid. And blinked down at a pair of purple and white polka-dot flip-flops.

The tips of Brady's ears were red. "They were out of pink," he said almost defiantly.

"That's okay," she whispered. "I love purple."

He scowled. "I wasn't sure of your size."

"They're fine. They're perfect," she said. "Thank you."

He inclined his head, the barest of nods. "Good night."

"Wait." She stepped onto the landing, pulling the door closed in case Daisy made a run for it. "Don't you want to come in?"

"Do you want me to come in?" he asked cautiously.

She clutched the box, holding it over her racing heart. "Yeah, I do."

He gestured for her to go ahead of him and she hurried inside. Before she changed her mind.

She kicked off her shoes. "Do you want a soda?" she asked, setting the box on top of her coffee table before making her way toward the kitchen. "I think I have regular—"

"How are you going to get the tree up here?"

She placed a hand over the fluttering in her stomach. "I'll call my dad tomorrow."

He glared at the sheet and tree stand under the window. "I can't bring the tree up."

"I didn't ask you to." And then she realized what he meant. What bothered him. "Is this about your knee? Because even if I wasn't pregnant, I couldn't drag that tree up all those stairs, either."

He tossed his jacket onto the sofa. "That's different."

"If that isn't one of the finest examples of the male ego at work, I don't know what is."

"It's not ego. Not all ego. More like I hate not being able to do all the things I used to."

"So you can't haul a large evergreen up a flight of stairs. At least you can still climb them," she said, sick to death of him focusing on what he couldn't do. What he didn't have, such as Liz. "You're able to get out of bed by yourself. You can work at a job—even if it's not the one you'd always planned on. You're surrounded by people who care about you. Who are more than willing to give you a hand when you need one. And if all of those reasons weren't enough for you to thank God each and every day," she said, her face hot, her voice breaking, "I'd think the fact that you're alive would be."

The room seemed too quiet after her outburst. All she could hear was the sound of her own ragged breathing. Her pulse kicked up as Brady closed the distance between them, the surprise on his face giving way to admiration.

He stopped a few inches from her. Close enough she could feel his body heat, smell the fresh winter air clinging to his clothes. "You're right. Those things weren't enough for me. I'm not sure they'll ever be." He tucked one of her stray curls behind her ear, his fingertip grazing her neck. "But you're wrong, too. Because right now, I can honestly say I'm very grateful to be alive."

"DID YOU FIND SOMETHING to drink?" J.C. asked as she came back out into the living room ten minutes later. After her impassioned speech and his own admission, she'd bolted with the excuse of changing out of her work clothes.

Sitting on the sofa, her cat curled up next to him, Brady held up his can of soda. He watched as J.C. walked past him. She'd pulled her hair back and had on the same clinging black pants she'd worn last week when she fell on the steps and a loose T-shirt the color of peaches.

As she disappeared into the kitchen, his fingers tightened on the can. He took a long swallow. "You hungry?" he called.

She came back into the room eating from a bag of pretzels. "What'd you say?"

He grinned. "I asked if you were hungry."

She sat on the other end of the couch. "Nowadays that's pretty much a yes no matter when you ask me."

"We could order some dinner," he said casually. "Maybe get some Chinese?"

"Sure," she said after a long moment, as if having takeout with him was some sort of momentous decision. "That'd be nice." Handing him the bag of pretzels, she stood. "Let me grab the take-out menu for The Golden Dragon."

"I don't need it. I'll have a number three and a number fifteen."

"You have the menu for the Chinese restaurant memorized?"

The cat stood and stretched, stepped onto Brady's lap and lay down again. "Just the dishes I like."

She rubbed the side of her stomach. "I take it you don't cook."

"Not if I can help it."

"Me, either. Between my parents, Grandma Rose and Liz and Carter, I—" She blushed, acting as guilty as if she'd admitted to hiding Al-Qaeda operatives under her bed. "I'll go order dinner," she said before rushing out of the room. Again.

He didn't call her back. Not when he had no idea what to say to her. He knew what he should say—that J.C. could go ahead and talk about her sister all she wanted. That Liz was a part of her life and as such, she shouldn't worry about bringing her up in an innocent conversation.

Leaning his head back against the couch, he stared at the ceiling. Yeah, he should say all of that. But he'd be lying. He didn't want to hear anything about Liz. Didn't want to be reminded of her existence. Not when he'd gotten to the point where he could go all day without once thinking about her.

Someone knocked, and Brady set the cat aside and stood. He opened the door, nodded at Matt and then noticed J.C.'s tree on the stairs behind his brother.

"Thanks," he said, figuring he could manage to drag it up the last few feet. "I've got it from here."

Matt pushed the door back open when Brady tried to shut it in his face. "Don't I even get invited in? After all, I dropped everything to do you a favor."

Dropped everything, his ass.

"Favor's appreciated," Brady said, refusing to fall for his brother's bait.

When he'd called Matt's cell phone fifteen minutes ago, Matt had been at The County Line, one of the higher end bars in Jewell. And Brady sure as hell didn't feel guilty for tearing him away from a watered-down drink and whichever local girl he'd been trying to charm into sleeping with him.

"Well, appreciation's great and all," Matt said, leaning against the door. "But I'd rather have a beer."

"J.C. doesn't have—"

"Food should be here in twenty minutes," J.C. said, coming up behind Brady. "Oh. Hi, Matt." She glanced curiously between the brothers. "I didn't know you were home."

"Since I had to fly back to Australia the day

after Thanksgiving, I thought I'd come in early for Christmas."

Funny how Matt's accent became thicker whenever a female was within hearing distance. His green eyes lit as he scanned J.C. head to toe and back up again. "Jane Cleo, you get prettier every time I see you."

Brady stopped himself from laying a proprietary hand on J.C.'s shoulder. "Any women stupid enough to buy your tired lines?" he asked.

Matt grinned, his hair, too long, blowing around his face. "You'd be surprised."

"I wouldn't," J.C. said. Brady scowled while Matt laughed. "What?" she asked. "I'm just saying there are plenty of stupid women out there."

He laid a hand over his heart. "You wound me, sugar. And after I hauled your Christmas tree up all those stairs. Your very heavy Christmas tree."

At that moment, Brady would've given anything to have full use of his leg back so he could kick Matt down the steps.

"You brought my tree up?" J.C. asked, her brow knit in confusion.

"Sure did. Now, why don't you hold the door open and I'll bring it the rest of the way in."

Brady stepped out onto the landing. "Better let me help you," he said. "Seeing as how this is one of those extra-heavy Christmas trees."

He carefully took a hold of a thick bottom branch while Matt did the same. Walking backward, they pulled the tree up over the doorstep and into the apartment. The sharp needles pricked and scratched his skin. The pungent scent of pine filled the room.

"Want me to set it up for you, Jane?" Matt asked.

"No," Brady said before J.C. could so much as open her mouth.

"You sure?" Matt hooked his thumbs in his pockets and sent J.C. one of his patented grins guaranteed to charm the ladies. "I'd be more than happy to stick around."

"We've got it," Brady ground out. "Thanks for coming over."

"Yes," J.C. added, giving his brother a warm smile. "Thank you so much, Matt. This was really sweet of you."

"No problem." He walked to the door and stood on the landing. "Call me if you need anything else," he said to J.C. "Come to think of it, why don't I give you my cell phone—"

Brady shut the door. "I don't suppose you have a hacksaw?" he asked, his hands on his hips as he studied the tree. The cat came over and delicately sniffed the trunk. "We're going to have to cut this down by—"

He broke off, went rigid when she pressed against his side. Stretching up, she kissed his cheek. "Thank you for getting my tree inside."

"I didn't do anything," he said, stepping back when what he really wanted was to pull her closer.

"You called your brother when it must've been hard for you to ask for help."

J.C. flinched, her hand going to her side.

"What is it?" he asked. "Are you sick?"

"No, I…I think I felt the baby move."

"You're not sure?"

"I'm new at this, remember? Dr. Owens said I'd know what it was like when I felt it, whatever that's supposed to—" She gasped, her face filled with wonder. "That had to be it."

Brady watched her stomach, as if he could somehow get a glimpse of movement through her clothes and skin. "Does it hurt?"

"No, it's...weird. Here." Shifting so they were toe to toe, she took his hand and slid it under her snug top.

His fingers grazed her warm skin and he clenched his fist. "J.C., I—"

"Don't you want to feel it, too?"

Forcing his fingers to uncurl, he let her guide his hand to her side. Her skin was incredibly soft and he couldn't stop himself from cupping the roundness of her stomach, his thumb by her belly button, his fingertips brushing her hip bone. They were so close, he breathed in the fresh scent of her hair. Had the torture of her breasts brushing against his chest with every small move she made.

He cleared his throat. "I don't feel anything."

"That's because he hasn't moved yet." Another second passed. And another. "There! Did you feel it?"

He shook his head. "What's it like?"

"The first few times, it felt as if there were butterflies in my stomach—literally." Making a sound somewhere between a laugh and a cry, she raised her head, bringing their faces to within inches of each other. Her smile faded.

"Butterflies, huh?"

"Uh...yes... It was this...sort of fluttering," she whispered, staring at his mouth. "But now it's more of a... rolling sensation. Sort of...how you feel when you're falling..."

She lifted her hand to his cheek. Her lush breasts pressed against him, her breath washed over his lips.

And then she kissed him.

She kept the kiss delicate. Light. But in that instant, with her mouth supple and warm against his, her lips tasting of salt and a sweetness that was uniquely her, his senses spun.

Yeah. He knew all about falling.

He also knew how much it hurt when you hit the ground.

She eased back. Her smile was so purely Jane—simple and honest and bright enough to chase away nightmares—it took all his waning willpower not to yank her to him.

"In case you were wondering," she said as she adjusted her shirt to cover her stomach again, "that was one of those happy kisses."

He frowned. Happy what? And then he remembered. That day when she'd kissed him in his mom's kitchen, she'd claimed she'd only done it because she was happy.

"Good thing I was here," he said.

"It was awfully convenient. Although if I'd felt the baby move a few minutes earlier Matt would've still been here so…"

"You would've still kissed me."

She laughed. "Well, you would've had a fifty-fifty chance."

He set his hands on her waist and pulled her forward. Sliding his arms around her, he held her to him, pressing his palms against the flat of her back.

"You would've kissed me." His gaze followed the movement of her throat as she swallowed, then shifted back to her eyes. "Say it," he demanded in a soft undertone.

She gripped his forearms, her short nails digging into his skin. "I would've kissed you."

He dipped his head in acknowledgment and dropped his arms. "I'll check in the garage for that hacksaw," he said. And maybe, if he helped her put up her tree, she'd be so happy she'd kiss him again.

"THIS IS MY FAVORITE PART," J.C. said late the next night as they watched the DVD of *It's A Wonderful Life*.

"You said that before."

Tossing popcorn into her mouth, she didn't even bother glancing at Brady. Not when Mary and George were about to kiss for the first time. And, okay, she may have said her favorite part was the scene after the school dance when Mary and George walk home, but this was her absolute favorite scene.

"You're not going to cry again, are you?" Brady asked.

On the screen, George stormed out and Mary smashed the record of their song into pieces.

"I haven't cried yet," J.C. said. She may have welled up a few times, but what did he expect when she was watching the most fabulous movie ever? "But if tears bother you, I should warn you that I bawl at the end for a solid five minutes."

"Great," he muttered, slouching down even farther on the opposite end of her couch, staring at the brightly lit Christmas tree across the room.

Setting the popcorn bowl aside, she picked up her water glass and took a sip. "Are you all right?"

He sent her an unreadable look. "Fine."

"Are you sure? You seem…distracted."

He lifted one shoulder in a shrug.

She huffed out a breath, trying to figure out why he was acting like his old brooding, angry self. It was as if he didn't want to be there—although when they'd talked at the Diamond Dust's gift shop earlier, he was the one who'd asked if he could stop by. She couldn't refuse him, not after last night when he'd helped put up her tree and then had kissed her so tenderly before he left.

And for once, she hadn't felt guilty for wanting to spend time with her sister's ex. Or worried about telling Liz she'd made a mistake when she'd promised to stay away from Brady.

She paused the movie. "We don't have to watch—"

"I said I'm fine."

She crossed her arms at his clipped tone. "Yes. That's obvious."

"I just…" He ran his palms up and down his jeans. "I really want a drink."

"Oh." She sipped more water, but it did little to ease the dryness in her throat. After pulling the hem of her shorts down, she tucked her legs underneath her. "Are you going to have one?"

"If I could stop at one drink, it wouldn't be a problem now, would it?"

"No, I suppose not."

When she remained silent, he sat up. "Aren't you going to tell me not to drink?"

"Is that why you're here?" she asked, proud of how calm she sounded, how rational. "So I can stop you from drinking?"

"You don't get it," he burst out. "I don't need you to

babysit me so I won't drink. I want a drink because...
because, maybe if I get drunk," he continued, the low
rumble of his voice scraping along her nerve endings,
"I can forget how much I want you. Even for a little
while."

She caught her breath. "I...I don't..."

"It's killing me to sit here and not touch you," he
admitted raggedly, his hands fisted on his thighs.

It all made sense now. How Brady had barely looked
her way all evening. Why he'd sat as far away on the
small sofa as possible.

She knew what was at risk. Her family wouldn't
understand. Wouldn't approve. And her sister? If J.C.
followed her heart, if she chose Brady, she may never
be able to salvage her relationship with Liz.

Her heart pounding, she unfolded her legs and knelt
on the cushion, facing him. He watched her warily, his
jaw taut. Swallowing back her trepidation, she said the
words that had the power to change everything between
them.

"Touch me, Brady."

For a moment, he didn't move. Other than the rapid
rise and fall of his chest, it was as if he were made of
stone. Then he groaned and pulled her forward for a
voracious kiss. She tumbled, catching herself against
his shoulders, and still he didn't release her mouth. His
kiss was hard. Hungry. Almost punishing.

When he lifted his head, they were both breathing
hard. He kissed her jaw up her cheek to her temple and
back down again. His fingers kneaded her neck, his
other hand squeezing her outer thigh. He captured a
fistful of her hair and tugged her head back. He pressed

his lips against the hollow of her throat before scraping his teeth across her collarbone.

She whimpered and clutched his shoulders, her nails digging into his skin. He kissed his way back up her throat to her mouth again, his tongue sweeping inside to touch hers.

He straightened and combed both hands through her hair, his touch incredibly gentle. "Where's that purple top?" he asked.

"What?"

"The tank top you wore with these shorts before."

"I'm wearing it."

He stared at her black sweatshirt so intently she half expected it to burst into flames. "Under that shirt?"

She nodded and he lowered his hands to the hem of her shirt. She lifted her arms as he pulled the fleece up, his knuckles grazing the sensitive skin on the inside of her arms as he pulled it over her head and let it drop.

She glanced down. The ribbed tank top clung to each curve, hugging the mound of her belly and her breasts, her hard nipples jutting out. She held her breath as he edged closer, his leg bumping her knees. He brushed his fingertips over the fabric covering the upper slope of her breasts and she exhaled softly.

"I really like this shirt," he said solemnly, dragging his fingernail down between her breasts and back up. His cupped her breasts in his hands, his thumbs brushing back and forth over her nipples.

"I'll…" But the promise to wear it more often died on her lips when he bent his head and his open mouth was over her breast. The heat of his breath washed over her, causing her nipple to tighten even more, if that was possible. His tongue rasped against the cloth and she jerked, her hands clutching his thigh.

He raised his head, got to his feet and held his hand out.

Though her nerves battled with her anticipation, she didn't hesitate. Linking her fingers through his, she stood and led him to her bedroom.

She let go of him to cross the room and turn on the lamp on her nightstand. Brady came up behind her. Wrapping an arm around her waist, he pulled her to him, his arousal pressing against her back. Reality about what they were about to do, how it was going to change everything—again—crashed over her and she stiffened.

"I won't hurt you, Jane," Brady said, brushing her hair aside and kissing her neck.

He would. Of course he would. Eventually. Because she wasn't who he really wanted. But he did want her tonight, right now. And that would be enough.

She forced herself to relax against him and felt his own tension ease, as well. He turned her around and kissed her deeply as he backed her toward the bed, helping her onto the mattress. Straightening, he quickly toed off his shoes and stripped his shirt over his head.

Her blood quickened. He was all lean muscles and golden skin, his mouth unsmiling, his eyes glittering. He was gorgeous. And as always, she was plain Jane Cleo.

But he didn't look at her as if she were plain, but rather as if she were…special.

Beautiful.

He climbed onto the bed and lay down on his side

next to her. He dipped his head for a kiss and she sighed. No more second-guessing. No more insecurities.

She ran her hands over him. Over his broad shoulders, down his arms and back up again, then trailed her fingertips down his back to the waistband of his jeans. He was so warm. His skin smooth, his muscles flexing under her hands. Then his kiss became more urgent.

In one quick motion, he sat up, pulling her up with him. He grabbed the bottom of her tank top and peeled it off.

"You're beautiful," he said huskily. Reverently.

Warmth filled her, grew to searing heat when he eased her back again, bent his head and sucked one nipple into his mouth. She whimpered, then bit down hard on her lower lip. Her hands curled around her bedspread. With each tug and pull on her breast, desire built inside her. He moved to her other breast, giving it the same attention until she squirmed.

He kissed his way down to the slope of her stomach, his hands on either side as if holding a precious—albeit large—egg.

"Hello, baby," he murmured.

J.C. felt the baby move as if he couldn't help but respond to Brady's deep voice.

Brady rubbed the sides of her stomach a moment longer, placed a kiss just under her belly button and then slid his hands to the waistband of her shorts. J.C. lifted her hips and he tugged the material, along with her underwear, down her legs.

It hurt to breathe as he stared down at her. She squeezed her eyes shut. As much as she wanted to watch him undress, as much as she wanted to see him—every part of him—she couldn't. Her stomach turned with nerves as she waited for him to enter her. What if the unsatisfying sex last time hadn't been Brady's fault? What if she'd somehow messed up? Moved the wrong way or—

Her eyes snapped open as his hand smoothed up her inner thigh. He was lying on his side next to her, still wearing his jeans. "Wha-what are you doing?" she asked.

"Touching you."

"Why?"

"Because you're soft." He nudged her legs farther apart with his hand then pressed his nose to the side of her neck and inhaled deeply. "Because you smell good." His hand trailed along the crease of her thigh up to her hip bone, then back and forth over her lower stomach. Her pelvis contracted. "Because I want to make you wet for me."

Heat suffused her at his words, said in such a dark, seductive tone. "I…" Her breath whooshed out when he brushed his fingertips over the tight curls between her legs. Back and forth. Back and forth. She lifted her hips but he didn't deepen those featherlight touches like she wanted. "I think I'm already there so if you want to…"

"I do want to," he said with such a wicked smile, she couldn't help but smile in return.

Until he slid his hand down. It was like an electric shock, feeling his hard, work-roughened hand on her most intimate place. She gripped his wrist, tried to pull his hand away, but he didn't budge.

"What's wrong?" he asked, looking so confused and sexy, for a moment she couldn't remember why she'd stopped him.

"Nothing," she managed to squeak out, her voice about three octaves higher than usual. "I... You don't have to... I've never done this before," she said, forcing the words out. "This...part...I mean..."

"J.C.," he asked slowly, "were you a virgin the night we—"

"No! No, there were...two other guys—"

His head snapped back. "Two?"

"Three...since we should count you," she added faintly.

For several long moments, Brady just watched her. Her body started to cool and all the reasons why they shouldn't be doing this seeped back into her brain.

Until he sat up. Keeping his hand above her center, with his other hand he brushed her hair away from her face. Then he kissed her. Their lips clung for one heartbeat. Then two. When he lifted his head, he traced the arch of her eyebrow, the slope of her nose with one finger. Her resistance and her doubts melted away.

"I want to touch you," he said quietly, his hand now in her hair massaging her scalp. Before she could point out that he was touching her, he continued, "I want to touch you like no other man has touched you. Make you feel things no other man has made you feel."

He was. He did. But she couldn't say that out loud. He rubbed large circles over her stomach as he swirled his tongue around her nipple. When he bit her nipple lightly, her hips rose off the bed.

Then his hand on her stomach moved between her legs. At his slow, sure strokes, her pleasure built, almost impossible to bear. Sweat coated her skin which suddenly felt too tight. Sensitive to his touch. Her need to find relief from his talented hands and tongue grew until her hips pumped up and down. Brady once again sucked on her breast, his teeth scraping the sensitive bud the same time he slipped a finger inside her.

She teetered on the edge, but then she looked down at the sight of his head at her breast and she fell. Her back arched off the mattress and her vision blurred as her orgasm flowed through her, a rush of pleasure followed by smaller tingles of electricity. Tears stung her eyes.

And she knew that her worst fear had come true after all.

She was one hundred percent, totally and unequivocally in love with Brady Sheppard.

CHAPTER FOURTEEN

HIS BODY ACHING, screaming for release, Brady raised his head and watched J.C. come down from her orgasm. Her eyes were closed, her full lips parted, her heavy breasts rising and falling as she panted softly, a sheen of sweat coating her skin.

At that moment, she was the most beautiful thing he'd ever seen.

As if of its own accord, his hand moved back up to her belly. He couldn't seem to stop touching her there, where she carried their child. Couldn't get past how... hard...her stomach was. He could only imagine what she'd look like next month. Or four months from now. How much more would her body grow and change?

And did it even matter if he wasn't sure he'd be around to see it?

He rubbed her stomach, his body growing harder as she wiggled and sighed. Her eyes slowly opened. She skimmed her hand over his shoulder and down his bicep, her touch hesitant. Shy, almost.

Which made sense, considering her sexual history. Obviously neither of the two guys she'd slept with had taken the time to give her pleasure. Idiots.

And he was idiot number three for not only neglecting J.C.'s satisfaction the first time they'd made love, but by not even remembering being with her and calling out her sister's name. Make that king of the idiots.

And yet, by some miracle, she hadn't turned him away tonight. Instead, she'd trusted him with her body.

I won't hurt you, Jane, he'd promised.

J.C. stared at him, or rather the bulge in his pants. She reached out, her hand a few inches above his arousal. Behind his zipper, his body twitched.

"Don't stop," he said in a husky whisper when she took her hand away without touching him.

"I'm not stopping," she said. "At least not until I've had my fill of you."

He swallowed in an attempt to work some moisture in his mouth.

J.C. rose onto her elbow, the movement causing her breasts to sway. He lightly pinched one hard, dusky tip and she moaned. He lifted his head to take her into his mouth again but she moved back, out of reach.

"Let me," she said, nudging his shoulders until he reclined on the bed once again.

He held his breath as she laid her hand against his cheek. She stroked the side of his neck, then his shoulder and down his arm. Outlining the edges of his USMC eagle tattoo with her fingertip, her frown thoughtful. He expected her to ask him about it, why he got it, what it meant. Instead, she smoothed her hand back up to his shoulder and down his chest. Under her soft, seeking touch, his heart skipped a beat before finding a steady rhythm that quickened as her fingers traveled down to his belly button.

He inhaled sharply, his stomach muscles contracting. With as much concentration as an explosive ordnance disposal unit defusing a bomb, her other hand went to the waistband of his jeans. Both his lungs and his groin tightened almost to the point of pain. But he forced himself not to move. To wait and see what she'd do next.

"Could you take your pants off?" she asked in a rush.

He thought she'd never ask. He undid his jeans, shimmied them and his boxers down his legs and kicked them off before sitting back up.

She blinked. "Wow. That must be some sort of land speed record."

"I aim to please," he managed. Not an easy feat when J.C. stared at his body as if he were one of her candies.

"So do I," she murmured. His mouth went dry.

J.C. rose to her knees. Lying flat on his back, he couldn't watch her like he wanted so he grabbed a pillow, folded it in half and shoved it under his head, the scent of her shampoo surrounding him.

As she sat back on her heels beside him, she looked confused, as if she had no clue what to do. He almost took her hand and placed it on a part of him where he'd love for her to start. And finish. And spend any amount of time and attention on.

She leaned forward and softly kissed his scarred knee.

He jerked, his hands fisting into her bedcovers.

She lifted her head and turned to him, her hair falling to the side, the ends tickling his lower thigh. "Does it hurt?"

"No."

But he couldn't stop himself from tensing when she laid her right hand above his knee. Blindly staring up at the ceiling, a lump formed in his throat as she traced each and every one of his scars, her touch as gentle, as soothing as a summer breeze. No one had touched his knee in a nonprofessional way since the attack. He couldn't remember anyone ever touching it, touching any part of him with as much compassion and tenderness as J.C. did now.

When she was done with his scar, she caressed his thigh. Up and down, from his knee, along his outer thigh to his hip bone and back again. Each time she seemed to get more confident. And a lot bolder as she worked her way toward his inner thigh, stopping shy of his erection. Grinding his teeth, he raised his head to look down at her only to find her watching him.

As soon as his eyes met hers, she wrapped her hand around him. His vision blurred. Then she started stroking him leisurely. He about went over the edge. He hissed out a breath and fought for control. But he couldn't take his eyes off her, the sight of her pale, small hands on him and the way she watched him carefully, her eyes bright, as if there were nothing she'd rather do than touch him, explore his body.

She was…amazing. Her generosity and warmth. Her sensuality. Her beauty—both inside and out. And she wanted to be with him. Even after all of his mistakes, she still wanted him. She humbled him.

She scared the hell out of him.

He lost the ability to think at all when J.C. did some sort of gentle twisting motion that felt so damned good that he groaned.

And she smiled.

That did it.

He jackknifed up, had a glimpse of her startled expression right before he took her mouth in a hungry kiss.

Clutching his biceps, she kissed him back as he lowered her to the mattress and followed her down, supporting his weight on his elbows.

Breaking the kiss, he shifted to the side, picked up his jeans and shook them until his wallet fell out of the pocket. He flipped it open and took out a condom.

"I'd say it's a little late for that," J.C. said, the lightness of her tone unable to completely cover her underlying nerves.

He opened the packet and covered himself. "It's never too late to be safe."

Besides, though he'd gotten a clean bill of health when he'd had a physical before starting physical therapy, he didn't want to take any chances with J.C.

He settled himself between her thighs, his arms shaking with the effort to hold himself back.

"Are you sure this is safe?" he forced himself to ask. "For the baby, I mean."

"Dr. Owens said it's safe."

She no sooner got the last word out when Brady lifted her hips and slid inside her. Her body tensed, her expression unsure. He withdrew slightly and didn't move. It took every ounce of self-control not to take what he needed so badly from her.

But he couldn't find any of those things at J.C.'s expense. Not again. Not when he was finding his way to who he was. He kissed her, careful to keep his weight off both the baby and his bad knee.

He continued to kiss her until some of the stiffness left her. When she combed her fingers through his hair, he rolled his hips, filling her. She gasped into his mouth and he smiled against her lips before pulling back and repeating the motion. Again. And again until the tension built to a fever pitch. Her hands pulled at his hair, her body soft and pliant under his. But still, he could feel her holding back from him.

He lifted his head but her eyes remained closed, her hands now at his hips. "Jane." Her eyes popped open, her nails digging into his skin. "It's just you and me here," he continued hoarsely, increasing his tempo as he moved in and out of her body. "No one else I want here. Only you, Janie."

Reaching between them, with the pad of his thumb he rubbed the hard nub at her center. Her mouth opened and her eyes grew cloudy. Her body squeezed around him. She tipped her head back but kept her eyes on his as she came, her body pulsing around him. Pushing him to follow.

He gripped her under her thighs and plowed into her. Again. And again. His concern for the baby, his vow not to hurt J.C. keeping his control in check. Keeping him from taking her as hard, as fast, as he wanted.

His climax built.

"No," he ground out when J.C.'s eyes began to close. "Watch me, Jane. Watch what you do to me."

Her eyes, so dark they seemed bottomless, locked on his. With a guttural groan, he threw his head back and emptied himself.

J.C. ROLLED OVER and reached for Brady but found his side of the bed empty. The sheets cold. Shoving her hair out of her face, she glanced at the glowing numbers of the digital clock on her nightstand. Two thirty-two. Flopping onto her back again, she flung her arm across her eyes. After she and Brady had made love, he'd pulled the comforter over them both and she'd immediately fallen asleep in his arms.

Hoping he'd still be there in the morning.

She tossed off her covers. Since she was up, she may as well get a glass of water, maybe use the bathroom. Swinging her feet over the edge of the bed, she sat up and flipped on the light.

"You okay?"

She yelped and almost fell off the bed. She spun around to find Brady, wearing only his jeans, sitting on the floor, his back against her closet, one leg bent, his injured leg out straight.

"Don't do that!" Grabbing the comforter, she wrapped it around herself.

"Sorry."

She frowned. Something was wrong. And it wasn't just that he sat on her floor in the middle of the night. His expression was tight. His hands clenched.

Holding the end of the comforter so she didn't trip, she walked over and sat next to him. "What are you doing on the floor?"

"I couldn't stay." His head fell back against her closet door with a thump. "But I couldn't leave, either."

"I'm sorry, I don't understand."

"I should go," he said. "But I don't want to."

She wouldn't read more into any of this—what he said or how he acted or how he'd looked at her when they'd made love. She was going to take it one day, one minute at a time.

And she wouldn't get her hopes up or start wishing for things that weren't going to happen. Like him loving her back.

"I'm glad you stayed," she said. "But I think you'll be more comfortable in the bed."

"I can't."

"Sure you can. It's plenty big enough for two."

"No. I mean, I really can't. I have these...dreams." He faced forward and wiped an unsteady hand down his face. "Nightmares. And sometimes I get...sometimes it's like I'm...back in Afghanistan and I...I'll throw a punch or..." He shook his head, and his voice dropped so low she had to strain to hear him. "I don't want to hurt you. Or the baby."

Oh, God. Unable to catch her breath, not strong enough to face the bleakness in his eyes, she curled her knees up to her chest and stared at the floor.

As much as it shamed her, as big as her feelings for Brady were, she wanted to run. She had no idea—absolutely no clue—how to help Brady, what to say or do.

"These dreams..." She cleared her throat. "Are your dreams like the flashbacks?" The flashbacks he never confirmed nor denied having.

Sometimes I think about what happened back there.

He remained silent. She didn't press. She waited, hoping he'd open up to her. Time passed and her toes got cold so she tucked the comforter around them.

"We were on patrol," Brady finally said, speaking in a slow monotone as if unaware she was even there. "Jonesy was driving, Thad was riding shotgun, and me and Van were in the back. One minute Van was telling us about when he'd accidentally hired a male stripper to show up at his brother's bachelor party, and the next...I was coming to on the side of the road. We'd all been laughing and then…" He swallowed. "The explosion was so loud, after it was as if I was listening to everything through a filter. But I could still hear Van yelling for help. Jonesy's cries of pain."

She shivered. God, she couldn't even imagine what he'd gone through. How close he'd come to dying. "What about your other friend?"

"Dead," he said flatly, his lips a thin line. "He had a wife and two little kids and now…" He blew out a heavy breath and lowered his head into his hands. "It should've been me."

"Don't say that." She scrambled onto her knees in front of him, cupping his face in her hands and raising it so he looked at her. "What happened was horrible for you all but—"

"He should've lived," he said, bracketing her wrists with his hands. "He had people to live for."

J.C.'s eyes stung but she wouldn't cry. Not when Brady sat there dry-eyed, thinking he had nothing to live for.

"Have you considered talking to someone about this?" she asked. "A psychologist or—"

"No."

Shaken and humbled he'd trusted her with this, she pressed her forehead against his. "I'm glad you told me. But I think," she said carefully, not wanting to say the wrong thing, "you should consider getting professional help."

He exhaled shakily, his breath washing over her face. "I know you're trying to help—"

"I am. And I won't push you, I swear, but could you at least think about it?"

"Yeah," he said gruffly. "Okay."

"Thank you," she said. Then she pressed a kiss against his mouth. As she stood, she let the comforter slide off her shoulders to pool at her feet. "Come on. Let's go back to bed."

After a moment's hesitation, he accepted the hand she held out and let her help him get to his feet.

As much as she wanted to, she couldn't heal him.

But she could help him get through tonight.

BRADY CARRIED HIS SHOES as he soundlessly made his way to the bedroom door. He glanced back at J.C. She was still asleep, the covers pulled up to her chin, her lips were parted, her hair a mass of wild curls.

He wanted more than anything to slip back into bed with her. To be here when she woke up so they could make love again.

He snuck out of the room. Sitting on the sofa, he put his shoes on, grabbed his jacket from the chair where he'd tossed it last night and stepped out into the cold. His leg had stiffened during the night and descending the stairs became an awkward and painful process. But less awkward than it would've been if J.C. had woken up while he was still there.

He couldn't face her. Not now. He needed time to sort things out. Like why he'd told her about the nightmares when he'd never told anyone else. Why he'd enjoyed holding her so much as she slept.

A black Lexus pulled into the driveway as Brady reached the bottom step. Goosebumps appeared on his arms as the driver got out.

Stopping below him, Liz glanced from him to J.C.'s apartment and back at him again.

As if she had any right to try to make him feel guilty.

"You slept with her? Again?" Liz asked, crossing her arms over her red jacket.

He moved to the left but she blocked his way. Her breath turned to a cloud before disappearing. "What's between me and Jane is none of your concern," he said.

"That's where you're wrong. Anything having to do with my family is my concern. Especially when someone is using my sister to get to me."

"Get to you? Why the hell would I do that?"

"To hurt me for what I did to you or…or maybe you think if you make me jealous, I'll come back to you."

"I'm not into revenge," he snarled. "And what makes you think I'd ever want you back?"

Liz tucked her hair behind her ear, her hand trembling. "From what I understand, you've made it clear you want nothing to do with the baby. Why else are you with J.C. if not to hurt me?"

"You act as if she has no redeeming qualities other than having you as a sibling."

Liz blushed, rubbed her gloves hands together. "J.C. is plenty special on her own but I'm not blind to her faults. She's a dreamer, unreliable and can't stick with one project, job or college for more than three months at a time."

"She's also sweet and funny and sexy…" Brady shook his head to clear his thoughts.

Liz's took a step back as if she'd been slapped. "Oh, my God," she breathed. "You're in love with her."

The back of his neck tingled, like it used to in Afghanistan before a firefight broke out. As it did moments before the bomb exploded. "I'm not in love with Jane Cleo," he growled, noticing the relief in Liz's eyes.

Loving one Montgomery sister had almost killed him. And he never made the same mistake twice.

"All the more reason to stay away from her," Liz said emphatically, the breeze lifting her hair. "Before she gets hurt. I mean it, Brady. Leave her be."

Damn it, he knew that. "You gave up any say into how I live my life when you wrote me that Dear John letter."

"This isn't about you and me," she said unsteadily.

"It's only ever been about us," he said, his voice rising. "I loved you, I wanted to marry you. We'd planned our life together and then suddenly you met someone new and it's over?"

Her mouth trembled. "It wasn't like that. With Carter, I mean. I never… We didn't…"

"You didn't what?"

"I never cheated on you."

"Is that supposed to make it all right?" he asked, taking that last step, forcing her to back up. She bumped into J.C.'s car. He kept walking until he stood mere inches from her. "How long after you sent that letter did it take the two of you to get together?"

Her eyes welled with tears. "Brady, please don't…"

A car drove by but both Brady and Liz ignored it. "I deserve to know," he said, his stomach in knots. He needed to know. "How long? A week? A month?"

She wiped her fingers over her cheeks, brushing away the tears. "One."

"One week?"

She stared at the ground. "One day," she said faintly.

His blood drummed in his ears. "So while I was over

seven thousand miles away, thinking you and I were still engaged, thinking you still loved me, you were back here screwing another guy?"

She blanched. "I never meant for it to happen. And I'm sorry I hurt you, Brady, but…people change. Feelings…change. You need to accept it and move on."

Accept it? She'd lied to him. Used him. And the best she could do was toss him an *I'm sorry?* And now she wanted him to move on—just not with her sister.

To hell with her.

"Just because it was that easy for you doesn't mean that's how it works for everyone." He started pacing, the breeze doing nothing to calm his anger. "You have everything you've always wanted." He spun to face her and she shrank back against the car. "Everything you were supposed to have with me. Instead, I'm five months away from becoming a father to a baby I don't want with a woman I'll never be able to love because she's not you!"

Behind him, he heard a sound—as if someone had just been punched in the stomach. Brady's scalp tingled, his skin grew clammy. He turned to find J.C. in the same pajamas she'd had on last night, standing on the next to last step, her feet bare, her eyes huge. With one hand she gripped the railing, with the other she held her stomach protectively.

His panic spiked. He sensed he was close to losing something important—something he might not be able to get back.

He didn't move.

Now, he wouldn't have to worry about facing her again. Trying to keep his distance. About the feelings he had for her he couldn't explain. Things between them could end here, now, before they became even more complicated.

Before he had to admit to himself that what he'd just said had been nothing but a lie.

CHAPTER FIFTEEN

TODAY WAS SUNDAY, J.C. thought stupidly as she stood there, the wind blowing her hair in her face, causing her eyes to tear. How could she forget it was Sunday. And that on Sunday mornings when Liz didn't work the night before, she took Grandma Rose to church.

"J.C., let's go inside where it's warm," Liz said as she walked toward her. J.C. didn't so much as glance Brady's way. She couldn't. If she looked at him now, she'd never get through the next few minutes without breaking down.

Liz climbed up to stand next to her. "Oh, honey, you don't even have any shoes on."

"I didn't think I'd need them," she said absently.

Liz put her arm around J.C.'s shoulder, either ignoring or not noticing how J.C. stiffened. "Come on. We'll go in, ask Grandma to make some of her blueberry pancakes. You'll feel better after you have something to eat."

J.C. blinked. "Yes, I'm sure some pancakes will make this all better."

"At least you'll be out of the cold and away from…"

Away from Brady.

Brady, who hadn't moved since he noticed her.

Brady, who didn't want the baby. Who still loved Liz.

A sob rose in the back of her throat and she covered her mouth to hide the sound.

"None of that," Liz admonished gently. "You don't want him to see you cry, do you?"

Why not? He'd already seen her at her absolute worst and best. She was about to tell Liz exactly that when she saw the pity in her sister's eyes. Any small pieces of her pride that'd survived Brady's impassioned speech died.

She shrugged Liz's arm off. "You go ahead, I'd like a few minutes alone with Brady."

"I don't think that's a good idea," Liz said.

J.C. stared hard at her sister. "I didn't ask your opinion. Or your permission."

Liz was taken aback. "If that's what you want…"

"It is."

"All right. But remember, I'm right inside if you need me."

"I won't," J.C. said with such conviction, she almost believed it herself. "I can handle this on my own."

Looking far more hurt than J.C. thought she had a right to, Liz rounded J.C.'s car and walked over to their grandmother's house. J.C. finally turned to Brady. As she'd suspected, his hooded gaze was on her, his hands in his front pockets, his hair still mussed from her bed. From her fingers.

Brady stepped toward her, stopping when she backed up a step.

"Jane…" he said in his deep voice.

"Is this where you tell me last night was a mistake?"

"It was."

"So it meant nothing to you? Or maybe you're too big of a coward to admit it did mean something."

"I'm sorry."

"Don't," she warned, unable to keep her voice from shaking. "Don't you dare patronize me by giving me some trite apology."

He glanced down at the ground. "It's the best I can do."

Her toes were numb, her legs shaking from the cold. "No. It's all you're willing to do." The baby moved, strengthening J.C.'s resolve not to let him see how much he'd hurt her. "I feel sorry for you."

His posture grew rigid. "Don't bother."

"Why not? Isn't that what you want, what this is all about? Poor Brady Sheppard lost his one true love and his plans for the future. Welcome to the real world, Brady, where people get their hearts broken every day. Where plans fall through, jobs are lost and loved ones pass away. The world where we don't always get what we want, but most people make the most of what they do have."

"I'm trying to," he said with a definite edge to his voice as he stepped onto the stair below her, bringing them eye-to-eye. "Once my knee heals more—"

"You'll what, be whole again? Be able to act like a human, like someone who stands up and brushes himself off when he falls? Your leg is an excuse, like your drinking."

His expression darkened and he walked away, his gait uneven.

"Oh, no, you don't," J.C. muttered. Careful of the damp stairs, she didn't start jogging until she stepped onto the cold, rough cement of the driveway. She rounded the garage and sped past him to stand in front of the driver's door of his truck.

His keys jingled in his hand. "Move," he ordered.

She swallowed. "Remember when I told you I've never seen anything through because it's easier to quit when things get tough?" He inclined his head. "Well, that's only part of it." She tried to slow her breathing, to get her heart rate back to where it belonged. "The truth is, if I quit, then I can't fail."

And if she never failed, that was almost as good as always succeeding. Like Liz did.

"But I've realized," she continued, pulling the sleeves of her sweatshirt down to cover her cold hands, "that by giving up so I don't fail, there's also no chance I'll ever succeed. And if succeeding means taking risks and putting myself out there, putting my pride on the line, then that's what I'll do."

She'd do it because, right now, success was more than getting what she wanted. It was proving to herself she had the courage to try.

"Brady, I…" She took a moment to regain her composure. "I'm in love with you."

He flinched. "No. You aren't."

"You don't have to love me back," she told him quietly. "You don't even have to like the fact that I'm in love with you. But don't you ever tell me what is or isn't in my heart."

He held his head with both hands, as if to stop it from exploding. "Damn it, Jane. Don't make this harder than it has to be."

"How could I? You're the one who made love to me last night then couldn't slip out of my bed fast enough this morning. You're choosing to hold on to Liz, to what you had. Wishing for things to be different, for a life you could've had if Liz hadn't fallen in love with Carter.

If you hadn't been injured. If you hadn't slept with me and gotten me pregnant."

Brady stared straight ahead, not showing even the tiniest flicker of emotion, of reaction to her words.

Tears stung the backs of her eyes. "I can't tell you what your life would've been like. But I can tell you what you could've had. Me. And our son. You could've had a home filled with laughter and love and hope. But you'd rather wallow in self-pity."

He glanced at her, took in the tears running freely down her cheeks. "Is that all?" he asked tightly, a muscle jumping in his jaw.

She used her sleeve to dry her face. "One last thing. If you ever start thinking you'd like to be a part of our lives after all—don't bother. My son and I will be fine without you. We don't need you." She'd make sure her baby had all the love and support she could give him. Hopefully it would be enough to make up for his father's abandonment. "But I wonder, Brady," she asked softly, "how do you think you'll be without us?"

LIZ WAS ADDING FROZEN blueberries to her grandma's pancake batter when J.C. finally walked into the kitchen. Her relief at seeing her sister died quickly once she noticed J.C.'s tear-streaked face, red nose and chattering teeth.

"You poor dear," Grandma Rose said, wrapping her arm around J.C.'s middle and leading her to the table. "Sit down while I fetch a blanket."

"How about getting a pair of socks, too, Grandma?" Liz asked. Grandma Rose waved her hand to indicate she'd heard as she hurried out of the room.

"Here," Liz said, setting a tea cup in front of J.C.

"Don't worry," she added when J.C. just stared at it, "it's decaf. And I added extra honey."

J.C. picked up the cup, sloshing tea over the side. Liz was about to help her when J.C. raised the cup and took a sip.

Grandma Rose came back into the kitchen carrying two blankets and a pair of fuzzy slipper-socks. "We'll have you warm again in no time," Rose said, wrapping a fleece blanket around J.C.'s shoulders while Liz pulled the socks over her cold feet. The second blanket they laid across her lap.

And that whole time, J.C. didn't move. She didn't even blink. Liz and her grandmother exchanged worried glances.

"Hey," Liz said, covering J.C.'s cold hand where it rested on the table. "Are you all right?"

"Fine." She pulled her hand away and put it on her lap. "And you'll no doubt be happy to know that Brady's gone. Once again, you get exactly what you wanted."

Liz sat back. "Excuse me?"

"You didn't want him in my life and now he's not."

"He never should've been there in the first place," Liz pointed out. "And as I remember, you promised me you wouldn't see him anymore." She lowered her voice so Grandma Rose couldn't hear. "And yet, there he was, sneaking out of your apartment not twenty minutes ago."

And the sight of Brady leaving her sister's place after having obviously spent the night had been enough to knock the air out of her lungs.

J.C. pulled the blanket tighter around her shoulders. "The only reason I agreed to that promise was because

I was willing to do anything to get you to forgive me. But you already knew that, didn't you?"

Liz flushed hot, then cold. "Don't be ridiculous."

"And then you added in that story about you and Carter—"

"What about Liz and Carter?" Rose asked, setting a plate of pancakes in the middle of the table.

"Nothing," Liz said, her cheeks burning. She sent J.C. a loaded look, one that clearly said, "Keep your mouth shut."

"Carter thinks Liz is still in love with Brady," J.C. said with more than a hint of venom in her voice. "Liz denies it, but either she's protesting too much or not enough, because Carter thinks they need to attend marriage counseling."

"Is that true, Elizabeth?" Rose asked.

"Carter and I are fine," she snapped, glaring at J.C. "And we'll be even better now that Brady Sheppard is out of the picture."

J.C. shook her head. "You'd like to believe that, wouldn't you? You'd like to pretend that Brady is at the root of all your problems."

Liz stabbed a pancake and set it on her plate. "Pretend? Brady *is* at the root of my problems and he has been ever since he crashed my wedding."

"So rude," Rose said, sitting opposite J.C. "You should've let your father have him escorted off the premises."

"I didn't want a scene," she insisted, pouring syrup over her pancakes though her appetite was quickly disappearing.

"You really don't see what you're doing, do you?" J.C. asked. "The reason Brady is a problem for you and

Carter at all is because of you. You put him between you and your husband because you haven't let Brady go yet."

Liz set her fork down so no one would notice her hands trembling. "That's not true. Just because I don't want my sister and my ex-fiancé to be together doesn't mean I'm holding on to Brady."

"No." J.C. stood and tossed the blanket over the back of her chair. "It means you can't stand the idea of Brady moving on. Of him wanting to be with someone besides you."

"But he doesn't want to be with anyone else, does he?" she snapped, immediately wishing she could take her words back when she saw J.C.'s stunned expression. The hurt in her eyes.

"You're right," J.C. said faintly, her face white. "I'll always be second choice to him." She rubbed at her temples. "Want to know the worst part? Up until this morning, that would've been enough for me."

Liz's chest burned. "J.C., I didn't mean—"

"Not now, okay? I…I can't handle much more this morning and I…" She brought her hand to her mouth, her fingers trembling. "I'm not feeling very well."

"Let me get you some ginger ale," Rose said, going around the table to the refrigerator.

J.C. was already backing out of the room. "No. Thank you. It's just a headache. I'll lie down until it goes away."

A moment later, they heard the front door close. Liz went to the sink and watched J.C. make her way up to her apartment, her steps slow, her shoulders shaking.

"She's crying," Liz said, pressing her fingers against her eyes. "I didn't mean to make her cry." She sighed and dropped her hands. "How did everything get so messed up?"

Rose set the dishes in the sink. "It got messed up because life is messy. People are fallible. They make mistakes, say things they shouldn't. And sometimes, they even hold on to a relationship, not because they still want to be with that person, but because there's unfinished business, unresolved feelings."

"My feelings for Brady are firmly resolved." *Liar*, a tiny voice inside her head whispered. She filled a glass with water and drank deeply, hoping to dislodge what felt like a pebble in her throat. "I love Carter, not Brady."

Rose smiled and patted Liz's cheek. "I believe you. And once you realize what's holding you back from fully committing to your husband, heart and soul, everyone else will believe you, too. Including yourself."

HIS MOTHER WAS getting married.

And instead of celebrating with her, her fiancé and their respective families, Brady was hiding upstairs in his father's office—in Aidan's office—where he could drink a few beers in peace.

Lying on the leather sofa, he stared out the window at the starry sky. Bing Crosby singing "White Christmas" floated upstairs, as did the muted sounds of laughter, conversation and general revelry.

He tipped his bottle of beer at the sky in a mock toast. Welcome to the Sheppards' annual Christmas Eve party, where more than one hundred of his mother's closest friends mingled downstairs. After his mother and Al had announced their engagement to wild applause, Brady had done his familial duty for about fifteen minutes before the press of bodies, the noise and smells—floral perfumes, musky colognes and rich, buttery desserts—forced him to find some solitude.

Sensory overload, he thought, drinking his beer.

But up here, with the lights off and no one asking him how his physical therapy was going or if he planned on sticking around Jewell now that his options were limited, he could breathe.

I'm in love with you.

The bottle slipped from his fingers, dropping with a thud. It rolled, spilling beer over the carpet before he could grab it. Damn it. Damn it! Why couldn't J.C. leave him alone? Every time he'd shut his eyes last night, he'd relived their lovemaking, the dreams so vivid he'd woken up reaching for her. Only to remember the look on her face when she overheard him claiming he didn't want the baby. That he couldn't love her because she wasn't Liz.

He tipped his head side to side until his neck popped. But he could still hear her voice in his head.

My son and I will be just fine without you. But I wonder, Brady, how do you think you'll be without us?

My son, she'd said, claiming their baby as effectively as if she'd said straight out she was keeping him. And he didn't doubt they'd be fine. J.C. was far more resilient than people gave her credit for. She'd be a terrific mother. And someday, she'd meet someone without so much baggage. A guy smart enough not to screw up what a good thing he had with her.

Sitting up, he finished his beer. He needed another one. Or twelve.

But to get one, he had to venture yet again into the

party. This time he was bringing a six-pack out with him instead of one bottle.

He got to his feet as the office door opened and someone flipped the lights on.

"I thought you might be in here," Matt said from the doorway. He looked at the beer bottle in Brady's hand, his eyes narrowing slightly. "There's a pretty brunette out on the porch to see you."

Jane.

"Why didn't you bring her up?" Brady asked roughly, already on his way toward the door.

"I tried. She said she didn't want to interrupt the party."

Brady brushed past Matt and was down the stairs in a few minutes. In the living room next to the foyer, the party was in full swing. Avoiding eye contact, he paused at the front door to comb his fingers through his hair and realized as he raised his hand he still held the empty beer bottle. He stuck it under the skinny fake tree in the corner his mother had decorated all in red.

He stepped outside. Between the porch light and the white Christmas lights his mother had wound around every available surface, the porch fairly glowed, making it easy for Brady to see her sitting on the wooden swing.

Just not the woman he'd hoped it'd be.

"Hello, Brady," Liz said, stopping the motion of the swing and standing.

He exhaled. Mouth tight, he nodded.

"I'm sorry to barge in on you this way," she said, hunching her shoulders against the cold. "I forgot about your mom's holiday party until I pulled in and saw all the cars."

"Is J.C. okay?"

Liz looked at him speculatively. "As far as I know, she's fine."

"Good. That's...good." He shoved his hands into his pockets. "Do you want to come inside?"

"I'd rather stay out here if you don't mind. This won't take long."

He lifted a shoulder, then leaned back against the porch rail while she retook her seat on the swing. She cleared her throat. "Brady, I...I owe you an apology."

"Mind telling me what, exactly, you're apologizing for?"

Tipping her head back, she searched his face. "I'm sorry I wrote you that letter."

Out of all the reasons he could think of for Liz to show up at his mother's house on Christmas Eve, her apologizing for writing him a Dear John letter hadn't made the list.

"After everything we'd been through," she continued when he remained silent, "you deserved more than a letter."

It didn't matter. No apology could change what happened or bring him back what he'd lost. But maybe he could get some answers to the questions that had plagued him for so long.

"Why'd you write it?" he asked. "Why not break off things when I was home for leave that summer instead of letting me go overseas thinking nothing had changed between us?"

She clasped her gloved hands together on her lap. "I should have. But I'd convinced myself my feelings for Carter weren't serious." She lowered her head, her gaze on the porch floor. "But the biggest reason I didn't end our engagement face-to-face or even over the phone was because I knew you'd try to talk me out of it. I was afraid if you did," she said thickly, "I'd let you. And then things would go on between us the way they always had."

"That would've been so bad?"

"Not bad," she said with a shaky breath, "but not what I wanted, either." She raised her head, tears sparkling in her eyes. "I loved you, Brady. I loved you for half of my life but I…I didn't want to marry you," she whispered.

"What the hell does that mean?" he growled, not giving a rat's ass that she winced at his harsh tone. "You accepted my proposal. You wore my ring. Now you tell me you never planned on marrying me?"

"It wasn't like that," she said, getting to her feet. "I didn't even realize it myself until…until after I met Carter."

Brady stared at Liz as if he'd never seen her before. "All those times you pushed the wedding date back," he said, "because you wanted to finish college first, then med school and your residency, those were excuses not to marry me?"

"I kept thinking, hoping, something would change." She pulled a tissue from her pocket and wiped her eyes then blew her nose. "I held on to you because I loved you too much to let you go."

"You loved me," he said in a monotone. "Just not enough to commit to making a life with me."

"I was wrong. That's why I'm here. It's time I let you go for good, for both our sakes." She reached past him and he stiffened. But she didn't touch him, just set the blue jeweler's box containing the ring he'd bought her on the porch rail. "Goodbye, Brady."

He watched Liz walk away and stood staring out over the driveway long after she left. But instead of thinking of Liz and what she'd confessed, one thought consumed him.

J.C. had been right.

He wiped a shaky hand over his mouth. He'd been holding on to his past because he couldn't imagine loving any other woman but Liz. He'd thought they had the perfect love, but it had been a lie. All those years of waiting for Liz to set a wedding date, to be ready to marry him, he'd pretended everything was great because he wanted to hold on to the fantasy rather than face reality.

While he'd been focused on what he'd lost, he'd ignored what he'd gained. A chance for the life he'd always dreamed of with a beautiful, warm, funny woman. A woman who'd give him a child. A woman who loved him.

And he'd pushed her away.

CHAPTER SIXTEEN

"YOU'RE LATE."

With a gasp, Liz whirled toward the sound of her husband's voice. "Carter. You scared me."

"Sorry."

Frowning, she shut the front door and walked into their living room. Carter was slouched in an armchair staring at the flames in the fireplace. Other than the fire and the colorful lights on their Christmas tree, the room was dark.

"I thought you were going to Mitch and Kelly's for dinner," she said, taking her coat off and laying it on the back of the sofa before switching on a floor lamp.

Carter's shirtsleeves were rolled up, the top three buttons of his collar undone. His pale hair stuck up at odd angles, as if he'd repeatedly run his hands through it. "I didn't want to go without you. I wanted to spend our first Christmas Eve as a married couple together."

She crossed to him. "I'm glad. I want that, too."

"How was work?" he asked, sipping red wine as he regarded her over the glass. "You must've been busy."

Sitting on the arm of the chair, she slipped off her shoes and wiggled her toes. "You know how it is during the holidays. The E.R. was a madhouse."

"Is that why you're late?" he asked in that calm way of his. "Why you've been crying?"

She rubbed at the aching arch of her foot. Though she'd done a quick repair job on her makeup in the car, she knew there were still traces of smudged mascara under her red-rimmed eyes. And the tip of her nose was still pink.

She helped herself to his wine, took a long drink and prayed she'd done the right thing for her marriage. "I went to see Brady."

His fingers dug into the arm of the chair by her leg. "Why?"

"To apologize." She tucked a strand of hair behind her ear. "And because...we both needed...closure."

She just hadn't realized how badly they'd needed it until yesterday after J.C. had left their grandmother's house.

Carter sat up. "You apologized for breaking up with him?"

"No. For how I handled it. How I handled everything." She stood and wandered to the tree. Traced a fingertip over a red ball before facing her husband. "He needed to know the truth about why I wrote that letter. And I had to return his ring."

"Did he take it back this time?"

"I didn't give him a choice." She clasped her hands. "I left it there. What he does with it isn't my concern. Not anymore."

"Why?" he asked quietly.

"I...I don't understand."

He rested his elbows on his knees. "Why worry about closure now, after all this time?"

She rubbed her hands over her suddenly chilled arms. "For you," she told him simply. "For us. I want us to get back to how we used to be. And because..."

When she'd seen Brady leave J.C.'s apartment, Liz hadn't just been angry, hadn't just felt betrayed. For one awful moment, she'd hated them both.

Her throat burned with tears. "Because yesterday I realized I couldn't move on with my life until I'd settled my past. Neither could Brady."

Carter watched her, his expression unreadable. "What if we can't go back?"

Fear immobilized her for one heartbeat. Two. Then she shook her head. "I'm not going to lose you," she told him fiercely.

Kneeling in front of him, she gripped his hands. Relief made her light-headed when he linked his fingers with hers. "Thanksgiving, when we argued about Brady, you…you asked me if I still loved him and I didn't answer." She drew in a breath, then said in a rush, "Ask me now."

Dropping his gaze, he rubbed his thumbs over the backs of her hands. "I'm afraid to hear the answer," he whispered.

She brought his hands to her mouth, kissed both in turn and waited until he met her eyes. "I don't love Brady. I made a mistake, a huge one, in not telling you that before. You are the only man I love. And that is never going to change."

Carter searched her eyes and this time, instead of feeling guilty, as if she was hiding something from him, she let him see the truth.

He pressed a soft kiss against her forehead, then on each closed eye before wrapping his arms around her and dragging her onto his lap. She curled into him and rested her head on his shoulder.

"I love you so much, Liz," he told her. "I never want to lose you."

"You won't," she promised, stroking her fingers through his hair. She took his wonderfully handsome face in her hands. "I love you," she told him again.

Then she tugged on his hand and pulled him to the floor. And in the flickering glow of the fire, she showed him just how much.

WELL AFTER 1:00 A.M., when all the guests had gone and most of the cleanup was completed, Brady sat back in a recliner in his mother's family room, staring at her tree so long, the lights began to dance and blur in front of his eyes. He shook his head and blinked several times until his vision cleared.

The only reason he was still here was because Matt was freaking out about their mother's engagement. And because he wasn't in any hurry to go back to the cottage where he'd spend a restless night dreaming of J.C. Wondering if there was any way he could make things right between them again.

Yeah, even listening to Matt bitch and moan was better than that.

"You think Al would mind if I call him Daddy?" Matt asked from his spot on the sofa, his head propped up on his bent arm as he stared at the ceiling.

Aidan was on the floor, his back resting against an armchair, his dog lying next to him, her head in his lap. He stared at his youngest brother. "You're an idiot."

"Me? Hey, I'm not the one in this family who's taking the marital plunge with a guy who looks like a horse when he smiles. All those teeth can't be real. And if a man lies about his teeth, who knows what else he'll lie about."

Aidan pinched the bridge of his nose. "He's not that bad."

"He's a politician," Matt pointed out. "There's nothing *but* bad about that."

"He's retired," Aidan said. "Trust me, he's a decent guy."

"How do we know he's not after Mom's money?"

"He could buy the Diamond Dust outright—twice— in cash, and still have money left over."

Matt raised his head and looked at Brady. "What about you? Do you think Mom's making a mistake?"

As if Brady had any right to judge someone else's choices. "If she is, it's her mistake to make."

"That's such a cop-out. You don't think it's risky for a woman Mom's age to jump into marriage with the first guy who asks her?"

"He might not be the first guy to ask," Brady said, lifting his bottle of beer to his mouth. Feeling Aidan watch his every move. "For all we know, it's just the first time she's said yes."

Scowling, Matt got to his feet. "If you two aren't going to take this seriously, I'm going to bed."

"Merry Christmas," Brady murmured as his brother left the room, adding to Aidan, "I would've thought out of the three of us, you'd be the one having the hardest time with Mom getting remarried."

While Tom Sheppard had loved his boys equally, he and Aidan had had a special bond. Probably because they were so much alike.

"I like Al. More importantly, he makes Mom happy."

Aidan leaned his head back on the chair cushion. "Besides, Dad would want Mom to move on."

Seemed to be the theme in Jewell. His mother getting remarried. Liz moving on with her new husband. And eventually, J.C. would move on, as well. She'd give birth to their baby, raise their son.

I'm in love with you.

Even that would change.

And that thought turned his blood to ice. He finished his beer and stood. "Want another?"

"I'm good."

Brady tossed his empty into the recycling bin and grabbed a full bottle from the fridge. He flipped the cap into the garbage and then sat back down. "You have something you want to say?"

"Do you hear me talking?" Aidan asked.

"No. But I can feel all those waves of disapproval."

Aidan stroked Lily's head, her eyes squinting in pleasure. "I'm wondering what happened to send you back to the bottle."

"Maybe I'm just thirsty."

"I thought Jane would be at the party," Aidan mentioned way too casually for the comment to actually be casual. "Did she have other plans?"

He scowled. "How the hell would I know?"

"Thought you two were…friends."

Cold sweat broke out on his forehead. Friends. Jeez. "We're not," he said.

Aidan bent one leg, resting his arm on his knee. "You blew it, huh?"

"There was nothing to blow. She wasn't what I wanted."

"Why not?"

He froze in the act of raising his beer to his mouth. "She's Liz's sister."

"You don't want her because she's Liz's sister? Or because she's not Liz?"

"Both. Neither." Hell. He carefully set the bottle on the table. "It would never work out."

Aidan raised an eyebrow. "Your crystal ball tell you that?"

"This isn't how my life was supposed to be," he said, feeling as if the words were being ripped from his throat. "Liz and me breaking up. My knee..." The nightmares. The drinking. J.C. and the baby. "None of it's what I wanted."

"And all this time I thought Matt was the idiot in the family," Aidan muttered as he stood. "You think you're the only person whose life is one hundred and eighty degrees from where you thought it'd be? If things went according to plan, Dad would still be alive and I'd be working my way up to partner at some high-end law firm in D.C."

"You could've still had that law career," Brady said, feeling as if he were backed into a corner and the only way out was to start swinging. "No one forced you to take over the winery after Dad died. The only thing you didn't choose was Yvonne leaving."

At the mention of his ex-wife, Aidan's expression hardened. "Why don't you take responsibility for yourself, for your decisions? It's not as if your life turned out the way it has through no fault or conscious choice of your own."

Brady wanted to deny it. He hadn't wanted Liz to end their engagement and he sure as hell hadn't asked for his vehicle to run over that bomb. But, damn it, he had stayed with Liz despite her repeatedly pushing their wedding date back. He'd joined the Marines, stayed in the Corps despite the risks involved.

He chose to spend time with J.C. even though his feelings for her grew more tangled, more confused with every one of her smiles. With every casual touch or soft kiss.

He'd let himself fall completely for Jane Cleo Montgomery.

Shaken, he rubbed the heel of his hand over his heart. "You were right the first time. I definitely blew it with J.C."

"So fix it."

If you ever start thinking you'd like to be a part of our lives after all—don't bother. My son and I will be fine without you. We don't need you.

His pulse pounded in his ears. "I don't think I can," he admitted.

"Want my advice?"

"No."

"Don't let her go. Do whatever you have to do or say to convince her to give you a second chance."

Brady brought his head up at the urgency in his brother's voice. "Is that the voice of experience talking?"

"It's the voice of a man whose wife walked out on him." Aidan's expression was grim. "And because he chose not to go after her."

CHRISTMAS MORNING, J.C. and most of the other congregation joined in as the First Presbyterian's choir sang "Joy to the World" at the end of the church service. She snuck a glance down the wooden pew, past her parents and Grandma Rose, to where Liz and Carter stood sharing a songbook. They'd arrived just before services started, harried, windblown and flushed. And obviously very much together.

As J.C. watched, Carter bent his head and whispered in Liz's ear. She smiled, then caressed her husband's cheek with her fingertips.

J.C. jerked her gaze back to the songbook in her hand but the words blurred. Maybe this loneliness was her penance for coveting her sister's ex.

Or maybe she'd just been simply foolish to fall in love with someone as lost and damaged as Brady Sheppard.

The song ended and as usual, her family was one of the last to leave, thanks to Grandma Rose being in no particular hurry to get out of the pew. How it could possibly take someone so long to put on a coat, button it, pull on some gloves and dig her house keys out of her purse—because God forbid she'd have to stand outside her own front door searching for her keys—J.C. had no idea. All she knew was that by the time her grandmother was ready to go, the church was half-empty.

J.C. followed her family out of the pew. Her parents walked down the aisle with their closest friends, Sandy and Dan O'Brien, while Carter escorted Grandma Rose.

Leaving Liz standing in the aisle waiting for her. J.C. considered exiting from the other end of the pew, even took a step in that direction before sliding her purse strap over her shoulder and moving forward.

Liz's smile was bright, her eyes uncertain. "Merry Christmas," she said, hugging J.C.

Though it was petty—petty and immature and not

in the Christmas spirit at all—J.C. kept her arms at her sides. "Merry Christmas."

Liz's smile faltered. She cleared her throat then swept her gaze over her sister. "Wow, you look really..."

So help her, if Liz said *tired* or commented on the dark circles under her eyes or the pallor of her skin, J.C. was going to hit her with a hymnbook.

"Pretty," Liz decided.

"Thank you." The baby moved—he'd been rolling around like mad in there all morning—and J.C. rubbed her stomach. "I take it everything's all right with you and Carter?"

Liz glanced over at her husband, who was waiting patiently for Grandma Rose to finish her conversation with the minister. "I wouldn't go that far, but we're trying. We..." Fidgeting with the buttons on her coat, Liz lowered her voice. "We're going to look into couples' counseling after the holidays."

"That's good," J.C. said, meaning it. She stepped into the aisle, forcing Liz to hastily move out of the way. "I hope...I hope you two work things out."

She walked toward the double doors. The church had cleared out quickly. The kids were itching to change out of their fancy clothes and play with the toys they'd unwrapped earlier. The adults were either hurrying from one relative's house to another's or racing home to start Christmas dinner. Her parents were probably speeding home themselves to host their annual Christmas brunch at noon.

She'd planned to attend. Had told herself she was tough enough to survive a couple hours surrounded by family and friends. But now she was panicked at just the thought of acting as if everything were okay.

She'd go back to her apartment. Once there, she'd call and tell her parents she wasn't feeling well and wouldn't make it to their party.

"Jane, wait," Liz called, stopping J.C. before she reached the doors. "I...I want to apologize for what happened the other day. For the things I said."

"It doesn't matter."

Liz's eyes filled with tears. "How can you say that? I was...horrible. What I said about Brady..." She swallowed convulsively. "About him not wanting anyone but me..."

"All you said was the truth."

Liz opened her mouth. Then shut it as she looked over J.C.'s shoulder, her eyes widening slightly. "No," she said, "I don't think that was the truth at all."

A ripple of awareness washed over J.C. Holding her breath, she turned slowly. And there he was—Brady Sheppard, leaning against the door, looking as sullen and dangerous and lost as he had on the day of Liz's wedding.

Except...he wasn't looking at Liz. No, he was looking at...her. Even when Liz brushed past him and walked out the door.

J.C.'s mouth went dry. Shock held her immobile as he straightened and strode toward her, his step purposeful despite his limp. He looked...well...he looked awful. As if he'd slept in his clothes—or hadn't gone to bed yet. His hair waved in disarray, his eyes were bloodshot and the thick stubble on his cheeks and chin did nothing to soften the harsh lines of his face.

He didn't stop until he was so close she had to tip her head back to meet his eyes.

"You're not at your apartment," he rumbled.

She blinked. Blinked again. "No. I'm not."

"You didn't stay there last night."

She gaped at him. "How do you—"

"I waited for you."

She remembered the other times he'd waited. Thanksgiving night. At the doctor's office for her appointment. "You…you waited all night?" He nodded curtly. "I…stayed over at my parents' house. They didn't want me to be alone."

"When you didn't come home I thought…" He looked away. "I thought I'd lost you. For good. Tell me I haven't. Tell me I'm not too late."

Shaking her head slowly, she backed away. But for each step she took, he followed.

"I'm not doing this," she said, her voice trembling when she'd meant to sound confident. Angry. Damn it, she was angry. And way too raw to give him even the slightest opportunity to hurt her again.

"Please." He reached out as if to touch her face but she jerked her head back. "Please," he repeated, curling his fingers into a fist. "Just let me explain—"

"Explain what, Brady? You've made it perfectly clear you don't anything to do with me or our baby. Oh, or maybe you'd like to tell me how you'd rather be with Liz, but hey, I'll do in a pinch, right? And if it's dark enough and you pretend real hard," she said, her voice cracking, "you can convince yourself you're really with her."

"Jane…no…God, I didn't…" He looked stunned. "You know that's not true. I made love to *you* that night. You're who I want."

"It's too late."

She started to walk away.

"I love you, Jane."

She stumbled and turned around, her eyes wide. "Don't say that," she snapped.

"It's the truth. I love you."

"You love Liz." She hugged her arms around herself. "You're always going to love Liz."

"I'm always going to care about her, but I don't love her. I'm not in love with her. Not anymore." He stepped toward J.C. "You were right. I couldn't see what had gone right in my life." Another step. "You, Jane. You and our baby are what's right."

She began to shake. "No."

He regarded her gravely. "What I said that morning after we made love…what you heard…" He blew out a shaky breath. "I was scared. Afraid of my feelings for you. I didn't know what to do with them. They were… too much. Too soon. I wanted to control them because so many parts of my life were out of my control."

"Stop. Please…" Her voice was raw. Her breathing shallow. "I can't do this again."

"You said you and the baby didn't need me," he said, relentlessly, stubbornly, as he closed the remaining distance between them. He gently lifted her chin. "You may not need me, but I need you. Both of you."

Afraid to believe, she searched his eyes. Joy and love, so much love for him, welled inside her and the tears she'd tried to hold back rolled down her cheeks.

"Don't cry," he said raggedly, wiping her face, his touch unsteady. "It rips me up when you cry."

Throwing her arms around him, she pressed her face into his neck. She inhaled his familiar, comforting scent. He stilled for a moment, then with a groan, wrapped his arms around her, pulling her close, holding her so tightly, she couldn't breathe. She clung to him harder.

"Thank you," he murmured. "Thank you."

He pulled back and kissed her, his lips warm, his mouth coaxing. When he straightened, he cupped her face in one hand, his thumb caressing her jaw. His other hand went to the soft swell of her stomach, his fingers spread wide. "Tell me."

Because he still seemed so unsure, so nervous, she kissed him. Then smiled. "I love you, Brady."

He nodded and she felt some of his tension drain away. "I love you, Jane Cleo," he said, his voice husky.

And then—disheveled, contented and, if she wasn't mistaken, mended—Brady Sheppard smiled. At her.

EPILOGUE

One month later

ABOUT A MILE AWAY from the turn to the Diamond Dust, Brady took a right down a narrow lane.

"Where are we going?" J.C. asked from the passenger seat as he passed two houses—one on each side of the road—and pulled to a stop in front of a large, well-maintained farmhouse where the street ended. "Brady, what's going on? You know how your mom gets if we're late for lunch."

Lunch with his mom, Al and Aidan had become a weekly Sunday event. Things were still…tense…with J.C.'s family, and he doubted he and Carter would ever be more than stiffly polite to each other, but J.C. and Liz seemed to be making inroads.

He unclenched his hands from around the steering wheel. "We'll be there on time. I…" His throat was dry. "I want to show you something."

Grinning, she rolled her eyes. "Like I haven't heard that line before."

When he couldn't return her smile, hers slid away.

"You okay?" she asked, laying a hand on his arm. "Do you need to do some breathing exercises?"

"I'm fine." He squeezed her hand. "I'm not having an…an episode."

He'd been seeing a therapist for the past three weeks who'd officially diagnosed him with PTSD—post-traumatic stress disorder. And while he couldn't say he was thrilled with the diagnosis or having to spill his guts every week in his therapy session, the techniques he'd learned for dealing with his memories, stress and flashbacks were helping.

"Come on," he said, then hurried around the car, opened her door and pulled her to her feet.

She laughed but followed him to the wooden porch. He dug a set of keys out of his pocket. Her eyes widened. "What are you doing? Who lives here?"

"It's empty," he said, pushing open the door and tugging her into the wide foyer. He swallowed. "Want to look around?"

"Uh…sure."

Holding her hand, he led her up the stairs, turned left and walked into a large room with deep burgundy walls and white trim. "Master bedroom," he said, repeating the information the Realtor had given him, "complete with walk-in closets, bath and a balcony."

"It's very…pretty," she said, looking at him as if he'd recently suffered a head injury.

"Two more bedrooms up here." Spinning her around, he walked down the hall and into the room on the right—this one smaller and painted a sunny yellow—only to walk right out again and into the third bedroom at the back of the house. He opened the door at the end of the hall. "Closet." Gestured toward the final door. "Bathroom."

By the time he'd gotten her back down the stairs she was silent and his knee was aching.

"Foyer," he said as they passed the tiled entryway again. "That's the family room." He pointed to the large room off the foyer, then, knowing where he wanted the tour to end, he went the way they came, pointing at rooms as they walked. "Another bedroom or office, half bath, dining room."

Finally, his heart pounding, they reached the last room. "This is the kitchen."

"Yes," J.C. said, tugging free of his hold, her brow furrowed. "I can see that."

He waited as she slowly walked around, checking out the stainless-steel appliances, granite counters and built-in pantry.

"Well?" he asked, his voice a low growl when she remained silent.

She leaned back against the sink and crossed her arms. "Well what?"

He ground his teeth together. "Do you like it?"

"The kitchen?"

"The house."

She shrugged. "Yes."

He narrowed his eyes. Yes? That was it? "The asking price is for the house plus ten acres. And since it's been on the market for over a year, the owners are ready to make a deal."

"Well, if I was in the market to buy a house, that would all be good to know." Smiling, she straightened. "You ready to go? I'm starving," she added as she walked toward the door. "Do you think your mom made that potato soup I like?"

"I'm in the market."

Almost to the door, she turned slowly. "Excuse me?"

He shoved his hands into his pockets. "I'm in the market to buy a house. To buy this house." She regarded him steadily. Sweat formed at the nape of his neck, a bead of it sliding down between his shoulder blades. "I want to buy this house for you and the baby. For…us."

"Why?"

"Because I love you," he ground out, crossing to her. "And you love me."

"Yes, I do." She tipped her head to the side, looking so serene and so damn beautiful, he caught his breath. "I want you to ask me," she said softly.

His chest tight, he pulled a ring box out of his pocket and opened it. "It was my great-grandmother's," he said of the round diamond set in a platinum scrolled band.

"It's beautiful." She kept her hands clasped in front of her. She met his eyes. "But I'm still waiting for you to ask me."

"I can't kneel."

"No." Her eyes glistened. "I don't want you to. I just want the words."

"Jane Cleo Montgomery," he said quietly, taking her left hand and sliding the ring onto her finger, "I love you. I want to make a life with you and our baby." He kissed her hand, then looked into her eyes. "Will you marry me?"

"Yes," she whispered, linking her fingers through his. She cleared her throat. "Yes, Brady. I'll marry you."

Humbled, grateful, he pressed his lips against hers. Her mouth softened. He lifted his head and grinned. "I know you're anxious to get to lunch, but what do you think about christening the house before we go?"

She laughed and linked her arms around his neck. "I think that's the second-best proposal I've had today."

* * * * *

COMING NEXT MONTH

Available December 7, 2010

REQUEST YOUR FREE BOOKS!

2 FREE NOVELS PLUS 2 FREE GIFTS!

HARLEQUIN®

Super Romance®

Exciting, emotional, unexpected!

HARLEQUIN®

A Romance

FOR EVERY MOOD™

Spotlight on
Classic

Quintessential, modern love stories
that are romance at its finest.

See the next page
to enjoy a sneak peek from
the Harlequin® Romance series.

*See below for a sneak peek from our classic
Harlequin® Romance® line.*

Introducing DADDY BY CHRISTMAS by Patricia Thayer.

Mia caught sight of Jarrett when he walked into the open lobby. It was hard not to notice the man. In a charcoal business suit with a crisp white shirt and striped tie covered by a dark trench coat, he looked more Wall Street than small-town Colorado.

Mia couldn't blame him for keeping his distance. He was probably tired of taking care of her.

Besides, why would a man like Jarrett McKane be interested in her? Why would he want to take on a woman expecting a baby? Yet he'd done so many things for her. He'd been there when she'd needed him most. How could she not care about a man like that?

Heart pounding in her ears, she walked up behind him. Jarrett turned to face her. "Did you get enough sleep last night?"

"Yes, thanks to you," she said, wondering if he'd thought about their kiss. Her gaze went to his mouth, then she quickly glanced away. "And thank you for not bringing up my meltdown."

Jarrett couldn't stop looking at Mia. Blue was definitely her color, bringing out the richness of her eyes.

"What meltdown?" he said, trying hard to focus on what she was saying. "You were just exhausted from lack of sleep and worried about your baby."

He couldn't help remembering how, during the night, he'd kept going in to watch her sleep. How strange was that? "I hope you got enough rest."

She nodded. "Plenty. And you're a good neighbor for

MAKING AMENDS

"What are you fellows doing in all those feathers?" Ramona Delpheen asked. She wasn't sure why the butler had let strangers through the door.

The men said nothing. Long robes of yellow feathers hung down to their knees. One of them carried what appeared to be a phallic symbol made of stone. "We are all of Indian blood—Actatl. All we wished for was to live. But you would not let us. You have violated what we hold precious and worthy, the stone of our ancestors, the life of our hearts, the most gracious and central inspiration of our being."

The next moment, the man with the phallic symbol of stone raised it above Ramona's head and rammed it into her chest. He worked quickly, severing the last arteries, and then with a rip he tore the heart out of her body. Then he left a note with its corners carefully smeared with her blood. She was the second victim . . .

The Destroyer Series:

The Destroyer

KING'S CURSE #24

by Richard Sapir & Warren Murphy

PINNACLE BOOKS   NEW YORK CITY

This is a work of fiction. All the characters and events portrayed in this book are fictional, and any resemblance to real people or incidents is purely coincidental.

THE DESTROYER: KING'S CURSE

Copyright © 1976 by Richard Sapir and Warren Murphy

An original Pinnacle Books edition, published for the first time anywhere.

ISBN: 0-523-00879-1

First printing, July 1976

Cover illustration by Hector Garrido

Printed in the United States of America

PINNACLE BOOKS, INC.
275 Madison Avenue
New York, N.Y. 10016

For:

Amnon, Judy, Sharon, Uriyah, Joseph, Gilli, Naomi, Ruthi, and most of all the awesome magnificence of the House of Sinanju (American drop P. O. Box 1149, Pittsfield, Mass. 01201).

KING'S CURSE

Chapter One

The stone was old before the pale men on four high legs with metal chests and metal heads followed the path of the sun in from the big water you could not drink.

Before the king-priests, the stone was; before the warrior-kings, it was. Before the Aztec and the Toltec and the Maya, it was. Before the Actatl, who served it and acknowledged it as their own personal god, the stone was.

The stone was a king's height, and if you did not know that the circle outlined in its belly was carved by the very gods themselves before man came from the mouth of the turtle, if you did not know that, then you were not Actatl. And you would not be allowed in the palace of the god, and you would not be allowed near the sacred stone, lest the god be enraged by an unbeliever's finger touching it.

And the people called the sacred stone Uctut.

But only the priests knew its real name.

In the first years of the pale men the warrior king of the Actatl called the five priests of Uctut to the palace, which was 142 steps high and protected Uctut from the north wind and the north light. He asked the priests what they thought of the new pale men.

"Moctezuma says they are gods," said one priest.

"Moctezuma thinks the gods breathe when he vents air after a feast," said the king.

"Moctezuma is a king that is more to god's way," said another priest reproachfully. "It is known that the Aztec of Moctezuma follow their gods better because their king is a priest."

"Life is too short to spend it preparing for its end," the king answered. "And I believe that the rain falls without a baby's heart being thrown into the well that feeds Uctut, and I believe that new babies come even if the hearts of women are not sent into the well, and I believe that I win victories, not because Uctut has been fed with blood, but because my men fight from high places and others from low."

"Have you never wanted to know the name of Uctut? The real name? So that he could speak to you as he speaks to us?" another priest asked.

"What for? Everyone has a name for something. It is just a breath of air. I have not called you here to say that after so many years I have

2

come to your way. Let it remain at this: You give the people your gods, and I do not take the people away from you. Now I ask you, what do you think of the men colored like clouds?"

"Uctut thinks he must have their hearts for his water," said one priest.

"Moctezuma thinks we should give the tall ones with four legs the yellow metals they seek," said another.

And another said, "Moctezuma has also said we should give the hearts of these white men to Uctut."

"Did Moctezuma say the Aztec should give the hearts of these white men with their death sticks?" the king asked. "Or did he say the Actatl should take these hearts?"

"He said it was such a good sacrifice, we should be pleased to make it to Uctut," said a priest.

"Then let the great Moctezuma take their hearts," said the king, "and he may offer them up to Quetzalcoatl, the plumed serpent god."

Another priest responded, "He said the Aztec honored the Actatl by not taking this rich sacrifice for themselves but allowing us to take it for Uctut, to make our god rich and red with the finest hearts."

"Then this I tell to Moctezuma, great king of the great Aztec, from his most respectful neighbor, king of the Actatl, holder of leopards, who protects Uctut from the winds of the north, conquerer of the Umay, Acoupl, Xorec. To Moctezuma, I say, greetings neighbor. We appreciate your generosity and in turn, we give gifts to the Aztec and their great king."

3

While the king spoke, the priests all made sacred marks, for they were knowing of the mysteries, how one man could place a mark on a tablet of stone, and how another man seeing that mark could divine a thought from it, even though the maker of the mark had gone many years before to the other world.

Five hundred years later, in a land where almost everyone read and there was no mystery to it, archaeologists would engage in a favorite pastime of wishing they could talk to inhabitants of the dead cultures they studied. They would say they could get more from a half-hour conversation with someone who lived in that culture than they could get from a lifetime of studying the marks on the tablets they had found.

Yet, if they had talked to the average Actatl, they would have gotten only that the marks were mysteries, that the king lived high, the people lived low, and the priests served Uctut, whose real name only the priests knew and were allowed to speak.

But the stone that was Uctut would last. The Aztec would be no more, the Maya and Inca would be no more. The name of the Actatl would be destroyed, and the Umay, the Acoupl, the Xorec, the inland people they had conquered, would not even be remembered.

All would be forgotten. Yet Uctut would survive and in that far-off time, in a land called the United States of America, blood and horror would be visited upon many, in a royal sacrifice by the Actatl to their god of the stone.

4

And that blood sacrifice started from what happened that day when the king of the Actatl attempted to avoid facing in battle the Spanish invader, whom he suspected was not a god, but just a man of a different color.

And so the priests made their marks and the king spoke. The gift he and his people would give to the Aztec would be the sole rights to the hearts of the pale men on four high legs with metal chests and metal heads.

One priest protested that this was too generous an offer, that Uctut would be jealous of Quetzalcoatl, the Aztec's chief god. But the king signalled for silence and the message was over.

For Uctut's approval a small sacrifice was chosen, a young girl of budding breasts from a fine family, and she was dressed in a royal robe of yellow feathers and placed upon the stone above the well that held the waters that fed Uctut.

Now if her family seemed to be forcing tears and only pretending to wail, there was good reason. For many generations now the Actatl had bought slaves and kept captives for just such a ceremony, and when the priests called for a sacrifice from the ranking soldiers and from those who directed the farmers and the building of roads, they would dress those slaves kept just for this purpose and offer them to Uctut.

One priest held one ankle, and another priest held the other ankle, and two other priests held the wrists. They were strong men of necessity because the bodies struggling for life often had great power. This girl's skin was smooth, and her

5

teeth were fine, and her eyes were shiny black. The fifth priest nodded approvingly at the family, who would be pleased with themselves later; now they lamented as if the child were their own daughter.

With delicate care, the fifth priest unfolded one side of the robe and then the other, and so careful were his hands that the girl smiled hopefully up at him. Perhaps he would let her go. She had heard other slaves say that sometimes they would bring you to the big rock and let you go. Not often but sometimes. And she had placed pebbles in a circle on a grassy bank to the gods of the streams who, while not as strong as Uctut, could sometimes outwit him. And her only request since she had been brought to the special building from the fields was that her god would outwit Uctut and let her live.

And did not the priest's smile above her and his gentle hands mean that he would say this girl is too small and too sweet to die this day? She did not know, nor did the other slaves, that victims were sent back only because of crossed eyes or chipped teeth or scars that would make them unseemly.

But this was a pretty little girl and so the Actatl priest ripped out her heart.

It was a good heart, still pumping in his gentle hands after it was cut and ripped out of the young chest, and she had given a good scream that would increase Uctut's appetite. The priest held the moving heart high so that all would see what a fine gift the family gave for the benefit of all.

The supposed mother wailed and collapsed to

her knees in supposed grief. A laudation chant filled the open cathedral of the rock, and before the heart was stilled the priest lowered it to the well, and the four other priests sent the body after, careful that the valuable robe did not go in with it.

Thus was the king's message to Moctezuma assured of the good will of Uctut.

The king watched all this with apparent approval, but his mind was not with the stupid, cruel little ceremony. Even as a little boy he had realized that it was not Uctut who wanted hearts, but the priests and the people. And since the only ones who suffered were slaves and captives, the ceremonies would continue.

He had other things on his mind this day as he looked out upon his people and their homes and fields, which he knew stretched twenty days run in all directions, beyond mountains and rivers and plains. All this was doomed. The people were doomed. Even the very words they spoke would disappear. And while he knew this must have happened to others and would happen to still others and that it was the way of things, some coming and some going, yet inside him something he could not fathom insisted that he not allow this.

He knew the visitors from the water you could not drink would take everything, for they wanted more than the yellow metal and more than slaves. They wanted, according to the king's spies, what they said was in every man and lived forever. Sort of a mind, but not a mind, the spies had said. And they wanted this thing for their god.

And their god was one god, yet three gods, and

7

one had died but had not died. The king had instructed his spy to ask if the pale men's new god would accept a fourth—Uctut—and when the spies returned with the words they had translated from the new language, the king understood that everything the Actatl and the Aztec and the Maya and all the rest had known was over and done. The words were: "You shall have no other gods before me."

This god would not take blood or food or ornaments. He wanted the living minds of his people. Not like Uctut, who could be fooled by a yellow feathered robe and an artificial wail from someone pretending to be a victim's mother.

The king had not mentioned anything to the priests, lest in their fear or anger they attempt something that would surely fail. This new thing was unlike anything the Actatl had ever known, and against it nothing they had ever known would be effective.

That evening of the sacrifice, the king announced he would stay in his high place for many days, but he dressed as a slave, and accompanied by his most fearsome warrior, and he left the high place with a bundle of yellow metal. Now the warrior had much difficulty treating the king as a slave at first, since from birth he had been trained to serve his king and lay down his life to save that of his king. But the king told him that now they must use the deception of rank as their cover, like they used the cover of the forest once. The warrior was puzzled by this as they ran along the roads at night. Everyone knew that the king was a king because he was king. He was not a slave, otherwise he would be a slave. And the pale newcomers would know this, for those who are kings are kings.

Now the king could not tell him what he had long suspected—that the differences in men were made up by men like children's stories were made up, except that differences among men were believed in. So the king told the warrior he had made a magic spell which would make pale men believe he was a slave and not the Actatl king. And this satisfied the warrior.

They ran through the night and in the morning they slept. For twenty-two days they did this, passing the home city of Moctezuma. And one morning they saw a fearful thing.

A pale man, twice as tall as other men, with much hair on his face and shiny metal on his head and chest, and two legs fore and two behind, walked past them, and instinctively the warrior shielded his king. But the king warned him again that he was to be treated as a slave, not a king, and there would be no more warnings. He could not give him another warning.

And they walked out of their hiding place and the tall pale man pointed at them a spear without a point but with a hole in it. And the king noticed that there was another head the same color as the body, and then he realized why the pale man had four legs and was so incredibly tall. He sat on an animal.

Had not the Inca to the south trained animals to carry bundles? This strange new animal had been trained to carry a man. And the king realized the metal was just something that was put on

9

the pale man's head. This was confirmed when
they entered a large camp, and the king saw some
men with metal on their heads and some men
without. He also saw the pale men and the
strange animals separated, and not joined together.

He saw a queen of the coastal people sitting on
a high chair next to a pale man, and he and the
warrior were brought to them. The woman spoke
the language of the Aztec, and she spoke to the
warrior. As he had been instructed, the warrior
gave his name and his function as an Actatl, then
waited.

The woman questioned in Aztec and then spoke
to the pale man in another language. And the king
memorized each sound as it came from her lips
for there was much he had to learn to save his
people. And then the warrior said he had captured this slave fleeing from the city of Moctezuma.

The warrior paused, and the woman talked the
strange language, and while she pronounced Moctezuma correctly, the pale man could not. When
he repeated it, he said "Montezuma" with different emphasis.

The warrior said the slave was worthless and
had nothing because Moctezuma and the Aztecs
were poor. And the woman spoke in the other language, and the pale man spoke, and there was tension in their voices. And the woman said to the
warrior that the Aztec was not poor, that Moctezuma himself had rooms of gold. And the warrior
said, no gold. Just worthless slaves. And when the
woman spoke again, the king of the Actatl,

dressed as a slave, let loose the many heavy weights of gold he had run with for many days, and he paid scant attention to them, brushing off his poor rags as though the gold was but the dust of the earth.

And, as he had planned, this caused great commotion, and the pale ones even tried to eat the gold by pressing their teeth into it. And the king pretending to be a slave laughed and cried out: "Oh, great queen, why do these pale ones love the yellow dirt so much?"

"Did this come from Moctezuma's city?" she asked, and the king nodded low like a slave and said, "Yes. It comes from the rooms of gold."

And when she repeated this to the pale one, he jumped up and danced, and from then on the pale man wanted words from the slave and ordered the warrior put to death for telling untruths. And thus was the slave-king trusted and taken into the camp of the pales, and thus did this pale man, whom the king later found out was named Cortez, proceed to his long and difficult siege of Moctezuma's city, finally taking it.

During the months of siege, the king thought to be a slave gave bits of information about the Aztec, like a lake letting only a little stream flow out each day. And he watched and learned. Like his own people, few here could read, although the secrets were not guarded. He learned the new language from a priest of the new god. He learned that it was not the sound from the sticks that killed, but a projectile that came at great speed from a hole in the stick. He learned that there were bigger sticks that fired bigger projectiles.

11

One night he learned to ride a horse and almost got killed.

The pale men's metals were harder than the Actatl's. Their military formations were not superior, but being able to stand twenty to thirty paces off and kill with the sticks called guns, the formations did not have to be superior. Their writing was not symbols of things but symbols of sound, and in this, the Actatl king knew, there was a great power. Lighter people were treated better than darker people, and these pale men did not, as his spies had correctly told him, sacrifice people or animals, although at first when he saw the statue of the man stretched out on crossed bars, he was not sure.

He saw the city of Moctezuma fall and its people enslaved, and he was sure that even as the stronger Aztec were doomed, so were his own people. There would be hardly a trace.

These pale men from a land called Europe were robber warriors, and while it was not unusual for new tribes to move into old land, these pale men were different because they did not share ways, they imposed theirs. And theirs was a better way that did not demand the silliness of the sacrifice.

But he must not let his people die.

Among the camp of the pales were many tribes that sided with the newcomers against Moctezuma. One man recognized the Actatl king, and he went to the woman of Cortez and said, "That is not a slave but king of the Actatl." And the woman called the king to her and asked why he had come as a slave when as a king he would have been welcome.

12

"Have you told this to Cortez yet?" asked the king.

"I will tell him before sunrise," said the queen of the coastal people. And with the sharper, harder metal of the pale men, the king slit her throat. He did not take her heart.

When his hands were dry, he went to Cortez and told him of what he had heard as a young slave—that there were cities to the north of Moctezuma's that were of pure gold. The walls were gold. The ceilings were gold. The streets were gold.

Cortez asked why he had not told him this earlier.

"Oh, great lord of the pale men, I was asked by your woman for rooms of gold. In these cities of the north, they do not keep gold in rooms. They make bricks of gold and they build with it, so plentiful is this strange metal."

And with a glorious laugh, Cortez ordered his expedition to prepare. In the excitement the death of one translator, even a coastal queen, was not taken as an undue tragedy. There were many translators now.

Fifteen days north did the king take Cortez and his party and on the fifteenth, while in the mountains, the king slipped away at night.

Losing his guide, Cortez would give up the expedition, but for centuries after, those who followed him would continue to search for the Seven Cities of Cibol, cities that never existed except in the imagination of a king who wished to keep the greedy Spaniards away from him and his people.

On that fifteenth night the king left with a horse and one gun with powder and bullets and flint and many books.

And a month later, he arrived at the main city of the Actatl. The king had been gone for four full seasons.

There was a new king now, and the priests of Uctut, in their confusion, announced one king would have to be killed. So the new king, who was a son of the old king, gathered his warriors and prepared to sacrifice his father. But when the first warrior approached, the old king used the thunder stick and, throwing nothing at all, killed the man. All seeing this turned on the new king to make him sacrifice for the old, but the old king would not have this. He had not returned to be king but to bring a message of a new undertaking that Uctut should approve.

The old king would take fifty women and ten young male children and ten young female children, and he would go off with them. But the priests would not have this for that would mean two kings lived and Uctut would be angered.

"Within but a few generations, Uctut will not be," said the old king. "This city will not be. The words we use will not be. The way priest greets king and king priest and people greet their lords will not be. Nothing of the Actatl will be."

They asked if a god had spoken to him in a sacred vision, and so they would understand, he said that Uctut had told him.

This greatly worried the priests, who ordered each family to give a sacrifice so that Uctut would speak to the priests.

When the sacrifices were over, a person could not walk on the stone above the well for it sloshed with blood.

Basins of blood filled the cracks and crevices in the steps to the high stone. Red was the well that fed Uctut. Strong was the stench that came from the high stone.

And then there was knowledge. The old king could live, but each who left with him would have to become a priest of Uctut who would have to know the real name of the stone, and should the king's predictions be true, each would have to promise a priest's service to protect Uctut.

In this promise, in a civilization soon to die, in the lush green hills between Mexico and South America, was a seed planted that would sprout more than four hundred years later. Its flower would feed on human life, and nothing in that future world that could put a man on the moon would be able to defend against the descendants of those who still looked upon the shiny yellow moon in the night as another god.

The old king took his new family away toward an uninhabited valley he had seen once on a march. He bred well and he taught well. Each learned language and writing and numbers and the primitive science of the west. And when the new generation of his loins was ready, he sent them out in groups to find the pale invaders—not to kill them for there were too many—but to reproduce with them, taking the best child of each brood and teaching it that it was Actatl. Even if its hair were yellow, still it was Actatl.

For the king had discovered that the only way

15

his people could live was to camouflage themselves in the colors of others, whoever they were.

Only one thing bothered him. He could not break them of Uctut, the silly rock. For while he taught them everything, Uctut and its real name became the one thing even the children knew, but not he. And thus it was prized even more. The more he said it was just a silly rock, the more important Uctut became to them as the symbol of what they had been and what they would preserve in their future lives. So he just stopped talking about it.

One day the last of the original women died, and he realized he was alone. He gave her ritual burial, although piling the stones was hard because he was an old man.

The new village was empty, and the clay tablets upon which Actatl sounds and European speech were written had not been used for many years, since the last trained group of youths had left. The older ones had not taken well to the new language and way of things, and most had stayed with him here in the hidden village. It was empty now, but for an old dog that could hardly move and had cried very much when its master had left years before.

"Done," said the last king of the Actatl. He tried to coax the dog to come with him, but he could not. He put as much food as he could carry into a small bundle and opened the storehouse to the dog, who would probably be a meal for one of the cats of the jungle, now that the man was gone.

The king made the trek back to the city of the

Actatl. Even before he set foot there, he knew the kingdom was gone. The roads were grassed over and the fields untilled. Great plants grew in stone watchtowers.

Perhaps a few old friends would be biding their last days, hiding in the remains of the city. But there was no one, not even dogs, left in the great city from which once the empire of the Actatl had been ruled. And something else was strange. There was no sign of the fires that usually accompanied a siege.

He thought, Yes, the Spaniards have been here. All the gold had been removed. But the pieces, he saw, had not been torn away or hacked away or ripped away but were carefully taken out. He thought for a moment, with great happiness, that one of the later kings had wisely taken the people away, something the old king knew he never could get the priests to agree to. But when he arrived at the high stone altar, he knew otherwise, and he let out from his stomach a deep wail. Whitened bones covered the steps and formed in great piles, already mingling with plants. A small tree grew from the mouth of a grinning skull.

He knew what had happened. Hearing of the Spaniards nearby, they had all come to the high place, hiding what they knew would be of value to the pale men invaders. And they had killed themselves here, their last offering to Uctut. Probably one group killing another, until the last made himself sacrifice to Uctut. He noticed the chest bones chipped on the lower bodies, but higher up there was no such bone breakage. Probably the first were sacrificed ritually, and as the days of

17

blood wore on the killing became like the tilling of a field, something to be gotten over with as quickly and effectively as possible. At the top stones he saw skulls with holes in them, and this confirmed his guess. At the end they were smashing in heads.

He was tired, more of spirit than of his old body.

He looked up at the carved rock, a king's height, and said, "Uctut"—for he did not know its secret name—"you are not even stupid because people are stupid and you are not people. You are a rock. A rock made special by people. You are like a pebble that gets in the way of a plow. Rock. Stupid rock."

He sat down, pushing bones aside, amazed at how light they were, now dried, and he was tired. And on the fourth day he felt something sharp at his heart and reached weakly to his chest just to assure himself that there was no blood. There was none, of course, and he shut his eyes and he felt good and wanting of death in a natural way. And he slipped away into that deepest sleep, knowing his job was well done.

Centuries passed, and with nothing special to preserve the bones of all who were there, they blended into the natural substances from which they came. Not even the dreams remained when a heavy rope crane dragged the king-high stone with the carving from the high place. Other men chopped up stones with carvings on them, but this stone would be worth more uncut, even though it took four mules to drag it through the jungles and over the mountains, where men with Aztec faces and Spanish names sold it to the highest bidder.

Uctut, the stone, came to a large museum in New York City on Central Park West and was incorrectly put into a display of Aztec art. One day a German businessman saw it and suggested that it have a room of its own. A wealthy Detroit industrialist made a large contribution to the museum and, on becoming a trustee of that institution, moved to follow the suggestion of the German.

The curator objected, saying it was a rather insignificant piece of pre-Aztec work and didn't deserve a whole room, and shortly thereafter, to his surprise, he was dismissed for his "surly and unprofessional attitude."

A Japanese architect designed the new room for the stone with a rather gross, heavy wall blocking out the north light from what had been a fine window. And the architect even put in a large water fountain, although there was a drinking fountain just outside.

Apparently, the new trustee and architect knew what they were doing because this stone received many visitors from all over the world. A fiery Arab radical visited it on the same day as an Israeli paratroop colonel, and apparently the stone had some sort of soothing effect because they not only seemed to get along, but they embraced just before leaving. Both, when asked if this had happened by their countrymen, denied the incident. Of course, none seemed as enamored of this pre-Aztec stone as Count Ruy Lopez de Goma y Sanches, who came every day.

19

One October evening, a guard discovered that someone with a spray can of green enamel-glow had written in large letters on the stone: "Joey 172."

The next day, the congressman from the district was found in his Washington office with his chest over a pool of blood.

His heart had been ripped out.

Chapter Two

His name was Remo, and he was disbelieving his ears.

"Remo, this is Smith. Get back to Folcroft right away."

"Who's this?" Remo asked.

"Harold W. Smith, your employer."

"I can't hear you. The waves here are too loud," said Remo, looking at the quiet gentle roll of the sea green Atlantic coming onto the white sandy beach of Nag's Head, South Carolina.

The motel room was quiet also but for the faint scratching of goose quill against parchment. A wisp of an aged Oriental worked the quill quickly, yet his long-nailed fingers scarcely seemed to move. He would pause and look off into that well of creativity and write again, hardly moving his golden morning kimono.

"I said you've got to come back to Folcroft right away. Everything is coming apart."

"You said you want to speak to a Harold Smith?" Remo said.

"I know this is an open line but ..." Remo heard buzzing. Someone had cut them off. He put down the receiver.

"I'll be back in a while, Little Father," Remo said, and Chiun turned regally from his scriptures.

"Were you cringing and fat, or were you lying in the dirt when I found you?" asked Chiun. The voice was squeaky and hit highs and lows like a mountain range of slate with giant paws scratching across it.

"Neither," said Remo. "I was coming out of unconsciousness. I was pretty healthy for this civilization. As a matter of fact, I was pretty healthy for almost any time or place. Except one place."

"And lo," intoned Chiun—the quill had become a blur of speed, yet each Korean character of the writing remained clear and precise—"did Chiun, the Master of Sinanju, see the groveling white amid the garbage of his birth. Deformed of limb he was. Dull of eye he was with strange round orbs set in his head. But most deformed, saw the Master of Sinanju, was this white in his mind. A dull, sodden, lifeless mass in his ugly pale skull."

"I thought you had already contributed your section about me to the history of Sinanju," Remo said.

"I am revising it," Chiun said.

"I'm glad I see you writing this because now, with great certainty, I can reject the whole history of your village as bilge and fantasy and nonsense. Remember I've seen the village of Sinanju. We have better-looking sewer systems in this country."

"Like all whites and blacks, you are prejudiced," said Chiun, and his voice became scriptural again. "And, lo, the Master of Sinanju said unto this wretch, 'Arise, I shall make you whole. You shall know your senses and your mind. You shall breathe clean air fully in your whole body. You shall have life in you as no white has ever had.' And the wretch knew that grace was upon him, and he said, 'Oh, Awesome Magnificence, why do you bestow such gracious gifts upon one as low as I?'"

"Blow it out your ears," Remo said. "I've got work. I'll be back soon."

Late summer in Nag's Head, South Carolina, had all the charm of a roaster bag in an overheated oven. Remo saw car windows rolled up with people preserved by air conditioning. Those who were on the street this steamy day lagged as if their feet were weighted with lead.

Remo moved briskly. He was just short of six feet and thin but for the extra thickness in his wrists. He had sharp features and high cheekbones that seemed a platform for dark penetrating eyes that some women had told him made their stomachs "liquidy."

"Hey, don't you sweat?" asked the clerk as Remo stepped into a small luncheonette and asked for change.

"Only when it's hot," said Remo.

"It's a hundred and five outside," said the clerk.

"Then I'm sorry, I forgot to," Remo said. Actually he knew that sweating was only one form of cooling the overheated body and not the most efficient form. Breathing was, but most people did not know how to breathe, treating it like some function that had to be looked after only when you noticed it wasn't working right. From proper breathing came the rhythms of life and power.

"Funny, ah ain't ever seen nobody not sweat on a day liken today, not even a nigra," said the clerk. "How you do it?"

Remo shrugged. "You wouldn't understand if I told you, anyhow."

"You think ah'm dumb. You some smart yankee, come down hyeah, think ah'm dumb."

"Not until you opened your mouth," said Remo and went to the telephone booth. He piled up the change in front of him. He dialed the 800-area code emergency feed number. It was designed more for availability than security, but he could always leave a message for the real Harold W. Smith to call him back at the phone booth.

"I am sorry sir," came the distant voice of a tape recording. "The number you have reached is not in service at this time. If you need assistance, please wait and an operator will be with you in a moment."

Remo hung up and dialed again and got the same message again. This time he waited. A live operator answered with a nonregional sort of voice—neither the guttural consonants of the northeast, the syrup of the south, or the twang of

24

the midwest. California, thought Remo. The drop phone number is in California.

"Can I help you?"

"Yes," said Remo. And he gave the number he had tried to dial.

"You're where, now?" asked the operator.

"Chillicothe, Ohio," lied Remo. "Why is that number not working?"

"Because, according to our records, this number has never worked. You're not in Chillicothe."

"Thank you," said Remo.

"But we do have some information on this number." And she gave him another number, and this was even stranger because if Smith had set this up, he would never have given out an alternate number. And it occurred to Remo that the operator was not there to give him information but to find out where he was. He hung up.

Outside a gray and white police car with a red bubble atop parked at the curb. Two heavy officers with hands on pistols were out of the car lumbering into the luncheonette. The clerk ducked. Remo left the booth.

"Were you in that booth making a telephone call?" asked the first officer. The other moved to one side so Remo would be facing two guns.

"No," said Remo.

"Who was in that booth then?"

"How should I know?" Remo said.

"He was in that booth," said the clerk from behind the counter. "He's a weirdo, Jethro. Watch him. He don't sweat."

"I want to talk to you," said the officer.

"You seem to be accomplishing that," said Remo.

"Down at headquarters," said the officer.

"Are you arresting me or what?"

"Just to talk. People want to talk to you."

"Weirdo don't sweat, Jethro," said the clerk rising from behind the counter.

"Shut up, Luke," said the officer.

"I do too sweat," said Remo. "That's slander."

And when they were in the air conditioned offices of the Nag's Head Police Department, Remo perspired while others complained of the chill. Two men who said they were lawyers from a joint congressional committee investigating CIA and FBI abuses arrived and said they wanted to talk to Remo. They wore three-hundred-dollar suits and didn't comb their hair. Remo was not being charged with anything, but he had phoned a telephone number they were interested in, they said. This number had come to light on an FBI voucher no one could explain. Perhaps Remo could help. Why did he phone that number, who gave it to him, what was it used for?

"I can't believe this," Remo said. "You guys have come all this way to check some guy's expense account phone calls?"

"It's not exactly just a phone number. We have discovered that within the FBI and CIA there were whole units unaccounted for in their investigative work. Incomplete files on American citizens that seemed to lead nowhere and a loose tie-in to a computer system that the committee investigators could not locate," said one of the lawyers.

"That makes you pretty important, fella," the other lawyer told Remo.

"We've had our own experts check out leads into this system and they believe it is massive. Massive," said the first lawyer.

"That makes you very, very important," said the second lawyer.

"So do yourself a favor, fella, and tell us why you were dialing that number, and maybe we can do you a favor."

Remo stopped perspiring. He had to leave soon. He had promised Chiun he would be back quickly.

"Like what?" he said. "Not charging me with felonious dialing? Conspiracy to make a phone call? Aiding and abetting the Bell System?"

"How about material witness in a murder, fella? How about material witness, if not suspect, in the murder of a United States congressman investigating coverup operations? How does that thrill ya, fella?"

"Because I tried to make a phone call, I'm a murder suspect?"

"Because you tried to reach that phone number, fella. Now we know that number appeared on an FBI voucher no one seems to know about. We know that in the last three months of the investigation, only one person has called that number. You. We know there was a congressman looking into that computer network and intelligence money hidden in federal budgets. And we know that he's dead now with his heart ripped out of his body. It's not just any phone number anymore, fella."

"It's a gazelle?" asked Remo innocently.

27

"You know we can hold you as a material witness," said the second lawyer.

"Feel free," said Remo, and he gave the cover name and address, which was proper procedure for arrest. When this name and address was forwarded to FBI files to check for any previous arrests—a routine police function—the FBI clerk would find a forwarding number listed on it, and within twenty minutes the computers at Folcroft Sanitarium would spin out orders to another government agency to get Remo released officially from wherever he was being held in the United States.

The whole process, Smith had assured him, would take no more than two hours, possibly three if the jail were relatively inaccessible. The fingerprints, of course, would check with nothing in the vast FBI files. Not with a service record, a security clearance, or an arrest, because they had been permanently disposed of by the FBI itself more than a decade ago. They did not keep fingerprints of dead men.

So when Remo was told he had his last chance to shed some light on the telephone number he had dialed from the luncheonette in Nag's Head or the horror killing of the congressman who had been investigating covert government operations, Remo said they could throw away the key if they liked.

The cell was small with fresh gray painted iron bars set into the normal flat iron frame that locked by pushing a steel stud, click, into a receiver socket. It looked formidable if you did not understand it in the Sinanju way.

Remo sat down on the hard cot suspended from the wall and remembered the last cell he had been in more than a decade before.

He had been waiting for death then when a monk entered his cell to give him last rites and told him to swallow a pill at the end of the crucifix, right at the moment he was strapped into the electric chair. He did and passed out, and when he recovered there were burns on his arms and ankles, and the first people he'd found yet who believed he had not committed a murder were talking to him. They believed that because they had framed him, a neat plan by Harold W. Smith, director of CURE.

"Never heard of it," Remo had said and the lemony-faced Smith allowed that if Remo had heard of it, the country as they knew it would be finished. CURE had been set up because regular government agencies could not deal effectively with growing chaos within the constitution. CURE provided the extralegal help the country needed to survive. It lacked only one thing—a killer arm. Remo was it, the man who didn't exist for the organization that didn't exist. As one who had just been electrocuted, he was a nonperson. Dead men had no fingerprints.

At first Remo had thought he would just escape at the first opportunity. But one mission led to another, and then there was the training with Chiun, through which he really became someone else, and each day the person he had been before he was electrocuted died a little bit more. And he stayed on the job.

Now, more than a decade later, Remo Williams

waited in the southern jail cell for the computers at Folcroft Sanitarium, CURE's nerve center, to spin off their untraceable orders for his release. Two hours, three at the most.

So he waited. Two hours, three hours, four hours, as the water dripped into the sink and a lone fly made its erratic energized way up the cell block and down toward a fan that spun slowly enough to keep the air placid, hot, and steamy. Humidity droplets formed on the slick gray paint of the bars, and a drunk in the next cell with body odor pungent enough to rust aluminum began philosophizing about life.

"Enough," said Remo and joined two fingers of his left hand on top of the square metal lock. He felt the warm wetness of the slick paint against the skin grooves of his fingers. Beginning ever so lightly, for the rhythm of the pressure was the key to this move, he lowered the skin of the paint downwards, crushing the thin layer of rust underneath. More pressure and the frame strained at its hinges. The fly lit on a bar and popped off as if stung by electricity. A bolt of the bar frame lost a thread with a crack, and then the lock snapped with a dull snap like a piece of lead falling on a stack of mimeograph paper. Remo pushed the door open and it squealed off its bottom hinge.

"Sumbitch," yelled the drunk foggily. "They don't make 'em the way they used to. Can you open mine?"

And with two fingers pressing just on the lock, Remo released the second cell door. The drunk rolled his feet off the cot to the floor, and seeing he would have to take at least three steps to get out of his cell, decided to escape later. He thanked the generous stranger and passed out.

A guard poked his head into the corridor and, realizing what had happened, slammed the iron corridor door. He was bolting it when it slammed right back at him as if a jet plane were coming through it. Remo walked over him and down a long approach corridor until he found a door. It led to the police station. A detective looked up, startled.

"I didn't like the accommodations," said Remo and was off, down another corridor before the detective could get his gun out. He slowed to a casual walk, asked an officer filling out a form where the exit was, and was out of the building by the time someone shouted: "Prisoner escaped."

Nag's Head was not the sort of town in which one could get lost in a crowd, so Remo chose backyards and high palmettos, becoming one with the green and sandy landscape under the blood red sun of the late afternoon.

At the motel, Chiun was gazing at the Atlantic churning custard tops of foam as it came into the long white sandy beach, spread out flat, then slipped back into itself again, to come back in another green and white wave.

"We've got to run," said Remo.

"From whom?" Chiun asked, astonished.

"The local police. We've got to get back to Folcroft."

"Run from police? Does not Emperor Smith rule the police?"

"Not exactly. It's sort of complicated."

31

"What is he emperor of then?"

"The organization," Remo said.

"And the organization has no influence with the police?"

"Yes and no. Especially not now. I think he's in trouble."

"He reminds me of a Caliph of Samarkand who was so afraid to show weakness he would not even confide in his assassin, who was, of course, at that time a Master of Sinanju. When fortune turned against this Caliph, the Master was unable to help him. So too with Emperor Smith. We have done what we could do and we can help him no longer."

"He's in deep trouble."

"Because he did not confide in you," Chiun said, "and therefore it is not our responsibility. You have done everything you could for this silly man and now you must take your talents where they are properly honored. I have always thought that Sinanju was a waste for this man."

"As there are some things you cannot get me to understand, Little Father," Remo said, thoughtfully, "so too are there things that I cannot explain to you."

"That's because you are stupid, Remo. I am not stupid."

Remo looked at the large lacquered steamer trunks.

"We won't have time for those. We'll have to get them later."

"I am not leaving my meager possessions to go looking for an unworthy emperor who has not trusted the House of Sinanju."

32

"I'm sorry," Remo said. "I'll have to go myself."

"You would abandon a gentle aging man in the twilight of his golden years?"

"What twilight? What golden? What gentle?" asked Remo. "You're the deadliest assassin on earth."

"I provide honest service for honest proper tribute," said Chiun.

"Goodbye," said Remo. "See you later."

Chiun turned away.

Chapter Three

Undoubtedly there would be roadblocks and a statewide search for him, so Remo decided to use a passing tractor trailer until he was out of South Carolina.

He rode in between new Chromacolor televisions and automatic defrost refrigerators in the back of the trailer, black as a cave. He could not hear the driver in the motor cabin up front, and the driver had not heard him enter. Once out of the state there was little chance he would even be stopped. To a saddeningly large degree the only way fugitives got caught nowadays was if they told someone who they were and where they were, or if they were collared committing a major

34

felony, and their fingerprints were checked out properly with FBI files in Washington.

Once in North Carolina, there would be no worry.

Remo listened to the crates of appliances straining against their metal strappings. Something was wrong with the organization, terminally wrong, if it could not even get him out of a little jail cell.

That first frantic phone call over an open line to his motel room, that really had been Smitty's voice, and that was something Smitty never would do unless all his other channels had fouled up.

Maybe it was better anyway that the organization was coming apart. What had it done? Put a temporary crimp in a landslide that was taking the country with it anyhow? Maybe you couldn't change history. As Chiun had so often said: "Your greatest strength is knowing what you cannot do."

When the truck stopped and Remo heard two drivers get out talking about food, he slipped from the trailer and saw he was in the outskirts of a large city.

It was night and the offensive odor of greasy meat frying felt like it came from an aerosol can. He was near a large diner, and as he stopped a cab was just pulling out. The painted sign on the side of the taxi said, Raleigh, North Carolina.

"Airport," said Remo, and within twenty minutes he was at the small Raleigh-Durham airport and within an hour on a Piedmont Airlines flight to New York City, where he rented a car at

LaGuardia, and by three A.M. he was approaching the high stone walls of Folcroft Sanitarium in Rye, New York.

The one-way windows of Smith's office overlooking Long Island Sound seemed like dull yellow squares in the early morning blackness. The lights were on. No guard stopped him at the gate. The door to the main building was open. Remo skipped up a flight of darkened stairs and down a corridor to a large wooden door. Even in the darkness, he could see the staid gold lettering:

"Dr. Harold W. Smith, Director."

The door was unlocked. It led to a room of desks where Smith's secretaries worked during the day. Remo heard a familiar high-pitched voice come from Smith's inner office. It vowed eternal support in these times of trouble. It lauded Emperor Smith for his wisdom, courage, and generosity. It promised a bloodbath for his enemies.

It was Chiun.

"How'd you get here so fast?" asked Remo in Korean. Chiun's long fingernails stopped in the midst of an eloquent gesture. Smith sat behind the large, well-polished desk, his dry face precisely shaved. He wore a dark suit with vest and a fresh tie and a spotless white shirt.

Three A.M. The man was facing an obvious disaster and he looked as if he had only paused for a coffee break in a Wall Street office. He must have been the only baby ever to toilet train himself in the first week of life. Remo never remembered seeing Smith without a crease in his pants.

"It is of no importance how I got here. I must

extricate you from this idiot emperor and his disaster," Chiun answered in Korean.

"What about your trunks?"

"I have more invested in you. Ten arduous years without so much as a mite of repayment for the great gifts of knowledge I have bestowed upon you. I will not let you just run off with my investment."

"If I may interrupt," said Smith, "I think we have important business. I don't understand Korean."

"Neither does Remo, really," said Chiun in English. "But it is our thing to know things to serve you better."

"Thank you," said Smith. "Remo, I have what may be shocking news to you. We're not only just in trouble but I've had to—"

"Shut down most of the systems," Remo interrupted.

"Let him finish," scolded Chiun.

"Shut down most of the systems," said Smith.

"You see," said Chiun to Remo. "Now you know."

"We're virtually inoperative," Smith continued. "We could have survived those ignorant investigations of the CIA and FBI where we have linked systems that they don't know about. But after that gruesome insanity with the congressman, they started looking all over and they stumbled onto a few of our systems. I phoned you direct, hoping you wouldn't rely on one of our special phone numbers."

"I did."

"Lucky you didn't get picked up."

"I did," said Remo.

"Kill anyone?"

"Of course," said Chiun.

"No," said Remo.

"Good," said Smith.

"Of course not," said Chiun. "Peaceful as a monk. Awaiting only your word to slay your enemies."

"I'm afraid that just eliminating someone won't do here," Smith said. "It won't relieve the pressure on us. You've got to find out who or what did that killing of the congressman and then make it clear to the world. Have it or them confess or be convicted. That should take the pressure off this investigation."

"Are there any leads?"

"None," said Smith. "The congressman's heart was ripped out. And they didn't even find it."

"By hand?" asked Remo.

"Not exactly, as far as we could tell. It appeared like some very crude knife."

"No trace of the heart?"

"None."

"Sounds like some lover's quarrel," Remo said.

"Man didn't have a love life. He was married," Smith said, thinking of his own thirty-year marriage. "A normal happy marriage that just grinds on and on."

"Like the incessant dropping of water," said Chiun.

"Yes. Something like that," Smith said.

"I had one of those once," Chiun said, "but one day she slipped on a rock near the windy bay and drowned. So you see, patience makes all things turn out well."

"In any case," Smith said, "this congressman was clean. He didn't have any but political enemies. He was safely guarded, they thought. The man assigned to him by the Justice Department when this investigation started was outside his office door all night. He got suspicious at about five A.M., and when he checked, he found the congressman slumped over his desk. His shirt had been unbuttoned and the heart was out. Arteries and valves severed. Incredible amount of blood."

"Amateurs," said Chiun disdainfully. "The first sign is sloppiness."

"So you have to be careful," Smith said. "The FBI and the CIA are just as anxious as we are to get the right man. The only problem is that they think it may be us, some secret organization that they don't know anything about. If they suspect you're with our organization, they might just scoop you up."

"I'll be careful," Remo said.

"I'm going to start closing this place down for a while," Smith said. "The computers have been washed clean already, and most of the staff has been cut loose. In a few days there won't be a trace. Everything else is up to you."

"Okay," said Remo.

"More than okay," said Chiun. "We shall find this menace and destroy it."

"Not destroy," said Smith, clearing his throat. "Identify and have him publicly convicted. This is not an assassination."

"But of course," said Chiun. "Your wisdom is

39

beyond that of a simple assassin. You are truly an emperor, most formidable."

Outside in the cooler night with the salt wind coming in off the Long Island Sound, Chiun said in Korean to Remo:

"I have always said that Smith is a lunatic, and tonight he has proved it."

And this reminded him of a czar who, when he went insane, asked the court assassin to clean the stables. "That one wanted a stable cleaner, and this one wants I do not know what."

"He wants someone convicted," Remo said.

"Oh. A representative of justice, a speaker in the courts of law. A lawyer. I would rather clean stables."

"Not exactly," said Remo. "We've got to find out who and then get the evidence to some prosecutor."

"Oh, like soldiers, policemen, and detectives do?" asked Chiun.

"Sort of."

"I see," said Chiun. "We are looking for some one or something, but we are not exactly sure what or who, and we are not exactly sure what we are supposed to do to this someone or something, but we do know that if we don't succeed in what we do not know, Emperor Smith will suffer."

"I know what I'm doing," Remo said. "Don't worry."

"Worry?" said the latest Master of Sinanju. "One would have to stop laughing to worry. You whites are so funny."

Chapter Four

Mrs. Ramona Harvey Delpheen was examining a chart of bicentennial celebrations when a long yellow feather fell over a blue outlined box called "Columbus Circle Monument Parade." She looked up.

Mrs. Delpheen was a portly woman whose flesh had been pampered by expensive oils and skilled fingers so that when she smiled it looked as if delicate creases had jumped from hiding. She smiled intensely because she was surprised by these men and also they looked rather funny.

"What are you fellows doing in all those feathers?" she said, laughing. She thought she recognized one, a rather untalented lad who somehow had gotten control of a publishing company.

Met him at a party or somewhere. The other men were strangers, and she was not quite sure why the butler had let them through the main door of her Fifth Avenue residence without announcing them first. There was so much trouble nowadays on the New York City streets outside that one should never allow strangers access to the house proper. She was sure that she had made this very clear to the butler.

"We already have a group of Indians for the Columbus Circle affair," said Mrs. Delpheen. "Besides, it's an Italian-American day," she added.

The men said nothing. The long robes of yellow feathers hung down to their knees and were open in front, revealing bare chests and white loin cloths.

"I said we already have a very fine band of Mohawk dancers. Those aren't even American Indian trappings you're wearing. More South American, if you will. Aztec."

"Not Aztec," said the farthest man, who held what appeared to be a phallic symbol made of a light colored chipped stone. The other four men stood at the sides like a formation of twos.

"Well, we can't use Mayas either," she said.

"Not Maya."

"You don't look like Indians anyway," said Mrs. Delpheen, forcing the smile now. She fingered a pearl at the end of a strand that hung looping over her ample breasts enclosed in basic black. The pearls became sweat-slippery in her hands.

"We are all of Indian blood," said the man with the pointed stone.

42

"That's lovely," said Mrs. Delpheen. "I think the beauty of America is that so many groups have made such significant contributions. But you see, the . . . uh . . . Incas weren't one of them."

"Not Inca. Actatl."

"I've never heard of them."

"Because you would not allow us to live. Not in our real skins. So we chose your skins and your hair and your eyes, but we are all Actatl. All we wished for was to live. But you would not let us. Not in our real skins. Now you have violated what we hold precious and worthy, the stone of our ancestors, the life force of our hearts, the most gracious and central inspiration of our being. So holy that you may only know it as Uc-tut."

"Well, I'm certainly sorry for anything I have done. I'm sure we can make amends."

"You shall."

Two of the men in feathered capes latched onto Mrs. Delpheen's wrists, and she said there was no need to be physical. But when the other two reached for her ankles, she had another idea.

"All right, if it's kinky rape you want, I can't stop you. But at least let's go into the bedroom."

They hoisted her bulky frame to the desk top, and the man with the pointed stone chanted a monotone song in a language and tune she did not recognize. She tried twisting an arm from a locking grip, but it only was gripped even more firmly. She tried kicking, but she couldn't get a leg back far enough for a good forward thrust. She smelled the sharp odor of fear and excitement, like urine mixed with a stale perfume. The man holding her right wrist had pupil-wide eyes, just like her first husband had had at orgasm. Sweat made his yellowish forehead glisten in the gentle light from the crystal cut chandelier overhead. A small stone replica of an Egyptian pyramid she had used for a paperweight cut painfully into her right hip, but she could not get her body shifted to avoid it. The two men at her ankles joined their free hands, pinning her belly also.

Looking up at the chandelier, she had a strange thought. It had not been dusted for a long while, and that was all she could think of. The chandelier had not been dusted, and probably the one in the main hall was the same.

Both of the men holding at her hands simultaneously reached to her neck and with a single rip tore down the top of her basic black dress. They also unleashed the pearls which clicked across the desk top and fell chattering to the wood parquet floor. Then one unsnapped her bra.

"Talk about kinky," said Mrs. Delpheen. "Do you fellows need feathers to get it up?"

The man with the phallic symbol of stone raised it above her head, and to Mrs. Delpheen, her dress half-off down to her waist, the downward thrust of the stone seemed very slow until it rammed into her chest. Not cut, rammed. Like someone had hit her chest with a ball peen hammer that kept going inside, and then she saw very clearly the stone move slowly toward her navel, and it felt like pulleys were ripping her insides out, taking her shoulders into her body, and then she screamed—a wail stifled by a lack of air com-

44

ing into her. She saw a big grin on the face of the fifth man, pulling the stone around her chest.

"More," he said. "Scream more."

And then the chandeliers didn't matter any more because they were now away, going far away down a long tunnel that became gray, then black, and quickly nothing to worry about any more.

The man with the stone knife saw the fat face become flat and almost waxy, and he knew there would be no more screams of honor to Uctut. He worked quickly, severing the last arteries, and then with a rip he tore the heart out of the body cavity and held it aloft, still pumping bloodily in his hands. There was no need for the two at the arms to hold on any longer, and they reached behind them under their robes where leather thongs held clay bowls.

Each unsnapped his bowl and waited while the heart pumped violently and then with a small flutter stopped. The man with the stone knife delicately placed the mass of bloody muscle into one upturned bowl. The second bowl went on top with a neat interlocking click.

The men at the ankles turned the lifeless hulk over so that the open chest cavity faced downward over the desk. And the man who had cut out the heart left a typewritten note with its corners carefully smeared with Mrs. Delpheen's blood.

Remo heard about the killing in New York City just as he and Chiun entered Dulles Airport outside Washington. They had gone there, Remo had said, to examine "the scene of the crime" where the congressman had been killed.

"What crime?" Chiun had asked. "Smith said nothing of robbery or deceit, or worse, not paying a worker for his just efforts."

"The killing," Remo had said. "That's what crime."

"Was it not paid for?" Chiun asked.

"The killing was the crime," Remo had said.

"Then every leader of every country is a criminal. No, this is impossible. Emperors cannot be criminals because they make the laws. Those who defy emperors are criminals."

"It's against the law in this country to kill someone," Remo had said.

Chiun had thought a moment, then shook his head.

"Impossible. That would make us criminals, and we most certainly are not. A criminal is someone without our strong standards."

"It's complicated," Remo said. "Take my word for it. It's complicated."

"I do not need your word for it," Chiun had said, and he told a banker from Des Moines, sitting across the aisle from them, that the American way of life was incredibly inscrutable, but if it worked to America's satisfaction, Chiun was not one to complain.

That had been in the plane. Now in the airport Remo heard a pocket radio news report and caught the last words about the second such killing. The afternoon *Washington Star* had a small story:

New York (API)—A rich widow was discovered slain in her fashionable home here today in a manner similar to that of the congressman investigating legal abuses by the FBI and CIA. The woman, Mrs. Ramona H. Delpheen, 51, was found by her butler, slumped over her desk, her heart ripped from her body.

Remo paid for the newspaper but returned it to its stack.

"Well," said Chiun, "I await your brilliant plan to go looking for someone, you do not know who, to do something to him, you do not know what, in a place where he may or may not be, but was once."

"I've changed my mind," Remo said, somewhat embarrassed.

"How can you change what you have yet to show?" Chiun asked.

"We're going to New York."

"I like New York," said Chiun. "It has some restaurants that aren't foreign. Of course, the Korean restaurants are not the best, but very good considering how far they are from civilization."

The shuttle flight to New York took less than an hour, the cab ride from the airport twice that.

Chiun made a small comment that they had gone to four cities so far, and perhaps they might try Tacoma. He had not discovered Tacoma, Washington, yet. Remo said Chiun could go back and watch his trunks if he wished. Chiun said there was nothing worth more than seeing what Remo planned to do next. Perhaps he would like to clean a stable.

47

A uniformed patrolman stood in front of the Delpheen mansion. Remo walked by him with authority. Chiun stopped to chat. He asked the patrolman what he was doing there. The patrolman said there had been a murder committed there the night before. Chiun asked why the patrolman hadn't been there the night before instead.

He did not wait for an answer. The door opened for Remo. A gaunt man in a white jacket and dark pants refused Remo entrance. Chiun muttered in Korean how foolish it was to use doors that were closed to you when the windows in the upper floors were of such easy access and were always open to you. But, he added, the people who used windows usually knew what they were looking for.

"The family is not receiving visitors," said the butler.

"I'm not exactly a visitor," said Remo, sidestepping past the butler. As the butler turned to stop Remo, Chiun went by the other side.

"Where'd the killing take place?" Remo asked.

"I must ask you to leave," the butler said.

"We'll be going in a minute. Relax," Remo said.

"Miss Delpheen is in a deep state of shock, over grief for her mother. You must leave."

A young woman, her gray blue eyes staring dumbly into a far-off nowhere, padded into the main hall. She wore white shorts and a white blouse, and her small anklet sneakers moved sluggishly. A tennis racket hung limply from her right hand. She had sandy yellow hair and her skin was gently golden from much sun.

"I can't believe it," she said softly. "I can't believe it."

"I'm sorry to hear about your mother," Remo said. "She was your mother, wasn't she?"

"Who?" said the girl, pausing under a large chandelier that looked like an upside-down bush of glass.

"The tragedy. The woman who was killed."

"Oh. Mother. Yes. She's dead. I can't believe it."

"I've come to help," Remo said.

"I can't believe it," the girl repeated. "Six-four, six-two, six-love. And I double faulted four times. I never double fault. Once, maybe, if I'm on the verge of death."

"Tennis?" said Remo. "You're worried about a tennis loss?"

"Loss? It was a fucking massacre. I'm Bobbi Delpheen. What can I do for you?"

"I think you're involved in something far more sinister than you realize. I've come about your mother's death. I've come to help you."

"Mother's taken care of. She's at the morgue. Funeral's been taken care of too. Six-four, six-two, six-love. And I double faulted four times. Four times. Can you believe it?"

"Miss Delpheen," said Remo somberly. "Your mother's been murdered. I don't think the police can help, but I can."

"With what?" she said. She had a perky charm and a sweet face, as though she'd been designed by a cartoonist for a toothpaste company. Cute, thought Remo. White, thought Chiun.

"With your mother's tragedy," Remo said.

49

"Her problems are over. I've got my own. Leave me alone. Four double faults." She shook her head and turned away but Chiun spoke up.

"I can teach you to never twice error," he said, looking disdainfully at Remo. For, as he had often said, "To tell the truth to a fool is to be more the fool yourself."

"Double fault," corrected Bobbi Delpheen.

"Yes, that," said Chiun.

"You don't even know how to say it," she said.

"I did not say I would teach you to talk the game, but to play the game. All games of physical skill are the same."

"Tennis isn't like any other game."

"It is like all games. The winners are those who do not let their ignorance defeat them."

"I've been through twenty-eight professional instructors. I don't need some gook philosophy," said Bobbi.

"That instrument hits something, yes," said Chiun, motioning to her steel-framed racket.

"Get these two out of here," said Bobbi Delpheen to the butler.

Chiun's long fingers flickered in the shimmering light of the chandelier. The racket was out of Bobbi's hands and in his, leaving her groping at air. With no more than a gentle slow wrist action, Chiun waved the racket, and then gliding upward in a small leap, knocked crystal pieces from the chandelier above, like harvesting shiny berries from a tree. He was on the floor before the shiny glass pieces reached his open hand. Then, one by one, with a stinging whip of the racket, he hit each crystal down the long hall into the back of a

50

chair. Seven crystals made a single hole the diameter of an espresso cup in the back of a brocaded chair. A tuft of white down sprouted from the small hole.

"I notice you didn't shift weight, didn't drive into the shot," said Bobbi.

"I've come to help," said Remo.

"Shut up," said Bobbi.

"I'll remove them now," said the butler.

"Shut up," said Bobbi.

"Forget the nonsense you have learned," said Chiun. "Your feet do not hit. This instrument hits. I will teach you all, but first you must help me."

"Name it."

"Do as my pupil asks," said Chiun.

"What does he want?" Bobbi asked.

"I could not explain," Chiun said, "for I do not think he knows."

The first place Remo examined was Mrs. Delpheen's study. Chiun watched Remo. Bobbi slumped in a chair, drumming her fingers, bored.

"This is where your mother was killed then?" Remo asked.

"Yes, yes," said Bobbi and blew some air from her puffing cheeks. "The cops say nothing should be touched for a while."

The blood on the desk and floor had dried. And Remo noticed a clot covering a small pointed-up object. He lifted it up, breaking the brownish film around it. A pyramid paperweight. And an outline of its base had been pressed into the hard wood desk. Perhaps someone had leaned on it or had been held down on it. He noticed a bright yellow quill in an inkwell behind the desk. The room was sedate in brown polished wood, dark frames, and dark upholstery, yet the feather of this quill was bright yellow. He lifted it and saw it had no point.

"Was this feather here before your mother was killed?" Remo asked.

"I don't know. This was her study. I never went in," said Bobbi. She made a tennis stroking motion with her right arm, looking at Chiun.

"Later," he said.

"I want to talk to the police and see the body," Remo said.

A homicide lieutenant met the grieving daughter, Bobbi Delpheen, and her two friends at the city morgue, which looked like a gigantic white hospital room with large stainless steel files along one side.

"Look," said the homicide lieutenant, a cigar pegged in the center of his teeth, unlit and oozy. "I'm going out of my way for you people. But I need some cooperation, too. Now, miss, I hope you're sufficiently recovered to answer some of my questions."

Bobbi looked to Remo, who nodded.

"We don't think this was personally motivated, Miss Delpheen, but could you think of anyone who had any ill feeling toward your mother? Who just might want to kill her?" asked the lieutenant.

"Anyone who knew her intimately," said Bobbi. She made another tennis motion with her right hand. Chiun signaled—"later."

"Would that include you?" asked the detective.

"No. I say anyone who knew her intimately.

That would leave me out, and Mother's five husbands, too."

"She was a cold person then?"

"Only to relatives. To everyone else she was hostile and haughty."

"Was your mother engaged in any special activities that you know of?"

"Pick any six. She was a joiner. She was on more committees than that congressman who got it."

"We've already found one that overlapped," said the detective. "They were both on the monuments committee at the museum. Does that mean anything to you?"

"No," said Bobbi, and Chiun had to signal her again that tennis would be later.

"Do you think you're strong enough to view the remains? We're going to have an autopsy tomorrow."

"I thought her heart was ripped out," said Bobbi. "Who needs an autopsy? That probably killed her."

"It was a homicide. This is routine."

The lieutenant pulled back a stainless steel square that looked like a file. It was a morgue slab. A white sheet, dotted with drops of brown, covered a series of rises like miniature Wyoming foothills.

"Brace yourselves," said the lieutenant, then he pulled back the sheet. Mrs. Delpheen's face was a frozen, waxy twist of flesh. The mouth was locked open, but the wrinkles, well hidden in life, now streaked down her face, obvious. Her aging breasts hung like melted marshmallows in loose cello-

53

phane sacks. And where the middle of her chest had been was now a dark coagulated hole.

"We believe some sort of dull knife and forceps were used," said the detective. "That's what careful scientific analysis told us about the congressman. And the FBI spared no avenue of investigation. Even brought in heart specialists and surgeons."

"What are forceps?" asked Chiun softly.

"They're things you grab with, like pliers," said the detective. Chiun shook his head precisely once. The wisp of beard created a floating wave within itself, then quieted.

"No," said Chiun. "They are wrong. This wound was made by a stone knife."

"How the hell can you tell that?" said the detective disbelievingly.

"Because I look," said Chiun. "If you look, you will see no long tear of murder, which is what happens when the body is torn apart in anger. No. There are small horizontal tears across the arteries, and these are made by a stone knife. Have you ever made a stone knife?"

The detective allowed as he had not.

"A stone knife," said Chiun, "is made by chipping to sharp edges, not grinding straight like metal. And these sorts of knives are sharp at some points and not sharp at others. They are used more like saws after they go into something. Do you see?"

"No kidding?" said the detective. A cold ash fell from his unlit cigar into the chest cavity as he peered into the body. "Sorry," he said. The detective puzzled a moment.

54

"Maybe you can help us with something else," he said. From the left breast pocket in his shiny seersucker jacket he took a photocopy sheet rolled up like a scroll.

It was about eight inches wide but twenty-four inches long and had twelve dark sections of writing when it was unrolled.

"What's this?" asked the detective, handing the sheet to Chiun. "We made it from an original found under the head of the body."

Chiun looked at the long sheet carefully. He examined the edges. He felt the surface of the paper, then nodded wisely.

"This is a copy of a document produced by an American machine that makes such copies."

"Yeah, we know it's a photocopy, but what does the note mean?"

"It is in twelve different languages," said Chiun. "And one of them I do not understand, nor have I seen. The Chinese I know, the French and Arabic I know, the Hebrew and Russian I know. Here it is again, in real language. In Korean. The Sanskrit and Aramaic I know. The Swahili and the Urdu and Spanish I know. But the first language I do not know."

"We think it's a ritual murder and the note is part of the ritual. Death for kicks sort of thing," said the detective. Remo glanced over Chiun's shoulders at the note.

"What do you think, Remo?" asked Chiun.

"Is he an expert?" asked the detective.

"He is learning," said Chiun.

"I don't know," said Remo, "but I'd guess all those languages say the same thing."

Chiun nodded.

"But what is this symbol here?" Remo pointed to a rough rectangular drawing in the middle of the text of the unknown language.

"In the other languages on this paper, it is called an Uctut," said Chiun.

"What is an Uctut?" asked Remo.

"I do not know. What is a Joey 172?" Chiun asked.

"I don't know. Why?" said Remo.

"Because that is in the note, too," Chiun said.

"So what does it all mean?" asked the detective. "We've had trouble making heads or tails out of it."

Chiun raised his delicate hands and signaled ignorance.

Outside, in the muggy, grimy New York City streets, with traffic jammed to a horn-blaring standstill, Chiun explained.

"It was a note of demand for reparations," he said. "It was not clear because it was written in the lofty language of a religion. But whoever wrote it demands that a 'Joey 172' be punished for some sort of offense to an Uctut. And until this country punishes this Joey 172, then the servants of Uctut will continue to ease his pain with blood."

"I still don't understand," said Remo.

"Your country gives up Joey 172, whatever that is, or more will die," said Chiun.

"Who gives a shit?" asked Bobbi.

"I do," said Remo.

"This bright, beautiful, and charming young woman makes much sense," said Chiun.

"If you care, then do your thing," Bobbi said to Remo. "Find Joey 172."

"She makes sense," Chiun said, "when she is not talking stupid. Like now."

Remo smiled. "I think I know how to find Joey 172. Have you ever ridden on a New York City subway?"

"No," said Chiun, and he was not about to.

Chapter Five

Antwan Pedaster Jackson felt he had an obliga-
tion to bring wisdom to whites. For example, the
old woman with the frayed brown shopping bag
riding on the rear of the "D" train after seven
P.M. Didn't she know that whites weren't supposed to ride the subways after that hour? She
sure enough seemed to realize it now as he
moseyed into the empty car with Sugar Baby
Williams, both seniors at Martin Luther King
High School, where Sugar Baby was going to
graduate as valedictorian because he could read
faster than anyone else and without moving his
lips either, except on the hard words. But even
the teacher couldn't read the hard words at Martin Luther King.

"You know where you is?" asked Antwan.

The old woman, her face lined with years of toil, looked up from her rosary, fingering a Hail Mary. A faded yellow and red babushka cradled her heartlike face. She moved the paper shopping bag tighter between her knees.

"I am sorry I do not speak the English well," she said.

"This the Noo Yawk subway," said Sugar Baby, the valedictorian.

"This aftah the rush hour, honkey," said Antwan.

"You not s'posed to be being hyeah," said Sugar Baby.

"I am sorr,   'o not speak English well," said the woman

"Wha you got in that there bag?" said Sugar Baby.

"Old clothes which I mend," said the woman.

"You got bread?" asked Antwan. To her look of confusion, he explained: "Money?"

"I am a poor woman. I have just coins for my supper."

To this, Antwan took great umbrage and brought a flat smacking black hand across the woman's white face.

"Ah don't like liars. Ain't nobody tell you lying a sin?" asked Antwan.

"It shameful," said Sugar Baby and smacked her in the other direction.

"No. No. No. Do not hit," cried the woman as she tried to cover her head.

"Get yo' hand down," demanded Antwan, and he banged her a shot in the head. Then he tried his latest karate chop on her right shoulder, but a fist proved better. It knocked the babushka off and sent blood trickling from her right earlobe. Sugar Baby hoisted the old woman to her feet and rammed her head against the window behind the train seat while Antwan rummaged through her pockets. They got $1.17, so Sugar Baby hit her again for being so cheap.

They got off at the next stop, commenting on how they had made the subways once again free of whites after nightfall. It did not occur to them that they had also helped make the subway system of New York City equally free of blacks and Puerto Ricans after that hour. They watched the empty train roll by, headed for Mosholu Parkway, the last station on the D train with the next stop the open yards.

There was not much to do with $1.17, but they went upstairs to the street anyway. It was a white neighborhood, which meant the racist storeowners didn't have everything locked up or hidden away out of reach, as in the black neighborhoods. Antwan and Sugar Baby, free of this racist store-owner mentality, enjoyed themselves like free men in these stores and markets where goods were displayed openly for people to handle, inspect, and then decide upon purchasing. At the end of this small sojourn off the Grand Concourse, they had three cans of aerosol spray paint, three bottles of Coke, four Twinkies, eight candy bars, a nudie magazine, and a bar of Cashmere Bouquet soap. And they still had their $1.17 left.

"Wha you rip that soap off for?" demanded Sugar Baby.

"Maybe we can sell it," said Antwan.

"That stupid," said Sugar Baby. "Who gonna buy a bar of soap around our neighborhood?"

"We could use it, maybe?" said Antwan thoughtfully. He had seen a television show once where a woman ran water over soap and then rubbed the resulting foam onto her face.

"Wha fo?"

"With water and s⁞ ff," said Antwan.

"You dumb. That Uncle Tom stuff. You Uncle Tom," said Sugar Baby.

"Ah ain' no Tom," said Antwan. "Don' you call me no Tom."

"Then wah yo' doin' with soap?"

"Ah thought it was a candy bar, is all."

"Well, get rid of it."

Antwan threw it through the ground floor window of an apartment building and then they both ran, laughing. They had to run because, as everyone knew, racist cops would bust you for no reason at all.

There was a reason for the spray paint. Sugar Baby was one of the better artists at Martin Luther King. He had painted the ceiling of the gymnasium by hanging suspended by ropes one night with Antwan holding a flashlight from the floor below. And there it was for the big game against DeWitt Clinton. A masterpiece laid on a $30,000 acoustical ceiling. In red and green spray paint: SUGAR BABY.

"Beautiful," Antwan had said.

"Oh, no," the principal had said.

"Ah'm king lord over all de planet," Sugar Baby had said then, and now, running down a side street in the Bronx, he was going to do his masterwork. Instead of painting "Sugar Baby" on a ceiling or just one car of a subway train, he was going to invade the yards and put an entire train to his spray paint—if the cans lasted.

The yard stretched beside an elevated track, and in the darkness he could tell he would have his pick. He needed the right train, one which was without other's works, but it seemed impossible to find one free of "Chico," "RAM I," "WW," and "Joey 172."

Sugar Baby finally made the hard decision. He would paint over. To make the cans last, he decided to omit the usual border and substitute one long thin line in script. He was good at handwriting, making the best B's in the school, and a guidance counselor had told him his handwriting was good enough to make him the president of a college or at least of a corporation.

He was on the first loop of the S, a bright fluorescent green crescent, when a face popped out from between two cars. It was a white face. It was a man. Sugar Baby and Antwan started to run. Then they saw the man was alone. And he wasn't that big. Thin, in fact.

"Hi," said Remo.

"Who you, mother?" said Antwan.

"I'm looking for somebody," said Remo, and he hopped down off the car onto the cinders of the yard.

Neither Antwan nor Sugar Baby noticed that

this man landed on the crunchy cinders with the silence of a balloon touching felt.

"You looking for a bruisin'," said Sugar Baby.

"You grin, you in, mother," said Antwan.

"I really don't have time to rap," said Remo, "and I don't think coaxing will work."

Antwan and Sugar Baby giggled. They spread apart so Antwan could come at the front and Sugar Baby at the back. The white man stood quietly. Sugar Baby tried his karate chop. The hand came down perfect on the white man's head. He imagined himself splitting a brick. He imagined the head opening. He imagined how he would tell how he killed a honkey with one blow. His imaginings were interrupted by a decided pain in his right wrist. The skin was there but the fingers would not move, as if the hand were connected to the forearm by a bag of jelly. Sugar Baby dropped the spray paint. Antwan saw this and put his feet to action, heading out of the yards. He got four steps. On the fifth, his hip failed to cooperate. He went skin-splitting burning across the gravel, crying for his mother, professing innocence, vowing cooperation, and generally expressing fond feelings for the world and a desire to live in peace with all mankind.

"Who is Joey 172?" Remo asked.

"Ah don' know, man. Hey, ah square wif you, baby. Ah love you, baby," moaned Antwan.

"Try again," said Remo.

And Antwan felt a sharp stabbing pain in his neck but he saw no knife in the white man's hands.

"Don' know, man. Ah knows a Chico and a Ramad 85. They south city men."

"Joey 172, ever hear of him?"

"No, man. He nothing."

"Then you know him?"

"Ah say he nothing. Hey, Sugar Baby, tell mah man hyeah whuffo Joey 172."

"He nuffin'," said Sugar Baby, holding his painful right arm as vertical as possible. If he held it straight down and breathed very gently he could make the wrist pain almost bearable, if the elbow were cradled just right. When Sugar Baby said "nuffin'," he said it very softly.

"Where's he from?" Remo asked.

"Nowhere, man. He's nothing."

"Try," said Remo.

"Ah'm tryn, man. He ain' big enough to be from somewheres."

"Where's nowhere?" asked Remo.

"Lotsa places nowhere, man. You dumb or something?" said Sugar Baby.

"Name some," said Remo and gave Sugar Baby's dangling right arm a gentle touch.

Sugar Baby screamed. He suddenly remembered someone saying once that Joey 172 was from the Stuyvesant High School.

"All right, we'll all go there," said Remo.

"Bronx High School of Science," Sugar Baby corrected quickly. "He one of them Toms. Bronx High School of Science. Ah seen a Joey 172 there. They say that where he from."

"Are you sure?" asked Remo.

And even in the next great pain, Sugar Baby allowed as how nobody could be sure, and Antwan too allowed as how it was probably Bronx High School of Science. Now, if the man wanted Chico, they could get him Chico for sure. Everybody knew Chico. For Chico they could give him the address.

"Thank you," said Remo.

As an afterthought he took the can of green glow spray paint and, ripping off their shirts, made a neat artistic "Remo" on each of their chests.

"I'm an artist myself," said Remo and went whistling off to find the Bronx High School of Science building, which as it turned out was nearby. On all the walls, there was no Joey 172. It was a big city and finding one graffiti artist in a plague of them was like singling out a locust in a swarm. And then he had an idea. He bought a can of white spray paint from a hardware store open late and convinced a cab driver to take him to Harlem. This required a fist full of twenty-dollar bills and a gentle stroking of the cab driver's neck. When Remo told the driver to let him off in front of an empty lot, the driver tried to nod but his neck hurt too much.

Remo skipped into the lot from the silent street. If night crime had thinned the street population of the rest of New York City, it had made Harlem into a desperately quiet enclave of citizens bunkered precariously for the night. Almost nothing moved except occasional packs of youngsters or convoys of grownups.

Stores were shuttered with metal shields, occasionally working streetlights illuminated empty littered sidewalks, a rat scurried soundlessly along a wall. And it was the wall Remo wanted.

Even in the dim half-light, he could make out the strong lines of powerful colors blending into a mosaic of fine black faces, set like a monument of a new generation against the decaying brick of a preceding one. It was a "wall of respect," and it hurt Remo a bit to deface it.

With the white paint, he sprayed a neat and glaring "Joey 172" across the wall and then faded back across the street to wait. The first person to spot the desecration of the wall that was, by custom and mutual consent, not to be touched was a youngster with a key around his neck. He stopped as if hit in the stomach with a pail of water. Remo lounged on a stoop. The gray dawn was succumbing to light. The youngster ran off. Remo smelled the ripe aroma of day-old greasy ribs, combined with week-old oranges and rotting chicken bones.

The street lights went off. The youngster came back with three others. By the time the sun was high, Remo had what he wanted. A large crowd formed in front of the wall spilling out into the street. Young men in gang jackets, older ones in rainbows of reds and yellows and platform shoes, a few winos careening precariously in place, a fat woman with layers of clothes like tenting over haystacks.

And down the street, his arms pinned by two burly men with raging Afroes, was a young man, his eyeglasses askew, his eyes wide with terror, his sneakers kicking helplessly in the air.

66

"That him," yelled a woman. "That Joey 172."

"Burn the mother," yelled a man.

"Cut him," shrieked a kid. "Cut him. Cut him good."

Remo eased himself from the stoop and cut into the mob, some of whom had been loudly discussing what to do about the white man across the street.

He wedged himself toward the opening where the two burly men were slapping the youngster into place. Remo cleared a small area in front of him quickly. To the crowd it looked like hands floating and bodies falling. The front of the crowd, after making some useless swings with knives and knuckles, tried to retreat from Remo. The back pushed forward and the front pushed back. Swinging started in the center of the crowd. Remo yelled for quiet. He wasn't heard.

"I don't suppose," he said, in a voice smothered to insignificance, like a pebble rolling uphill against an avalanche, "that you would consider this graffiti an expression of culture and ethnic pride?"

Not getting a response, he dropped the young man's handlers with two backhands flat to the side of the skull, just compressing the blood flow momentarily. Each dropped like a ripe plum. Remo grabbed the boy and cut his way through a wing of the crowd. Two blocks away, he avoided a police column that was waiting for the mob to fight out its energy before moving in.

"Hey, man, thanks," said the youngster.

"You're not going anywhere, kid," said Remo,

stopping the lad by cementing the boy's wrist to his palm. They were in a deserted alley now with crumbled bricks rising toward the end like refuse from a bombing raid.

"Are you the painter of the Joey 172's?" Remo asked.

"No, man, I swear it," said the boy. He was about twelve years old, a foot shorter than Remo. His Captain Kangaroo tee shirt was torn off his left side revealing a skinny chest and bony shoulders.

"All right," said Remo. "I'll take you back to the mob, then."

"I did it," said the boy.

"Now we're talking."

"But I didn't mess up no wall of respect, man."

"I know," said Remo. "I did it for you."

"You mother," said the boy. "What'd you do that for?"

"So that I could enlist the aid and resources of the community in meeting you."

"You ain't much with a spray can, man. You got a weak hand. A real weak hand."

"I never defaced anything before," said Remo.

"Why should I help you?" asked the boy logically.

"Because on one hand I'm going to give you two hundred dollars cash if you do, and on the other, I'm going to puncture your ear drums if you don't," said Remo, just as logically.

"You make a sweet offer. Where's the money?"

Remo took a wad of bills from his pocket and counted out exactly two hundred dollars.

"I'll be back in a minute," said the boy. "I just want to see if this money's real. Can't be too careful nowadays."

Remo took a flat hand and, pushing it up against the boy's spinal column like a concentrated jet of force, catapulted the boy into the air so the floppy sneakers paused momentarily above Remo's head.

"Eeeow," yelled the boy and felt himself turn over and head for the rubble below him, skull first, until he was caught like a parachute harness an eyelash away from ground collision and righted.

"Money's good," he said. "What can I do for you, friend?"

"I've got a problem," said Remo. "I'm looking for some people who are mad about something."

"I feel for those mothers, man," said the boy honestly.

"These people are mad over something you wrote 'Joey 172' on. Like the mob back there at the 'wall of respect.'"

"That's a mean group back there."

"This group is meaner," said Remo.

"Here's your money back, man," said the boy wisely.

"Wait. If I don't get them, sooner or later they're gonna get you."

"You're not gonna hand me over to them?"

"No," said Remo.

"Why not?" asked the boy. He cocked his head.

"Because they have pretty stiff penalties for defacing property."

69

"Like what?"

"Like they cut your heart out."

The boy whistled. "They the ones that offed the politician and the rich lady?"

Remo nodded.

The boy whistled again.

"I've got to know what you defaced."

"Improved," said the boy.

"All right, improved."

"Let's see. Bathrooms at school."

Remo shook his head.

"Two cars on an A train."

"I don't think so," said Remo.

"A bridge."

"Where?"

"Near Tremont Avenue. That's real uptown," said the boy.

"Any church or religious monument nearby?"

The boy shook his head.

"Did you do it on a painting or something?"

"I don't mess over someone else's work," said the boy. "Just things. Not works. Rocks and stuff."

"Any rocks?"

"Sure. I practice on rocks."

"Where?" asked Remo.

"Central Park once. Prospect Park a lot. Rocks are nothing, man."

"Any place else?"

"A museum. I did one on the big museum off Central Park. With the guy on the horse out front."

"What did the rock look like?" asked Remo.

"Big. Square like. With some circles and birds on it and stuff. A real old rock. The birds were shitty like some real little kid carved them."

"Thanks," said Remo.

Chapter Six

Off Central Park Remo found the Museum of Natural History, a massive stone building with wide steps and a bronze statue of Teddy Roosevelt on a horse, facing fearlessly the onslaught of the wilds, namely Fifth Avenue on the other side of the park. The bronze Roosevelt presided over two bronze Indians standing at his side, equally fearless in their unchanging stare across the park.

Remo made a contribution at the entrance and asked for the exhibit of stones. The clerk, drowsy from the mind-smothering passing out of buttons, which labeled the donor as one of those keenly aware of the importance of nature and of the Museum of Natural History, said the museum had a lot of stones. Which one did he want?

"A big one," said Remo. "One that has some graffiti on it."

"We don't feature graffiti, sir," said the clerk.

"Well, do you have any stones? Large ones?" asked Remo. He felt heat rising in his body, not because the afternoon was muggy but because if the organization was still operating, they could probably have had this whole thing worked out in an afternoon and just given him the name of whoever or whatever he was supposed to connect with, and that would be that. Now he was looking for rocks in a museum. If he were right, he would have this whole little mess wrapped up in a day. Give him the sacred rock and the killers would have to come to him.

"We don't just collect rocks, sir," said the clerk.

"This is a special rock. It's got engraving on it."

"Oh. You mean the South American artifacts. That's the ground floor. Turn right."

Remo wandered past a stuffed bear, an imitation jungle, two dried musk oxen, and a stuffed yak eating a plastic peony into a dark room with large stones. All were intricately carved. Massive heads with flattened noses and almond eyes. Curving serpents weaving among stilted birds. Rock remnants of peoples who had disappeared in the western onslaught. But as Chiun had said, "The sword does not destroy a people; only a better life does. Swords kill. They do not change."

But on South American cultures Chiun had never shed any light, and Remo was sure it was because those cultures had been cut off from the rest of the world until the coming of the Euro-

73

peans in 1500. Which meant to Chiun, since an ancestor had probably never done business there, that the area was still undiscovered.

"You mean you didn't have book on any of them," Remo had said.

"I mean the area is undiscovered," said Chiun. "A wilderness with strange people, like your country, until I came. Although your birthplace is easier because of so many descendants of Europeans and Africans. But now that I have discovered it, future generations of Sinanju will know of your inscrutable nation."

"And what about South America?" Remo had asked.

"So far undiscovered," Chiun had said. "If you should find out anything, let me know."

Now Remo was in the museum, finding out, and finding out very little at that. The carvings seemed very Egyptian, yet Egyptians used softer stone. These stones were hard.

Two guards stood before a large unmarked door at the north end of the display room.

"I'm looking for a special stone," Remo said. "It's been marked over recently."

"You can't go in," said one guard.

"So it's in there?"

"I ain't saying that. Anyone who goes in needs special permission from the Antiquities Department."

"And where's the Antiquities Department?"

"That's closed today. Just the assistant is on."

"Where's the department?"

"Don't bother, mister. They won't let you in.

74

They never let anybody in who just walks up anymore. Just special people. Don't bother."

"I want to bother," Remo said.

The assistant was in a small box of an office with a desk that made moving around difficult. She looked up from a document, focusing above blue-framed eyeglasses. Her reddish hair formed a bouquet around her delicate face.

"He's not in and I'm busy," she said.

"I want to see that stone in the locked room."

"That's what I said. He's not in and I'm busy."

"I don't know who you're talking about," Remo said, "but I just want to see that stone."

"Everybody who sees it goes through the director, James Willingham. And he's not in as I said."

"I'm not going through James Willingham, I'm going through you."

"He'll be back tomorrow."

"I want to see it today."

"It's really nothing much. It hasn't even been classified into a culture yet."

Remo leaned across the desk and, holding her eyes with his, smiled ever so slightly. She blushed.

"C'mon," he whispered in a voice that stroked her.

"All right," she said, "but only because you're sexy. Academically this makes no sense."

Her name was Valerie Garner. She had an M.A. from Ohio State and was working toward her Ph.D at Columbia. She had everything in her life but a real man. She explained this on the way down to the South American exhibit area. There were no real men left in New York City, she said.

"All I want," she said plaintively, "is someone who is strong but gentle, sensitive to my needs, who will be there when I want and not be there when I don't want. Do you see? Is that asking too much?" asked Valerie.

"Yes," said Remo, beginning to suspect that Valerie Garner, assuming she ever met a man, would not be able to see him because the sound waves rising incessantly from her mouth would obscure her vision.

Valerie motioned the guards away from the door and unlocked it with a key from around her neck.

"The director goes bananas about this stone and there's no reason for it. It's nothing. Nothing."

The nothing she described was about Remo's height. It rested on a polished pink marble pedestal with soft crystal lights bathing it in a deep artificial glow like a far-off morning. A small flowing fountain, carved from what appeared to be a solid five-foot piece of jade, bubbled gently, its clear water coming from carved lips above a perfectly round basin.

The stone itself looked like a random block of igneous rock with incredibly inept scratching of circles and lines, and only by the greatest tolerance could Remo make out a circle, birds, snakes, and what might have been a human head with feathers above it. But the rock had what Remo wanted.

A graceful, glowing green signature of "Joey 172" ran diagonally across the circle from the chunky snake to the stiff bird.

"The graffiti is the only piece of art in it," said Valerie.

"I think so, too," said Remo, who had seen enough. The stone looked like the symbol in the note the police had recovered from under Mrs. Delpheen's body, the symbol that was called an Uctut in the other eleven languages of the note.

"You should have seen Willingham when he saw the graffiti on it," Valerie was babbling. "He couldn't talk for an hour. Then he went into his office and stayed on the phone for a half-day. A full half-day. Long distance calls, overseas and everything. More than a thousand dollars in phone calls that one afternoon."

"How do you know?" asked Remo.

"I handle the budget. I thought we were going to get killed by the trustees but they approved it. Even approved two guards for the doors. And look at the stone. It's nothing."

"Why do you say that?" Remo asked.

"For one thing, I don't think it's more than a thousand years old, which would therefore not justify such shoddy craftsmanship. For a second, look at the Aztec and Inca work outside. Now those are gorgeous. This looks like a scribble compared to them. But you want to know something crazy?"

"Of course," said Remo, sidestepping Valerie's hand, which somehow alighted on his fly as she said the word "crazy."

"This stone has had more groups of visitors from all over the world than any other special exhibit. There's no reason for it."

77

"I think there is," Remo said. "Why didn't you people clean off the graffiti?"

"I tried to suggest that but Willingham wouldn't hear of it."

"Can you reach him today?"

"He never comes in on his day off. He's got an estate up in Westchester. You can't pry him out with crowbars."

"Tell him someone is defacing the statue."

"I can't do that. I'd be fired."

With two fingers, half curled and pressed together like a single instrument, Remo snapped his nails downward across the raised circle, carved by stone implements in a time that preceded even the memory of the Actatl tribe. Crumpled chunks of pinkish rock sprayed from the path of his fingers. A small white scar the size of an electric cord cut a curve in the circle.

"Now you've done it," said Valerie, pressing her hand to her forehead. "Now you've done it. This place is going to be a madhouse."

"You're going to phone Willingham, right?" said Remo pleasantly.

"Right. Get out of here. You don't know what you've done."

"I think I do," Remo said.

"Look," Valerie said, pointing to the scar. "That's bad enough. But if you're still here, there may be murder."

Remo shrugged. "Phone," he said.

"Get out of here."

"No," said Remo.

"You're too cute to die."

"I'm not leaving."

78

Since he was thin and Valerie was one of the toughest defensive guards in field hockey at Wellesley, she put her shoulder into his back and pushed. The back didn't move. She knew he couldn't weigh more than 150 pounds, so she tried again, this time getting a running start and throwing her body at the back.

When she was bracing for the thump of impact, it seemed as if the back suddenly dropped beneath her and she was hurtling horizontally toward a wall, and just as suddenly there were hands about her waist, soft hands that seemed to caress her as they guided her softly to her feet again.

"Make love, not war," said Valerie.

"Phone Willingham."

"Do that thing with the hands again."

"Later," Remo said.

"Just a touch."

"Later, I'll give you everything you want."

"There's no man who has that much."

Remo winked. Valerie glanced down at his fly.

"You're not one of those machismo types who's great with his fists and duds out in bed, are you?"

"Get Willingham and then find out."

"There won't be anything left of you. I mean it," said Valerie and with a shrug she went to the wall with a green metal cabinet. The cabinet housed a phone.

"It's not bad enough this rock's had to have running water in the room, but it's got its own private line, too. You ought to see the phone bills that come off of this line. It's incredible. Visitors come and make these free calls at museum expense and Willingham doesn't do anything about it."

Valerie's conversation with Willingham quickly dissolved into her pleas for Mr. Willingham to stop screaming. Waiting for him to arrive, Valerie took eighteen drinks of water, fourteen cigarettes, often lighting three at a time, went to the lavatory twice, and muttered "Oh God, what have we done?" every seven minutes.

Willingham was there in an hour.

He spotted the stone immediately. He was a large lumbering man with large freckles suntickled from their winter hibernation. He wore a tan suit and a blue ascot.

"Oh," he said, and "no" he said. His dark brown eyes rolled back into his forehead, and he weaved momentarily in place. He shook his head and gasped.

"No," he said firmly, and as his body regained its normal circulation, his lips tightened. His eyes narrowed and he moved methodically to the stone, ignoring Valerie and Remo.

He lowered himself to both knees and pressed his head to the marble base three times. Then with great force of will he turned to Valerie and asked: "When did you discover this?"

"When I did it," Remo said cheerily.

"You did this? Why did you do this?" Willingham asked.

"I didn't think it was a true yearning of man's cosmic consciousness," said Remo.

"How could you do it?" asked Willingham. "How? How?"

So Remo pressed two fingers tight together in a

80

light curve and with the same loose wristed snap made another line through the circle on the great stone. It crossed the first line at right angles, leaving an X.

"That's how," Remo said. "It's really not too hard. The secret, as in all better use of your body, is in breathing and rhythm. Breathing and rhythm. It looks fast, but it's really a function of the slowness of your hand being slower than the rock. You might say the rock moves out of the way of your fingers."

And with snapping fingers and rock dust flying from the great stone, Remo carved neatly through the spray of Joey 172 and the stiff bird and the curving raised snake: REMO.

"I can do it left-handed, too," he said.

"Ohhh," moaned Valerie, covering her eyes.

Willingham only nodded silently. He backed out of the display room and shut the door behind him. Remo heard a whirring. A large steel sheet descended from the ceiling, coming to a neat clicking stop at the floor. The room was sealed.

"Damn," said Valerie, running to the phone in the wall. She dialed. "I'm getting the police," she said to Remo over her shoulder. "This place is built like a walk-in safe. We'll never get out. Can't reason with Willingham after your insanity. He'll leave us here to rot. Why did you do it?"

"I wanted to express myself," said Remo.

"The line's dead," said Valerie. "We're trapped."

"Everyone is trapped," said Remo, remembering a talk long ago in which Chiun had explained

81

confinement. "The only difference between people is in the size of their trap."

"I don't need philosophy. I need to get out of here."

"You will," said Remo. "But your fear isn't working for you."

"Another religious nut, like Willingham and his rock. Why do I always meet them?" asked Valerie. She sat down on the pedestal of the great stone. Remo sat down next to her.

"Look. All your life you've been trapped. Everyone is."

She shook her head. "Not buying," she said.

"If you're poor, you can't afford to travel, so you're trapped in your home town. If you're rich, you're trapped on earth unless you're an astronaut. And even they are trapped by the air they have to bring with them. They can't leave their suits or their ship. But even more than that, every human being is trapped by his life. We're surrounded on one end by our birth and the other by our death. We can't get out of our lives. These walls are just a small period in our trapped lives anyhow, see?"

"I need a way out of here, and you're giving me a pep talk."

"I could get you out of anything but your ignorance," Remo said, and it surprised him how much like Chiun he was sounding.

"Get me out of here."

"I will after I'm finished with it," said Remo.

"What do you mean by that?"

"I'm the one who's got Willingham and his friends trapped."

"Oh, Jesus," said Valerie. "Now not only are we trapped, Willingham is too."

"Exactly," said Remo. "He's trapped by his devotion to this ugly hunk of stone back here. I've got him."

"I'd rather be him," said Valerie, and she lowered her head into her hands and moaned about how she always met them. From the man in Paterson, New Jersey, who had to strap on a five foot medieval sword before he could get it up, to the Brooklyn dishwasher who had to lather her up with foaming Liquicare before he would do it. And now, the worst. Locked in a disguised safe with a guy who thinks the outside world is trapped because they have a rock inside with them.

"Why do I always meet them?" screamed Valerie, and she knew her screams would not be heard because the whole freaking room was lined with lead. They had even sealed off the beautiful north windows. Willingham had muttered something about protection from the north wind as though the ugly box of a rock was going to catch a headcold.

"Why me, Lord?" cried Valerie Gardner. "Why me?"

"Why not you?" asked Remo just as logically, and when he tried to comfort her with his hands, she shrugged away, saying she would rather do it with a walrus in aspic than with Remo.

Her anger turned to boredom and she started yawning. She asked Remo what time it was.

"Late," he said. "We've been here about five

hours and forty-three minutes. It's eight-thirty-two and fourteen seconds."

"I didn't see you look at a watch," Valerie said.

"I'm the best watch there is," said Remo.

"Oh, great," said Valerie, and she curled up in front of the stone and dozed off. An hour later, the square metal slab locking them in raised with a whirring sound. Valerie woke up. Remo smiled.

"Mr. Willingham, thank god," said Valerie, and then she shook her head. Mr. Willingham was nude except for a loincloth and a draping of yellow feathers in a robe around his body. He carried a stone knife in front of him. Six men followed him. Two ran to Valerie, throwing her to the floor and pinning her arms. The other four rushed to Remo, two grabbing one foot each and the other two going for his wrists.

"Hi, fellas," Remo said. He let himself be lifted. They brought him to the very top of the stone called Uctut. Willingham approached, the knife held high. He spoke in a language Remo couldn't recognize. It sounded like stone clicking against stone, popping sounds with the tongue of a language kept in secret over the centuries.

"Your heart will not recompense your foul deed for it is not enough for the desecration you have performed," said Willingham in English.

"I thought I improved the stone," Remo said.

"No, Mr. Willingham, no," cried Valerie. The two men stuffed part of their robes in her mouth.

"You may save yourself pain if you tell us the truth," said Willingham.

"I like pain," Remo said.

The man on his right wrist was gripping too

84

tightly and would lose control of his strength shortly. The one on the left was too loose, and the men at Remo's feet had no protection from his yanking his legs back and driving their ribcages into their intestines if he wished. He did not wish—yet.

"If you do not give me the information I seek, we will kill the girl," said Willingham.

"That's even better than giving me pain. I can live with that," said Remo.

"We will kill her horribly," said Willingham.

"What will be will be," said Remo philosophically.

He glanced down over the stone edge to the floor, where Valerie tried desperately to shake loose. Her face turned purple in fear and rage and hysteria.

"Let her go," said Remo, "and I'll tell you everything you want to know."

"Why you did this awful thing and everything?" asked Willingham.

"And even where you can reach Joey 172," said Remo.

"We know where we can reach Joey 172. We've known since the day after he did his horror. It is for the American people to make restitution, not us. Uctut wants proper restitution, not for his priests to soil their hands with unclean blood, but for the people of the offender to offer up to us the offender. To make the sacrifice through our hands but not by our hands."

"Why didn't you say so?" said Remo, feigning an air of enlightenment. "Through your hands but not by your hands. Now everything is crystal

85

as cement. Through, not by. Why are we even arguing? Why didn't I see this before? And here I was thinking it was simple revenge."

"We have restored the sacrifices and will continue to do so until America acts properly," said Willingham.

"Would you like the Attorney General to hold down Joey 172 while the Secretary of State rips out his heart? Like you did to the congressman and Mrs. Delpheen?"

"They were in charge of monuments here at the museum. They refused my request to station guards in this room. And thus the desecration followed. It was their failure."

"Just who the hell do you expect to take this revenge for the writing on the stone?" Remo asked. "The FBI, the CIA? The Jersey City Police Department?"

"You have secret agencies. It could be done. We know it could be done. But your government has to realize what it has allowed to happen and then set about making amends. We would have allowed your government to do this quietly. Your government has done this before, many times and secretly. But your government has not acted to avenge the insult upon Uctut."

Remo noticed that Willingham held the stone knife in a strange grip. The back of the thumbnail drove the handle tight against the inside pads of the other fingers. From Orient to Western Europe, there was no grip like it. Not the Mecs in Paris or the stiletto in Naples. Even the many variations of tuck fist grip so prevalent in the American west, never used the thumb as the compressor. And yet this was a highly logical grip for a blade, allowing a good downward stroke.

Remo saw it coming from Willingham's flabby stomach, the slight twitch that meant he was getting his back into the thrust. And then he stopped at the top of the stroke as if generating power, which would be logical because a stone knife needed tremendous force to crack a chestbone.

"Now," said Willingham, his body tightened like a spring on the flicker of explosion. "Who sent you?"

"Snow White and the seven dwarfs. Or is it dwarves?"

"We will mutilate Valerie."

"You'd do that to your assistant?"

"I would do anything for my Uctut."

"Why do you call it Uctut? What does Uctut mean?" asked Remo.

"It is not the real name of the stone, but it is the name that men are privileged to speak," said Willingham. "We will mutilate Valerie."

"Only if you promise to start with her mouth," said Remo.

The stone knife hitched and started down with Willingham's shoulder under it. The thrust was perfect, except the body didn't cooperate. For the first time since the great stone had been served by the people of the Actatl, an Actatl knife struck the stone itself.

Remo's two feet yanked back, drawing the robed priests with them, and when his heels drove into their chests, they were going forward into the blows. Blood exploded out of their mouths with bits of lung. The two men holding his arms felt themselves yanked over his body, and Remo was on his feet, softly on the pedestal as the Actatl knife committed the sacrilege of striking Uctut, the stone which it served.

Using thumbs brought together from a wide inward arc, Remo caught the soft temples of the two men pinning Valerie. The thumbs went in up to the index fingers, touched hair, and then squished out. The men were dead in the midst of holding, and they looked up dumbly, their eyes focused on eternity, their minds shattered midthought.

The men who had held Remo's arms were still dazed, crawling on the floor, looking for their balance. Remo snapped one vertebra on one man, and he suddenly stopped crawling and flattened out on the floor. His legs stopped responding, and shortly thereafter his brain stopped, too.

Remo dropped the other man with a short shattering chop to the forehead. The blow itself did not kill. It was designed to use the thick part of the skull as fragments, driving them into the frontal lobes. It did the job without getting the hands sticky.

Remo wiped his thumbs off on the golden feathers of the robe. He noticed the knots tying the feathers into the cape were strange. He had never seen knots like that before. He knew something about knots, too.

Valerie spit feathers out of her mouth. She coughed. She brushed herself off. She spit again.

"Fucking lunatics," she muttered.

Remo went over to Willingham who leaned against the stone like a man having a heart at-

Here's Max.

The maximum 120mm cigarette.

Great tobaccos. Terrific taste.
And that long, lean,
all-white dynamite look.

*"Max, I can take
you anywhere."*

After all I'd heard I decided to either quit or smoke True.

I smoke True.

Regular: 11 mg. "tar", 0.6 mg. nicotine;
Menthol: 13 mg. "tar", 0.7 mg. nicotine
per cigarette FTC Report Nov. 1975.

© Lorillard 1976

The low tar, low nicotine cigarette.

tack. His cheek pressed against the uppermost bird, his robe drawn tightly over his chest.

"Hi," said Remo. "Now we can talk."

"With my own hand I have desecrated Uctut," moaned Willingham.

"Now let's start at the beginning," said Remo. "This stone is Uctut, right?"

"This stone is the life of my fathers and their fathers before them. This stone is my people. In many skins and many colors are my people because you would not let us keep our own skins and our own hair and our own eyes. But our souls have never changed, and they reside in the infinite strength of our beautiful god, who is eternal and one with his people, who serve him."

"You're talking about the rock?" asked Remo.

"I talk about that which is us."

"All right," said Remo. "We got the rock is holy. And you people are the Actatl and you worship it, right?"

"Worship? You make it sound like lighting some candle or not playing with women. You do not know worship until your very life is sacrifice."

"Right, right," said Remo. "Moving right along, we know you killed the congressman and Mrs. Delpheen. What I don't know is why I never heard of you guys before."

"Our protection was your lack of knowledge of us."

"You keep talking about other skins. What does that mean?"

"You would not let us keep our own skins. If I were brown with high cheekbones as once the Ac-

89

tatl were, would I be a director of this museum? Would DeSen or DePanola be ranking generals in the armies of France and Spain?"

"They're Actatl, too?" said Remo.

"Yes," said Willingham. He looked past Remo at the bodies on the floor, and his voice trailed off like an echo. "They came with me."

"I don't think they're ranking now," said Remo, glancing at the stone dead stillness of the bodies, limp as leftover string beans.

"Would we have been able to worship our precious and awesome stone in your society? People are not allowed to worship stones."

"I take it you've never been to the Vatican or the Wailing Wall or Mecca," said Remo.

"Those are symbols. They do not worship them. This stone god we worship and would never have been allowed to love and serve it as we do."

"Are there a lot of you Actatl?"

"Enough," said Willingham. "Always enough. But we made a mistake."

"Yeah?"

"We did not find out who you were."

"I'm your friendly neighborhood assassin," said Remo.

"They will find you and destroy you. They will tear your limbs. They will obliterate you. For we Actatl have survived the test and we are strong and we are many and we are disguised."

"You're also as flippy as dandelions," said Remo. He noticed the separations in Willingham's lower teeth oozed red, threatening to spill over his lower lip.

"We will survive. We have survived five

90

hundred years," said Willingham, and he smiled, releasing the dam of blood over his lips, and let his yellow feathered robe slide from his shoulders. The handle of the stone knife, a round block of chipped stone, stuck from his belly and underneath his heart. Willingham, who was so expertly trained to rip out the hearts of others, had missed his own and was bleeding to death.

"I have bad news for you," said Remo. "I come from a house thousands of years old. While your Actatl had yet to use the stone, Sinanju was. Before Rome, Sinanju was. Before the Jews wandered in the desert, Sinanju was."

"You have taken other skins, too, to survive?" Willingham hissed.

"No," said Remo.

"*Eeeeah,*" cried Willingham. "We are doomed."

"Hopefully," said Remo. "Now where is your headquarters?"

And then Willingham smiled his death smile. "We are not doomed. Thank you for telling me so."

Willingham went down in a mess of blood and feathers as though he were a goose caught at close range by double barrels of birdshot. Valerie spat the last feather out of her mouth.

"You were going to let them mutilate me, weren't you?"

"Only your mouth," said Remo.

"Men are turds," yelled Valerie.

"Shhh," said Remo. "We've got to get out of here."

"You're damned right. I'm calling the police."

"I'm afraid you're not," said Remo and touched

91

a spot on the left side of her throat. She tried to speak, but all that came out was a dry gurgle.

Remo led her from the room. Under a painting on the wall outside he found the switch that lowered the steel door. He heard it thump and click into place, then he closed the wooden outside doors. On the door he hung a sign he took from a nearby men's room: CLOSED FOR REPAIRS.

Then Remo led Valerie from the darkened, closed-for-the-night museum and delivered her to the hotel where Chiun and he were staying at Fifty-ninth Street and Columbus Circle. Then he massaged her throat in such a way that her voice came back.

Chiun sat in the middle of the living room of the suite. Bobbi Delpheen practiced her new forehand stroke, allowing the racket to float into an imaginary ball.

"You here for tennis lessons, too?" Bobbi asked Valerie.

"The world is mad," shrieked Valerie.

"Shut up or your voice goes again," said Remo.

"They've got a great system," Bobbi reassured the worried Valerie. "You don't hit the ball. The racket hits it."

Quietly, Valerie began to cry. She would have preferred screaming, but she did not like being voiceless.

Remo spoke softly to Chiun. He told him of the stone. He told him of the new grip on the knife. He told him of Willingham's sudden last joy when he had asked for the location of the Actatl headquarters.

Chiun thought a moment.

"That lunatic Smith has led us into ruin," he said.

"You saying we should run?"

"The time to run has passed. The time to attack has begun. Except we cannot attack. He smiled when you asked about his headquarters because I am sure he does not have one. We are set against the worst of all enemies, the formless unknown."

"But if they are unknown to us, we are unknown to them, Little Father," said Remo.

"Perhaps," said Chiun. "Once, many of what you call your centuries ago, there was a Master, and he did disappear for many years, and the stories were told that he had gone to a new world, but he was not believed because he was much given to exaggeration."

"So?"

"I must search my memory," said Chiun, "and see if something there may help us." And he was quiet. Very quiet.

"Can I talk now?" said Valerie.

"No," said Remo. Valerie started crying again.

Remo looked out over the night lights of Central Park. His plan had worked so well until Willingham. When you grabbed hold of an organization, you planned on working your way to the top. You didn't expect someone to kill himself along the way and break the chain.

Remo walked away from the window. Chiun had often warned him against thinking too much, lest his greater senses be dulled to the subtleties of the moment.

And in this way Remo did not see the binoculars trained on the window of his hotel suite. He did not see the man raise a rifle, then lower it.

"I can't miss," said the man to another person in the room across the street from Remo's.

"Wait until you're inside the room. We want his heart," said the other man.

"Willingham probably couldn't miss either. But this guy came out of the museum and Willingham didn't," the second man said.

"I still can't miss."

"Wait until you're inside his room. We want his heart," said the second man. "When we get the word."

Chapter Seven

The spectacular failure at the Museum of Natural History was outlined in detail to a senior vice-president of a computer company branch office, Paris, Rue St. Germain.

Monsieur Jean Louis Raispal deJuin, vice-president for corporate development of international data and research, nodded with all the feigned interest his finely etched patrician face could muster. Uncle Carl, from the German side of the family, had always been rather peculiar and one had to be patient with him. Jean Louis reacted instinctively with the politeness beaten into him by his governess and ordered by his mother, who had always said one could not choose one's family, but one could certainly choose one's manners.

So Jean Louis listened on about all sorts of mayhem and two formidable Americans, except one was an Oriental, and all the while his mind worked at an adjustment he would make in a research team that was stymied by a computer problem.

Occasionally he glanced out at Rue St. Germain with its bookshops and restaurants. He had always considered his university days his happiest, and since his work was entirely cerebral and could be done anywhere, the firm had allowed him to select the office site and furnishings, which were largely Napoleonic period combined with Chinese. The ornate gilded forms mixed so well. Robust, mother had called them.

Uncle Carl sat on a chair, ignoring the center extended portion of the seat, which allowed men to sit sideways so that their sword pommels could hang conveniently across their laps. Uncle Carl sweated like a stuffed red sausage this fine autumnal day, and Jean Louis wished he would suggest a walk, perhaps in the direction of Invalides, where Napoleon was buried, along with all those who had directed la belle France in one disastrous war after another. Uncle Carl liked those things. Even though he often railed about things European and often trailed off into some South American nonsense. This was surprising because Uncle Carl was an ardent Nazi, and it had taken awesome family pull to get him off unindicted by the War Crimes panels. Fortunately Cousin Geoffrey was a lieutenant general on Field Marshal

Montgomery's staff and Uncle Bill was in the American OSS.

Jean Louis deJuin had been a teenager at the time, during the German occupation of Paris, and even though Cousin Michel was on the most wanted list as a leader in the Maquis resistance movement, Jean Louis' family had lived quite well during the occupation, by some order from within the German general staff.

As mother had said, one did not choose one's family, and Jean Louis had thought little about it until now, when Uncle Carl said those strange words.

"So now it is up to you, Jean Louis Raispal de-Juin."

"What is up to me, dear Uncle?" asked Jean Louis.

"Our hopes, our fortunes, our honor, and our very survival."

"Ah well, very good," said Jean Louis. "Would you care for coffee?"

"Have you been listening?"

"Yes, but of course," said Jean Louis. "Terrible happenings. Life can be so cruel."

"Willingham is gone now."

"The pale fellow who worked in the museum?"

"He was the foremost priest," said Uncle Carl.

"Of what?" asked Jean Louis.

Uncle Carl's face burst crimson. He slammed a large fat fist down on the pressed leather of an eighteenth century desk. Jean Louis blinked. Uncle Carl was getting violent.

"Don't you know who you are? What your family is? Where you came from? Your roots?"

"We share some great, great, great uncle who was in South America for a while. Is that what you mean? Please don't be violent. Perhaps some anisette, Uncle?"

"Jean Louis, tell me now, for this answer must be truthful . . ."

"Yes, Uncle Carl."

"When we took those walks when you were a child, and I told you things about your ancestors, was your mind paying attention to me, Jean Louis? Tell me truthfully now."

"Well, you know how children are, Uncle Carl."

"The truth."

"No, Uncle Carl. I went with you because as a German you could get the best patisserie at the time. I thought about chocolate."

"And the manuscripts I gave you?"

"I must confess, I drew pictures on them. Paper was scarce, Uncle Carl."

"And the name of our possession? That all of us share?"

"That stone. Uctut?"

"Yes. Its real name," said Uncle Carl.

"I forgot, Uncle Carl."

"I see," said Carl Johann Liebengut, president of Bavarian Electronics Works. "So you think I am a German uncle of a French nephew, and this is such a fine autumn day, what is this crazy uncle doing talking about death in New York City, yes?"

"You put it rather harshly, Uncle."

"True, no?"

"All right, true," said Jean Louis. His gray vest tailored precisely to his lean form hardly

98

wrinkled as he brought one leg over the other and formed an arch with his long delicate fingers in front of his face. He rested his chin on this arch.

"You are no more French than I am German, Jean Louis," said Carl Johann Liebengut, and such was the coolness of his voice that deJuin forgot about the sunshine and the bookstores and the autumn green of the leaves outside on Rue St. Germain.

"I said you are not French," said Carl.

"I heard you," said deJuin.

"You are Actatl."

"You mean, I share a bit of this blood."

"Actatl is what you are. Everything else is a disguise because the world would not let you be Actatl."

"My father is a deJuin. So am I."

"Your father was a deJuin and he gave you that disguise. Your mother gave you the blood. I gave you the knowledge, and you apparently rejected it. I am too old to wage the war of survival that is now required, and you, Jean Louis, apparently do not want to. So a thousand years of our heritage, maybe more, dies this day. Monsieur deJuin, may you have a long and happy life. I go."

"Uncle Carl, wait."

"For what, Monsieur deJuin?"

"For me to listen. Come, I will go with you. If I was unattentive as a child, let me listen now. I am not saying I will take up the standards of the war of our tribe, but I am saying I will not let a millenia of history succumb without even access to my ear."

As a child, the tale of the last king of the Actatl has amused Jean Louis because of the discrepancies of his childhood memory—the attenuation of unimportant things.

They walked along Rue St. Germain, up the Left Bank, past restaurants and cinemas and coffee shops and tobacco shops, strung along the way like so many minor potholes to collect loose change. At Rue du Bac, they turned right and crossed the Seine over the Pont Royal Bridge. Now as deJuin heard the story of the last king he could appreciate the man's brilliant assessment of a sociological avalanche, one that would crush the existing Indian culture to pumice. The Maya had not known this. The Inca had not known this, nor had the all-powerful Aztec. And they were no more.

But here was Uncle Carl, talking to him about symbols on a sacred stone. Every nuance, every meaning was as clear as on the day the priests of the Actatl had made their last sacrifice in the verdant Mexican hills.

"Why have we not made sacrifices until recently?" asked deJuin. "Back in our ancestors' time, it was a monthly thing. And now we use it only for revenge?"

"It was not thought wise on one hand. And on the other, the sacrifice of the last of the Actatl city was interpreted as the final eternal sacrifice. But if you should look upon the stone and see the living lines as I have done, if you had gone last year as you were supposed to, you would have seen everything in the stone. The meaning of the earth and rivers and sky. To see everything we have heard about. There it is, our history. Shared by no one else, Jean Louis. Ours. You don't know how insufferable those Nazi rallies were, but I had to do it for the tribe, just in case Hitler should win. What had started out as a protection society for the tribe eventually became a network of each of us helping the other. Then came the desecration of Uctut."

"And just the death of this one boy would not do?"

"Of course not. First, Uctut demands that the United States bear the responsibility for the desecration. And what is the life of a Negro worth?"

"You forget, our real skin is brown, Uncle," said deJuin.

"Have you decided to take up the case of our family?"

"I want to show you something," Jean Louis said. "That is all. Do you know why I went into computers?"

"No," said the older man, who was having difficulty keeping up with the long strides of the tall, thin man who moved so effortlessly and so quickly while seeming just to stroll.

"Because, it was untainted by what has made me feel uncomfortable all my life. Computers were pure. I will now show you what is not pure for me."

And this bridge led to the Louvre, a giant square of a castle with an immense courtyard that had been transformed into a museum more than two hundred years before. A gaggle of Japanese tourists coming on in phalanx marched into a side exhibit following a leader with a flag.

101

Four Americans laughing noisily brushed aside a vendor who offered to take their pictures.

"It takes a full week just to properly peruse, not even to examine, the contents of this museum," said deJuin.

"We don't have a week," said Uncle Carl.

The younger man smiled. "We don't need a week." He spread his right arm slowly in a wide arc, as if offering the entire museum. "I spent, if you would total the time, literally months here in my student days. China, ancient Greece, Europe, even some modern South American painters are all represented here."

"Yes, yes." Carl was becoming impatient.

"I never felt at home with any of them. None. Since childhood, even though Father told me our family went back to Charlemagne, I never felt at home in France. I felt a little bit at home in computers because it was a life without a past."

"So what are you saying?"

"I am saying, dear Uncle, that I am no European."

"So you will help?"

"Help, yes. Run at someone with a stone knife, no."

Uncle Carl became flustered. He angrily announced he had not come to Paris to organize a committee but to seek help in fighting a holy war of the tribe.

"And how is that war going, Uncle?"

"Disastrous," said Carl.

"So let us get it going right, eh? Come. We think."

"The knife is holy," said Carl, lest his nephew think he was surrendering a point.

"Success is holier," said Jean Louis deJuin. He looked around the spacious and awesomely elegant stone courtyard of the Louvre for the last time as a Frenchman and silently said his goodbye to Europe in his heart.

Listening to Uncle Carl, it did not take deJuin long to see what had gone wrong with the family. The Actatl had been content to hide, not only for generations, but for centuries, and when a time came that action was demanded, action was beyond the capacity of the family.

He hailed a cab and ordered it to the small apartment he kept for his mistress on Avenue deBretuil, a spacious two floors of rooms with large rococco molding on the ceiling. The houseboy, a North African dressed in a silver embroidered waistcoat, served them coffee with heavy dollops of sweet cream. Uncle Carl ate three patisserie, gleaming in syrupy sugar over candied fruit set in an exquisitely light flaky crust, while Jean Louis took a pad from his pocket and wrote down several formulas. DeJuin, oblivious to his uncle, did not answer questions about what he was doing. At one point, he phoned into his office and asked for computer time. He read several formulas to an assistant over the phone and fifteen minutes later got his answer.

"Ordure," he mumbled when he got the answer. He tore up his notes, flinging them into the air. The houseboy attempted to pick up the pieces, and deJuin shooed him from the room. He paced. And as he paced he talked.

103

"The trouble, dear Uncle Carl, is that the tribe is not fit to rule." He went on without waiting for an answer.

"We have hidden so long that when the moment comes when we must make a just demand, not only is it ignored, but we do not even know how to make it. All has been disaster, from start to finish."

Jean Louis deJuin walked to the window and looked out onto the sunlit street.

"What must we do?" asked Uncle Carl.

"We start over," said deJuin. "From now on, the goal of the Actatl is power. In the future, when our names are known, our demands will be met."

"What of our demands for reparation?" asked Carl.

"From the beginning that was stupid," said deJuin. "The notes demanding reparations were unclear. Written in twelve languages and none of them English. Forget that. We ourselves will take care of the reparations at the proper time. But our main problem now is these two very dangerous men, the American and the Oriental."

DeJuin drummed on the crystal bright window pane with his fingers as he talked.

"We were unlucky that we bumped into them," said Carl.

"No," said deJuin. "They came looking for us, and like fools, we went rushing into their trap. There is one highly probable course of events, and this is it: After the descration of Uctut, our actions in the sacrifices somehow stepped on something or someone in a highly sensitive area that

104

employs killers. Men of that skill do not just go wandering into museums on pleasure trips. We must have caused a danger to them. Now, whoever or whatever we have endangered wants us to attack those two. They could hope for nothing better. We will attack, and we will be destroyed."

"So we will not attack?" said Uncle Carl.

"No. We *will* attack. But we will attack our way, on our terms, at our time. And we will use these killers as they would use us. We will trace from them the secret organization they work for, and then we will seize that organization's power. That power will become the tribe's power, and then the Actatl will hide no more."

DeJuin paused at the wind͡ow, waiting for a comment from Uncle Carl. But there was only silence.

When he turned, he saw that Carl had gotten off his chair and was kneeling on the floor, his head touching the carpet, his arms extended in front of him.

"What is this, Uncle Carl?"

"You are king," Carl said. "You are king." Carl looked up. "Come to me."

DeJuin moved close to the older man, and Carl leaned forward and whispered in his ear.

"What is that?" said deJuin.

"You are a believer now. That is the true name of Uctut and only believers may speak that word. Should an unbeliever say it aloud, the skies will darken and the clouds will fall. You may say it."

DeJuin was careful not to smile and spoke the word aloud. As he had suspected, the skies did not

105

darken and the clouds did not fall, which Uncle Carl took as proof that deJuin believed truly and well.

Uncle Carl rose. "You are king. For thirty years I have waited for you, because you are blood of blood, soul of soul, of that ancient Actatl king of centuries ago. Now you must lead the family to victory."

DeJuin was surprised that he did not regard his uncle's words as foolish.

"We will do that, Uncle," he said.

"And we will avenge the desecration?"

"When we work all this out, Uctut will have all the hearts it ever wanted," deJuin said.

And that night, before he fell asleep, he said the secret name of Uctut again. And when the skies did not darken and the clouds did not fall, he knew.

He did not know if he was a believer, but he knew that the Actatl had at last gained a king who would lead them to glory.

Chapter Eight

When Jean Louis deJuin and his Uncle Carl arrived in New York, they went directly to a Fifth Avenue hotel where a battery of bellhops waited to handle their luggage, where they were not required to register, where the presidential suite had been vacated for them, and where the hotel manager gave Uncle Carl a large knowing wink, convincing deJuin that no matter what it might mean as a tradition and religion, the international brotherhood of Uctut followers had a great deal of secular clout.

"I had never realized the family was so extensive," deJuin said after he and Carl had dismissed the bellboys and sat in the drawing room of the large five-room suite.

"We are everywhere," said Uncle Carl. "You would have known if you had paid more attention when you were young." He smiled, more critical than mirthful.

"But I am here now," said deJuin, returning the smile.

"Yes, Jean Louis, and I am grateful for that and will indulge in no more recriminations, no matter how pleasant they may be."

"Recriminations are pleasant only for losers," deJuin said, "as an explanation to themselves of why their lives went wrong. You are not a loser and your life has not gone wrong. In fact, it will now go most extremely right, and so recriminations do not become you."

Then deJuin directed the older man to begin immediately to call in members of the family to speak to deJuin. "We must plan now better than we have ever planned before, and I must study our resources. I will be ready to speak to people in two hours."

He went into a bedroom and on a large oaken desk spread out papers from the alligator leather briefcase he had carried with him.

Before sitting down, he removed the jacket of his gray chalk-striped suit. He carefully undid his monogrammed French cuffs and turned his shirt sleeves up two precise folds. He undid his collar and carefully removed his black and red silk tie and hung it over a hanger with his jacket, which he placed in one of the large, oil-soaked cedar closets.

DeJuin clicked on the wood-framed fluorescent light and took the caps off two broad-tipped marking pens, one red and one black. The red was for writing down possibilities; the black was for crossing them out after he decided they would not work.

He held the red marker toward his lips and looked through the window at the early afternoon sun shining down on the busy street, then he fell upon the pile of blank white paper as if he were an eagle plummeting down onto a mouse that had the misfortune to wander across a patch of land that offered no cover.

When again he looked up, there was no sun. The sky was dark, and he realized afternoon had slipped away into evening.

The wastepaper basket was overflowing with crumpled sheets of paper. The top of the desk looked like the overflow from the wastebasket.

But one sheet was squared neatly in front of deJuin. On it was written one neat word, printed in red block capitals: INFILTRATE.

When he went back into the drawing room, a dozen men were there, sitting quietly. They were mostly middle-aged men, wearing business suits with vests buckled down by university chains, straight-legged pants, and the highly polished leather shoes favored by practical men who can afford any kind of shoe they wish and choose the same kind they grew up wearing.

All rose as he entered the room.

Uncle Carl rose too from his chair near the window.

"Gentlemen. Our king. Jean Louis deJuin."

The dozen men sank slowly to their knees.

DeJuin looked at Uncle Carl questioningly, as if

for the command that would bring the men to their feet. But Carl too had gone to his knees, his bowed head extended toward deJuin.

"The name of Uctut cannot be defiled," said de-Juin. "It is all holiness and beyond the dirtying touch of men. But for those who have tried, Uctut calls for sacrifice, and we of the Actatl shall provide that sacrifice. This I vow—this we all vow. On our honor and our lives." He paused. "Rise."

The men got slowly to their feet, their faces illuminated with an inner glow, and came forward to shake deJuin's hand and to introduce themselves.

DeJuin waited, then waved the men to seats on the couches and chairs in the room.

"Our first goal is to get close to these two, this American and the aged Oriental. From them we will move against their organization and expropriate its power. The question is, how do we infiltrate? How do we get close to these two men?"

He looked around the room. He had expected puzzled looks, but instead he found smiles that showed satisfaction. He looked to Uncle Carl.

Carl rose. "We have ways of getting to those two."

He smiled.

"Two ways," he said.

Chapter Nine

Remo carefully addressed the large trunk to an oil company operating in Nome, Alaska. By the time the trunk reached the company, it would be winter in Nome. The trunk would go into the warehouse, and not until summer would someone notice the funny smell and eventually the body of the Justice Department official. Who had almost caught Remo off guard. But in this business, "almost" meant flying to Nome in a trunk because you kept better till next summer.

"Return address, sir?" said the clerk at the railway station.

"Disneyworld, Florida," said Remo. The clerk said he had always wanted to go to the place and asked if Remo worked there, and Remo said he was president of the Mickey Mouse union.

"Mickey Mouse for short," said Remo. "Actually it's the International Brotherhood of Mickey Mice, Donald Ducks, Goofies, and Seven Dwarfs of America, AFL-CIO. That's dwarfs, not dwarves. We may go on strike next week over our mistreatment by cartoonists. Not enough lines."

"Oh," said the clerk suspiciously. But he nevertheless sent William Reddington III, assistant director, northern district, New York, on his Nome vacation with two loud pounds of a rubber stamp.

Reddington had been the strangest assault. He came padding in to Remo's hotel suite in a four-hundred-dollar blue striped suit with vest, a Phi Beta Kappa key, and light brown hair immaculately combed to casualness.

He was sorry to bother Remo at that hour, and he knew the tension everyone in the room must be suffering, but he had come to help.

Chiun was asleep in one of the bedrooms. Remo had not been sure the two women would be safe if he just turned them free after the slaughter at the museum, so he told them they must stay with him for a while. Valerie had started sobbing at that moment, and when Reddington arrived, she was still sobbing, staring straight ahead in a state of shock. Bobbi Delpheen watched the late late show, starring Tyrone Power as a handsome but destitute Italian nobleman. She had also watched the late show where Tyrone Power had starred as a handsome but destitute French nobleman. Power had died, Bobbi commented, while making the greatest picture of his life—the story of a handsome but destitute Spanish nobleman.

Remo nodded for Reddington to enter.

"I'm from the Department of Justice," he said. "I hear you've been having some trouble."

"No trouble," said Remo, shrugging.

"Whaaaaa," said Valerie.

"Are you all right, dear?" asked Reddington.

"Oh, my god," said Valerie. "A sane person. Thank God. Thank God. A sane human being." And her gentle sobs released in a heave of tears, and she stumbled to Reddington and cried into his shoulder as he patted her back.

"She's all right," said Remo. "You're all right, aren't you, Valerie?"

"Drop dead, you freaking animal," cried Valerie. "Keep him away from me," she said to Reddington.

"I think someone is trying to kill you," said Reddington. "And I don't even know your name."

"Albert Schweitzer," said Remo.

"He's lying. It's Remo something. I don't know the last name. He's a lunatic killer. You don't even see his hands move. He's murderous, brutal, cold, and sarcastic."

"I am not sarcastic," said Remo.

"Don't listen to that broad," called out Bobbi. "She doesn't even play tennis. She sits around and cries all day. She's a punk loser."

"Thank you," said Remo. Bobbi raised her right hand in an okay sign.

"He kills people with his hands and feet," said Valerie.

"I take it you're a karate master of some sort," said Reddington.

"No," said Remo, and in this he was honest. "I am not karate. Karate just focuses power."

"And you use it for self-defense?" Reddington asked.

"He uses it on anyone in sight," said Valerie.

"I haven't used it on you," said Remo.

"You will."

"Maybe," said Remo, imagining what Valerie would look like with a mouth removed from her face. It would be an improvement.

"As I said," Reddington explained, "I've come to help. But first I must see your weapons. Are your hands your only weapons?"

"No," Remo said. "Hands are just an extension of the weapon we all share. That's the difference between man and animals. Animals use their limbs; man uses his mind."

"Then you're an animal," said Valerie, creating a large wet spot of tears on Reddington's lapel.

"Just your body, then?" said Reddington musingly. He excused himself for backing away from Valerie Gardner, and she was the first to see the .45 caliber automatic come out of Reddington's neat pinstriped jacket. She realized she was between the gun and the lunatic behind her and all she said was "To hell with it." A man from the Justice Department was making her a shield in a shooting gallery. Her, Valerie Gardner, she had to go and meet the only US Attorney who doubled as a hit man.

"Go ahead and shoot the damned thing," she yelled.

114

"Come on, fella. Is this any way to act?" Remo said.

"Right," Valerie shrieked, wheeling from Reddington to Remo and back. "Right. That's the way to act. Shoot the damned thing. Get this homicidal maniac before he gets us all."

"Quiet," said Remo. "I'm going to get to you later." He smiled at Reddington. "We should sit and reason together," he said hopefully.

Reddington backed off a step, beyond the reach of Remo's arm and leg, so he could not be disarmed by a sudden move.

"There is nothing to discuss," he said, "with one who has laid hands on the high priests of Uctut."

"What priests?" said Remo. "Those loonies who were trying to open my chest without a key?"

"Shoot," shrieked Valerie. "Shoot."

Reddington ignored her. His eyes seemed fixed on Remo with a cold stare, his lids too icy to blink.

"Through the ages, there has been Uctut," he said to Remo. "And there have been those of us who have defended him against the desecrators who would do our God evil."

"Wait a minute," Remo said. "You were the guy standing guard outside the congressman's office when he got it, weren't you?"

"Yes. And I lifted his heart from his chest myself," Reddington said.

Remo nodded. "I thought so. I wondered how a flock of two-hundred-pound canaries could have sneaked past a guard."

"And now it is your turn," Reddington said.

115

"Nixon made me do it," Remo said.

"It is past excuses."

"Bobby Kennedy?" Remo offered. "Jack Kennedy? J. Edgar Hoover?"

"It will not do," said Reddington.

"Don't say I didn't try," Remo said.

Reddington backed up another step.

"Shoot, will you?" yelled Valerie. "Off this violent lunatic."

Reddington held the gun professionally, near his right hip. This was the way taught by the Justice Department to prevent its men from being disarmed by someone just reaching out and slapping or kicking the gun away.

But for every counter there is a counter, and when Remo went into a sudden move to Reddington's left, Reddington found that the gun could not home in on Remo as it should because Reddington's own hip was in the way. He wheeled to his left to keep the gun on Remo, but when he turned, Remo was not there anymore. He turned again, this time to the rear, and there he found Remo, but he had no chance to celebrate his discovery with a one-gun salute because the gun, still held properly against his hip, was pushed back above the hip, through his side, past his abdominal cavity, and into the center of Reddington's right kidney, where it came to rest.

Reddington fell, eyes still iced over.

"Killer! Killer!," Valerie shrieked.

"Quiet," Remo said. "You're going to get yours."

Bobbie looked up from the television set. "Do it

now," she said. "Get rid of this twit and let's go out and hit a few. There's an all-night court over on the East Side. Clay court too. I don't like playing on hard surfaces. And you don't get a true bounce on grass. Unless you've got a big serve. If you've got a big serve, then I'd probably give you a better game on grass because it'd slow down your serve."

"I don't play tennis," Remo said.

"That's revolting," Bobbi said. "This one was right. He should have killed you."

"Quiet. Both of you," Remo said. "I'm trying to think."

"This should be good," Valerie said.

"Think about taking up tennis," Bobbi said.

Remo decided instead to think about how much he remembered the boy scout adviser who had come to the orphanage in Newark to start a scout troop. All the orphans over twelve, Remo included, had joined because the nuns had ordered them to. That had lasted only until the nuns found out that the scoutmaster was teaching the boys how to start fires with flint and steel, and three mattress fires in an old wooden building with a flash point somewhat lower than butane gas convinced the nuns to evict the boy scouts and think about affiliation with a 4-H club.

Remo had never learned how to build a fire with flint and steel. He hadn't been able to steal a lump of flint from any of the other boys, and the little pieces that came in cigarette lighters were too small to get a good grip on.

But Remo had learned knots. The scoutmaster

117

had been a whiz on knots. Bowlines and sheepshanks and clove hitches. Square knots. Right over left and left over right. Reno thought about those knots. Bowlines were best, he decided. The knot was designed for tying together two different thicknesses of rope and this would come in very handy when he trussed up Bobbi and Valerie with the thick pieces of drapery rope and the thin cord from the venetian blinds.

"We'll scream for help," Valerie threatened.

"You do that and I'll tie a sheepshank on you, too," said Remo.

He tied up Valerie with bowlines. He tied another drapery cord over her mouth in a gag and fastened it with a clove hitch. It came loose so he changed it to a square knot tied tightly behind her neck.

"You?" he said to Bobbi.

"Actually I was planning to be quiet," she said.

"Good," said Remo, tying her up but leaving off the gag. "The old gentleman is sleeping inside. If you're unlucky enough to wake him up before he chooses to rise, it's going to be game, set, and match point for you, kid."

"I understand," she said, but Remo wasn't listening. He was wondering what had gone wrong with the clove hitch he had tried to use to tie Valerie's mouth. He tried it again when he packaged Reddington for his Alaskan sabbatical and was pleased when the knots held very tightly.

It gave him a warm feeling of accomplishment that he kept all the way to the railway station, where he mailed Reddington to Alaska, and on a long all-night walk through Central Park, where he fed a mugger to the ducks, and all the way back to his hotel suite, when he found out that Bobbi was gone.

She had been kidnapped.

Chapter Ten

Chiun was sitting in the center of the floor watching television. Valerie was trussed in a corner of the room.

"Where's Bobbi?" Remo said.

Valerie mumbled through her gag. *"Gree-grawkgra. Neargh, graw, graw."*

"Shut up," said Remo. "Chiun, where's Bobbi?"

Chiun did not turn. He raised a hand over his head as if in dismissal.

Remo sighed and reluctantly started to untie the gag from Valerie's mouth. It was triple-knotted, and the square knots he had used had given way to some other kind of knot Remo had never seen before. His fingers had to pick tightly at the strands of drapery sash before he got the gag off.

"He did it, he did it," said Valerie. She nodded at Chiun.

"*Shhhhh,*" Chiun hissed

"Shut up," Remo said to Valerie. "Where's Bobbi?"

"They came for her. Three men in the yellow feathered robes. I tried to tell him, but he tied me up again. Pig!" she shouted across the room at Chiun.

"Kid, do yourself a favor and knock that off," Remo said.

A commercial came on the television. For the next two minutes and five seconds, Remo had Chiun to himself.

"Chiun, did you see them take Bobbi?"

"If you mean was I awakened from my few golden moments of rest by uncalled for intrusions, yes. If you mean when I came out here, did this disciple of the open mouth verbally abuse me with her noise, yes. If you mean—"

"I mean did you see the three men take the other girl away?"

"If you mean, did I see three creatures who looked like the big bird on the children's program, yes. I laughed, they were so funny."

"And you just let them go?" Remo said.

"This one was making enough noise for two persons, even through the gag that was so ineptly tied. I did not need a second female here to make even more noise. If they had promised to come back for this one, I would have put her outside the door to await them, as if she were an empty bottle of milk."

"Dammit, Chiun. Those were the people I wanted. We've been looking for them. What do you think we've had these girls here for? In the hope that those Indians would come to us."

"Correction. You have been looking for those people. I have carefully avoided looking for them."

"That girl's going to be killed. I hope you're proud of yourself."

"There are too many tennis players in the world already."

"She's going to have her heart cut out."

"Perhaps they will settle for her tongue."

"That's right. Make fun," Valerie shrieked. "You miserable old man."

Chiun turned around and looked behind him.

"Who is she talking to?" he asked Remo.

"Ignore her."

"I try to. I came out of my room and I was so kind as to untie her mouth. That proves that even the Master is not beyond error. The noise that came out. So I retied her."

"And you just let those three yellow ostriches take Bobbi away?"

"I was getting tired of talking about tennis," said Chiun. "It is a stupid game anyway."

The commercial ended, and he turned his face away from Remo and back toward the television set, where Dr. Rance McMasters was congratulating Mrs. Wendell Waterman on her elevation to acting chairman of the Silver City Bicentennial Commission, a post she was hastily named to when the permanent chairman, Mrs. Ferd Delanettes, contracted a terminal case of syphilis, given her by Dr. Rance McMasters, who was now talking softly to Mrs. Waterman, preparatory to giving her a dose of her own in the twenty-three hours and thirty minutes between the end of this day's episode and the start of tomorrow's.

"Is there any chance, any slight chance," Remo asked Valerie, "that while those dingdongs were here, you kept your mouth shut long enough to hear anything they said?"

"I heard every word, freak," she said.

"Give me a few."

"The biggest one—"

"Did you ever see any of them before?" Remo asked.

"What a stupid question!" Valerie said. "How many people do you see in New York wearing yellow feathers?"

"More this year than last. They weren't born with feathers, you know. Underneath there are men. They look like men. Did you recognize any of them?"

"No."

"Okay, what'd they say?"

"The biggest one said, 'Miss Delpheen?' and she nodded, and he said, 'You are coming with us.' "

"And what happened?"

"They untied her and—"

"Did she say anything?"

"No. What could she say?"

"I'll bet you could have thought of something. What else?"

"Then they took her by the hands and walked

123

out the door. That one—" She nodded to Chiun. "He came out of the bedroom. He saw them, but instead of trying to stop them, he went and turned on the television set. They left. I tried to call him, and he untied my mouth, but when I told him that she had been kidnapped, he tied my mouth again."

"Good for him," said Remo. "So you don't know where they went?"

"No," said Valerie. "Are you going to untie me?"

"I'm going to sleep on it," Remo said.

"They went to the Edgemont Mansion in Englewood, wherever that is," Chiun said softly without turning from the television.

"How do you know that?" Remo asked.

"I heard them, of course. How else would I know that? Be quiet now."

"Englewood's in New Jersey," Remo said.

"Then you will probably still find it there," Chiun said. "Silence."

"Finish it up," Remo said. "Then put on your tape machine. You're coming with me."

"Of course. Order me around."

"Why not? It's all your fault," said Remo.

Chiun refused to answer. He fastened his gaze onto the small color television screen.

Remo went to the telephone. His first call to the private line in Smith's office drew a screeching whistle that indicated he had dialed wrong. After two more tries resulted in the same response, he decided the telephone had been disconnected.

On a chance, he called a private number that

rang on the desk of Smith's secretary in his outer office.

The telephone rang eight times before it was picked up and the familiar voice answered.

"Hello?"

"Smitty, how are you?"

"Remo—"

Remo saw Valerie watching him. "Just a minute," he said.

He picked up Valerie by her still-bound legs.

"What are you doing, swine?"

"Quiet," said Remo. He put her in a clothes closet and shut the door.

"Bitch. Bastard. Rotten bastard," she yelled, but the heavy door muffled the noise and Remo nodded with satisfaction as he picked up the telephone.

"Yeah, Smitty, sorry."

"Anything to report?" Smith asked.

"Just for once," Remo said, "couldn't you say something pleasant? Like 'hello' and 'how are you'? Couldn't you do that just for once?"

"Hello, Remo. How are you?"

"I don't want to talk to you," Remo said. "I just decided I don't want you to be my friend."

"All right, then," said Smith. "With that out of the way, have you anything to report?"

"Yes. The girl Bobbi Delpheen has been grabbed by those Indians."

"Where did this happen?"

"In my hotel room."

"And you let it happen?"

"I wasn't here."

"And Chiun?" asked Smith.

"He was busy. He was turning on his television set."

"Wonderful," said Smith dryly. "Everything's coming down around our ears, and I'm dealing with an absentee and a soap opera freak."

"Yeah, well, just calm yourself down. As it happens, we have a lead. A very good lead, and now I don't think I'm going to tell you about it."

"Now or never," said Smith and allowed himself a little chuckle that sounded like a bubble escaping from a pan of boiling vinegar.

"What does that mean?"

"I've finished dismantling this place now. There are too many federal agents around and we're just too vulnerable. We're closing down for a while."

"How will I reach you?"

"I've told my wife we're going on vacation. We've found a little place near Seboomook Mountain in Maine. This will be the number there." He gave Remo a number which Remo remembered automatically by scratching it into the varnish of the table with his right thumbnail.

"Do you have it?"

"I've got it," Remo said.

"It's odd for you to remember something first try," Smith said.

"I didn't call so you could bitch about my memory."

"No, of course not." Smith seemed to want to say more, but no more words came.

"How long are you going to be up there?" Remo asked.

"I don't know," Smith said. "If it looks like

126

people are getting too close and that the organization might be exposed, well . . . we might just stay there."

Smith spoke slowly, almost offhandedly, but Remo knew what he meant. If Smith and his wife "stayed there," it would be because dead men did not move, and Smith would choose death before risking exposure of the secret organization to which he had devoted more than ten years.

Remo wondered if he would ever be able to look forward to death with Smith's calmness, a calmness born of knowing he had done his job well.

Remo said, "I don't want you staying up there too long. You may get to like the idea of vacations. You might retire."

"Would it bother you?"

"Who'd pay off my expense accounts? My Texaco card?"

"Remo, what is that noise?"

"That's Valerie," Remo said. "She's in a closet, don't worry about her."

"She's the woman from the museum?"

"Right. Don't worry about her. When are you going to Maine?"

"I was just leaving."

"Have fun. If you want to know where the skiing's good, I know a great guidebook."

"Oh, really?" said Smith.

"Right," said Remo. "It tells you all about the illimitable skills and the indomitable courage of the author. It tells you all about the politics of the downslope trade and rips the mask of hypocrisy off the faces of the ski resort owners."

"I'll be at Seboomook Mountain. How's the skiing there?"

"Who knows?" Remo said. "The book doesn't get into things like that."

After hanging up, Remo gave Valerie her choice of options. She could go with them to the Edgemont Estate or she could stay tied up in the closet. If she were anyone else, there might have been a third option. She could be set free on the condition that she keep her mouth shut and not tell anybody anything.

He paused. Twice, he thought. Twice in five minutes he had worried about someone else's life. He savored the emotion before deciding he did not like it.

For her part, Valerie decided to go with Remo and Chiun, working on the assumption that she could never escape from a closet, but if she were outside with them, she might be able to slip away.

Or, at least, yell loud and long for a cop.

Jean Louis deJuin smoked a Gauloise cigarette in a long ebony filter that tried manfully but unsuccessfully to hide the fact that Gauloise cigarettes tasted like burned coffee grounds. He looked through the sheer draperies from the third floor window of the red brick mansion out onto the grounds between the building and the road beyond.

Uncle Carl stood alongside deJuin's red leather, high-backed chair and watched with him. DeJuin casually flicked ashes from his cigarette onto the highly polished wood parquet floors that had been set in place, individual piece by individual piece, back in a day when wood was something that craftsmen used, and not just a temporary stop on the road to the discovery of plastic.

"It was too bad about Reddington," Uncle Carl said.

DeJuin shrugged. "It was not unpredictable; still it was worth the attempt. Today we try again. All we need is one of those two men, and from him we can learn the secrets of the organization he works for. Do we have people looking through their rooms?"

"Yes, Jean Louis. As soon as they left, our men went up to look through the rooms. They will call if they find anything."

"Good. And the computers in Paris are analyzing the various capacities of American computer systems. If that secret organization is, as it must be, tied tightly into a computer system, our own computers will tell us where."

He looked up at Carl and smiled. "So there is nothing to do but enjoy the day's sport."

DeJuin snuffed his cigarette out on the floor and leaned forward to look through the open window. Three stories below him, twelve-foot-high hedges crisscrossed each other at sharp right angles, in the form of a geometric maze covering almost an acre.

Eliot Jansen Edgemont, who built the estate, had been an eccentric who made a fortune out of jokes and games, and during the twenties, half of America's families had owned one Edgemont game or another, back in the days before America had been mesmerized into thinking that sitting next to each other and sharing a communal stare at the photoelectric tube constituted a rich and full family life.

He invented his first game at age twenty-two. When no game manufacturer would buy it, he himself produced and sold the game to department stores. At twenty-six he was wealthy. At thirty he was "America's Puzzle Master," spinning out from his fertile mind game after game, all of them bearing the Edgemont emblem, a large block E set into the middle of a geometric maze.

For the maze had been the linchpin of Edgemont's success. While his early games had been successful, the first that had swept America in a craze had been a board game built around a maze. It was inevitable that the maze motif be built into Edgemont's life, and when he built his estate in Englewood, New Jersey, he copied a European idea for a maze of hedges on the grounds. Life Magazine had done a full color spread on it once: "The Mysterious Mansion of America's Puzzle King."

The story did not mention any of the more unusual aspects of Eliot Jansen Edgemont's life. Most specifically it did not mention the orgies that took place in the maze that separated the house from the road.

Then, on one fine summer day in the late 1940's, two male guests caught the same girl in the maze at the same time, and in the resulting argument over property rights, one of the men was killed.

The scandal could not be hushed up, and various legions aimed at preserving America from the godless hordes organized boycotts of Edgemont products. The puzzle and home game business had been on the downs anyway, slowly being destroyed by America's new toy, television, and so the old man took his games and went home.

He sold his business and retired to Europe, where people were more broad-minded, and he died there in the mid 1960's of a stroke suffered while tupping a fifteen-year-old girl in a haymow. It took the girl six minutes to realize he was dead.

She told police that Edgemont said something before he died, but she could not hear the word clearly. Even if she had, she would not have been able to repeat it, for it was the secret name of the stone god Uctut.

For Edgemont had been an Actatl.

In the disposition of his estate, the mansion in Englewood passed into the hands of a corporation that was controlled by the tribe.

It was usually seen only by workmen who kept the hedges trimmed and the buildings in good repair, except on days like this, when the Actatl needed a place to conduct some business.

Today there were no workmen on the grounds, and as Jean Louis deJuin looked down into the center of the maze that covered more than an acre, he smiled in satisfaction.

Everything was going very well.

He looked up as a blue Ford pulled up outside the spike-topped high metal gates two hundred yards from the house. Raising field glasses to his eyes, he watched as Remo, Chiun, and Valerie got out of the car. The two men, he thought, did not really look impressive. Except for the thick wrists on the white man, neither showed any indication of special physical prowess. But he remembered that the white man had gone through some of the Actatl's best warriors like a Saracen blade through flan, and he did not make judgments on appearances anyway.

The gate to the estate had been locked at deJuin's order with a new heavy-duty chain and padlock. As he watched, deJuin saw the padlock and chain fall away under the hands of the Oriental as if they were paper.

Then the two men and the woman were walking between the twelve-foot-high walls of hedge toward the house, which sat on a small rise two hundred yards away. The alley through which they walked was about six feet wide.

DeJuin moved back from the window, set down his binoculars, and glanced down into the main body of the maze. Everything was ready.

The three people had reached the end of the hedge-lined walkway. A wall of hedge prevented their going farther ahead and they must choose now to turn left into the maze or go back. The Oriental looked behind them at the gate. He spoke, but deJuin could not hear the words.

The white man shook his head no, grabbed the girl roughly by the elbow, and turned left. The Oriental followed slowly.

Then they were into the maze, turning right, turning left, the white man leading the way, following the small paths down blind alleys, then turning back, slowly, steadily working their way toward the center.

The telephone on the floor next to deJuin

132

buzzed slightly, and he nodded for Uncle Carl to answer it.

He stared at the three, and when they were deep in the heart of the labyrinth, deJuin pulled the sheer curtain back a few inches and leaned forward toward the open window.

He made a small gesture with his hand, then leaned onto the windowsill to watch. This was going to be interesting.

"Why are we here?" Chiun demanded. "Why are we in this place of many turns?"

"Because we are going to that house to get Bobbi back. Remember her? You let them take her because you were busy watching your television shows?"

"That's right," said Chiun. "Blame it on me. Blame everything on me. It's all right. I'm used to it."

"Stop carping and—"

"So it's carp again, is it?" said Chiun.

"Stop complaining," said Remo, holding Valerie tightly by her elbow, "and help me find our way to the house. I'm getting confused in here."

"You were confused before you got here," said Chiun. "You have always been confused."

"Right, right, right. You win. Now will you help me get to the house?"

"We could go over the hedges," Chiun suggested.

"Not with this one," Remo said, nodding toward Valerie.

"Or through them," Chiun said.

133

"She'd get cut. Then she'd probably start yelling. I couldn't take it if her mouth was going."

Remo reached a blank wall of hedge. Another dead end.

"Dammit," he said.

"If we cannot go through or over," Chiun said, "there is only one thing to do."

"Which is . . ."

"Find our way through this growth."

"That's what I'm trying to do," Remo said.

"Actually it is a simple little toy," Chiun said. "Once there was a master, this was many years ago in what you would call the time of the pharaohs, and while in the land of the Egyptians, oh, to what a test he was put with one of these labyrinths and it was only his—"

"Please, Chiun, no puff pieces for great masters you have known and loved. Bottom line. Do you know how to get through this thing?"

"Of course. Each master is privileged to share the learnings of all the masters who have gone before."

"And?"

"And what?" asked Chiun.

"And how the hell do we get through this thing?"

"Oh." Chiun sighed. "Put out your right hand and touch the wall of hedge."

Remo touched the spiny green bush. "Now what?"

"Just move forward. Be sure your hand is against a wall at all times. Follow it around corners, into dead ends, everywhere it takes you. You must eventually find the exit."

Remo looked at Chiun with narrowed eyes. "Are you sure this will work?"

"Yes."

"Why didn't you tell me before?"

"I thought you wanted to do it your way. Running down alleys until they disappeared and then yelling at the plants. I did not know you wanted to do this efficiently. It has never been one of the things you are most interested in."

"No more talk. Let's get to the house." Remo moved away at a trot, keeping Valerie close to his left side, his right hand extended, fingertips on the hedge wall.

Chiun moved along after them, seeming only to amble, but staying just a step behind.

"They found a telephone number in the room," Uncle Carl hissed to deJuin. "It is a number in the state of Maine for a Dr. Harold Smith."

"Smith?" mused deJuin, still staring into the maze. "Call Paris and have our computer run the name of Smith through its memories." He smiled as he watched Remo reach out his hand and touch the hedge. DeJuin had nodded. So the secrets of a maze were no secret to the old man.

DeJuin raised his hand slightly in a small gesture, careful not to call attention to himself.

"And let the fun begin," he said.

"There is someone in that window, Remo," Chiun said.

"I know. I saw."

"Two persons," Chiun said. "One young, one old." He was interrupted as a voice rang out over

135

the maze. It echoed and seemed to come from all around them.

"Help. Help." And then there was a scream.

"That's Bobbi," Remo said.

"Yes," said Chiun. "The voice came from over there." He pointed at the wall of the hedges, in the general pilot's direction of ten o'clock.

Remo broke away into a run. He let Valerie go. She was unsure of herself, but suspecting she was safer with Remo than away from him, she ran after him.

As deJuin watched from the window, he saw something that even later he would find difficult to believe.

The old Oriental did not run after the white man. He looked around him, then raced into the hedge to his left. DeJuin winced. He could imagine what the prickers and thorns were doing to the old man's flesh. Then the old man was in the passageway on the other side of the hedge, moving across the six feet of gravel and charging again into another of the five-foot-thick growths of shrubs. And then he was through that, too.

"Help, Remo, help," Bobbi's voice came again.

When the maze was built, it had been designed around a small central court, and Bobbi Delpheen was there. She was tied to a high marble bench. Her tennis shirt had been ripped open and her bare breasts were exposed.

Behind her stood two men wearing the yellow feather robes. One held a wedge of stone, its two edges chipped into a knife blade.

They stood looking down at her, and then they looked up. Coming through the hedge directly

136

facing them was a small Oriental in a golden robe.

"Hold," he called. His voice rang out like a whipcrack.

The men froze in position momentarily, then both turned and fled into one of the pathways leading away from the central court. Chiun moved to the side of the girl, whose arms and legs were tied to the corners of the bench.

"Are you all right?"

"Yes," Bobbi said. Her lips trembled as she spoke.

She looked up at Chiun then past him as Remo suddenly raced into the clearing. A few paces behind him came Valerie.

Chiun flicked at the ropes binding Bobbi's wrists and ankles and they fell away under his fingernails.

"Is she all right?" Remo asked.

"No thanks to you," Chiun said. "It's all right that I have to do everything around here."

"What happened?" Remo asked.

"She was here. The feathered men fled as the Master approached," Chiun said.

"Why didn't you chase them?" Remo asked.

"Why didn't you?"

"I wasn't here."

"That was not my fault," Chiun said.

Bobbi stood up from the marble slab that served as a bench. Her tennis shirt hung open and her bosom jutted forward.

Oblivious to that, she rubbed her wrists, which were red and chafed.

"You'll never be a tennis player," Remo said.

Bobbi looked up, startled. "Why not?"

"Too much between you and your backhand."

"Cover yourself up. That's disgusting," Valerie shrieked—again proving that beauty is in the eye of the beholder and that "disgusting" is a 38-C being viewed by a 34-B.

Bobbi looked down at herself as if at a stranger, then took a deep breath before pulling her shirt closed and tucking the ends into the waistband of her tennis shorts.

"Did they hurt you?" Remo asked.

"No. But they ... they were going to cut my heart out." The last words came out in a gush, as if speaking them slowly would have been impossible, but there was less horror in haste.

Remo glanced toward the house. "Chiun, you get these girls out of here. I'm going after those two canaries."

"Girls?" shouted Valerie. "Girls? Girls? That's patronizing."

Remo raised his left index finger in a caution. "You've been a very good girl up until now," he said. "Now if you don't want your jaw patronized by my fist, you'll shut off that perpetual motion machine you call a mouth. Chiun, I'll meet you at the car."

Behind him, deJuin heard the two men in feathered robes enter the room. Without looking, he waved them forward to the window. "This will be good now," he said.

The four men leaned forward to watch.

"Be careful," Chiun said to Remo.

"You got it," Remo said.

He turned, but before he could take a step

138

away, the corridors of the maze resounded with a deep angry baying. The sound was answered by another howl. And another.

"Oh, my god," said Valerie. "There are animals here."

"Three," said Chiun to Remo. "Large."

The baying changed now into angry excited barks that moved closer.

"Take the girls, Chiun. I'll watch the rear."

Chiun nodded. "When you leave," he said, "place your left hand against the wall. It will bring you back the way you came."

"I know that," said Remo, who did not know that.

Chiun led the girls away down one of the gravel paths leading from the central courtyard.

The barking was louder now, growing more frenzied. Remo watched as Chiun and the two women hurried down the passageway, then turned left and vanished from sight.

Along one of the paths to the right, Remo caught his first glimpse. It was a Doberman Pinscher, black, brown, and ugly. His eyes glinted savagely, almost taking on a blood-red glow, as he saw Remo standing in front of the marble slab bench. Behind him came two more Dobermans, big dogs, one hundred pounds each of muscle and teeth that glistened white and deadly, like miniature railroad spikes covered with dental enamel.

When they all saw Remo, they drove forward even faster, each trying to be first to get to the prize. Remo watched them coming, the most savage of all dogs, a breed created by intermingling other dogs selected for their size, their strength, and their savagery.

They moved together now in a straight line, coming at Remo shoulder to shoulder, like three tines of a deadly pitchfork.

Remo leaned back against the marble slab.

"Here, poochie, poochie, poochie," he called.

Remo moved a few feet farther to his right, away from the path Chiun and the women had taken. He did not want the dogs to be diverted from him and go off chasing a random smell.

With one final growl delivered almost in unison, the three Dobermans moved into the clearing. They crossed the space between themselves and Remo in just two giant strides, and then they were in the air, their muzzles close together, their hindquarters separated, looking like deadly feathers attached to an invisible dart.

Their open jaws all went for Remo's throat.

He paused until the final instant, then moved down under the three soaring dogs.

He sent the center one up over his head with his shoulder. The dog did a slow, almost lazy flip in the air and landed on its back on the marble slab with a splat. He yelped once, softly, then slid off onto the gravel on the far side.

Remo took out the dog on the right with an upward thrust of the bent knuckle of his right middle finger. He had never struck a dog before, and he was surprised at how much a dog's belly felt like a man's belly.

The results of the stroke were the same, too, as with a man. The dog dropped dead at Remo's feet.

The Doberman on the left missed Remo, hit the

marble slab, skidded on its paws, fell off the slab, scrambled to its feet again, and turned back with a snarl toward Remo, who was backing away.

He came through the air at Remo just as Remo decided he did not like killing dogs, even Dobermans who would gladly kill him just to keep their teeth cavity-free.

As the dog's massive head turned to the left so its powerful open jaws could encircle Remo's throat, Remo leaned back, pulling his neck away, and the jaws closed harmlessly with a loud click as tooth surface contacted tooth surface.

Remo reached down and with his left hand dislocated the beast's right front leg. The dog yelped and hit the ground. Remo walked away.

The dog got up on three feet, and dragging its dislocated leg, ran toward Remo again. Remo heard the injured limb scudding through the white gravel. He turned as the dog growled and reared up on its two hind legs, trying to bite him.

He slapped the big dog's wettish nose with his left hand and dislocated the other front leg with his right hand. This time, when the dog hit the ground, it stayed there, whining and whimpering.

In the window high above Remo, deJuin moved back from the curtain. He felt the feathers of the two men on his sides brush his face. "Marvelous," he said softly.

Below, as if he had heard the Frenchman, Remo turned, remembering the men who had been watching from the window, and he pointed an index finger as if to say "you're next."

Then he darted up one of the paths leading away from the central courtyard to the house.

141

Forty yards away from Remo, but separated by many twists and turns, Chiun had heard the dogs' frenzied barking and yelping and then the screeches and then the silence.

"It is well," he said, continuing to shuffle forward with the two women.

He stopped suddenly short and spread his arms to prevent the two women from lurching forward. The women bumped into his thin arms, extended outward from his sides. Each let out an "oof" as if they had walked stomach first into an iron guardrail.

Valerie got her breath back first. "Why are we stopped? Let's get out of here." She looked to Bobbi for agreement, but the buxom blonde stood silent, still apparently shaken from her near miss cardiectomy on the marble slab.

"We will wait for Remo," Chiun said.

From the window, Jean Louis deJuin saw the old Korean stop. He saw Remo now, atop the hedges, racing along them as if they were a paved road, coming toward the house, and he shouted, "Withdraw." He and Uncle Carl and the two men in feathered robes fled from the window.

Ten seconds later Remo came through the open window in a rolling vault from the top of the tightly packed hedges.

The room was empty.

Remo went out into the hall and searched each room.

"Come out, come out, wherever you are," he called.

But all the rooms were empty. Back in the room he had first entered, Remo found a yellow

142

feather on the floor and consoled himself with the thought that even if he didn't find the men, the mange might yet carry them off.

He stuck the long feather into the hair over his right ear, like a plume, then dove through the window with a cry of "Excelsior!"

He turned a slow loop in the air, landed on his feet atop the hedge, and ran across the interstices of it toward where he saw Chiun and the two women up ahead.

DeJuin waited a few moments, then pressed the button which opened the wall panel in the room where they had been sitting. He and the other men stepped out from the secret room, and deJuin motioned to them for silence as they moved toward the window, standing alongside it, peering through the side of the curtain.

He saw Remo stop atop the hedges twelve feet above where Chiun and the two women still stood.

"Hey, Little Father," said Remo.

"What are you doing up there?" Chiun asked. "Why are you wearing that feather?"

"I thought it was kind of dashing," Remo said. "Why aren't you at the car?"

"There is a boomer down here," Chiun said.

Remo looked down. "Where is it? I don't see it."

"It is here. A wire buried under the stones. I saw the thin upraised line of rocks. I would not expect you to see it, particularly when your feathers get in your eyes. How fortunate that it was me leading these young people and not you."

"Yeah? Who took care of the dogs?" Remo asked. "Who always does all the dirty work?"

143

"Who is better qualified for dirty work?" Chiun asked. He liked that so he repeated it with a little chuckle. "Who is better qualified? Heh, heh."

"Where's the bomb?" said Remo, pulling the yellow feather from his hair and dropping it into the hedge.

"Right here," Chiun said. He pointed to a spot on the ground. "Heh, heh. Who is better qualified? Heh, heh."

"I ought to leave you there," Remo said.

As deJuin watched from the window, he saw Remo drop lightly from the top of the hedge to the outside of the tall iron fence that bordered one side of it. He could not see it, but he heard metal screeching as Remo separated the bars of the fence. A moment later he saw Remo stand up and he heard his voice.

"Okay, Little Father, it's disconnected."

"That means that it is safe?"

"Safe. I guarantee it."

"Say your final prayers," Chiun told the two women. "The white one guarantees your safety." But he led the two women past the wire imbedded under the gravel and toward the gate at the end of the pathway.

Remo walked along on the outside of the hedge.

"I have been thinking," Chiun said through the hedge to Remo.

"It's about time," Remo said. "Heh, heh. It's about time. Heh, heh."

"Listen to him," Chiun told the two women. "A child. Amused by a child's joke."

Which took all the fun out of it for Remo, and

144

he said to Chiun: "What were you thinking about?"

"About the Master that I told you about, who went to far off places and new worlds and was not fully believed."

"What about him?" Remo asked.

"I am still thinking," Chiun said and would say no more.

DeJuin watched as the old Oriental led the two women through the open gate. Remo had trotted along outside the fence, and then vaulted the twelve-foot-high fence with no more effort than if it had been the low right field handrail in Yankee Stadium.

They started to get into the car, but then the old man turned around, looked at the house, and began to speak words that gave deJuin an unexplained chill.

"May your ears burn as fire," Chiun called toward the house in a voice suddenly strong.

"May they feel the tingle of cold and then snap as glass. The House of Sinanju tells you that you will tear off your eyelids to feed your eyes to the eagles of the sky. And then you will shrink until you are eaten by the mice of the fields.

"All this, I, Master of Sinanju, tell you. Be fearful."

And then the old man stared at the window, and deJuin, even concealed by the curtain, felt as if those hazel eyes were burning into his. Then the old man entered the blue Ford and the American drove off.

DeJuin turned to the other men in the room, whose faces had turned white.

145

"What is it?" he said to Uncle Carl.

"It is an ancient curse, from the people of the plumed serpent in our land. It is very strong magic."

"Nonsense," said deJuin, who did not really feel such confidence. He had begun to speak again when the phone tingled softly at his feet.

He picked up the instrument and listened. Slowly his features relaxed and he smiled. *"Merci,"* he finally said and hung up.

"You have learned something?" asked Uncle Carl.

"Yes," said deJuin. "We will leave these two alone. We no longer need them to bring us to their leader. The computers never fail."

"The computers?" asked Carl.

"Yes. The name our kinsmen learned in the hotel room. Harold Smith. Well, Dr. Harold Smith is head of a sanitarium near here called Folcroft. And it has a computer system with access to most of the major computers in this country."

"And that means?" asked Uncle Carl.

"That means that this Dr. Smith is the head of the organization which employs these two assassins. And now that we know that, we will leave these two alone. We do not need them to attain our goals of power for the Actatl."

"But that leaves us always vulnerable," Carl protested.

DeJuin shook his head and let a slow smile take over his face.

"No. These two men are the arms. Strong and mighty arms, but only arms nevertheless. We will cut off the head of this secret organization. And

146

without the head, the arms are useless. So our trap did not work, but we have won anyway."

He kept his smile, and it spread infectiously to the other three men. DeJuin looked out into the maze at the central court, where two dogs lay dead and the third Doberman lay whimpering with two dislocated front legs.

Behind him, he heard the men say in unison: "You are king. You are king."

He turned. "That is true." And to one of the feather-wearing men, he said: "Go out and kill that dog."

In the car leaving the Edgemont Estate, Remo asked Chiun: "What was that all about? Eagles and mice and eyeballs of glass?"

"I thought of what that long-ago Master wrote in the histories. He said it was a powerful curse among the people he had visited."

"You don't even know, though, if these are the same people," Remo said.

Chiun formed his fingers into a delicate steeple. "Ah," he said. "But if it is, they will have sleepless nights."

Remo shrugged. When he glanced in the rearview mirror, Valerie was sitting sullenly against the door on the right side, but Bobbi Delpheen's face was white and drawn. She had really been frightened, Remo realized.

Chapter Eleven

The police found Joey 172 that night under a railroad bridge in the Bronx.

They did not find his heart.

There was almost a witness to the killing, who said that he was walking beneath the bridge when he heard a scuffle and a groan. He coughed and the sound stopped, and then he left. He came back fifteen minutes later and found Joey 172's body.

Alongside his body was a small note on the pavement, apparently written in his own blood by Joey 172. It said "Maine next." Police believed that in the brief reprieve Joey 172 got by the presence of the passerby, he had written this message on the ground.

This was all reported the next day by the *Post*, which Remo read.

That the *Post* took the message "Maine next" to mean that the killing was the work of a right wing lunatic fringe whose next mission was to go to Maine and make sure that the fascists won the Presidential election there was immaterial.

That the *Post* first and alone promulgated this theory on page one, and by page twenty-four, the editorial page, had promoted it to the status of fact by referring to it in an editorial entitled "Heartless in America" did not impress Remo at all.

What impressed him was the contents of the message. "Maine next."

What else could it mean but Dr. Harold Smith?

Throughout the Actatl tribe, the word had flashed on the death of Joey 172: The despoiler of the great stone Uctut is no more.

Another message flashed through, too. Soon the Actatl would be hidden no more; their proud historical traditions would no longer be kept secret by fear of annihilation and reprisal.

Soon the Actatl and their god Uctut, of the secret name, would stand high among the peoples of the world, proud and noble, for even now the leaders of the family were planning to humble a secret organization of the United States.

DeJuin sat in his hotel suite and gathered to him the bravest of the Actatl. They planned their trip. And when Uncle Carl insisted upon going, deJuin made no argument. The old man, he felt, deserved to be in on the moment of glory.

149

Chapter Twelve

Before Remo could pick up the telephone to call Dr. Harold Smith, the phone rang.

It was uncanny, Remo thought, how Smith sometimes seemed to be able, across many miles, to read Remo's mind and call just when Remo wanted to speak to him. But Smith had a far stronger track record of calling when Remo did not wish to speak to him, which was most of the time.

The phone rang again.

"Answer the instrument," Chiun said, "or else remove it from the wall. I cannot stand all this interruption when I am trying to write a history for the people of Sinanju."

Remo glanced at Chiun on the floor, surrounded by sheets of parchment, quill pens, and bottles of ink.

He answered the phone.

"Hello, Smitty," he said.

"Remo, this is Bobbi."

"What do you want? A fourth for doubles?"

"Remo, I'm frightened. I've seen men around the front of my home and they look like the men who were at Edgemont."

"Mmmmm," said Remo. He had sent Bobbi Delpheen home with orders to be careful, hoping he would never hear from her again. Happiness was never having to hear her Adidas tennis shoes scuffling along the rug in his room.

"Can I come and stay with you, Remo? Please. I'm frightened."

"All right," Remo said. "But be careful coming here. And wear something warm. We're going on a trip."

"I'll be right there."

Remo hung up with a grunt.

When he had sent Bobbi home, Remo had told her to be careful. When he had sent Valerie home, he had told her to be quiet. He wondered now if she were being followed also.

"Hey, Chiun, you writing anything good about me?"

Chiun looked up. "I am writing only the truth."

Remo was not going to stand there and be insulted, so he called Valerie. He found her at the desk in the museum.

"It's about time you called, freak," she said. "When are you going to get rid of all that ... all those ... you know, in the special exhibit room?

How long do you think this can go on? What do you think I am anyway?"

"That's nice. Have you had any problems? People looking for Willingham?"

"No. I put out a directive that he was going on vacation. But he can't stay on vacation forever. You've got to do something about it," she said.

"And I will. You have my absolute guarantee that I will," Remo said sincerely. "Have you seen anybody? Has anybody been following you?"

"Not that I know of."

"Have people been coming to see the exhibit?"

"No. Not since I've been back. I've kept the sign on the door that it's closed, but no one comes."

"And no one's been following you?"

"Are you trying to make me nervous? That's it, isn't it? You're trying to make me nervous. Probably to get me up to your room so you can have your way with me. That's it, right?"

"No, dear," Remo said. "That most certainly is not it."

"Well, don't think that some shabby trick is going to frighten me into going there. No way. Your silly maneuvers are transparent, do you hear me, transparent, and you can forget it, if, for a moment, you think you can frighten me and get me to—"

Remo hung up.

Valerie arrived before Bobbi, even before Remo was hanging up the phone from his conversation with Smith.

No, Smith had not heard anything about Joey 172. With the closing down of Folcroft, the flow

152

of information to him had stopped, except for what he was able to glean from the newspapers. When he wasn't snowed in at his cabin.

No, he had not seen anyone around his cabin, and yes, the skiing was fine, and if he stayed on vacation another month, his instructor told him, he would be ready to leave the children's slope, and he would be happy to see Chiun and Remo if they came to Maine, but they could not expect to stay in his cabin because a) it was small and b) Mrs. Smith after all these years still had no idea of what her husband did for a living, and it would be too complicated for her to meet Remo and Chiun. And there was no shortage of motel rooms nearby, and what was that awful yawking in the room?

"That's Valerie," Remo said. "She calls that speech. You be very careful."

He hung up, just in time to wave down Chiun, who was turning threateningly on the rug toward Valerie, who had interrupted his concentration. Even now he was holding the writing quill poised on the tips of his fingers. In another split second, Remo knew, Valerie was going to have another appendage, a quill through her skull and into her brain.

"No, Chiun. I'll shut her up."

"It would be well if both of you were to shut up," Chiun said. "This is complicated work I do."

"Valerie," Remo said, "come over here and sit down."

"I'm going to the press," she said. "I'm tired of this. *The New York Times* would like to hear my story. Yes. *The New York Times*. Wait until

Wicker and Lewis get through with you. You'll think you were in a meatgrinder. That's it. *The Times*."

"A very fine newspaper," Remo said.

"I got my job through *The New York Times*," Valerie said. "There were forty of us who answered the ad. But I had the highest qualifications. I knew it. I could tell when I first talked to Mr. Willingham." She paused. "Poor Mr. Willingham. Lying dead in that exhibit room and you, just leaving him there."

"Sweet old Mr. Willingham wanted to cut your heart out with a rock," Remo reminded her.

"Yes, but that wasn't the real Mr. Willingham. He was nice. Not like you."

"Swell," said Remo. "He tries to kill you and I save you and he's nice, not like me. Go to the *Times*. They'll understand you."

"Injustice," Chiun said. "You should understand it. You Americans invented it."

"Stick to your fairytales," Remo said. "This doesn't concern you."

The door to their suite pushed open and Bobbi came in. Her idea of cold weather garb was a full-length fur coat over a tennis costume.

"Hello, hello, hello, everybody, I'm here."

Chiun slammed a cork stopper into one of the bottles of ink.

"That's it," he said. "One cannot work in this environment."

"Were you followed?" Remo asked Bobbi.

She shook her head. "I watched carefully. Nobody."

She saw Valerie sitting on the chair in the corner and looked absolutely pleased to see her. "Hello, Valerie, how are you?"

"Happy to see you dressed," Valerie said glumly.

Chiun blew on the parchment, then rolled it up, and stashed it and the quills and the ink into the desk of the suite.

"Fine, Little Father, you can finish that later."

"Why?"

"We are going to Maine."

"Blaaah," said Chiun.

"Good," said Bobbi.

"I'm going to get fired," said Valerie.

"Why me, God?" said Remo.

Chapter Thirteen

From Europe they had come. From South America and Asia they had come.

They had come from all over the world, the bravest of the Actatl. Their strengths had been wasted in misadventures before Jean Louis deJuin had assumed leadership of the tribe, and this was what was left.

Twelve men, wearing the yellow feathered robes and the loin cloths, stood barefooted in ankle-high snow, oblivious to the cold, looking down a hill at a small cabin nestled in a stand of trees.

The cold Maine mountain wind whipped around them, and the gusts flattened the feathers of their robes against their bodies, but they neither shivered nor shook because the ancient traditions had held it that a child could not become a warrior until he had conquered a snake and a jungle cat and the hammer of the weather, and despite the passage of twenty generations all of them, even fat old Uncle Carl, knew they were Actatl warriors, and that warmed them and gave them strength.

They listened as one now as Jean Louis deJuin, dressed in heavy leather boots and a hooded fur parka, gave them their instructions.

"The woman is for sacrifice. The man I must speak to before we offer him up to Uctut."

"Will those two, the white man and the Oriental, come?" asked Uncle Carl.

DeJuin smiled. "If they do, they will be killed—from within their own encampment."

Chapter Fourteen

Mrs. Harold W. Smith was frumpy.

At thirty-two, she hadn't known it; at forty-two, she had known it and worried about it; and now, at fifty-two, she knew it and no longer cared about it.

She was, she often reminded herself, a grown woman and would act like one, and that included putting aside the childish fantasies about going through life doing exciting things with an exciting man.

So she didn't have that. She had something better. She had Dr. Harold W. Smith, and even though he might be dull, she no longer minded, because it was probably inevitable with all that dull work he did dull day after dull day at Folcroft Sanitarium, pushing dull piles of paper and worrying about dull educational studies funded by the dull federal government in Jacksonville, Arkansas, and Bell Buckle, Tennessee, and other dull places.

Harold—it wasn't Harry or Har, but Harold. Not only did she always call him Harold, but she had always thought of him as Harold. Harold might have been a far different man, she often thought, if he had simply been placed in different circumstances.

After all, in World War II he had done some kind of secret work, and while he would never say anything more about it than that he had been "in codes," she had once run across a personal letter from General Eisenhower, apologizing that circumstances made it impossible for the United States to award Harold W. Smith the Congressional Medal of Honor, adding that "no man who served on the side of the Allies deserved it more."

She had never mentioned to her husband that she had found this letter inside the front cover of a book on a shelf over his desk. To discuss it might have embarrassed him, but she often thought he must have been exceptional "in codes" to have merited such praise from Ike.

The day after discovering the letter she got to worrying that she might not have returned it quite exactly to its spot inside the cover of the book, and she went back to look at it again. But it was gone, and in the ashtray in his study she had found bits of burned paper—but that couldn't have been it. What kind of man would destroy a personal letter of praise from a man who went on to become President of the United States?

No one would do that.

She listened to the coffee percolating on the stove, filling the small kitchen of their rented Maine cabin with the oily sweet smell of coffee, on which she had come to depend to start the day, and she regretted nothing.

Harold might be, yes, admit it, dull, but he was also kind and a good man.

She turned off the electric burner and took the pot off the hot grill and placed it on the cool metal of the stove to stop the percolation and let the grounds settle.

It had been so nice of him to think about coming up here to Maine for a few weeks. She took two cups from a closet over the sink, rinsed them, and poured coffee into them.

She paused a moment.

Inside the bedroom she could hear Harold Smith's soft, methodical, regular breathing stop and surrender to a large sip of air, and then she heard the bed springs squeak. As he always did, Smith had awakened, had lain perfectly still for three seconds as if checking his surroundings, and then without any waste of time had clambered out of bed.

Seven days a week, it was the same. Smith never luxuriated in bed, not even for a moment, after he was fully awake: he climbed out as if late for an appointment.

Mrs. Smith carried the two cups back toward the small formica-topped kitchen table, glanced out the window, then stopped in her tracks.

She looked again, then set the two cups on the table, and walked to the window, pressing her face near the cold damp glass so she could see better.

That was odd, she thought. Definitely odd.

"Harold," she said.

"Yes, dear," he answered. "I'm up."

"Harold, come here, please."

"In a moment, dear."

"Now. Please."

She kept looking out the window and she felt Harold Smith move to her side.

"Good morning, dear," he said. "What is it?"

"Out there, Harold." She looked at the window.

Smith put his head close to hers and looked through the pane of glass.

Coming down the small slope of a hill toward the cabin were a dozen men, naked except for loincloths and feathered headdresses and robes.

They were dressed in the fashion of some sort of Indians, but they did not have the skin of Indians. Some were yellow, some white, some tan. They carried spears.

"What is it, Harold?" asked Mrs. Smith. "Who are they?"

She turned to her husband, but he was not there.

Smith had darted across the room. He reached up over the door and took down a .12 gauge shotgun that sat in a rack made of two sets of antlers. He locked the door's simple drop latch, then carried the gun to the small china closet in the room. From behind the dishes he took out a box of shotgun shells.

Mrs. Smith watched him. She had not even known those bullets were there. And why was Harold putting them in that gun?

"Harold, what are you doing?" she asked.

"Get dressed, dear," said Smith, without looking up. "Put on your boots and a heavy coat in case you should have to go out suddenly."

He looked up and saw her still at the window.

"Now!" he commanded.

Numbly, not really comprehending, Mrs. Smith moved toward their bedroom. As she stepped inside, planning to dress quickly, just to throw clothes on over the pajamas and robe she now wore, she saw Harold moving about the room, the shotgun folded in the crook of his arm like a hunter. He locked the windows of the small cabin, then pulled the curtains closed over the windows.

"Does it have something to do with the bicentennial?" she called as she slipped her heavy snow-pacs over her booted pajamas.

"I don't know, dear," he said.

Smith emptied the box of shells into the left pocket of his robe. Into his right pocket he placed a 9mm automatic that he took from a niche between the couch and the warm air radiator in the main living room.

He looked back into the bedroom. "Make sure that those windows are locked. Pull the curtains and stay in there until I tell you differently," he said, adding "dear" without meaning it. Then he slammed the bedroom door closed.

The dozen Actatl moved silently across the snow field toward the small house, nestled alone in the tiny valley alongside the hill.

162

On a snowmobile atop the hill, Jean Louis de-Juin watched as his men—his warriors, his braves—moved nearer the cottage. One hundred yards. Ninety yards.

He looked toward the snowed-over dirt road that cut its way through heavy pine growth to the cabin.

As the Actatl warriors moved nearer the house, deJuin saw what he had been expecting: a puff of snow coming along the dirt road to the Smith cabin.

A car.

This was it. The Actatl would win now or lose now. It was that simple. He smiled, for he had no doubt that the battle would be a victory for the Actatl.

Smith punched out a pane of glass from the kitchen window with the muzzle of his shotgun and put the barrel of the gun through the opening.

He sighted on the first of the feather-clad warriors, then coldly moved his aim toward the left, where a single shotgun blast might take out three men at once.

How long had it been since he had fired a gun? To kill? It all flashed through his mind in a split second, the days in World War II when he had to shoot his way out of a Nazi trap after he had spent four months in occupied territory in Scandinavia, organizing a resistance movement and training its members in sabotage, aimed at one target: the secret Nazi installation where heavy water experiments, needed to build an atomic bomb, were being undertaken.

A good cause then, a good cause now.

His finger began to tighten on the right trigger, but he stopped when he heard a car jerking to a stop before the front door of his cabin.

Was it more of them? Or was it Remo?

The door was locked. He would wait a moment. The warriors were now thirty-five yards away, stumbling ahead through heavy snow, and Smith again took dead aim.

At twenty-five yards he would fire.

Before he could squeeze the trigger, he saw a flash of color to the right of his window and then Remo, wearing only a blue tee shirt and black slacks, and Chiun, clad only in a green kimono, moved around the corner of the building and ran toward the dozen spear-carrying men.

The front pair of Indians stopped, set up quickly, and fired their spears. If Smith had not seen it with his own eyes, he would not have believed it. The projectiles sped toward Remo and Chiun. Both men seemed oblivious to them. At what seemed a fraction of a second too late, Remo's left hand moved before his face. The spear cracked in half and both parts fell harmless at his feet. He kept running toward the Actatl. The spear that went at Chiun seemed almost to have reached his stomach, seemed sure to penetrate, seemed certain to be deadly, when Chiun's long-nailed fingers reached down, and then Chiun was holding the spear in his own right hand. He had caught it in midflight.

164

Neither he nor Remo lost a step in their advance toward the Actatl. Then they were on them, and Smith realized that in all his years as the head of CURE, he had never before seen Remo and Chiun at work together. And as he watched them, he understood for the first time the terror that the Master of Sinanju and his disciple, Remo, could strike into so many hearts.

He understood too why Chiun believed Remo to be the reincarnation of the Eastern God, Shiva, the Destroyer.

Remo moved in a blur, in among the group of twelve warriors, who had stopped their charge on the house to dispose first of the two intruders. About Remo all was speed, as if he were surrounded by a special kind of turbulence, and bodies flew away from him as if they held a different magnetic charge from his and were thrust away by invisible forces.

While Remo charged into the center of the Actatl, Chiun worked around the perimeter of the group. His style was as different from Remo's as that of a rifle from a pistol. Chiun did not appear to move quickly; his hands and body were not blurred as he went from one spot to another. Smith noted almost scientifically that Chiun hardly appeared to be moving at all. But suddenly he was one place and then suddenly another place. It was like watching a film in which the camera had been stopped intermittently while shooting the picture, and Chiun's movement from one spot to the next had occurred while the camera lens was closed.

And the bodies piled up in a huge mound of yellow feathers, like some kind of giant canary graveyard.

Smith noticed another movement to his right and turned his head. A girl in a fur coat came around the corner of the cabin.

That would be Bobbi or Valerie, Smith thought. Bobbi, judging from the full length fur coat. She paused at the end of the cabin for a moment, watching as Remo and Chiun lay waste the Actatl warriors.

Not knowing she was being watched, she reached into the right pocket of her fur coat. She drew out a pistol.

Smith smiled. She was going to protect Remo and Chiun.

She raised the revolver at arm's length in her right hand. Smith wondered if he should call out to her and tell her to stop.

He glanced back at the battle. All the Actatl had fallen. Only Remo and Chiun still stood, ankle deep in the powdery snow. They had their backs to Bobbi. Remo pointed up to the top of a hill, where a man sat on a snowmobile, watching the carnage below. Remo nodded to Chiun and moved off in the direction of the man on the hill.

Smith glanced back at Bobbi. She extended her left hand and grasped her right wrist to hold the gun steady. She took deadly slow aim across the twenty feet between her and Remo and Chiun.

She was going to shoot them.

Smith wheeled in the window opening, moving to his left, and without aiming squeezed first the right trigger of his shotgun and then the left.

166

The first blast missed. The second caught Bobbi in the midsection, lifted her in the air, folded her as if she were a dinner napkin, and set her down into the snow eight feet from where she had been standing.

Remo turned, saw Bobbi lying on the snow, blood oozing out of her almost severed midsection, melting the snow where it touched it, creating a purplish brown paste. He looked at the window where Smith still held the gun.

"Nice work, Smitty," Remo said sarcastically. "She's with us."

Smitty passed by the bedroom door on his way outside. He called to his wife, "Stay inside there, dear. Everything's going to be all right."

"Are you all right, Harold?"

"I'm fine, dear. Just stay in there until I call you."

Smith put the gun against the wall and went outside onto the porch, which wrapped around the small cabin.

Remo looked up at him and laughed.

"What's so funny?" Smith said.

"Somehow I had this idea you slept in a gray suit," Remo said, gesturing toward Smith's pajamas. "I thought you always wore a gray suit."

"Very funny," Smith said.

Chiun was leaning over the girl. When Remo and Smith approached, she hissed to Remo: "You are one with the despoilers of the stone. You must die."

"Sorry, but it doesn't look like you're going to be able to carry it off," Remo said.

167

"She was trying to shoot you," Smith explained.

"She wouldn't have," Remo said.

"You had your back turned."

"What has that got to do with it?" Remo asked. He knelt closer to Bobbi. "What's your interest in all this? Just because I wouldn't play tennis with you?"

"I am a daughter of Uctut. Before me, my father and before him, his father, through many generations."

"So you helped them kill your own mother?" Remo said.

"She was not of the Actatl. She did not protect the sacred stone," Bobbi said. She sipped air heavily. It gurgled through her throat.

"Who's left to protect the stone now, kid?" Remo asked.

"Jean Louis will protect it and he will destroy you. The king of the Actatl will bring you death."

"Have it your way."

"Now I die with the secret name on my lips." She spoke again, and Remo leaned close and heard the secret name of Uctut as she spoke it. Bobbi's face relaxed into a smile, her eyes closed, and her head fell to the side.

Remo stood up. Lying on the ground in her fur coat, surrounded by bloody slush, she looked like an oversize muskrat lying on a red pillow.

"That's the biz, sweetheart," Remo said.

Remo looked up toward the hill. The man on the snowmobile was gone.

"Oh, my god! Oh, my god!" Remo turned. The

168

new noise was Valerie, who had finally worked up nerve enough to come see what was happening after having heard the shots.

She stood at the corner of the cabin, looking at the bodies lying about the snowfield.

"Oh, my god! Oh, my god!" she said again.

"Chiun, will you please get her out of here?" Remo asked. "Muzzle her, will you?"

"I do not do this thing because it is a command," Chiun said. "I do not take commands from you, only from our gracious and wise emperor in his pajamas. I do this thing because it is so worth doing."

Chiun touched Valerie on the left arm. She winced and followed him back to the car.

"Well, you've got to get rid of these bodies," Smith said.

"Get rid of your own bodies. I'm not the dog-warden."

"I can't get rid of the bodies," Smith said. "My wife's inside. She'll be nosing around in a minute. I can't let her see this."

"I don't know, Smitty," Remo said. "What would you do if I weren't around to handle all these details for you?"

He looked at Smith, self-righteously, as if demanding an answer that would not come. Remo went to the shed near Smith's front door and dragged out Smith's snowmobile. Every cottage and cabin in this part of the country came with one because the snow sometimes was so deep that people without snowmobiles could be cut off for weeks. And having guests freeze to death or die of starvation did nothing for Maine's tourist business.

Remo started up the snowmobile and drove it to the pile of corpses, which he tossed onto the back of the ski-equipped vehicle like so many sacks of potatoes. He put Bobbi Delpheen on the top and then used some random arms and legs to tuck everybody in so they wouldn't shake loose.

He turned the snowmobile around, aiming it toward the top of a hill, which ended at a big gulley with a frozen river in its bottom, then cracked the steering mechanism so the snowmobile's skis could not turn. He jammed the throttle and jumped off.

The snowmobile lumbered away up the hill, carrying its thirteen bodies.

Remo said to Smith, "They'll find it in the spring. By that time, you do something to make sure no one knows who rented this place."

"I will."

"Good. And why don't you go back to Folcroft? No need for you to keep hiding here."

Smith glanced up the hill. "What of the king of this tribe?"

"I'll take care of him back in New York," Remo said. "Don't worry."

"With you on the job, who could worry?" said Smith.

"Damn right," said Remo, impressing himself with his own efficiency.

He looked around at the blood-stained snow, then picked up a loose yellow feather and began brushing snow around to cover the stains. In a few seconds, the yard looked as pristine as it had before the start of the battle.

"What about Valerie?" Smith said.

"I'll keep her quiet," Remo said.

He walked away. A moment later Smith heard the car's motor start and begin to move away.

Smith waited a moment before reentering his house. He paused inside the front door and yelled out at the empty open countryside: "That's enough fooling around. If you fellas want to practice your games, go somewhere else. Before somebody gets hurt. That's right. Get moving."

He waited twenty seconds, then closed the front door, and went into his bedroom.

"You were right, dear," he said. "Just some fools practicing war games for the bicentennial. I chased them."

"I heard shots, Harold," Mrs. Smith said.

Smith nodded. "That warned them off, dear. I fired off into the trees. Just to get them moving."

"The way you were acting before, I thought there was really something dangerous happening there," Mrs. Smith said suspiciously.

"No, no. Nothing at all," Smith said. "You know what, dear?"

"What?"

"Pack. We're going home."

"Yes, Harold."

"These woods are boring."

"Yes, Harold."

"I don't think I'll ever be a good enough skier to get off the children's slope."

"Yes, Harold."

171

"I feel like getting back to work, dear."

"Yes, Harold."

When he left the room, Mrs. Smith sighed. Life was dull.

Dull, dull, dull.

Chapter Fifteen

Across the river from New York City, in Weehawken, New Jersey, is a small exercise in concrete called a park, which commemorates the murder of Alexander Hamilton by Aaron Burr.

The park is a postage stamp alongside a bumpy boulevard that snakes its way along the top of the Palisades, and it is supposed to commemorate the spot where Hamilton was shot, but it misses by some two hundred feet. Vertical distance.

Hamilton was shot at the foot of the Palisades cliff, down in a rock-strewn area of rubble and debris that used to be cleaned up regularly when the ferry to Forty-second Street in New York was running. Since the closing down of the ferry, it had been ignored.

So it was hardly likely that one more rock in that area would have captured anyone's attention.

If it had not been for Valerie Gardner.

After making good on his promise to clear the bodies of Willingham and the other dead Actatl out of the special exhibit room at the museum, Remo had found a way to put Valerie's big mouth to good use.

And while she still thought he was a homicidal maniac, he had explained carefully to her that a successor would soon have to be named for Willingham, and who would have a better shot at the job than the young female assistant director who had worked so hard to preserve museum property?

So after Remo had contracted with a special moving company in Greenwich Village, which was used to working at night because it specialized in getting people and their furnishings out of apartments between midnight and five A.M., when landlords slept, Valerie got on the telephone with the representatives of the New York TV stations, the newspapers, wire services, and news magazines.

At one o'clock the next afternoon, when the gentlemen of the press arrived at the rock-littered site of the Hamilton-Burr duel, they found Valerie Gardner and a giant eight-foot stone, carved with circles and awkward birds, which Valerie informed them had been kidnapped from the museum and held for a "sizeable ransom," which she had paid personally, since she had not been able to contact the director, Mr. Willingham, for authorization.

A strong north wind blew in the face of the

174

stone statue, as Valerie explained that it was the ritual god "of a primitive Mexican tribe named the Actatl, a tribe which distinguished itself by vanishing absolutely with the arrival of Cortez and his conquistadores."

"Any leads on who took the stone?" one reporter asked.

"None yet," said Valerie.

"How did they get it out of the museum? It must weigh a ton," another reporter asked.

"Four tons," said Valerie. "But our guard force was depleted last night because some of our men were ill, and the burglars were able to break in and remove this, probably with a fork lift truck."

The reporters asked some more questions, while cameramen took film of Valerie and the stone, and finally one reporter asked, "Does this thing have a name? How do we refer to it?"

"To the Actatl, it was god," Valerie said. "And they called it Uctut. But that was its public name. It had a secret name known only to priests of the Actatl."

"Yeah?" said a reporter.

"Yes," said Valerie. "And that secret name was . . ."

Cameras whirred almost noiselessly as Valerie spoke the secret name of Uctut.

The case of the kidnapped stone was on the press wires and on the television all over the country that night. And across the country, even around the world, people who believed in Uctut watched as Valerie spoke the sacred name. And when the skies did not darken, nor the clouds fall, they sighed sadly and began to think that perhaps, after almost five hundred years in the west, they should stop thinking of themselves as Actatl, a hardly remembered tribe that worshiped a powerless stone.

But not everyone saw the broadcast on television.

After Valerie and the reporters had left, three men stood at the park atop the Palisades looking down at the huge monument.

In the center, looking down upon Uctut, was Jean Louis deJuin, who smiled and said, "Very clever. But of course it was all clever. How did you find me?"

The man to his right answered.

"Your name was in Willingham's files," Remo said. "All the names were. You were the only Jean Louis, and that was the name Bobbi gave me."

DeJuin nodded. "Information will be the death of us all yet." He looked to the old Oriental at his left side.

Chiun shook his head. "You are an emperor and this is what you get for not hiring qualified help. Entrusting serious business to amateurs is always a mistake."

"Now what is to happen?"

"When this is all on the news tonight," Remo said, "sacred name and all, the Actatl will see that Uctut's a fake. And that's that."

"And your secret organization will just pick up the pieces and continue as before?" deJuin said.

"Right," Remo said.

"Good," said deJuin. "Done is done and over is over. I don't think I was ever really cut out to be

176

a king. Certainly not king of people who worshiped a rock."

He smiled, first at Remo, then at Chiun, as if sharing a private joke with them.

They did not smile back. Remo thrust a hand into deJuin's pocket, leaving there a piece of paper. And Chiun threw deJuin off the cliff down onto the statue of Uctut, which deJuin hit with a splat.

"Good," Chiun said to Remo. "Over is over and done is done."

DeJuin's body would be found that evening by sightseers who watched the news item on television and hustled to the foot of the Palisades to see the big stone.

Police would find in deJuin's pocket a typewritten note that admitted that he had planned and carried out the murders of the congressman, Mrs. Delpheen, and Joey 172, in retribution because they had not prevented the stone Uctut from being defaced. The note would also say that Uctut was a false god, and that Jean Louis deJuin, as king of the Actatl, renounced the ugly hunk of rock and was taking his own life in partial penance for his part in the three savage, senseless murders.

The press would cover all these events thoroughly, just as thoroughly as they would ignore the return to Folcroft Sanitarium of Dr. Harold W. Smith, sanitarium director, well rested after his vacation trip to Mount Seboomook in Maine and now busy revamping the sanitarium's sophisticated computer system.

And Remo and Chiun would sit in their hotel room and argue about dinner.

"Fish," said Chiun.

"Duck would be nice," Remo said.

"Fish."

"Let's have duck. After all it isn't every day we kill a king," said Remo.

"Fish," said Chiun. "I am tired of looking at feathered things."

ALL NEW DYNAMITE SERIES

THE DESTROYER

by Richard Sapir & Warren Murphy

CURE, the world's most secret crime-fighting organization created the perfect weapon — Remo Williams — man programmed to become a cold, calculating death machine. The super man of the 70's!

Order		Title	Book No.	Price
	# 1	Created, The Destroyer	P361	$1.25
	# 2	Death Check	P362	$1.25
	# 3	Chinese Puzzle	P363	$1.25
	# 4	Mafia Fix	P364	$1.25
	# 5	Dr. Quake	P365	$1.25
	# 6	Death Therapy	P366	$1.25
	# 7	Union Bust	P367	$1.25
	# 8	Summit Chase	P368	$1.25
	# 9	Murder's Shield	P369	$1.25
	#10	Terror Squad	P370	$1.25
	#11	Kill or Cure	P371	$1.25
	#12	Slave Safari	P372	$1.25
	#13	Acid Rock	P373	$1.25
	#14	Judgment Day	P303	$1.25
	#15	Murder Ward	P331	$1.25
	#16	Oil Slick	P418	$1.25
	#17	Last War Dance	P435	$1.25
	#18	Funny Money	P538	$1.25
	#19	Holy Terror	P640	$1.25
	#20	Assassins Play-Off	P708	$1.25

and more to come . . .

PINNACLE
BOOKS

THE INCREDIBLE ACTION PACKED SERIES

DEATH MERCHANT

by Joseph Rosenberger

His name is Richard Camellion, he's a master of disguise, deception and destruction. He does what the CIA and FBI cannot do. They call him THE DEATH MERCHANT!

Order		Title	Book #	Price
____	# 1	THE DEATH MERCHANT	P751	$1.25
____	# 2	OPERATION OVERKILL	P085	.95
____	# 3	THE PSYCHOTRON PLOT	P641	$1.25
____	# 4	CHINESE CONSPIRACY	P168	.95
____	# 5	SATAN STRIKE	P182	.95
____	# 6	ALBANIAN CONNECTION	P670	$1.25
____	# 7	CASTRO FILE	P264	.95
____	# 8	BILLIONAIRE MISSION	P339	.95
____	# 9	THE LASER WAR	P594	$1.25
____	#10	THE MAINLINE PLOT	P473	$1.25
____	#11	MANHATTAN WIPEOUT	P561	$1.25
____	#12	THE KGB FRAME	P642	$1.25
____	#13	THE MATO GROSSO HORROR	P705	$1.25

the Executioner

The gutsiest, most exciting hero in years. Imagine a guy at war with the Godfather and all his Mafioso relatives! He's rough, he's deadly, he's a law unto himself — nothing and nobody stops him!

THE EXECUTIONER SERIES by DON PENDLETON

Order		Title	Book #	Price
_____	# 1	WAR AGAINST THE MAFIA	P401	$1.25
_____	# 2	DEATH SQUAD	P402	$1.25
_____	# 3	BATTLE MASK	P403	$1.25
_____	# 4	MIAMI MASSACRE	P404	$1.25
_____	# 5	CONTINENTAL CONTRACT	P405	$1.25
_____	# 6	ASSAULT ON SOHO	P406	$1.25
_____	# 7	NIGHTMARE IN NEW YORK	P407	$1.25
_____	# 8	CHICAGO WIPEOUT	P408	$1.25
_____	# 9	VEGAS VENDETTA	P409	$1.25
_____	#10	CARIBBEAN KILL	P410	$1.25
_____	#11	CALIFORNIA HIT	P411	$1.25
_____	#12	BOSTON BLITZ	P412	$1.25
_____	#13	WASHINGTON I.O.U.	P413	$1.25
_____	#14	SAN DIEGO SIEGE	P414	$1.25
_____	#15	PANIC IN PHILLY	P415	$1.25
_____	#16	SICILIAN SLAUGHTER	P552	$1.25
_____	#17	JERSEY GUNS	P328	$1.25
_____	#18	TEXAS STORM	P353	$1.25
_____	#19	DETROIT DEATHWATCH	P419	$1.25
_____	#20	NEW ORLEANS KNOCKOUT	P475	$1.25
_____	#21	FIREBASE SEATTLE	P499	$1.25
_____	#22	HAWAIIAN HELLGROUND	P625	$1.25
_____	#23	ST. LOUIS SHOWDOWN	P687	$1.25

AND MORE TO COME . . .

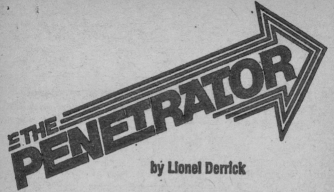

THE PENETRATOR

by Lionel Derrick

Mark Hardin. Discharged from the army, after service in Vietnam. His military career was over. But *his* war was just beginning. His reason for living and reason for dying became the same—to stamp out crime and corruption wherever he finds it. He is deadly; he is unpredictable; and he is dedicated. He is The Penetrator!

Read all of him in:

Order		Title	Book No.	Price
_____	# 1	THE TARGET IS H	P236	$ .95
_____	# 2	BLOOD ON THE STRIP	P237	$ .95
_____	# 3	CAPITOL HELL	P318	$ .95
_____	# 4	HIJACKING MANHATTAN	P338	$ .95
_____	# 5	MARDI GRAS MASSACRE	P378	$ .95
_____	# 6	TOKYO PURPLE	P434	$1.25
_____	# 7	BAJA BANDIDOS	P502	$1.25
_____	# 8	THE NORTHWEST CONTRACT	P540	$1.25
_____	# 9	DODGE CITY BOMBERS	P627	$1.25
_____	#10	THE HELLBOMB FLIGHT	P690	$1.25

TO ORDER

Please check the space next to the book/s you want, send this order form together with your check or money order, include the price of the book/s and 25¢ for handling and mailing to:

PINNACLE BOOKS, INC. / P.O. Box 4347
Grand Central Station / New York, N.Y. 10017

☐ CHECK HERE IF YOU WANT A FREE CATALOG

I have enclosed $_____ check_____ or money order_____
as payment in full. No C.O.D.'s

Name_____

Address_____

City_____ State_____ Zip_____
(Please allow time for delivery)